"Like Santa's annual journeys, Smith's anthology is exhaustive, including virtually every story about Santa. Collectively they create the story of not only an American icon, but a British icon as well. Anyone interested in the history of Santa Claus should have this on their book shelves."

Tom A. Jerman, author of *Santa Claus Worldwide: A History of St. Nicholas* and *Other Holiday Gift-Bringers.*

"Thomas Ruys Smith doesn't just search for Santa Claus; he finds him in the forgotten corners of the 19th-century American imagination. *Searching for Santa Claus* is a fascinating trove of stories, poems, and images chronicling the creation of an icon. Essential reading for anyone who's ever wondered where Santa really came from."

Brian Earl, host of the Christmas Past podcast and author of *Of Christmases Long, Long Ago.*

"Santa Claus is the most important fictional character in history, a legendary figure who fills our media, drives our economy, and lives in the imagination of millions upon millions of children. In this splendid book, Thomas Ruys Smith traces the development of the magical gift-bringer through the art, poetry, and stories of the nineteenth century. This is a wonderful trip through time for lovers of Christmas and an indispensable anthology for lovers of history."

Gerry Bowler, author of *Santa Claus: A Biography*.

"*Searching for Santa Claus* is both a lovely gift book for serious Santa fans and an important resource for anyone studying the history of American children's literature."

Linda Raedisch, author of *The Old Magic of Christmas*.

THOMAS RUYS SMITH

SEARCHING FOR
SANTA
Claus

AN ANTHOLOGY OF THE POEMS, STORIES AND ILLUSTRATIONS
THAT SHAPED A GLOBAL ICON

Searching for Santa Claus
Thomas Ruys Smith

First published by Boiler House Press, Norwich, 2025
Part of UEA Publishing Project

All rights reserved
Author © Thomas Ruys Smith, 2025

Cover design, typesetting and
digital restoration of source material
Glen Robinson, Rebecca Robinson
(www.glenandrebecca.com)

Design Copyright © 2024
Glen Robinson, Rebecca Robinson

The rights of Thomas Ruys Smith to be identified as the author of this work have been asserted in accordance with the Copyright, Designs and Patents Act, 1988. This booklet is sold subject to the condition that it shall not, by way of trade or otherwise, be lent, resold, hired out, stored in a retrieval system, or otherwise circulated without the publisher's prior consent in any form of binding or cover other than that in which it is published and without a similar condition including this condition being imposed on the subsequent purchaser.

ISBN: 978-1-915812-84-1

Thomas Ruys Smith

SEARCHING

for

SANTA
Claus

for my family

Contents

	PAGE
Searching for Santa Claus	14
Introduction Thomas Ruys Smith	15-33

1. *First Footings* — 34

"Old Santeclaus With Much Delight", *The Children's Friend: A New-Year's Present, to the Little Ones from Five to Twelve* (New York: William B. Gilley, 1821) — 36-39

Clement Clarke Moore, "Account of a Visit from St. Nicholas", *Troy Sentinel* (December 23rd 1823) — 40-43

James Kirke Paulding, from *The Book of St. Nicholas* (New York: Harper and Brothers, 1836) — 44-46

A Gallery of Santas:

PAGE 57

Robert Walter Weir, *St. Nicholas*, ca. 1837, oil on wood, Smithsonian American Art Museum	58-59
Illustration for "A Visit from St. Nicholas" in *The Poets of America*, edited by John Keese (New York: S. Colman, 1840)	60-61
Charles C. Ingham, "St. Nicholas", *The New York Mirror*, January 2 1841.	62-63
"Santa Claus", *The New Mirror*, December 30 1843.	64-65
T. C. Boyd, illustrations from *A Visit from St. Nicholas* (New York: Henry M. Onderdonk, 1848)	66-70
"Santa Claus Paying His Usual Christmas Visit to His Young Friends", *Harper's Weekly*, December 25, 1858	71
F. O. C. Darley, illustrations from *A Visit from St. Nicholas* (New York: James G. Gregory, 1862)	72-75
"A Letter for the Children", *The Mother's Magazine and Family Library* (February 1843)	76-77

		PAGE
2.	*Taking Stock of Santa*	*78*

Susan Fenimore Cooper, from *Rural Hours* (New York: George P. Putnam, 1850)	80-86
"The Drolleries of Santa Claus", *Woodworth's Youth's Cabinet* (1853)	87-89
"Is Not Santa Claus a God?", *Youth's Penny Gazette*, January 7 1846.	90-91
"Uncle Maynard's Stories, No 2: Santa Claus", *The Student* (December 1851)	92-93

3.	*Building Santa's World*	*94*

Joseph Holt Ingraham, from *Santa Claus, or The Merry King of Christmas* (Boston: H. L. Williams, 1844)	96-103
Caroline H. Butler, "A Visit to the Dominions of Santa Claus", from *The Little Messenger Birds* (Boston: Phillips, Sampson & Company, 1850)	104-120
Susan and Anna Warner, from *Carl Krinken, His Christmas Stocking* (New York: G. P. Putnam & Co., 1853)	121-126
"A. W. H.", "A Christmas Ballad", *The Book of One Thousand Tales* (New York: Dick & Fitzgerald, 1858; first published in The Schoolfellow Magazine, 1856)	127-129
Ralph Hoyt, "The Wonders of Santa Claus", *Harper's Weekly*, December 26 1857	130-135

		PAGE
3.	**Building Santa's World**	**94**
	Julia F. Snow, "Santa Claus's Ball; or, A Plea for the Children", *Harper's Weekly*, January 3 1863	137-146
	J. B. Greene, *An Adventure of Santa Claus* (Boston: Lee & Shepard, 1871)	147-152
	Margaret Mason, "Santa Claus", *Our Young Folks*, January 1872	153
4.	**The Thomas Nast Era**	**154**
	A selection of Thomas Nast's Santas	156-160
	George P. Webster, *Santa Claus and His Works* (New York: McLoughlin Bros., c1869)	161-173
5.	**"Dear Santa…"**	**174**
	Emily Huntington Miller, "Lilly's Secret", *The Little Corporal* (December 1865)	176
	"Santa Claus's Correspondents", *St. Nicholas* (December 1893)	177-179
	"Dear Santa": Letters from Young Readers	180-185
	Elizabeth Bigelow, "Kitty's Letter", *Ballou's Monthly Magazine* (December 1887)	186-190

		PAGE
6.	**Meeting Santa Claus**	192

M. Angier Alden, "Santa Claus in a Dilemma", *Children's New Church Magazine* (January 1869)	194-199
Anne R. Arran, "A Night With Santa Claus", *Our Young Folks* (January 1871)	200-205
Edward Eggleston, "The House of Santa Claus: A Christmas Fairy Show for Sunday Schools", *St. Nicholas* (December 1876)	206-219
Lucy Larcom, "Visiting Santa Claus", *St. Nicholas* (December 1884)	211-214
Tudor Jenks, "A Gentle Reminder", *St. Nicholas* (January 1891)	215

7.	**Introducing Mrs. Claus**	216

"The Marriage of Santa Claus", from *Dick's Recitations and Readings, No. 13* (New York: Dick & Fitzgerald, c.1869)	218-219
"Mrs Santa Claus and Jessie Brown", *Harper's Weekly* (January 9 1869)	220-221
"Why Two Christmases Came in One Year," *Harper's Bazaar* (December 30 1871)	222-226
M. B. Horton, "A New Departure", *Godey's Lady's Book and Magazine* (December 1879)	227-235

		PAGE
7.	*Introducing Mrs. Claus*	216

    Margaret Eytinge, "Mistress Santa Claus",   236
    Harper's Young People (December 20 1881)

    Sarah J. Burke, "Mrs. Santa Claus Asserts Herself",   237
    Harper's Young People (January 1 1884)

    Katherine Lee Bates, "Goody Santa Claus   239-243
    on a Sleigh Ride", *Wide Awake* (December 1888)

| 8. | *A New-Fashioned Christmas* | 244 |

    H. C. Dodge, "Santa Claus at the Telephone",   246
    Detroit Free Press, December 21 1890

    Mary Bissell Waterman, *"Hello! Santa Claus!"*   247-253
    or, How a Telephone Upset Christmas (Utica: D,
    Waterman, 1886)

    Rev. Washington Gladden, "Santa Claus in the Pulpit",   254-262
    St. Nicholas (December 1887)

    "Snap-shots by Santa Claus", *St Nicholas* (January 1894)   263

    Julie M. Lippman, "A New-Fashioned Christmas",   264-265
    St. Nicholas (January 1890)

		PAGE
9.	*Literary Luminaries, Literary Experiments*	266

Frances Hodgson Burnett, "Behind the White Brick", *St. Nicholas* (January 1879)	268-277
Mary E. Wilkins Freeman, "Santa's Narrow Escape", a composite of its appearances in *The Sunday News* (Detroit), December 25 1892; *The Cleveland Leader*, December 25 1892; *The Courier-Journal* (Louisville), December 25 1892; *The Inter-Ocean* (Chicago), December 25 1892.	278-284
Willa Cather, "The Strategy of the Were-Wolf Dog", *The Home Monthly* (December 1896)	284-291
L. Frank Baum, "A Kidnapped Santa Claus", *The Delineator* (December 1904)	292-299

10.	*So…is there a Santa Claus?*	300

Francis Church, "Yes, Virginia, There Is A Santa Claus", *The Sun* (New York), September 21 1897	302-303
Jacob Riis, *Is There A Santa Claus* (New York: Macmillan, 1904)	303-306
"The Spirit of Santa Claus": Nell Nelson of the New York *Evening World* (1891-3)	307-314
John Kendrick Bangs, "A Toast to Santa Claus", *A Little Book of Christmas* (Boston: Little, Brown & Company, 1912)	315

11. *"My pack is ready"*

PAGE 316

Abby Morton Diaz, "A Letter from Santa Claus to the Children", *Our Young Folks* (December 1870) — 318-320

INTRODUCTION
Thomas Ruys Smith

> Among the golden tales of youth,
> There's none so vague and yet so dear,
> As that of good old Santa Claus
> Who brings the children Christmas cheer.
>
> —"The True Story of Santa Claus", 1869[1]

Searching for Santa Claus

1 "The True Story of Santa Claus", *Dick's Recitations and Readings, No. 13* (New York: Dick & Fitzgerald, c.1869).

Every year when the weather turns wintry, one figure dominates the thoughts of countless millions of children (and their parents) across the world. Representations of this jolly Christmas gift-bringer permeate popular culture: he appears to us on television, in movies, in books, on packaging and Christmas cards; his human avatars pop up in department stores and on street corners. We write him letters; we tell him our secret wishes; all the while, he watches us from afar. On Christmas Eve, in a ritual that must count as one of the most unifying experiences of childhood, his expected arrival is heralded by the hanging of stockings and the offering of food and drink (including, perhaps, some sustenance for his animal companions). And even though he moves unseen, his magic hidden from our eyes, each new generation of children is initiated into what we know of his mysteries as they pose the questions that generations of children have asked before them: Where does he live? How does he travel? How does he make his toys? Is he married? Can we meet him? Is he a saint? Is he a god? Is he real? Suitably trained in the responses to that catechism, children—in America alone, roughly 80% of five year olds—know this to be true: Santa Claus is coming to town.

For many of us, Santa Claus is such a defining presence in our experiences of both childhood and parenting that it is difficult to imagine a time when his visit was not a confirmed fixture on the calendar. But in truth, his Christmas reign as a social and cultural icon traversing the globe is only two centuries old. In the last few decades, a series of books have helped to reshape our understanding of how Santa Claus came into focus in the early nineteenth century out of a festive mélange of winter traditions and competing gift-bringers transplanted from Europe to the New World.[2] To quote Tom Jerman's definitive summary:

▼

[Santa Claus] evolved, like a living organism, from the Winter Solstice festivals and pagan gods of Roman and Germanic mythology, to Christian notables like St. Martin and St. Nicholas, to a variety of secular figures who emerged throughout Europe following the Protestant Reformation and, eventually, immigrated to America [...] European gift-givers and their descendants coalesced into a single, American gift-giver with the elements of his European predecessors: the stateliness and holiness of St. Nicholas and his Dutch doppelganger, Sinterklaas; the rough, back-woods features of the secular gift-givers like Knecht Ruprecht and Pelznickle, who replaced St. Nicholas in Protestant regions of Germany following the Reformation; the stern disciplinarian look of Der Weihnachtsmann; the alcohol-induced jolliness of Father Christmas; the sparky elfin attitudes of the Scandinavian Julenisse and Jultomten.[3]

It is telling that in one of the poems that follows, a young girl offers Santa a representative European spread in an attempt to tantalise his taste buds, a nod to these multicultural roots: "Strong waters out of Holland, and old wine rosy red, / A pudding made in Nuremberg, an English Christmas pie." Undoubtedly, much of this evolution took place away from the public realm, spreading orally from child to child and household to household with much local variation. But from the moment that a recognisable Santa Claus appeared in print in 1821—in the poem and illustrations of *The Children's Friend: Part III, A New-Year's Present to the Little Ones from Five to Twelve*, the first extract in this collection—much of it also happened on the pages of magazines and books which reached a huge national and international audience. "The cult of Santa," Sarah Tooley noted perceptively in 1905, "owes much to literature."[4] It was there that American authors and artists puzzled through Santa's secrets and provided the answers to the questions with which children still pester the adults in their lives. It was there that a distinctive American gift-bringer emerged, shaking off the darker superstitions of his Old World predecessors. It was there that children and their families learned his secrets and emulated the seasonal rituals

2 See, for example: Phyllis Siefker, Santa Claus, *Last of the Wild Men: The Origins and Evolution of Saint Nicholas, Spanning 50,000 Years* (Jefferson, North Carolina: McFarland & Company, 1997); Gerry Bowler, *Santa Claus: A Biography* (McClelland & Stewart, 2005), Linda Raedisch, *The Old Magic of Christmas: Yuletide Traditions for the Darkest Days of the Year* (Woodbury, Minnesota: Llewellyn Publications, 2013); and Tom Jerman, *Santa Claus Worldwide: A History of St. Nicholas and Other Holiday Gift-Bringers* (Jefferson, North Carolina: McFarland & Company, 2020). The development of Santa's place in American life has also been traced in broader histories of Christmas, most essentially: Penne L. Restad, *Christmas in America: A History* (New York: Oxford University Press, 1995); Stephen Nissenbaum, *The Battle for Christmas* (New York: Vintage Books, 1997); Karal Ann Marling's *Merry Christmas! Celebrating America's Greatest Holiday* (Cambridge, MA: Harvard University Press, 2000). Significant expansions of our understanding of Santa's place in American culture can be found in E. James West, "Searching for Black Santa: The Contested History of an American Holiday Tradition", *Comparative American Studies*, 20:3-4 (2023), 251-271, and Jack Hodgson, "'The Santy Claus myth': The Politicisation of Santa Claus During the Great Depression", *Comparative American Studies*, 20:3-4 (2023), 291-307. And anyone interested in the wide-world of holiday gift-bringers and Santa's place in the pantheon should also consult Benito Cereno and Chuck Knigge's *The Alphabet of Christmas*: available on Tumblr.com.

3 Jerman, *Santa Claus Worldwide*, 2.

4 Sarah A. Tooley, "The Life Story of Father Christmas", *The English Illustrated Magazine*, December 1905, 205-215, 210-211.

that they read about. It was there, too, that Santa Claus rose from a figure of regional American interest to the ubiquitous global icon that we know so intimately today—a character with both a rich outer world and a complex inner life. And it was there that Santa Claus became more famous than any other seasonal gift-bringer, before or since. Yet despite Santa's outsized place in our lives and our culture, these stories, poems and drawings have largely been forgotten, hidden away in the books and magazines that once defined the festive season.

This anthology, then, is the first of its kind: collecting together the most pivotal portraits of Santa Claus from across the nineteenth century, it is a unique attempt to define a Santa Claus canon. Rather than seeking origins, this book recreates for readers the tangled, messy and often contradictory accounts that emerged when American creators went searching for Santa Claus. Here, we can witness the discovery of a seasonal superstar as that process played out in print culture up to the turn of the twentieth century. It brings together familiar texts and images that still come to life each Christmas—like Clement Clarke Moore's "A Visit from St. Nicholas" (1823) or the illustrations of Thomas Nast, reproduced here—with forgotten stories, poems and images which, though now unfamiliar, also contributed indelibly to our understanding of this enigmatic annual visitor. Across these texts, writers and artists competed to define all the elements of Santa's life that we now know so well. In magazines that reached an international audience, some of the century's most prominent authors attempted (not always successfully) to put their stamp on his legacy. Out of their communal efforts, the modern Santa Claus emerged, a powerfully intertextual creation composed of layer after layer of myth-making which solidified into accepted truths. Throughout this collection, therefore, crucial creative leaps are juxtaposed with narrative dead-ends which are no less significant. Santas who we immediately recognise as our own festive friend tussle with Santas who now seem strange to us, but whose creation

5   For more on the broader literary development of Christmas, see my other anthologies: *Christmas Past: An Anthology of Seasonal Stories from Nineteenth Century America* (Baton Rouge: Louisiana State University Press, 2021); *The Last Gift: The Christmas Stories of Mary E. Wilkins Freeman* (Baton Rouge: Louisiana State University Press, 2023).

6   See Frank Stockton, *The Bee-Man of Orn & Other Fanciful Tales*, edited by Hilary Emmett and Thomas Ruys Smith (Norwich: UEA Publishing Project, 2024).

7   Caroline M. Hewins, "Children's Books of the Year", *North American Review* (January 1866), 236-249, 236.

8   Gillian Avery, *Behold the Child: American Children and their Books, 1621-1922* (London: The Bodley Head, 1994), 131.

9   Caroline M. Hewins, *A Mid-Century Child and Her Books* (New York: The Macmillan Company, 1926), 27.

nevertheless helped to push forward our communal understanding of the man with the bag. And, then as now, Santa is put to work in a variety of different roles as society, and technology, shifts around him. Taken together, the texts in this volume should rightly be considered the equal of Charles Dickens's *A Christmas Carol* (1843) in terms of their impact on the way that we understand and experience Christmas today.

What emerges from this stuffed stocking of Santa-shaped delights is a new sense of Santa's vital importance as a literary figure, particularly in the field of American children's literature.[5] He begins this collection as a mysterious and potentially threatening nighttime intruder; thanks to the work of these artists and writers, he ends it as a familiar friend. It is a truism that as writing for young Americans developed in the early nineteenth century, it lacked—particularly in relation to its European counterparts—a shaping concern for the fantastic. Didactic realism was the dominant mode of American children's writers until the arrival of the groundbreaking work of figures like Frank Stockton late in the nineteenth century.[6] As author and children's librarian Caroline Hewins noted in 1866, "In the way of fairy stories, it must be humbly owned that American writers [...] have contributed very little."[7] But Santa Claus seems to have escaped these strictures: in Gillian Avery's words, he was "an honorable exception" to the prevailing piety.[8] His enigmatic persona inspired American writers, early in the century, to open the door to a magical world that touched the lives of all young Americans. For example, in her memoir of *A Mid-Century Child and Her Books* (1926), Hewins herself remembered that the fantastical traditions of Santa Claus had certainly been a part of her own youth: "The first Christmas tree that any of us ever saw was a hat-tree covered with pine branches and hung with toys, books and whatever children would like best. Santa Claus came with it to distribute the gifts [...] I remember that there were waiting for me a doll's iron bedstead, with beautifully made sheets and blankets, a wax doll beautifully dressed, a gold pencil and a silver fruit-knife which I have to this day."[9]

If we reposition this corpus of Santa writings and sketches as a body of fantastic literature designed for young readers, consumed avidly for decades before a fully-formed American fantasy tradition is supposed to have emerged, the trajectory of American children's writing starts to look very different. Throughout the century, Santa clearly provided an excuse for American children's writers to flex their imaginative muscles outside of their normal strictures, and offered children themselves profound moments of imaginative escape. Indeed, occupying a position adjacent to fairy-land, and sometimes stepping over into it, the world that American writers communally constructed around Santa Claus must be considered as one of the most important fantasy creations of all time, beloved and familiar around the globe, rich with magical creatures and numinous wonder. It is certainly telling that in one of the extracts that follow, Santa Claus takes Mother Goose to be his bride, and the pair serve as mother and father to the inhabitants of America's fairyland—just as we might position them as the parents of America's fantasy literary traditions.

Examples abound of the ways that the power of Santa on the page played out in the lives of children throughout the nineteenth century, shaping seasonal behaviour in ways that echo down the decades. In 1875, for example, the era-defining children's magazine *St. Nicholas*—whose name was itself a testament to the power of Santa Claus in the emergent children's literary culture of the American Gilded Age, and from whose pages many of the stories in this collection have been collected—reprinted Clement Clarke Moore's "A Visit from St. Nicholas" with the following encomium: "Just think of it! Jolly old St. Nicholas, with his sleigh and his bags full of all sorts of good things, made his first appearance to many of us in this poem. Until we had heard or read this, we didn't know much about him."[10] In 1903, one anonymous editor and writer reminisced about his enjoyment of Susan and Anna Warner's *Carl Krinken: His Christmas Stocking* (1853) (an extract from which is included in this volume): "It was only a little book, but that little book has made me happier every Christmas for fifty years. It was the reading of that story in our house which began, for us in the old home, the practice of hanging up Christmas stockings."[11] Caroline Hewins was also a fan. British readers may be surprised to learn that the Warners' Christmas book had no less of an impact across the Atlantic. Looking back at the changing landscape of her mid-Victorian childhood Christmases in 1905, British writer Susan Tooley clearly recalled: "Boys and girls read with wonderment how poor little Carl hung up an old woollen stocking [...] by the fire-place on Christmas Eve, and went to bed in happy faith [...] the delightful mystery of the stocking filled by Santa Claus caught their imagination, and 'St. Nick' is now almost as popular in London as in New York."[12] (Father Christmas had been established as a reigning spirit of the festive season in Britain at least as far back as the fifteenth century, but he had never had truck with stockings or presents. It was only after the emergence of his American rival in both Transatlantic print culture and the lives of English children that he slowly started to assume those duties on Christmas Eve. In Scotland and Northern Ireland, he largely remains Santa.)

Equally powerful were writer and biographer Albert Bigelow Paine's reminiscences of the intense and lasting effect—indeed, the expansion of his mental universe—that was sparked by coming across one of Thomas Nast's illustrations of Santa Claus in *Harper's Weekly*—"Santa Claus and his Works" (1866), also included in this volume:

▼

It is nearly forty years ago that a boy of five, whose home was a square, white farm-house on one of the big bleak prairies of the middle West, was lying flat on the rag carpet before the open wood-fire, poring over a wonderful double-page picture in Harper's Weekly. It was really a combination of several pictures, each of which depicted some important scene in the daily life of the merry old fellow whose home is at the North Pole, and who toils busily all the year through that good children everywhere may be made happy on Christmas Day. The little boy had the firmest faith in Santa Claus, and this picture, coming as it did just before the holidays, was of immense value. There was the interior of Santa Claus's shop, with the old chap busily at work and about him a number of finished toys. The little boy had tried to imagine this scene. Now here it was, all truly set down [...] Indeed, he scarcely realized that they were merely pictures. The Santa Claus they presented henceforth became his Santa Claus through all the coming years.[13]

10 "A Visit from St. Nicholas", *St. Nicholas*, January 1875, 160-1.

11 J. H. Willard, "Introduction", *The Christmas Stocking* (Philadelphia: Henry Altemus Company, 1903), vii-viii.

12 Sarah A. Tooley, " The Life Story of Father Christmas", *The English Illustrated Magazine*, December 1905, 205-215, 210-211.

13 Albert Bigelow Paine, *Thomas Nast: His Period and His Pictures* (New York: The Macmillan Company), 1-2.

Such scenes were multiplied as Santa took shape in the stories and illustrations that make up this volume, opening young minds and inspiring emulation in families everywhere. As Eugene Giddens has described, and as this collection powerfully highlights, "Christmas is not merely an agreed set of static family experiences, but changes dynamically because of the influence of print media."[14] The same is undoubtedly true of Santa Claus.

In this collection, therefore, we can now experience that creation process and meet Santa anew as we witness his extraordinary emergence on the page as a literary creation without equal. The stories, poems and illustrations that follow have been arranged both chronologically and thematically to trace the construction of Santa's image, the building of his world, and the definition of the narrative tropes that were shaped around him. Then as now, established traditions and imaginative experimentation sit side by side. We begin at the beginning—or thereabouts, for pinpointing a definitive debut for the Santa we know and love is no easy task. On the one hand, it is well understood that a group of well-to-do New Yorkers with antiquarian interests made a conscious effort to revive the figure of St. Nicholas in the early years of the nineteenth century. In Washington Irving's 1812 edition of *A History of New York*, for example, he positioned the saint as a founding figure in the history of New York and pictured him "riding jollily among the tree tops, or over the roofs of the houses, now and then drawing forth magnificent presents from his breeches pockets, and dropping them down the chimneys of his favourites."[15] John Pintard, President of the New York Historical Society, did even more to position St. Nicholas as a presiding spirit for the city. He featured his image on an 1810 broadside to mark the organisation's first annual St. Nicholas Dinner on December 6. Also included was a poem, apparently drawn from the memory of an old Dutch American, which tantalizingly referred to the Saint as "Sancte Claus." While St Nicholas himself resembles an orthodox bishop in Pintard's broadside, and while this celebration is taking place much earlier in December than Christmas, stockings are shown hanging by the fireplace—one filled with toys, one filled with a bunch of switches to hand out a punishment to naughty children. Of course, these men were playing with Dutch traditions for their own literary and social purposes; did any of this represent live folk traditions that were actually part of people's seasonal celebrations? Was Santa Claus yet a distinct personage? One small (and sadly dismissive) reference in Samuel Wood's 1813 *False Stories Corrected* suggests that something was certainly going on which involved chimneys, stockings, and a strange visitor with a name that seems familiar:

[14] Eugene Giddens, *Christmas Books for Children* (Cambridge: Cambridge University Press, 2019), 1-2.

[15] Washington Irving, *A History of New York* (Philadelphia: M. Thomas, 1819), 2 vols, 1:135.

[16] Quoted in Jerman, *Santa Claus Worldwide*, 157.

▼

Old Santaclaw, of whom so often little children hear such foolish stories, and once in the year are encouraged to hang their stockings in the Chimney at night, and when they arise in the morning, they find in them cakes, nuts, money, etc., placed there by some of the family, which they are told Old Santaclaw has come down the chimney at night and put in.[16]

▶ Broadside produced for the New York Historical Society to mark its first annual St Nicholas Dinner, December 6 1810.

Other variants of "Santa Claus" popped up fleetingly here and there in the years that followed, but it wasn't until the 1820s that a recognisable American Christmas gift-bringer emerged in print. In 1821—in the selection that opens this anthology—a children's book was published in New York which either reflected a well-established seasonal American tradition or helped to create one—probably both. In The *Children's Friend: Part III, A New-Year's Present to the Little Ones from Five to Twelve*, published by William B. Gilley with illustrations by Arthur Stansbury, American children could finally see their friend "Old Santeclaus" in print: dressed in red, he arrives on Christmas Eve in a sleigh pulled by a reindeer, lands on the roof, and secretly fills stockings with presents—or "a long, black, birchen rod" for naughty children. Clearly, Santa wasn't yet quite the wholly benign spirit that we know and love today—but he was already taking his place as a vital figure in the development of children's literary culture in America. And children didn't have to wait long for a wholly benevolent Santa to emerge. In 1823, Clement Clarke Moore's poem "A Visit from St Nicholas" appeared in the *Troy Sentinel* newspaper, introduced as a "description of that unwearied patron of children [...] Sante Claus." The rest was history: the popularity of Moore's depiction of a jolly, chubby Santa who was accompanied by eight named reindeer—and offered only treats, no tricks—gained momentum through the century and was soon ubiquitous at Christmas time, a by-word for seasonal domestic delights. As *St. Nicholas* magazine put it in 1875, "No matter who writes poetry for the holidays, nor how new or popular the author of such poems may be, nearly everybody reads or repeats '"Twas the night before Christmas" when the holidays come round; and it is printed and published in all sorts of forms and styles, so that the new poems must stand aside when it is the season for this dear old friend."[17] Still, it took a number of decades for Santa's image to truly coalesce. Prominent writers like James Kirke Paulding continued the attempt to fit St. Nicholas into a (largely imagined) Dutch-American tradition. An extract from

[17] "A Visit from St. Nicholas", *St. Nicholas*, January 1875, 160-1.

[18] "The Holidays", *The New England Offering*, February 1849, 46.

[19] "A New-Year's Tete-a-Tete with our Patrons", *Southern Literary Messenger*, January 1849, 61.

[20] "Some Christmas Thoughts", *Birmingham Journal*, December 24 1856, 4.

[21] Maria Susanna Cummins, *The Lamplighter* (Boston: John P. Jewett & Co., 1854), 106–7.

[22] "Old Santa Claus", *The Mother's Magazine*, September 1846, 28.

his *Book of St. Nicholas* (1836), in which John Calvin makes the real-life Nicholas a Protestant Saint and New Year's Day (his birthday) is the gift-bringer's favoured holiday, is included here. Similarly, visual artists were divided in their understanding of what Santa looked like; also included in this section are a number of contradictory paintings and illustrations which attempted to capture his likeness in the decades before the Civil War, all of which circulated widely—from the sublime (F. O. C. Darley's luminous Santas from 1862, perhaps the first real images of a Santa we can fully recognise) to the ridiculous (the Santa from *Harper's Weekly* in 1858 with a raffish moustache being pulled along by a turkey). Here again, the central importance of Moore's poem is clear: many of these important images were prompted by reprintings of "A Visit from St. Nicholas," across the decades. Something else started to take shape in this period too, something distinctive which helped to distinguish Santa from any other gift-bringer, before or since: a sense that he was not simply a seasonal sprite, but potentially a character with an inner-life. As he tells us in "A Letter for the Children" that was published in *The Mother's Magazine* in 1843, "I think I am not always appreciated, for few deem me a man of deep feeling, and no one gives me credit for being interested, as I really am, in things which are serious and important." It was this kind of creative leap that would propel the figure of Santa Claus through the decades that followed.

By the 1840s, Santa Claus had clearly become a firm fixture of Christmas and a national American phenomenon, North to South. In 1849, the *New England Offering* remarked of Christmas Day: "This has become, even with the descendants of the Puritans, a day of gifts and greetings; when Momus and Santa Claus are sure to have the tribute due, and the little children wonder how St. Nicholas has come through chimneys, funnels, heaters, and grates, with his unsoiled tokens of affections."[18] That same year, the editor of the *Southern Literary Messenger* hailed the traditions of the "blest season of innocent enjoyment" including "the kindly superstition of old Santa Claus, riding in his chariot above the tops of the houses and descending the chimney at midnight to dispense bon-bons to all good boys and girls, who hang up their stockings to receive them."[19] It wasn't long before the fashion for Santa crossed the Atlantic, either. In 1856, for example, the *Birmingham Journal* acknowledged that "Santa-Claus has had the temerity to scale the wooden walls of old England, of late years."[20] Maria Susan Cummins's bestselling novel *The Lamplighter* (1854) dramatized the way that Santa's manifold literary appearances must have stoked these trends and influenced young readers' understanding of his ways: "Gerty did not know anything about Santa Claus, that special friend of children; and Willie, who had only lately read about him in some book, undertook to tell her what he knew of the veteran toy-dealer."[21]

Yet mysteries remained. "Who is old Santa Claus? has been asked a thousand times by the little urchins," declared The *Mother's Magazine* in 1846—and the urchins were not the only ones still pondering that question.[22] Faced with the omnipresence of this new festive figure who had spread like a seasonal virus through young Americans and literary culture both, writers and commentators began to try and pin down this mercurial character about whom much was said but little was truly known. As the author of "The Drolleries of Santa Claus" pondered in 1853, "It quite puzzles my brain how such a personage as our merry friend Santa Claus ever found his way into the calendar." Or as Susan Fenimore Cooper put it in her beautiful exploration of the man and the myth in *Rural Hours* (1850): "most of the wisest people in the land know little more about Santa Claus than the children. There is a sort of vague, moonlight mystery still surrounding the real identity of the old worthy." Cooper also demonstrates the degree to which Santa had already taken shape as an intertextual figure springing from the extracts and images contained in this volume: "we have the portrait by Mr. Weir, and the verses of Professor Moore, as confirmation of nursery lore", she writes, turning to those earlier descriptions of Santa as points of authority in her examination of a character whose "domain" had recently "very much extended itself." Indeed, for some, Santa had extended his domain, and his hold on young Americans, rather too far. Some Scrooge-like commentators were keen to remind American children, in bald terms, that while Santa Claus was a jolly festive friend, he was certainly not a god. Parental discretion is advised!

With the fundamentals of his character in place, writers and artists began to delve deeper into the workings of Santa Claus's life and world, using him as a figure for flights of fancy and developing him into a fully fledged character with enormous narrative potential. Increasingly, he incarnated the animating concerns of the era: love of children, domesticity, charity. The decades surrounding the Civil War were a period of remarkable invention as a sense of the essentials of Santa's daily existence in the frozen north also took shape—with some compelling diversions along the way. In 1843, Dickens's *A Christmas Carol* had an enormous impact on the seasonal literary landscape, and it is certainly plausible that his depiction of the jolly, avuncular, philanthropic Ghost of Christmas Present—himself an avatar of the British Father Christmas—had an influence on this process.[23] When popular novelist Joseph Holt Ingraham imagined King Santa Claus in 1844, that influence seems evident. Accompanied by a horde of tiny minions, Ingraham's King Santa bursts forth from a tree on Christmas eve like a miniature version of the ancient wild hunt. After touring scenes of urban poverty, this regal Robin Hood sends out his helpers—not to deliver presents, but to unabashedly redistribute wealth: "Equity ruleth over this mighty city," King Santa declares, at the end of their evening's work: "From the rich hath been taken that, and only that, which was surplus to their wants, and it is given to him whose need was farthest removed from the rich man's fullness."

Other writers were more concerned with the logistics of Santa's operation—where did he live, and who made all those toys? Caroline Butler (1851) is the first—but certainly not the last—writer to take us inside Santa's workshop; her Santa Claus is decked out like a military leader and behaves like a factory owner, exhorting his little helpers to work ever harder. Ralph Hoyt (1857) gives us a glimpse of Santa's "wonderful house of snow" where "a great many elves" work tirelessly to "make a million of pretty things"—before sending him out on a global delivery route. For Julia Snow (1863), Santa lived in "an immense snow-cave in the side of Mount Hecla" in Iceland; Margaret Mason (1872) pictured a "crystal palace in the Polar Sea." Most extraordinary of all, however, is J. B. Greene's poem *An Adventure of Santa Claus*, in which the ritual gift-bringer announces himself to be the son of Odin, ordered by his father to spread Christmas cheer to make restitution for the mischief of his brother Thor. Greene's Santa has to battle bears, panthers and wolves as he makes his way from unexplored Arctic regions to deliver his presents, but he is helped in his quest by a series of woodland animals. Greene's illustrations of Santa are no less idiosyncratic than his plot. Yet all of these innovations pushed forward our contemporary vision of Santa's home, his workshop, and his attendant helpers. Away from the frozen north, other writers turned to Santa's interior life: Susan and Anna Warner let their readers in on Santa's ruminations when he visits Carl Krinken (1853), and "A.W.H." imagined a similarly meditative (and intriguingly attired) Santa in "A Christmas Ballad" (first published in *The Schoolfellow* magazine in 1856). Both of these depictions addressed head on the tricky question that echoed through the decades to come: why did Santa, the children's special friend, leave fewer gifts—or sometimes even nothing at all—at the houses of poor children, however good they might have been? For the rest of the century—and still today—writers grappled with that troubling Santa paradox.

The Civil War proved another pivot point in the place of Santa in the life of the nation. He became embroiled in America's sectional rivalry. Parts of the South turned against him as a yankee creation—a figure that Southern novelist William Gilmore Simms dismissed as a "little Manhattan goblin."[24] Of more lasting significance was the appearance of Santa Claus distributing presents to Union soldiers on the cover of

[23] For more on *A Christmas Carol*'s impact in the nineteenth century, see Thomas Ruys Smith, "A Christmas Carol in Nineteenth Century America, 1844-1870", *Comparative American Studies*, 20:3-4 (2023), 205-229.

[24] William Gilmore Simms, *The Golden Christmas* (Charleston, SC: Walker, Richards and Co., 1852), 153.

Harper's Weekly, January 3 1863. This was just the first of many seasonal *Harper's* covers produced by Thomas Nast, and the beginning of what can only be termed the Thomas Nast era in the life of Santa as the artist made the figure his own in the decades to come.

As we can see in this collection, Nast was certainly not the first to depict a recognisable Santa in print. However, the prominence and regularity of his seasonal illustrations on the cover of one of the nation's most important weekly journals means Nast must still take significant credit for proliferating the image of a rapidly standardising Santa. They also proliferate through this collection, introducing each section of the book. Nast's illustrations proved to be a springboard for other creators, too. In 1869, using Nast's influential "Santa Claus and His Works" (1866) illustration as inspiration, George P. Webster crafted a long narrative poem for a children's picture book which shared the same title and used Nast's illustrations throughout. This poem was reprinted frequently in the years that followed (just as it is reprinted here), and might be considered a second "Visit from St. Nicholas" in terms of its influence—even if its reputation has proved less enduring.

As early as 1904, however, Nast's role in the cultural life of Santa Claus was already a topic that could inspire hot debate. That summer, what became known as "The Nast Controversy" exploded in the pages of the *New York Times* book review section. The argument began when Albert Bigelow Paine published a preview of his biography of Thomas Nast in the June issue of *Pearson's Magazine*. In that article, Paine made multiple assertions that Nast was solely responsible for "the first published conception of Santa Claus as [...] the fat, fur-clad type which the world has accepted as the only genuine portrayal of its favourite saint."[25] Immediately, the *New York Times* sensed that such a statement would prove to be a flashpoint, and predicted "a controversy of some moment" about the issue: "We surely have clear memories of the same white-bearded, genial old person in popular pictures long before Nast began to exert his influence."[26] In itself, the fact that this question could generate partisan disagreement was a significant testament to Santa's significance in American culture. Sure enough, in the letters page, fellow artist Arthur Lumley asserted that he could "remember distinctly pictures of Santa Claus done to order in my boyhood [...] The subject was naturally always popular,

[25] Albert Bigelow Paine, "Thomas Nast: Civil War", *Pearson's Magazine* (June 1904), 530-543, 539.

[26] No title, *New York Times*, May 21 1904.

[27] Letter from Arthur Lumley, *New York Times*, June 4 1904.

[28] Letter from Albert Bigelow Paine, *New York Times*, July 2 1904.

[29] Giddens, *Christmas Books*, 1.

[30] Mary Mapes Dodge, "Dear Girl and Boy," *St Nicholas*, November 1873, 1.

but there is no evidence that anything like an original conception of St. Nick can be attributed to Thomas Nast." Indeed, Lumley excoriated Nast's Santas as "stiff and clumsy", claiming that "Nast was an indifferent draughtsman."[27] Paine resolutely blasted back that, wherever the real credit for Santa's definitive image might lie, one truth remained inarguable: "for years the Christmas pictures of Nast" were "made familiar to English-speaking children the world over."[28] He was right, and still today they help to shape our sense of Santa and his world.

In the years after the Civil War, with the explosion in publishing for children that followed, stories about Santa Claus saturated seasonal print culture. Santa was now simply ubiquitous, a constant presence on the pages of newspapers and magazines at Christmas-time. As Eugene Giddens has asserted, "The Christmas market played a large part in the emergence of the 'golden age' of children's literature."[29] But what hasn't been fully acknowledged is the starring role that Santa himself played in this process. It is no coincidence that the era's premier magazine for children, *St. Nicholas*, pointedly borrowed the gift-bringer's name. When editor Mary Mapes Dodge launched the publication in 1873 she paid a fulsome tribute to the titular figure in a welcome message to her young readers that emphasized the profound place that Santa Claus occupied in the lives of the young: "Dear old St. Nicholas, with his pet names—Santa Claus, Kriss Kringle, St. Nick, and we don't know how many others. What a host of wonderful stories are told about him—you may hear them all some day—and what loving, cheering thoughts follow in his train! [...] Is he not the boys' and girls' own Saint, the especial friend of young Americans?"[30] In turn, befitting his ability to visit all children in one night, children's magazines like *St Nicholas*, with a large Transatlantic audience, were filled with Santa stories and poems in the winter months. As adults shaped new tales about Santa he became a figure that children felt they could communicate with directly; alongside poems and stories framed around direct addresses to Santa, a smattering of real letters to Santa from the readers of children's magazines in this period are also included here. While most of this correspondence was directed to the North Pole, as a newspaper report about Santa's mailbag from 1893 reveals, plenty of children seemed to think that he lived in New York city (perhaps a nod to his literary and cultural roots). Other key narrative themes soon emerged in this feverishly creative era. The question of what it would be like to actually meet Santa Claus was, then as now, a popular trope that was answered in a variety of ways. Perhaps most intriguing—and even a potential source of fun at Christmas time—is Edward Eggleston's dramatic treat, "The House of Santa Claus: A Christmas Fairy Show for Sunday-Schools," written for *St. Nicholas* in 1876. You, too, could involve your friends and family in a revival of this antiquarian trip to Santa's domain.

One of the most pressing topics in the post-war years was the question of Santa's marital (and even parental) status: the existence and role of Mrs Santa Claus was imagined and reimagined as the question of women's rights came to the fore in the national conversation. In 1869, she could be depicted as both Mother Goose, in "The Marriage of Santa Claus", and a far more glamorous fairy godmother figure in "Mrs Santa Claus and Jessie Brown." More typically, though, Mrs. Claus was pictured as a domestic helper in various states of disgruntlement with her subordinate lot. On the one hand, M. B. Horton's "A New Departure" (1879) positioned Mrs. Claus as a frustrated women's rights activist whose misadventures beyond the domestic threshold served to bolster *Godey's Lady's Book's* disdain for those agitating for social change. On the other, Sarah J. Burke (1884) could produce a lament for Santa's "desolate wife", who never gets her due, and is driven "to sounding her own little horn." A more festive vision of marital harmony can be found in Katharine Lee Bates's famous "Goody Santa Claus on a Sleigh Ride" (1888), where Mrs Claus successfully lobbies her husband to join him on a Christmas Eve adventure, and finds her own important role in the distribution of presents. A story from 1871—"Why Two Christmases Came in One Year"—even imagines a son for Santa and Mrs. Claus: the appropriately named Kriss.

As the century neared its close, Santa Claus also had to contend with a whole range of new technology: how, writers pondered, would Santa fare with inventions like the telephone and the camera? Would a new-fashioned Christmas replace cherished tradition? In "Santa Claus at the Telephone" (1890), a distinctive shape-poem by popular versifier H. C. Dodge (nephew of *St. Nicholas's* Mary Mapes Dodge), Santa merrily announces his imminent arrival, before being abruptly cut off. In Mary Bissell Waterman's *"Hello! Santa Claus!" or, How a Telephone Upset Christmas* (1886), Santa is rather less thrilled at the constant cold-calling of his demanding young acolytes. Thereafter, he gets to grips with a new Kodak camera and even invents his own moving picture device.[31] In reality, new technology would create new traditions without displacing the old: as early as 1898, young viewers were able to witness Santa himself on the big screen in a British silent film, clearly inspired by "A Visit from St. Nicholas", directed by George Albert—the first of many movie Santas that still multiply each year.

Even as a common understanding of Santa coalesced in popular culture, he remained a source of experimental fun, even for some of the era's most important writers for children. Frances Hodgson Burnett imagines a very different home for Santa "Behind the White Brick" (1879), in her first published story for children. Mary E. Wilkins Freeman, whose popular Christmas stories were avidly consumed for decades around the turn of the twentieth century, constructs a Christmas tale that is part fairy-story, part political allegory

(1892), when a reformer obsessed with realism attempts to ban Santa Claus. Willa Cather, in an early-career story for *The Home Monthly* magazine, leaned into the Gothic traditions of Christmas for younger readers. Parental discretion is once again advised as the terrifying Were-Wolf Dog—with his red hair, long teeth and bright eyes "like ominous fires"—attempts to stop Santa and his friendly White Bear from delivering their presents (with some devastating consequences for Santa's reindeers). L. Frank Baum, fresh from writing *The Wizard of Oz* (1900), also turned his attention to Santa Claus, constructing a potently pagan vision of *The Life and Adventures of Santa Claus* (1902); here, in a short story from 1904 set in the same world, Baum imagines a plot which is still reworked regularly: what would happen if Santa was kidnapped?

By the twentieth century, the stories and poems in this collection—and countless others—had enshrined Santa Claus as a key figure in the lives of children across the globe, and an equally key character in the development of children's literary culture.

And yet, one question seemed to be pressing again: was there really a Santa Claus? Two famous affirmative answers to that question by Francis Church (who coins the resonant phrase, "Yes, Virginia, there is a Santa Claus", 1897) and Jacob Riis (who meets a sort-of Santa at the White House, 1904) are reprinted here. Still, the stark wealth disparities of the Gilded Age, exacerbated by a depression in 1893, meant that it wasn't always easy for children living in poverty to maintain a perfect faith in Santa Claus. One woman certainly did more than most towards "increasing the popularity of Santa Claus" among their number, as she put it herself.[32] Nell Nelson—really Helen Cusack Carvalho—was a pioneering journalist who made her name exposing poverty and injustice in urban America. When she joined the staff of Joseph Pulitzer's New York *Evening World* in 1888, she became the spokesperson for the newspaper's annual drive to provide Christmas presents for children who would otherwise go without— for, as Nell Nelson explained to her young readers, "St. Nick will never find them,

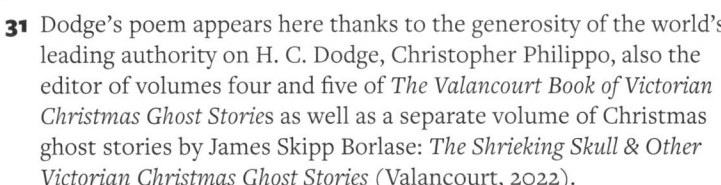

[31] Dodge's poem appears here thanks to the generosity of the world's leading authority on H. C. Dodge, Christopher Philippo, also the editor of volumes four and five of *The Valancourt Book of Victorian Christmas Ghost Stories* as well as a separate volume of Christmas ghost stories by James Skipp Borlase: *The Shrieking Skull & Other Victorian Christmas Ghost Stories* (Valancourt, 2022).

[32] Nell Nelson, "Hello, Santa Claus!", *The Evening World* (New York), November 17 1893.

because the poor people have no time to write to him."[33] Each Christmas throughout the late 1880s and early 1890s, she penned multiple columns (a selection of which are included here) exhorting her readers to donate to the *Evening World's* Christmas Tree Fund: "There must be no poverty," she declared peremptorily, "Santa must abolish it."[34] Donations duly flooded in, and each year the paper handed out tens of thousands of presents on Christmas morning at seven locations around New York. In turn, Nelson gained a devoted young readership who gave her their pennies and offered her, as well as Santa, their loyalty. As one young reader put, sending in two dollars for the fund, "I want to learn to write just like Nell Nelson to cheer the poor little tots. I think she is next to Santa Claus himself."[35] Nelson's instruction to her readers rings as true now as it was then: "The game of Santa Claus is immense. Suppose you play it. All you need is a generous impulse."[36] Popular humorist John Kendrick Bangs leaves us with "A Toast to Santa Claus" (1912) and a set of useful instructions about what to do when meeting someone whose belief in Santa has lapsed:

"I straightway cut that fellow out, And don't believe in him."

The final word in this collection, though, is left to the big man himself—in a letter to children from 1870—in which he pledges that "Santa Claus will be your friend always, always." Many decades later, the figure of Santa Claus still offers children an imaginative escape into a different and often better world; the confirmation of his stealthy nighttime visit through the discovery of a full stocking on Christmas morning is perhaps the closest to magic that most of us get. We still go searching for Santa Claus on the page and on the screen, hoping to unlock and expand the wonders of his world; each Christmas brings us new interpretations of his role in our lives. As in the nineteenth century, some of those innovations will become part of our traditions, some will be forgotten. But the core of his unchanging essence was forged in the stories and poems in this collection—during the extraordinary era when "Old Sancteclaus with much delight" first made his midnight deliveries to young Americans. Happy Christmas to all, and to all a good night.

[33] Nell Nelson, "Hello, Santa Claus!", *The Evening World* (New York), November 17 1893.

[34] Nell Nelson, "Hello, Santa Claus!", *The Evening World* (New York), November 17 1893.

[35] "To Keep Santa Claus on Top", *The Evening World* (New York), November 24 1893.

[36] Nell Nelson, "Merry Christmas", *The Evening World* (New York), December 3 1890.

1.

First Footings

Old Santeclaus with much delight
His reindeer drives this frosty night,
O'er chimney tops, and tracks of snow,
To bring his yearly gifts to you.

"Old Santeclaus With Much Delight",
The Children's Friend: A New-Year's Present, to the Little Ones from Five to Twelve
(NEW YORK: WILLIAM B. GILLEY, 1821)

Old Santeclaus with much delight
His reindeer drives this frosty night,
O'er chimney tops, and tracts of snow,
To bring his yearly gifts to you.

The steady friend of virtuous youth,
The friend of duty, and of truth,
Each Christmas eve he joys to come
Where peace and love have made their home.

Through many houses he has been,
And various beds and stockings seen;
Some, white as snow, and neatly mended,
Others, that seemed for pigs intended.

To some I gave a pretty doll,
To some a peg-top, or a ball;
No crackers, cannons, squibs, or rockets,
To blow their eyes up, or their pockets.

Through many houses he has been,
And various beds and stockings seen;
Some, white as snow, and neatly mended,
Others, that seem'd for pigs intended.

Where e're I found good girls or boys,
That hated quarrels, strife and noise,
I left an apple, or a tart,
Or wooden gun, or painted cart;

No drums to stun their Mother's ear,
Nor swords to make their sisters fear;
But pretty books to store their mind
With knowledge of each various kind.

But where I found the children naughty,
In manners crude, in temper haughty,
Thankless to parents, liars, swearers,
Boxers, or cheats, or base tale-bearers,

I left a long, black, birchen rod,
Such as the dread command of God
Directs a Parent's hand to use
When virtue's path his sons refuse.

Clement Clarke Moore, "Account of a Visit from St. Nicholas", *Troy Sentinel* (DECEMBER 23 1823)

We know not to whom we are indebted for the following description of that unwearied patron of children—that homely, but delightful personification of parental kindness—Sante Claus, his costume and his equipage, as he goes about visiting the fire-sides of this happy land, laden with Christmas bounties; but, from whomsoever it may have come, we give thanks for it. There is, to our apprehension, a spirit of cordial goodness in it, a playfulness of fancy, and a benevolent alacrity to enter into the feelings and promote the simple pleasures of children, which are altogether charming. We hope our little patrons, both lads and lasses, will accept it as proof of our unfeigned good will toward them—as a token of our warmest wish that they may have many a merry Christmas; that they may long retain their beautiful relish for those unbought, homebred joys, which derive their flavor from filial piety and fraternal love, and which they may be assured are the least alloyed that time can furnish them; and that they may never part with that simplicity of character, which is their own fairest ornament, and for the sake of which they have been pronounced, by authority which none can gainsay, the types of such as shall inherit the kingdom of heaven.

For the Sentinel.

Account Of A Visit From St. Nicholas.

'Twas the night before Christmas, when all thro' the house,
Not a creature was stirring, not even a mouse;
The stockings were hung by the chimney with care,
In hopes that St. Nicholas soon would be there;
The children were nestled all snug in their beds,
While visions of sugar plums danc'd in their heads,
And Mama in her 'kerchief, and I in my cap,
Had just settled our brains for a long winter's nap—
When out on the lawn there arose such a clatter,
I sprung from the bed to see what was the matter,
Away to the window I flew like a flash,
Tore open the shutters, and threw up the sash.
The moon on the breast of the new fallen snow,
Gave the lustre of mid-day to objects below;
When, what to my wondering eyes should appear,
But a miniature sleigh, and eight tiny rein-deer,
With a little old driver, so lively and quick,

I knew in a moment it must be St. Nick.

More rapid than eagles his coursers they came,

And he whistled, and shouted, and call'd them by name:

"Now! Dasher, now! Dancer, now! Prancer, and Vixen,

"On! Comet, on! Cupid, on! Dunder and Blixem;

"To the top of the porch! to the top of the wall!

"Now dash away! dash away! dash away all!"

As dry leaves before the wild hurricane fly,

When they meet with an obstacle, mount to the sky;

So up to the house-top the coursers they flew,

With the sleigh full of Toys—and St. Nicholas too:

And then in a twinkling, I heard on the roof

The prancing and pawing of each little hoof.

As I drew in my head, and was turning around,

Down the chimney St. Nicholas came with a bound:

He was dress'd all in fur, from his head to his foot,

And his clothes were all tarnish'd with ashes and soot;

A bundle of toys was flung on his back,

And he look'd like a peddler just opening his pack:

His eyes—how they twinkled! his dimples how merry,

His cheeks were like roses, his nose like a cherry;
His droll little mouth was drawn up like a bow,
And the beard of his chin was as white as the snow;
The stump of a pipe he held tight in his teeth,
And the smoke it encircled his head like a wreath.
He had a broad face, and a little round belly
That shook when he laugh'd, like a bowl full of jelly:
He was chubby and plump, a right jolly old elf,
And I laugh'd when I saw him in spite of myself;
A wink of his eye and a twist of his head
Soon gave me to know I had nothing to dread.
He spoke not a word, but went straight to his work,
And fill'd all the stockings; then turn'd with a jirk,
And laying his finger aside of his nose
And giving a nod, up the chimney he rose.
He sprung to his sleigh, to his team gave a whistle,
And away they all flew like the down of a thistle:
But I heard him exclaim, ere he drove out of sight—
Happy Christmas to all, and to all a good night.

THE

Author's Advertisement

WHICH IS EARNESTLY RECOMMENDED
TO THE ATTENTIVE PERUSAL

of

THE JUDICIOUS READER.

James Kirke Paulding, from *The Book of St. Nicholas*
(NEW YORK: HARPER AND BROTHERS, 1836)

You will please to understand, gentle reader, that being a true descendant of the adventurous Hollanders who first discovered the renowned island of Manhattan—which is every day becoming more and more worth its weight in paper money—I have all my life been a sincere and fervent follower of the right reverend and jolly St. Nicholas, the only tutelary of this mighty state. I have never, on any proper occasion, omitted doing honour to his memory by keeping his birthday with all due observances, and paying him my respectful devoirs on Christmas and Newyear's eve.

From my youth upward I have been always careful to hang up my stocking in the chimney corner, on both these memorable anniversaries; and this I hope I may say without any unbecoming ebullition of vanity, that on no occasion did I ever fail to receive glorious remembrances of his favour and countenance, always saving two exceptions. Once when the good saint signified his displeasure at my tearing up a Dutch almanac, and again on occasion of my going to a Presbyterian meeting house with a certain little Dutch damsel, by filling my stockings with snow balls, instead savoury oily cookies.

Saving these manifestations of his displeasure, I can safely boast of having been always a special favourite of the good St. Nicholas, who hath ever shown a singular kindness and suavity towards me in all seasons of my life, wherein he hath at divers times and seasons of sore perplexity, more than once vouchsafed to appear to me in dreams and visions, always giving me sage advice and goodly admonition. The which never failed of being of great service to me in my progress through life, seeing I was not only his namesake, but always reverently honoured his name to the best of my poor abilities.

From my youth upward I have, moreover, been accustomed to call upon him in time of need; and this I will say for him, that he always came promptly whenever he was within hearing. I will not detain the expectant reader with the relation of these special instances, touching the years of my juvenility, but straightway proceed to that which is material to my present purpose.

The reader will please to comprehend that after I had, with the labour and research of many years, completed the tales which I now, with an humble deference, offer to his acceptance, I was all at once struck dumb, with the unparalleled difficulty of finding a name for my work, seeing that every title appertinent to such divertisements hath been applied over and over again, long and merry agone. Now, as before intimated to the judicious reader, whenever I am in sore perplexity of mind, as not unfrequently happens to such as (as it were) cudgel their brains for the benefit of their fellow-creatures—I say, when thus beleaguered, I always shut my eyes, lean back in my chair, which is furnished with a goodly stuffed back and arms, and grope for that which I require in the profound depths of abstraction.

It was thus I comported myself on this trying occasion, when, lo! and behold! I incontinently fell asleep, as it were, in the midst of my cogitations, and while I was fervently praying to the good-hearted St. Nicholas to inspire me with a proper and significant name for this my mental offspring. I cannot with certainty say how long I had remained in the bonds of abstraction, before I was favoured with the appearance of a vision, which, at first sight, I knew to be that of the excellent St. Nicholas, who scorns to follow the pestilent fashions of modern times, but ever appears in the ancient dress of the old patriarchs of Holland. And here I will describe the good saint, that peradventure all those to whom he may, in time to come, vouchsafe his presence, may know him at first sight, even as they know the father that begot them.

He is a right fat, jolly, roistering little fellow—if I may make bold to call him so familiarly—and had I not known him of old for a veritable saint, I might, of a truth, have taken him, on this occasion, for little better than a sinner. He was dressed in a snuff-coloured coat of goodly conceited dimensions, having broad skirts, cuffs mighty to behold, and buttons about the size of a moderate Newyear cooky. His waistcoat and breeches, of which he had a proper number, were of the same cloth and colour; his hose of gray worsted; his shoes high-quartered, even up to the instep, ornamented with a pair of silver buckles, exceedingly bright; his hat was of a low crown and right broad brim, cocked up on one side; and in the buttonholes of his coat was ensconced a long delft pipe, almost as black as ebony. His visage was the picture of good-humoured benevolence; and by these marks I knew him as well as I know the nose on my own face.

The good saint, being always in a hurry on errands of good fellowship, and especially about the time of the holydays of Paas and Pinxster; and being withal a person of little ceremony, addressed me without delay, and with much frankness, which was all exceedingly proper, as we were such old friends. He spoke to me in Dutch, which is now a learned language, understood only by erudite scholars.

"What aileth thee, my Godson Nicholas?" quoth he.

I was about to say I was in sore perplexity concerning the matter aforesaid, when he courteously interrupted me, saying,

"Be quiet, I know it, and therefore there is no special occasion for thee to tell me. Thou shalt call thy work 'THE BOOK OF ST. NICHOLAS,' in honour of thy patroon; and here are the materials of my biography, which I charge thee, on pain of empty pockets from this time forward, to dilate and adorn in such a manner, as that, foreseeing, as I do, thy work will go down to the latest posterity, it may do honour to my name, and rescue it from that obscurity in which it hath been enveloped through the crying ignorance of past generations, who have been seduced into a veneration for St. George, St. Dennis, St. David, and other doughty dragon-slaying saints, who were little better than roistering bullies. Moreover, I charge thee, as thou valuest my blessing and protection, to dedicate thy work unto the worthy and respectable societies of St. Nicholas in this my stronghold in the New World. Thou mightst, perhaps, as well have left out that prank of mine at the carousing of old Baltus, but verily it matters not. Let the truth be told."

Saying this, he handed me a roll of ancient vellum, containing, as I afterwards found, the particulars which, in conformity with his solemn command, I have dilated into the only veritable biography of my patron saint which hath ever been given to the world. The one hitherto received as orthodox is, according to the declaration of the saint himself, little better than a collection of legends, written under the express inspection of the old lady of Babylon.

I reverently received the precious deposite, and faithfully promised obedience to his commands; whereupon the good St. Nicholas, puffing in my face a whiff of tobacco smoke more fragrant than all the spices of the East, blessed me, and departed in haste, to be present at a wedding in Communipaw. Hereupon I awoke, and should have thought all that had passed but a dream, arising out of the distempered state of my mind, had I not held in my hand the identical roll of vellum, presented in the manner just related. On examination, it proved to contain the matter which is incorporated in the first story of this collection, under the title of "The Legend of St. Nicholas," not only in due obedience to his command, but in order that henceforward no one may pretend ignorance concerning this illustrious and benevolent saint, seeing they have now a biography under his own hand.

Thus much have I deemed it proper to preface to the reader, as some excuse for the freedom of having honoured my poor fictions with the title of The Book of St. Nicholas, which might otherwise have been deemed a piece of unchristian presumption.

The Legend Of St. Nicholas

Everybody has heard of St. Nicholas, that honest Dutch saint, whom I look upon as having been one of the most liberal, good-natured little fat fellows in the world. But, strange as it may seem, though everybody has heard, nobody seems to know anything about him. The place of his birth, the history of his life, and the manner in which he came to be the dispenser of Newyear cakes, and the patron of good boys, are matters that have hitherto not been investigated, as they ought to have been long and long ago. I am about to supply this deficiency, and pay a debt of honour which is due to this illustrious and obscure tutelary genius of the jolly Newyear.

It hath often been justly remarked that the birth, parentage, and education of the most illustrious personages of antiquity, are usually enveloped in the depths of obscurity. And this obscurity, so far from being injurious to their dignity and fame, has proved highly beneficial; for as no one could tell who were their fathers and mothers on earth, they could the more easily claim kindred with the skies, and trace their descent from the immortals. Such was the case with Saturn, Hercules, Bacchus, and others among the heathens; and of St. George, St. Dennis, St. Andrew, St. Patrick, and the rest of the tutelaries, of whom—I speak it with great respect and reverence—it may justly be said, that nobody would ever have heard of their progenitors but for the renown of their descendants. It is, therefore, no reflection on the respectable St. Nicholas, that his history has hitherto remained a secret, and his origin unknown.

In prosecuting this biography, and thus striving to repay my obligations for divers, and I must say unmerited favours received from this good saint, after whom I was christened, I shall refrain from all invention or hyperbole, seeking the truth industriously, and telling it simply and without reserve or embellishment. I scorn to impose on my readers with cock and bull stories of his killing dragons, slaughtering giants, or defeating whole armies of pagans with his single arm. St. Nicholas was a peaceful, quiet, orderly saint, who, so far as I have been able to learn, never shed a drop of blood in his whole life, except, peradventure, it may be possible he sometimes cut his finger, of which I profess to know nothing, and, therefore, contrary to the custom of biographers, shall say nothing.

St. Nicholas was born—and that is all I can tell of the matter—on the first of January; but in what year or at what place, are facts which I have not been able to ascertain, although I have investigated them with the most scrupulous accuracy. His obscurity would enable me to give him a king and queen for his parents, whereby he might be able to hold up his head with the best of them all; but, as I before observed, I scorn to impose such doubtful, to say no worse, legends upon my readers.

Nothing is known of his early youth, except that it hath come down to us that his mother dreamed, the night before his birth, that the sun was changed into a vast Newyear cake and the stars into *oily cooks*—which she concluded was the reason they burned so bright. It hath been shrewdly intimated by certain would-be antiquaries, who doubtless wanted to appear wiser than they really were, that because our worthy saint was called Nicholas, that must of course have been the name of his father. But I set such conjectures at naught, seeing that if all the sons were called after their fathers, the distinction of senior and junior would no longer be sufficient, and they would be obliged to number them as they do in the famous island of Nantucket, where I hear there are thirty-six Isaac Coffins and sixteen Pelegs.

Now, of the first years of the life of good St. Nicholas, in like manner, we have been able to learn nothing until he was apprenticed to a baker in the famous city of Amsterdam, after which this metropolis was once called, but which my readers doubtless know was christened over again when the English usurped possession, in the teeth of the great right of discovery derived from the illustrious navigator, Henricus Hudson, who was no more an Englishman than I am.

Whether the youth Nicholas was thus apprenticed to a baker on account of his mother's dream, or from his great devotion to Newyear cakes, which may be inferred from the bias of his after life, it is impossible to tell at this distant period. It is certain, however, that he was so apprenticed, and that is sufficient to satisfy all reasonable readers. As for those pestilent, curious, prying people, who want to know the why and wherefore of everything we refer them to the lives of certain famous persons, which are so intermingled and confounded with the lives of their contemporaries, and the events, great and small, which happened in all parts of the world during their sojourn on the earth, that it is utterly impossible to say whose life it is we are reading. Many people of little experience take the title page for a guide, not knowing, peradventure, they might almost as safely rely upon history for a knowledge of the events of past ages.

Little Nicholas, our hero, was a merry, sweet-tempered caitiff, which was, doubtless, somewhat owing to his living almost altogether upon sweet things. He was marvellously devoted to cakes, and ate up numberless gingerbread alphabets before he knew a single letter.

Passing over the intermediate years, of which, indeed, I know no more than the man in the moon, I come to the period when, being twenty-four, and the term of his apprenticeship almost out, he fell desperately in love with the daughter of his worthy master, who was a burgomaster of forty years standing. In those unprecocious times, the boys did not grow to be men and the girls women, so soon as they do now. It would have been considered highly indecent for the former to think of falling in love before they were out of their time, or the latter to set up for young women before they knew how to be anything else. But as soon as the worthy Nicholas arrived at the age of twenty-four, being, as I said, within a year of the expiration of his time, he thought to himself that Katrinchee, or Catharine, as the English call it, was a clever, notable little soul, and eminently calculated to make him a good wife. This was the main point in the times of which I am speaking, when people actually married without first running mad either for love or money.

Katrinchee was the toast of all the young bakers of Amsterdam, and honest Nicholas had as many rivals as there were loaves of bread in that renowned city. But he was as gallant a little Dutchman as ever smoked his way through the world pipe foremost, and did not despair of getting the better of his rivals, especially as he was a great favourite with the burgomaster, as, indeed, his conduct merited. Instead of going the vulgar way to work, and sighing and whining out romance in her ear, he cunningly, being doubtless inspired by Cupid himself, proceeded to insinuate his passion, and make it known by degrees, to the pretty little Katrinchee, who was as plump as a partridge, and had eyes of the colour of a clear sky.

First did he bake a cake in the shape of a heart pierced half through by a toasting fork, the which he presented her smoking hot, which she received with a blush and did eat, to the great encouragement of the worthy Nicholas. A month after, for he did not wish to alarm the delicacy of the pretty Katrinchee, he did bake another cake in the shape of two hearts, entwined prettily with a true lover's knot. This, too, she received with a blush, and did eat with marvellous content. After the expiration of a like period, he did contrive another cake in the shape of a letter, on which he had ingeniously engraven the following couplet:—

"Wer diesen glauben wöhlt hat die vernanft verschworen, Dem denken abgesaght sein eigentham verlohren."

The meaning of which, if the reader doth not comprehend, I do hereby earnestly advise him to set about studying the Dutch language forthwith, that he may properly appreciate its hidden beauties.

Little Katrinchee read this poesy with a sigh, and rewarded the good Nicholas with a look which, as he afterward affirmed, would have heated an oven.

Thus did the sly youth gradually advance himself in the good graces of the little damsel, until at length he ventured a downright declaration, in the shape of a cake made in the exact likeness of a little Dutch Cupid. The acceptance of this was conclusive, and was followed by permission to address the matter to the decision of the worthy burgomaster, whose name I regret hath not come down to the present time.

The good man consulted his pipe, and after six months' hard smoking, came to the conclusion that the thing was feasible. Nicholas was a well-behaved, industrious lad, and the burgomaster justly concluded that the possession of virtuous and industrious habits without houses and lands, was better than houses and lands without them. So he gave his consent like an honest and ever to be respected magistrate.

The news of the intended marriage spoiled all the bread baked in Amsterdam that day. The young bakers were so put out that they forgot to put yeast in their bread, and it was all heavy. But the hearts of the good Nicholas and his bride were as light as a feather notwithstanding, and when they were married it was truly said there was not a handsomer couple in all Amsterdam.

They lived together happily many years, and nothing was wanting to their felicity but a family of little chubby boys and girls. But it was ordained that he never should be blessed with any offspring, seeing that he was predestined to be the patron and benefactor of the children of others, not of his own. In good time, and in the fullness of years, the burgomaster died, leaving his fortune and his business to Nicholas, who had ever been a kind husband to his daughter, and a dutiful son to himself. Rich and liberal, it was one of the chief pleasures of the good Nicholas to distribute his cakes, of which he baked the best in all Amsterdam, to the children of the neighbourhood, who came every morning, and sometimes in the evening; and Nicholas felt his heart warm within his bosom when he saw how they ate and laughed, and were as happy, ay, and happier, too, than so many little kings. The children all loved him, and so did their fathers and mothers, so that in process of time he was made a burgomaster, like his father-in-law before him.

Not only did he entertain the jolly little folk of the city in the manner heretofore described, but his home was open to all travellers and sojourners who had no other home, as well as those who came recommended from afar off. In particular the good pilgrims of the church, who went about preaching and propagating the true faith, by the which I mean the doctrines of the illustrious reformers in all time past.

The good Nicholas had, in the latter part of his life, embraced these doctrines with great peril to himself, for sore were the persecutions they underwent in those days who departed from the crying abominations of the ancient church; and had it not been for the good name he had established in the city of Amsterdam, among all classes, high and low, rich and poor, he might, peradventure, have suffered at the stake. But he escaped, as it were, by a miracle, and lived to see the truth triumph at last even throughout all the land.

But before this came to pass his faithful and affectionate helpmate had been taken from him by death, sorely to his grief; and he would have stood alone in the world had it not been for the little children, now grown up to be men and women, who remembered his former kindness, and did all they could to console him—for such is ever the reward of kindness to our fellow-creatures.

One night as he was sitting disconsolate at home, thinking of poor Katrinchee, and wishing that either she was with him or he with her, he heard a distant uproar in the street, which seemed approaching nearer and nearer. He was about to rise and go to the door to see what was the occasion, when suddenly it was pushed open with some violence, and a man rushed past him with very little ceremony. He seemed in a great hurry, for he panted for breath, and it was some time before he could say,

"I beseech thee to shut the door and hide me, for my life is in danger."

Nicholas, who never refused to do a good-natured act, did as he was desired, so far as shutting and barring the door. He then asked, "What hath endangered thy life, and who art thou, friend, that thou art thus afraid?"

"Ask me not now, I beseech thee, Nicholas—"

"Thou knowest my name then?" said the other, interrupting him.

"I do—everybody knows thee, and thy kindness of heart. But ask me nothing now—only hide me for the present, and when the danger is past I will tell thee all."

"Thou art no murderer or fugitive from justice?"

"No, on my faith. I am sinned against, but I never injured but one man, and I was sorry for that. But hark, I hear them coming—wilt thou or wilt thou not protect me?"

"I will," said the good Nicholas, who saw in the dignified air and open countenance of the stranger something that inspired both confidence and awe. Accordingly he hastily led him into a remote apartment, where he secreted him in a closet, the door of which could not be distinguished, and in which he kept his money and valuables, for he said to himself, I will trust this man, he does not look as if he would abuse my confidence.

"Take this key and lock thyself in, that thou mayst be able to get out in case they take me away."

Presently there was heard a great hallooing and banging at the outward door, with a cry of "Open! open!" and Nicholas went to the door and opened it. A flood of people rushed in helter-skelter, demanding the body of an arch heretic, who, they said, had been seen to take refuge in the house. But with all their rage and eagerness, they begged his excuse for this unceremonious proceeding, for Nicholas was beloved and respected by all, though he was a heretic himself.

"He's here—we saw him enter!" they cried.

"If he is here, find him," quoth Nicholas, quietly. "I will not say he is not here, neither would I betray him if he were."

The interlopers then proceeded to search all parts of the house, except the secret closet, which escaped their attention. When they had done this, one of them said.

"We have heard of thy having a secret place in thy house where thy money and papers are secured. Open it to us—we swear not to molest or take away aught that is thine."

The good Nicholas was confounded at this demand, and stood for a moment not knowing what to say or what to do. The stranger in the closet heard it too; but he was a stout-hearted man, and trusted in the Lord.

"Where is thy strong closet?" cried one of the fiercest and most forward of the intruders. "We must and will find it."

"Well, then, find it," quoth Nicholas, quietly.

They inspected the room narrowly, and knocked against the walls in hopes the hollow sound would betray the secret of the place. But they were disappointed, for the door was so thick that it returned no hollow sound.

They now began to be impatient, and savage withal, and the ferocious leader exclaimed,

"Let us take this fellow then. One heretic is as good as another—as bad I mean."

"Seize him!" cried one.

"Away with him!" cried another.

"To the stake!" cried a third.

They forgot the ancient kindness of the good man; for bigotry and over-heated zeal remember not benefits, and pay no respect to the obligations of gratitude. The good Nicholas was violently seized, his hands tied behind him, and he was about to be carried away a sacrifice to the demon of religious discord, when the door of the closet flew open, and the stranger came forth with a step so firm, a look so lofty and inspired, that the rabble quailed, and were silent before him.

"Unbind this man," said he, in a voice of authority, "and bind me in his stead."

Not a man stirred. They seemed spell bound, and stood looking at each other in silent embarrassment.

"Unbind this man, I say!"

Still they remained, as it were, petrified with awe and astonishment.

"Well, then, I shall do it myself," and he proceeded to release the good Nicholas from his bonds, while the interlopers remained silent and motionless.

"Mistaken men!" then said he, looking at them with pity, mingled with indignation, "you believe yourselves fulfilling the duties of your faith when you chase those who differ from you about the world, as if they were wild beasts, and drag them to the stake, like malefactors who have committed the worst crimes against society. You think that the blood of human victims is the most acceptable offering to your Maker, and worse than the ignorant pagans, who made martyrs of the blessed saints, sacrifice them on the altar of a religion which is all charity, meekness, and forgiveness. But I see you are ashamed of yourselves. Go, and do so no more."

The spirit of intolerance quailed before the majesty of truth and genius. The poor deluded men, whose passions had been stimulated by mistaken notions of religious duty, bowed their heads and departed, rebuked and ashamed.

"Who art thou?" asked Nicholas, when they were gone.

"Thou shalt soon know," replied the stranger. "In the mean time listen to me. I must be gone before the fiend, which I have, perhaps, only laid for a few moments, again awakens in the bosoms of these deluded men, or some others like them get on the scent of their prey, and track their victim hither. Listen to me, Nicholas, kind and good Nicholas. Thou wouldst have endangered thy own life for the safety of a stranger—one who had no claim on thee save that of hospitality—nay, not even that, for I was not thy guest by invitation, but intrusion. Blessed be thee and thine, thy house, thy memory when thou art dead, and thy lot hereafter. Thou art worthy to know who I am."

He then disclosed to him a name with which the world hath since rung, from clime to clime, from country to country. A name incorporated inseparably with the interests of truth and the progress of learning.

"Tell it not in Gath—proclaim it not in the streets of Askalon," continued he, "for it is a name which carries with it the sentence of death in this yet benighted city. Interests of the deepest nature—interests vitally connected with the progress of truth—the temporal and eternal happiness of millions living, of millions yet unborn, brought me hither. The business I came upon is in part performed; but it is now known to some that I am, or have been in the city, who will never rest till they run me down and tear me in pieces. Farewell, and look for thy reward, if not here, hereafter—for, sure as thou livest and breathest, a good action, done with a pure and honest motive, is twice blessed—once to the doer and once to him to whom it is done.

The good Nicholas would have knelt to the mighty genius that stood before him, but he prevented him.

"I am no graven image, nor art thou an idolater that thou shouldst kneel to me. Farewell! Let me have thy prayers, for the prayers of a good man are indeed blessings."

Saying this, the illustrious stranger departed in haste, and Nicholas never saw him more for a long time. But he said to himself,

"Blessed is my house, for it hath sheltered the bright light of the universe."

From that time forward, he devoted himself to the good cause of the reformation with heart and soul. His house was ever the refuge of the persecuted; his purse the never-failing resource of the distressed; and many were the victims of bigotry and intolerance whom his influence and entreaties saved from the stake and the torture. He lived a blessing to all within the sphere of his influence, and was blessed in living to see the faith which he loved and cherished at length triumph over the efforts of power, the arts of intrigue, and the fire of bigotry.

Neither did he forget or neglect the customary offices of kindness and good will to the little children of the city, who continued still to come and share his goodly cakes, which he gave with the smile and the open hand of kind and unaffected benignity. It must have been delightful to see the aged patriarch sitting at his door, while the little boys and girls gathered together from all parts to share his smiles, to be patted on the head, and kissed, and laden with his bounties.

Every Newyear's day especially, being his birthday, as it came round, was a festival, not only to all the children, but to all that chose to come and see him. It seemed that he grew younger instead of older on each return of the season; for he received every one with smiles, and even his enemies were welcome to his good cheer. He had not the heart to hate anybody on the day which he had consecrated to innocent gayety, liberal hospitality, and universal benevolence. In process of time, his example spread among the whole city, and from thence through the country, until every village and town, nay, every house, adopted the good custom of setting apart the first day of the year to be gay and happy, to exchange visits, and shake hands with friends and to forgive enemies.

Thus the good Nicholas lived, blessing all and blessed by all, until he arrived at a happy old age. When he had reached fourscore years, he was sitting by himself late in the evening of the first of January, old style, which is the only true and genuine era after all—the new style being a pestilent popish innovation—he was sitting, I say, alone, the visitors having all departed, laden with gifts and good wishes. A knock was heard at the door, which always opened of itself, like the heart of its owner, not only on Newyear's day, but every day in the year.

A stately figure entered and sat down by him, after shaking his hand right heartily. The good Nicholas was now old, and his eyesight had somewhat failed him, particularly at night.

"Thou art welcome," quoth the old man.

"I know it," replied the other, "every one is welcome to the house of the good Nicholas, not only on this, but every other day. I have heard of thee in my travels."

"Thou knowest my name—may I not know thine?"

The stranger whispered a name in his ear, which made the heart of the good Nicholas leap in his bosom.

"Dost thou remember the adventure of the closet?" said the stranger.

"Yea—blessed be the day and the hour," said the old man.

And now they had a long conversation, which pertained to high matters, not according with the nature of my story, and therefore I pass them by, more especially as I do not exactly know what they were.

"I almost fear to ask thee," at length said Nicholas; "but thou wilt partake of my cheer, on this the day of my birth. I shall not live to see another."

Old people are often prophetic on the duration of their lives.

"Assuredly," replied the other, "for it is neither beneath my character nor calling to share the good man's feast, and to be happy when I can."

So they sat down together and talked of old times, and how much better the new times were than the old, inasmuch as the truth had triumphed, and they could now enjoy their consciences in peace.

The illustrious visiter staid all night; and the next morning, as he was about to depart, the aged Nicholas said to him,

"Farewell—I shall never see thee again. Thou art going a long journey, thou sayst, but I am about venturing on one yet longer."

"Well, be it so," said the other. "But those who remain behind will bless thy name and thy memory. The little children will love thee, and so long as thy countrymen cherish their ancient customs, thou wilt not be forgotten."

They parted, and the prediction of the good Nicholas was fulfilled. He fell asleep in the arms of death, who called him so softly, and received him so gently in his embrace, that though his family knew he slept, they little thought it was for ever.

When this news went abroad into the city, you might see the worthy burgomasters and citizens knocking the ashes out of their pipes, and putting them quietly by in their buttonholes; and the good housewives, ever and anon lifting their clean white aprons to their eyes, that they might see to thread their needles or find the stitches, as they sat knitting their stockings. The shops and schools were all shut the day he was buried; and it was remarked that the men neglected their usual amusements, and the little children had no heart to play.

When the whole city had gathered together at the side of his grave, there suddenly appeared among them a remarkable and goodly-looking man, of most reverent demeanour. Every one bowed their bodies, in respectful devotion, for they knew the man, and what they owed him. All was silent as the grave, just about to receive the body of Nicholas, when he I have just spoken of lifted his head, and said as follows:—

"The good man just about to enter the narrow house never defrauded his neighbour, never shut his door on the stranger, never did an unkind action, nor ever refused a kind one either to friend or foe. His heart was all goodness, his faith all purity, his morals all blameless, yea, all praiseworthy. Such a man deserves the highest title that can be bestowed on man. Join me then, my friends, old and young—men, women, and children, in blessing his memory as *the good Saint Nicholas*; for I know no better title to such a distinction than pure faith, inflexible integrity, and active benevolence." Thus spake the great reformer, John Calvin.

The whole assembled multitude, with one voice and one heart, cried out, "Long live the blessed memory of the good St. Nicholas!" as they piously consigned him to the bosom of his mother earth.

Thus did he come to be called St. Nicholas; and the people, not content with this, as it were by a mutual sympathy, and without coming to any understanding on the subject, have ever since set apart the birthday of the good man, for the exercise of hospitality to men, and gifts to little children. From the Old World they carried the custom to the New, where their posterity still hold it in reverence, and where I hope it will long continue to flourish, in spite of the cold heartless forms, unmeaning ceremonies, and upstart pretensions of certain vulgar people, who don't know any better, and therefore ought to be pitied for their ignorance, rather than contemned for their presumption.

GALLERY

of *Santas*

Robert Walter Weir, *St. Nicholas*, ca. 1837, oil on wood,
SMITHSONIAN AMERICAN ART MUSEUM.

◀ Weir's faintly goblinish portrait of *St. Nicholas*, inspired by Moore's poem, was influential in its moment and beyond. Susan Fenimore Cooper, for example, referred to it in her account of Santa Claus in 1850 (see later in this volume). A review of this picture, following its appearance in the National Academy of Design, was published in the *The New-York Mirror* on June 17th 1837: "Mr. Weir has represented the children's Christmas friend with great humour. The arch expression is most admirable. In drawing the picture is perfect, and it is rich and transparent in colouring. The accessories tell the story as plainly as the attitude and face. This composition sustains the artist's high reputation."

Illustration for "A Visit from St. Nicholas" in *The Poets of America*, edited by John Keese
(NEW YORK: S. COLMAN, 1840)

▶ This illustration, accompanying a reprinting of Moore's poem, is a notably recognisable Santa Claus—including sleigh and reindeer.

A VISIT FROM ST. NICHOLAS.

BY C. C. MOORE.

'T was the night before Christmas, when all thro' the house
Not a creature was stirring, not even a mouse:
The stockings were hung by the chimney with care,
In hopes that St. Nicholas soon would be there;

NEW-YORK MIRROR.

A WEEKLY GAZETTE OF LITERATURE AND THE FINE ARTS.

Embellished with fine Engravings, and Music arranged with Accompaniments for the Pianoforte.

FIVE DOLLARS A YEAR.] SUBSCRIPTIONS RECEIVED AT THE OFFICE OF PUBLICATION NO. 148 NASSAU-STREET. [PAYABLE IN ADVANCE.

VOLUME NINETEEN. NEW-YORK, SATURDAY, JANUARY 2, 1841. NUMBER ONE.

ST. NICHOLAS, ON HIS NEW-YEAR'S EVE EXCURSION, (AS INGHAM SAW HIM,) IN THE ACT OF DESCENDING A CHIMNEY.

Charles C. Ingham, "St. Nicholas", *The New York Mirror* (1841).

◂ When this illustration was published in the *New York Mirror* in 1841, the editors prefaced its appearance with an apology: they had commissioned Robert Walter Weir to provide them with an engraving of his painting of St. Nicholas (see above), but they had been let down by the artist. Instead, another notable New York artist, Charles Ingham, had stepped into the breech, and purported to have drawn the gift-bringer "just as he saw him one bright, frosty, moonlight night, as he was returning home late from a party of friends [...] we feel that our friend Ingham has been a very highly favoured mortal in being permitted to see him whom we have so many years longed to get a peep at." Though hardly agreeing with our idea of an ideal Santa, the illustration proved a hit. One reader described what happened when he took the paper to his neighbours: "I can't stop to tell you how glad they were to see me, and how quickly the arm-chair was dusted off and pushed in front of the stove for me, that all the young tow-heads might cluster around me, and see *Santa Claus himself*! Oh how the young urchins gazed at Nick's queer phiz! how they scanned his budget and recognized *just such* things as they had; how they questioned me as to how Mr. Ingham *could* take his picture *so plain*, when they knew the kind of old saint only travels about at *night* [...] and then how they rattled on, and questioned the old folk as to *whether it was all true!*"

SANTA CLAUS.

THE NIGHT BEFORE NEW YEAR

Designed and Engraved expressly for the New Mirror by Shennon & Sonth

For 1844

"Santa Claus",
The New Mirror,
DECEMBER 30 1843

◂ The New Mirror accompanied this illustration of Santa Claus with the following description of his visit on New Year's—not Christmas—Eve: "Santa Claus has doffed his cocked-hat and assumes one in unison with the weather. The sign of the saint is stamped on his forehead as the genuine impress of heaven. He wears his snow-boots and fur-tipped mantle, which are the very same with which he journeyed over the hills of Holland. The artist has represented him about the midnight hour, on his last call; and, from the position of the saint, we should judge that he had heard, or thought he heard, the cock crow; or the rats, which are the great antipathy of the Dutch. Saint Nicholas is smothered with *gooderies*, and is prepared to be very lavish upon those who live in *expectancy* of presents. The family have retired, the little ones are dreaming most intensely of crammed stockings, which they have hung so as to attract the attention of the saint. We fancy ourselves looking upon the little, short limbs, on tip-toes, straining to place their hose out of the way of rats. Jane can scarcely reach higher than one of these animals; the larger boys and girls have obtained a better position; and one appears to tower above the rest, who, no doubt, has received the friendly aid of grandfather. The mother has coaxed them off to bed earlier than usual, and has saved a ration of gingerbread. Neither tears, words, sobs, nor petulance disturb them now; they know the saint visits only good children; and Bob, Sally and Peter find it difficult to hold their tongues. Their mother promises them, even though they have been violent transgressors throughout the year, that, for one night's peace, she will bribe the saint for them. They fancy they hear the sound of whistles, penny-trumpets and drums; the cries of dolls, the singing of wooden birds, and the ticking of pewter watches; then boxes of tools are already at work repairing houses built in air; and they fairly stagger under the inheritance of a new-year. When sound asleep, emblems of innocence and the kingdom of heaven, they are blessed with a diffusion of presents; the morning dawns, and the family are disturbed by their up-risings. On other mornings it may have been difficult to arouse them, but, on new-year's, trumpets and drums bring them down, scarcely half awake. John (who is advanced to the age of small boots) takes the lead; he misses his way, or runs against the door. Sally and Mary, aided by the bannisters, come down crying with impatience. The little ones seize their stockings with eagerness, Sally substituting a chair for her grandfather. The day is consumed. with comments, eyes sparkle with delight, and the faces of all beam with happiness."

T. C. Boyd, illustrations from
A Visit from St. Nicholas
(NEW YORK: HENRY M. ONDERDONK, 1848)

▼▶ These jaunty illustrations by T. C. Boyd accompanied the first stand-alone, illustrated edition of *A Visit from St. Nicholas*.

66   SEARCHING FOR SANTA CLAUS

First Footings

SANTA CLAUS'S VISIT.

"Santa Claus Paying His Usual Christmas Visit to His Young Friends",
Harper's Weekly,
DECEMBER 25, 1858

▼ This oddity graced the cover of *Harper's Weekly* in 1858. Substituting turkey for reindeer was not an innovation that caught on.

F. O. C. Darley, illustrations from
A Visit from St. Nicholas
(NEW YORK: JAMES G. GREGORY, 1862)

▼▶ It's arguable that these illustrations by F.O.C. Darley—accompanying another illustrated edition of *A Visit from St. Nicholas* in 1862—were the first to really capture a likeness of the Santa Claus that we are familiar with today.

"Now, Dasher! now, Dancer! now, Prancer and Vixen!
On! Comet, on! Cupid, on! Dunder and Blitzen—
To the top of the porch, to the top of the wall!
Now, dash away, dash away, dash away all!"
As dry leaves that before the wild hurricane fly,
When they meet with an obstacle, mount to the sky,
So, up to the house-top the coursers they flew,
With a sleigh full of toys—and St. Nicholas too.
And then in a twinkling I heard on the roof,
The prancing and pawing of each little hoof.
As I drew in my head, and was turning around,
Down the chimney St. Nicholas came with a bound.

He was dressed all in fur from his head to his foot,
And his clothes were all tarnished with ashes and soot;
A bundle of toys he had flung on his back,
And he looked like a peddler just opening his pack:
His eyes how they twinkled! his dimples how merry!
His cheeks were like roses, his nose like a cherry:

His droll little mouth was drawn up like a bow,
And the beard on his chin was as white as the snow;
The stump of a pipe he held tight in his teeth,
And the smoke, it encircled his head like a wreath.
He had a broad face, and a little round belly
That shook when he laughed, like a bowl full of jelly.

"A Letter for the Children",
The Mother's Magazine and Family Library
(FEBRUARY 1843)

A happy new-year to you, kind friends. My name is St. Nicholas, though I love better the more familiar title which all the little children give me, and by which I am best known: my name with them is *Santa Claus*.

I am an independent old man. I always do as I please. I go where I choose. I ask no leave or license, and I give no reasons. If it suits my fancy, I take my seat unbidden at the fireside, and mingle unasked in the gay party. Sometimes (for I am not always the jesting, frolicking person I am supposed) I stand by the couch of the suffering, and my tears fall with weeping friends over the dying bed of the dear ones to whom their hearts were bound. I think I am not always appreciated, for few deem me a man of deep feeling, and no one gives me credit for being interested, as I really am, in things which are serious and important. I find a great advantage in being devoid of all bashfulness, for I do not fear to introduce myself when and where I please. I make no apologies, and I never consider myself an intruder. Many of my friends deem me imprudent, and are very anxious lest I should some day so injure my reputation as to lose my influence, and thereby the world be deprived of the good which I am now able to accomplish. But I have no fears. I find many friends and few foes; and having no unkind feelings myself toward any living being, I seldom meet with any in others.

Even now, while I am writing, some considerate ones are warning me of my danger in presuming to address a letter to the Editors of the Mother's Magazine, and prophesying that I shall be speedily dismissed from such company. "You will be obliged to retreat in haste," say these whisperers, "if you presume to show yourself among such august and sedate dignitaries. What! do you think they will welcome you to deliberate with them—you, the imaginary patron of toys and playthings? Are you so bereft of all reason as to suppose that those who send out that valuable but grave publication will listen to your suggestions? What if you do love little children, and know a great deal about them? What if you do spend your life in devising means for their happiness? What if you can relate tales almost innumerable concerning their life and death? Do you fancy they will listen to your stories? No, no. You had better mind your own business, and go on in your own way. Although your object is the same as that of these good people, yet they will never tolerate your modes of proceeding. Although your influence is vast among the youthful members of every family and your experience great, you will never be allowed to cooperate with them. If you are not careful, you will get severely punished for your impudence, and be effectually banished from many a circle which is now gladdened by your yearly visit."

I heed them not. They mean well, but they are not over wise, and in spite of all their croaking, I write on. I send my letter to wish you most respectfully a happy new-year, and to tell you how I love the little children, and all the young people whom you are trying to benefit. I have also another object, which is to offer my services in aid of your work. I have travelled through many countries and seen various people . I have witnessed many a spirit-stirring incident, and many a heart thrilling scene. I have mingled in the merriest circles of merry England, and the gayest festivities of gay and laughing France. I have found a resting-place in the happy house of the pilgrims, and had many a frolic in the sunny South. My presence is welcomed in palace and cot; by the fire-side of the farmer and beneath the hospitable roof of the planter. I can tell tales of many lands, and in this way I may perhaps do good. If, then, you will allow me, I will send you now and then a letter, and if the stories of the old man should interest any of the youthful readers who may chance to turn over your pages, or increase the desire to do them good in the breast of a single individual, he will be satisfied. Do not fear that laughter and fun will be the sum of their contents, for he who has travelled as far as I have through this mingled scene of life, cannot fail to have many a serious thought, and he who sets himself to the task of relating what he has seen, though he may choose to look chiefly on the bright and happy spots, will yet be obliged sometimes to dip his pencil in deeper colors and to cast upon the picture some dark and sorrowful shades. I will tell the truth—may it do good.

ST. NICHOLAS.

2.

Taking Stock of Santa at Mid-Century

Susan Fenimore Cooper, *Rural Hours*
(NEW YORK: GEORGE P. PUTNAM, 1850):

Saturday, 23d.—Winter in its true colors at last; a bright, fine day, with a foot of snow lying on the earth. Last night the thermometer fell to 8° above zero, and this morning a narrow border of ice appeared along the lake shore.

Sleighs are out for the first time this winter; and, as usual, the good people enjoy the first sleighing extremely. Merry bells are jingling through the village streets; cutters and sleighs with gay parties dashing rapidly about.

It is well for Santa Claus that we have snow. If we may believe Mr. Moore, who has seen him nearer than most people, he travels in a miniature sleigh "with eight tiny rein-deer:"

"Now Dasher, now Dancer! Now Prancer, now Vixen!

On Cupid, on Cornet! On Donner and Blixen!

Now dash away, dash away, dash away all!

As leaves, that before the wild hurricane fly.

When they meet with an obstacle mount to the sky;

So up to the house-top the coursers they flew,

With the sleigh full of toys, and St. NIcholas too;

And then in a twinkling I heard on the roof,

The pawing and prancing of each little hoof."

▼

The domain of Santa Claus has very much extended itself since his earliest visits to the island of Manhattan, when he first alighted, more than two hundred years ago, on the peaked roofs of New Amsterdam, and made his way down the ample chimneys of those days. In this part of the country he is very well known. One has regular applications on Christmas-eve for permission to hang up stockings about the chimney for Santa Claus to fill; Sunday-scholars and other little folk come stocking in hand as a matter of course, and occasionally grown persons follow their example. It seems at first rather singular that Santa Claus should especially favor stockings and chimneys; one cannot easily account for the fancy; but a notion of this sort has spread far and wide. In France the children put their shoes on the hearth Christmas-eve, with the hope that during the night they will be filled with sugar-plums by the "Bon-Homme Noel," who is evidently a twin brother of Santa Claus. But these are matters in which experience sets reason at defiance. The children will all tell you that Santa Claus comes down the chimney—in this part of the world he will even squeeze through a stove-pipe—and that he fills stockings with good things, always looking after that particular part of their wardrobe, though why he should do so remains a mystery yet unfathomed. It seems a silly notion, perhaps. If you belong to the wondrous-wise school, you will probably despise him for it; a sensible man, you will say, would put the sugar plums in the child's pocket, or leave them with the parents. No doubt of it; but Santa Claus is not a sensible man; he is a funny, jolly little old Dutchman, and he and the children understand each other perfectly well. Some of us believe that he comes down the chimney expressly to make wise people open their eyes at the absurdity of the thing, and fills stockings because you would never dream of doing so yourself; and there cannot be a doubt that the little people had much rather receive their toys and sugar-plums by the way of the chimney than through the door, and that they find it far more delightful to pull treasure after treasure from the stocking than to take them in a matter-of-fact way from the hands of their respected parents.

Some people use harsh language toward our old friend; they call him an impostor, and even accuse him of being, under false colors, an enemy of the little folk; they say he misleads them. Not he, indeed; he is just as far from desiring to deceive his little friends as Mother Goose, or the historian of Jack the Giant-killer, and little Red Riding Hood; such an idea never enters his head. Moreover, if he tried it, he would fail. Children are not so easily deceived as you think; for, in all simple matters, all that comes within their own sphere of judgment, the little creatures have a remarkable instinct which guides them with the nicest tact in deciding upon the true and the false. They know, for instance, who loves them, and who only makes believe; they understand fully that this friend must be respected and obeyed, while that one can be trifled with all day long; they feel they can trust A— with the whole confidence of their loving little hearts, and B—is an individual of whom they have a very indifferent opinion, though they do not choose, perhaps, to express it in words. As for Santa Claus, they understand him well enough; they feel his kindness and they respect his reproofs, for these are always made with justice; they know he is a very great friend of children, and chief counsellor of papas and mammas; they are perfectly sure he will come to-night, and that their stockings will be filled by him. Tom is a little afraid he will bring a new birch twig with him, and Bessie has some fears of a great bitter pill to cure her of crying; still, they would not have him stay away for the world, and they go to sleep to dream of him. But at this very moment, if you were to step into the nursery and tell Tom and Bessie that Santa Claus is in the next room, and wishes to see them, they would not believe you. If you were to repeat the assertion, it is probable that Bessie would reprove you for telling a story, and Tom might go so far as to enter into a logical disquisition on the subject, informing you that nobody ever sees Santa Claus, for the reason that there is no such person; who ever heard of an old man's driving up the side of a house, over the roof, and down the chimney! Such things can't be done; he knows it very well. Nevertheless, next year Tom and Bessie will be just as eager as ever for a visit from Santa Claus, and they will continue to think his sugarplums the sweetest, and his toys the most delightful of all that are given to them, until they have quite done with toys and sugarplums—with those of the nursery, at least. Happy will it be for the little people if they never have a worse enemy, a worse friend either, among their acquaintances, whether real or fictitious. In fact, there is no more danger that the children should believe in the positive existence of Santa Claus, than there is a probability of their believing the Christmas-tree to grow out of the tea-table. We should be careful, however, to make them understand every Christmas, that the good things they now receive as children are intended to remind them of far better gifts bestowed on them and on us.

But most of the wisest people in the land know little more about Santa Claus than the children. There is a sort of vague, moonlight mystery still surrounding the real identity of the old worthy. Most of us are satisfied with the authority of pure unalloyed tradition going back to the burghers of New Amsterdam, more especially now that we have the portrait by Mr. Weir, and the verses of Professor Moore, as confirmation of nursery lore. It is only here and there that one finds a ray of light falling upon something definite. We are told, for instance, that there was many hundred years ago, in the age of Constantine, a saintly Bishop by the name of Nicholas, at Patara, in Asia Minor, renowned for his piety and charity. In the course of time, some strange legends sprang up concerning him; among other acts of mercy, he was supposed to have restored to life two lads who had been murdered by their treacherous host, and it was probably owing to this tradition that he was considered the especial friend of children. When the Dominican fraternity arose, about 1200, they selected him as their patron saint. He was also—and is, indeed, to this day—held in great honor by the Greek Church in Russia. He was considered as the especial patron of scholars, virgins, and seamen. Possibly, it was through some connection with this last class that he acquired such influence in the nurseries of Holland. Among that nautical race, the patron saint of sea-faring men must have been often invoked before the Reformation, by the wives and children of those who were far away on the stormy seas of Africa and the Indies. The festival of St. Nicholas fell on the 6th of December, but a short time before Christmas. It seems that the Dutch Reformed Church engaged in a revision of the Calendar, at the time of the Reformation, by a regular court, examining the case of each individual canonized by the Church of Rome, something in the way of the usual proceedings at a canonization by that Church. The claims of the individual to the honors of a saint were advanced on one hand, and opposed on the other. It is said that wherever they have given a decision, it has always been against the claimant. But in a number of instances they have left the case still open to investigation to the present hour, and among other cases of this kind stands that of Sanctus Klaas, or St. Nicholas. In the mean time, until the question should be finally settled, his anniversary was to be kept in Holland, and the children, in the little hymn they used to sing in his honor, were permitted to address him as *"goedt heyligh man"*—good holy man. It appears that it was not so much at Christmas, as on the eve of his own festival, that he was supposed to drive his wagon over the roofs, and down the chimneys, to fill little people's stockings. For these facts, our authority is the Benson Memoir. A number of years since, it may be thirty or forty, Judge Benson, so well known to the old New Yorkers as the highest authority upon all Dutch chapters, had a quantity of regular "cookies" made, and the little hymn said by the children in honor of St. Nicholas, printed in Dutch and sent a supply of each as a Christmas present to the children of his particular friends. But though we have heard of this hymn, we have never yet been able to meet with it. Probably it is still in existence, among old papers in some garret or storeroom.

Strange indeed has been the two-fold metamorphosis undergone by the pious, ancient Bishop of Patara. We have every reason to believe that there once lived a saintly man of that name and charitable character, but, as in many other cases, the wonders told of him by the monkish legends are too incredible to be received upon the evidence which accompanies them. Then later, in a day of revolutions, we find every claim disputed, and the pious, Asiatic bishop appears before us no longer a bishop, no longer an Asiatic, no longer connected with the ancient world, but a sturdy, kindly, jolly old burgher of Amsterdam, half Dutchman, half "spook." The legend-makers of the cloister on one hand, the nurses and gossips of Dutch nurseries, black and white, on the other, have made strange work of it. It would be difficult to persuade the little people now that "Santa Claus" ever had a real existence; and yet, perhaps, we ought to tell them that there was once a saintly man of that name, who did many such good deeds as all Christians are commanded to do, works of love and mercy. At present they can only fancy Santa Claus as Mr. Moore has seen him, in those pleasant, funny verses, which are so highly relished in our nurseries:

"His eyes, how they twinkled! His dimples, how merry!

His cheeks were like roses—his nose like a cherry;

His droll little mouth was drawn up like a bow,

And the beard on his chin was as white as the snow.

The stump of a pipe he held tight in his teeth,

And the smoke it encircled his head like a wreath.

He had a broad face, and a little, round belly,

That shook, when he laughed, like a bowl full of jelly;

He was chubby and plump, a right jolly old elf;

And I laughed, when I saw him, in spite of myself."

"The Drolleries of Santa Claus", *Woodworth's Youth's Cabinet* (1853)

It quite puzzles my brain how such a personage as our merry friend Santa Claus ever found his way into the calendar. He is sometimes called Saint Nicholas, I believe. But is this Nicholas the same saint as the one held in especial repute by the Russians? If so, he is a famous patron of virgins and seafaring men; and besides though that is not very much to his praise, and I don't set it down to his credit-the arch-fiend somehow got his name of Old Knick from him. How is it? Shades of our Dutch ancestors! solve the enigma, and let not the terrible fate happen to us that Hamlet was afraid would happen to him, in case his father's shade did not speak to him. Santa Claus seems to have been a fast friend of the Dutch boys and girls, from time immemorial; and I mistrust that some of our citizens, with names so long and guttural that an out-and-out Yankee would make sad work pronouncing them, could tell us how he came to be canonized, and when and where that great event took place. I hope they will dispel all the fog that hangs about our minds on this subject, and that they will do it very soon indeed, if not sooner. But I cannot "pause for a reply."

My head is at present so full of this veteran Santa Claus and his drolleries, that I must chat a minute about him, at all events. In the absence of the authentic chronicles concerning his birth, early education, and wonderful exploits, while in the flesh, it may not be amiss to collect in a compact ball what we do know about him, and to wind around that ball some threads of tradition. In so doing, it is to be hoped I shall not fall into a track like that reputed to have been pursued by a rather queer parson, who divided his discourse into three separate parts, thus: "First," he said, "I will tell you, my hearers, what you and I both know of this subject; secondly, what I know and you don't know; and thirdly, what neither you nor I know much about."

It has been said, by those who have unquestionably very tolerable means of forming a correct judgment, that this Santa Claus is, after all, a fabulous character, something like the St. George who is famed for dragon-killing, and something like the St. Valentine who performs such service in love affairs on a certain day in the year. But be that as it may—whether our generous old friend Santa Claus be purely a creature of the fancy, as I half suspect he is, or not—it cannot be denied that he has got the credit of doing wonderful, almost miraculous things for good boys and girls during the Christmas and New Year holidays. He cuts endless capers with them. He is as sly as a very thief in bestowing his favors. He comes not with the sound of the trumpet, as the hypocrites do, when he chooses to open his heart or his pocket for the benefit of the little people. Santa Claus—mark that—is never seen. Nobody ever saw him, though everybody has heard of him, and handled, perhaps tasted, the good things he has left behind him, while his little friends were sound asleep. Endless stories are current about his mysterious egress to the family circle. Now-a-days, we hear of his coming down the chimney. This mode of entering a house would be deemed rather improper for any other personages besides Santa Claus and the chimney-sweep. But how did the notion get wind that this jolly saint came down the chimney? Probably because it must seem so plain that there is no other way, when the doors and windows are closed, for him to get in. But how did he manage, in the very olden time, when our ancestors in Britain had no chimneys to their houses? That is a question over which I have never heard any learning expended. Would it not be well for our wise men to call up the subject, and shed some beams of light upon it?

Santa Claus has generally been supposed to be a near blood relative of old Father Christmas, whom he greatly resembles, as all the world knows. But I have been pondering over that matter, and I have come to the conclusion that Father Christmas and Santa Claus are one and the same individual, with different names. I don't ask any one else to believe this, without examining the question; but my mind is thoroughly made up. Our English ancestors, long time ago, made a great account of Father Christmas. Precisely where they discovered the merry old fellow, may be a matter of doubt. It may be he turned up among a multitude of rather fabulous characters, which our forefathers imported from Scandinavia. At all events, the outward appearance and turn of mind with which they invest him are entirely in keeping with those of a personage famed in the mythology of those northern regions. Father Christmas, by those who seem to have the best acquaintance with him, is represented with an elf-like face, a crown of mistletoe on his head, a very long and snowy beard, a great log on his back, with which to make a huge fire on the kitchen hearth, and a mammoth bowl in his hand, the contents of which are supposed to be capable of making all the mouths in the kingdom water at once. It would be a curious and profitable problem for you to try to solve, by reading history and by conversation with older persons, how and when all the customs connected with the observance of the Christmas and New Year festivals originated. No doubt they came into vogue gradually, not all at once, and they were imported, too, we have reason to believe, from different portions of the world. Some might have come from the old Druids. Are not the oak log which old Father Christmas carries on his back, and the crown of mistletoe on his head, relics of the Druidical notions? Some of the associations connected with these festivals came from the Northmen, and some from the ancient Romans. But, wherever they came from, and however they originated, I confess I have a great respect for them. To my mind, whether they had their origin among Pagans or Christians, they seem innocent, and as they make the little folks happy, I respect them, and vote for them. No matter if the genius sometimes called Santa Claus, sometimes St. Nicholas, and sometimes Father Christmas, is an imaginary personage, having no real existence, except in the imagination of children. There is no harm in talking, in sport, as if your nice things came through such a medium as that of Santa Claus. When, after hanging up your stocking at night, you find it crowded full of beautiful and valuable presents, it is well enough to say, in fun, "See what Santa Claus has done for me!" In fun-—not seriously. I want all my young friends to get in the habit of looking to another Being as the source of all the good things they receive. He is invisible, too. We cannot see his hand, when he bestows his gifts. We cannot hear his voice. But, unlike the fabled genius we have been talking of, he is a living, acting, loving Spirit, nevertheless. All that we enjoy comes from him. Let us ever remember this. Let us learn to say, with the Psalmist, "Bless the Lord, O my soul, and forget not all his benefits."

"Is Not Santa Claus a God?",
Youth's Penny Gazette,
JANUARY 7 1846.

(A question actually asked by a little child.)

"It's a thing that has troubled my head all day,
  Whether out with the boys or alone,
I am sure, that I often have heard you say,
That there's one God above to whom we pray,
  And that there is only One.

"And is it so, father? Please tell,
  For I very much wish to know."
"Why sure, my son, you remember full well
That one God alone in heaven doth well,
  And reigns o'er the earth below."

"Well! I can't understand it!" at last Philip sighed,
  And it puzzles my poor little head,
For there must be more than one; and beside,
If old Effie says true, there is!" he cried.
"Well, come tell me, my boy, what she said."

"Why, father, I've been with her an hour or more,
  And such beautiful stories she tells,
About Santa Claus and his sleigh and four,
And that loads of toys that he has in store,
  And his merry, jingling bells!

"And he rides o'er the roofs with a skip and a bound,
  And down every chimney he goes,
And wherever the good children's stockings are found,
He brings down a load and goes quietly round
  And stuffs them clean down to the toes."

"And I have been told, if I'm cross and don't mind,
 That Santa Claus all will know,
 And that leaving the toys, meant for me, all behind,
 To my poor empty stocking his eyes will be blind,
 And away up the chimney he'll go.

"Now, please, father, tell me: pray how can it be,
 If he can go all abroad,
 And over the land, and over the sea,
 And all the time can be looking at me,
 Why Santa Claus is not a God?"

"Ah, I now see the reason of all that you've said,
 And I'm not much surprised at the cause
 Of the trouble there's been in your 'poor little head,'
 From the foolish stories you've heard and read,
 Of this wonderful Santa Claus.

"My boy, believe me, when I say to you,
 That these stories all are made,
 By people who have no better to do,
 Than to tell children tales not one word of them true,
 To please them or make them afraid."

"Then, it seems, no such being as Santa Claus lives,
 And there is but one God after all!"
"Yes, my boy, to us all our blessings he gives,
 From him every creature its comfort receives,
 And He can look down upon all.

"He to one giveth life, and another he kills,
 And gives to each creature his food,
 To one the sad portion of sorrow he wills,
 While the cup of another with blessings he fills,
 For he does 'what to him seemeth good.'

"Oh, make Him your friend, child, while you've life and health,
 For joy, or for sorrow, or pain,
 And then in the hour of sickness or death,
 You can look up with hope and rejoice, for He saith,
 That our friend He will ever remain!"

"Uncle Maynard's Stories, No 2: Santa Claus", *The Student* (DECEMBER 1851)

Without doubt all of my little friends have heard much of Old Santa Claus, that little, fat, chubby, old fellow.

And I suppose you all expect him next Christmas to pay his compliments to you by some fine toys in your stockings.

If you are good children, I dare say you will have something when the time comes; but I want to ask if any of you ever saw Santa Claus?

I suppose not, and I have never heard of anybody that has seen the old gentleman.

When I was a little boy, about the age of some of you, I used to hear much about Old Santa Claus, and I had a great curiosity to see him.

One Christmas eve, while my older brothers and sisters were talking of him, telling how he came down the chimneys and stove-pipes, how he knew good children's stockings from bad ones', and how he always left the best children his biggest sugars, and his finest toys, I began to think that what they said of him was not always true.

I remembered how John Jones, one of the worst boys on our bench, in the school, one morning, after Christmas, brought to school more fine things than all the rest of us together had received.

He had his pockets quite full of nuts, candies, and spices. Beside these, he had a little pewter horse, with a tin cab hitched to it.

He had, also, a wooden soldier, and a paste-board goose, that would squall when he squeezed it.

I thought, as I desired to know if Old Santa Claus really did bring so many things, that I would not go to bed on the Christmas eve that my brothers had been talking about him; so I concluded to sit up until he came.

But what was my disappointment, when

I was told that if I did so he would not come at all; also, that if I wished him to stop I must go to sleep as soon as I could after going to bed.

Well, I did so; and after dreaming about him most of the night, I got up quite early, hastened to my stockings, and found some nice cakes, a paper of raisins, and a little blue handkerchief.

My handkerchief had printed on it the story of George Washington when a boy, with a picture of him in the garden, with his little hatchet.

But I had seen some cakes like mine, before. I remembered having seen sister Maria take some from the stove, just like them, only the day before, and I told her that she put them in my stockings.

She laughed, and seemed to think strange of my idea. But soon I went and found the little tins in which they had been baked.

Then I made her acknowledge that it was not Old Santa Claus who had given me my presents.

Now, children, I would never have you forget the name of Old Santa Claus; but you must remember that there is really no such being.

The presents which you receive in your stockings, the night before Christmas, are given you be some one who *does* know whether you have been good children or not.

And when they do right, they will leave empty the stockings of such boys and girls as have not behaved well in school, or who have been naughty at home.

3.

Building Santa Claus's World

Joseph Holt Ingraham, from *Santa Claus, or The Merry King of Christmas*
(BOSTON: H. L. WILLIAMS, 1844).

The scene of our Christmas Tale now changes to the Common. The moon still shines cold and clear in the deep blue skies; and the stars sparkle like gems. Fewer lights are seen in the windows and fewer passengers in the streets. The well-wrapped-up watchman walks slowly up and down his beat warming his fingers with his breath. The Common is silent and still. Not an object moves on its white floor of alabaster. In its midst the "OLD OAK" stood in stern majesty like the monarch of the wintry scene. Far and wide he flung abroad his massive limbs beneath whose leafy shelter in a summer's day, a thousand men might stand in shade. His huge, dark trunk of vast circumference, firmly rooted in the earth, stood like some mighty column of an ancient ruin, out of which a forest had up-grown, and flung wide their branching antlers to the storms.

All was dazzling moonlight! No sound was heard save the occasional dropping of an icicle from a limb, striking with a sharp noise into the crystal snows beneath the trees.

Suddenly comes from one of the far off streets that, like arteries, diverge from the Common, the deep, mellow cry of a watchman—

"*Twelve o'clock, and a merry Christmas morning!*"

At the same time, mingling with his sonorous voice came the deep-mouthed clock-tongues tolling the midnight hour from steeple and tower far and near.

As the first stroke rung clearly out upon the moonlit air and was borne towards the OLD OAK, all at once a strange movement was visible throughout the whole tree! Its branches began to wave and bend, and the icicles which were hung upon them in glittering fringes, striking together, tinkled with soft wild music, like a myriad of little silver bells. As the last stroke of twelve floated through the air, the tree was as full of music as an organ. The huge limbs as they swayed against each other, gave out deep bass notes, and from the lighter branches and more slender tendrils, came the sweet notes of a glauichord.[37] Never was heard such unearthly harmony. It seemed as if a choir from fairy-land had lit upon the tree, and filling its branches, like birds, were playing for joy that 'merry Christmas' had come!

Suddenly this strange, harmonious music, died away, and a silence followed as if some great event was about to happen. All at once from the vast trunk came forth a deep sound like that of a bassoon, and the tree on the side towards the city, slowly opened, leaving an arched way like the entrance to some Lilliputian gothic temple. As soon as this door in the trunk was wide open there came out of the body of the tree as if from a great distance, the notes of a trumpet. It came nearer and nearer, and as it approached other instruments of music was mingled with it, till at length a whole band of musicians seemed rapidly advancing from the deep recesses of the Oak towards the entrance!

Still nothing was yet visible to the eye, save the dark cavernous opening into the bowels of the tree, that resembled the vista of a long cathedral aisle dimly lighted.

Louder and nearer sounded the instruments of music, and although I could distinctly hear clarions and horns, bugles and drums, serpents and cymbals, yet they appeared to me to be Lilliputian players, and from the noise they made, I felt satisfied that the instruments could not be much larger than children's toys. All at once I heard the rattling of wheels and the shouting of tiny voices, and amid the shadows that enveloped the opening in the oak I beheld lights flashing, and then came galloping out a chariot and six horses, accompanied by out-riders and followed by a dense multitude, some on horseback, others on foot, and others riding astride upon humming birds and flying over the heads of the others. The out-riders bore flambeaux and before the horses rode at full speed, playing a merry peal, at least three-score musicians clad in green with silver helmets upon their heads.

A more beautiful and rare a sight than this brilliant and dashing cavalcade never was seen! The greatest wonder of it was that not one of the persons composing it was bigger than my thumb, except him who sat in the chariot and seemed the chief personage, who might have been half an inch taller than the rest. This personage was dressed magnificently in furs softer than the richest velvet. A white fur cap covered his head with a silver star glittering in the front; and about his person was wrapped a purple robe lined with ermine. In his hand he held a wooden cross and upon it was suspended an empty purse. His countenance (for I saw it distinctly by the light of the flambeaux carried by the out-riders) was very pleasing and inclined to mirthfulness; for joy sparkled in his black eyes and mirth

---

37 Presumably a variant of "clavichord" —or simply a typo!

played around his mouth. His countenance, nevertheless, was majestic and commanding, and as he wore a long, white beard, with snowy locks floating upon his shoulders, his appearance was at the same time pleasing and venerable. It at once irresistibly prepossessed me in his favor.

The mounted band of musicians, after galloping on their miniature but spirited horses about a yard or a little more from the tree, drew rein and formed in line with military accuracy, while they still continued to play the most delightful strains of martial music. The chariot wheeling, dashed on past the line, and thrice drove round the oak upon the sparkling surface of the snow, the whole train, which must have numbered full ten thousand, following at full speed; some on foot running like the wind; others mounted on fleet coursers no larger than a mouse; other borne through the air on the backs of gorgeous hummingbirds! The noise of their progress was like that of the wind stirring the autumn leaves, as it circles among the trees of the forest. It was a brilliant sight, with their waving plumes, their flaunting mantles, their gold, silver and steel ornaments and armor glancing in the moonlight, and reflecting back, with increased splendor, the flashing rays of the hundred tiny flambeaux!

After the third circle around the oak from which he had so strangely issued with his train, the person in the chariot waved his furred hand, and the whole cavalcade halted in front of the door in the tree, between it and the musicians. The out-riders ranged themselves on either side of the chariot, and those who were so fortunate as to be mounted on their green and gold winged coursers flew up into the branches of the tree; and as there was more than a thousand of this troop, the tree seemed to be covered with gold and emeralds, for these were the prominent colors that met the eye.

At a wave of the hand of the personage in the chariot, the music ceased and a deep silence reigned. Santa Claus, for this distinguished individual was none other than the merry King of Christmas, then rose up in his seat and thus spoke:

"Friends and followers! Once more we have come forth from our year-long retirement within the heart of this mighty Oak, to hail the dawning of merry Christmas! Without me—without you and our gifts, what would Christmas be? *Sad* instead of *merry* I wot. We administer to the happiness of millions, and this night of all nights in the year, myriads of children bless good king Claus!"

"Long live good King Claus! Long live the merry king of Christmas!" shouted ten thousand tiny voices; while loud and right merrily sounded horn, trumpet and clarion, till the very welkin rung again!

"Thanks, good friends and true hearts," answered the merry monarch of the Holidays. "Now are you ready all to do my bidding and fly to hovel and hall to gladden the hearts of my little friends, with presents from Santa Claus?"

"We are ready, we're ready, one and all,
To fly at thy bidding to hovel and hall!"

"Right glad am I to have such faithful and loyal subjects. Now prepare your sacks!"

When he had spoken thus, I saw now for the first time, that nearly every little imp, for I know not what else to call the miniature creatures, had, slung across his shoulder, an empty stocking. Some of them were so long and large that the burden was quite as much as they could stagger under, while others were smaller and more portable. All, except the musicians and the guard about the chariot, had these socks dangling over their backs.

"Now, my children," said Santa Claus looking around him very gravely, "I see you expect to have your stockings filled as heretofore, from my great stocking; for I know every one of you to have a favorite child whom you design this Christmas morning to make happy by a stocking full of presents. But you see my stocking. It is empty!"

As Santa Claus thus spoke he took from the cushion of his chariot a large gray stocking, so large that it would hold hundreds of such stockings as his attendants carried, and held it up to the view of all.

At seeing it in this condition, for he turned it upside down and held it by the toe and shook it that they might be convinced it contained nothing whatever, there was a general murmur of surprise which sounded like the rustling of the leaves of the Oak when agitated by an autumnal wind. Hitherto they had always been accustomed to see the merry king's huge gray stocking crammed and sticking out and over-running with Christmas 'gifts,' from which one and all filled his own sack and flew with the gifts, each to the chamber of his own favorite; for, we are told, each of these little servants of good King Claus, chooses a child as soon as it is born, and continues to be its Christmas 'Fay' year by year, deserting it only when it commits its first sin: and then weeping, it ceases to visit it more!

"You are grieved, my merry children, to see that I have assembled you here before me beneath our Christmas tree, with no annual gifts to pour into your sacks. But cease your lamentations; for not one of you shall want that to give! nor shall one of your favorites fail to be made happy tomorrow morning as on former Christmas days! I will now tell you how this shall be accomplished. Last night as I was counting out, in my palace beneath the oak, the gold which was to fill my stocking with gifts as on other Christmas Eves, I saw, all at once, standing before me a beautiful and youthful female in silvery robes and a crown of light encircling her brow. I knew that she was an inhabitant of one of the stars, and bowing before her in awe I awaited her message. 'Oh king,' said she to me, in a voice sweetly toned with the accents of benevolence and universal love, 'Thou art busy preparing thy generous donations for Christmas morn. I am come to thee to tell thee that for this time thou needest not trouble thyself to gather together gifts either for the old or young, for the rich or the poor!'

"At hearing these words, I looked very sad, thinking how many tears would be shed if I had no gifts for my little ones.

"'How then can there be a merry Christmas,' I said 'without Santa Claus and his presents?'

"'Listen, good king Christmas!' she replied, smiling. 'My name is CHARITY. I am sent from Heaven, with power to rule, for this Christmas day among men. Thou art also to obey me, not because I command thy obedience, but because thy great heart will prompt thee to submission; for I see, with pleasure, my own image reflected in thy breast. Wilt thou obey me this day? Shall my will be thine?'

"'I and my subjects, sweet Charity, are at thy disposal,' I said, laying my hand upon my heart; and kneeling I kissed the hem of her robe, in token of my free submission.

"'Thou shalt now hear my plan of ruling for this Christmas festival, merry King Claus. Put up thy gold for this time for I want it not. The gold I shall make use of I shall seek for in men's hearts. Hitherto thou hast expended vast sums for this occasion and thousands of hearths have been gladdened by thy bounties. Thou hast done enough for thy part; men must, this Christmas, do their part. When the midnight hour shall toll, which ushers in Christmas morn, ride boldly and gaily forth from thy OAK, as heretofore, with all thy train, and when thy people throng around thee for gifts to scatter through every habitation, say to them that for this merry Christmas time they must make mankind the givers! 'I am,' said Charity to me with a celestial smile, 'I am this day the almoner of the rich man's wealth and the reliever of the poor man's woe. Go forth with thy people, good king, and tell them they must take this night from the rich the gifts they would bestow upon the poor, and from the poor the gifts they would bestow upon the rich. Now farewell to thee, King Santa Claus,' she added, 'and see that thou showest thyself, this merry Christmas, both a faithful servant and friend of Heavenly Charity!'

"While she was thus speaking, my children, she was gradually lost to my sight, slowly ascending upon a bright cloud, towards the skies."

As all the little subjects of King Santa Claus had kind hearts, and delighted in nothing so much as doing good, the words of their king gave them the greatest pleasure; for they at once perceived (being as intelligent as they were benevolent) how noble and beautiful was the design which Charity had originated for—not only enabling them to pursue as before their delightful employment of distributing gifts upon every threshold, but of making the rich instead of the purse of King Santa Claus the involuntary dispensers of these bounties.

"Now disperse ye, messengers of sweet Christmas charity, all! Enter every abode in this vast city the halls of the rich and the hovels of the poor. Mark well each beholds! Report where thou seest the rich man have more than his need—where thou seest the miser hoarding his gold while the poor man perishes for want of it; where thou seest the powerful oppress the weak, and the wicked plot the ruin of the innocent! For Charity careth for all these things! Now fly each on his message and be ye all faithful and speedy. In ten minutes report to me what ye discover! For this night Charity holdeth judgment upon earth, and I am her prime minister! Do well thy work and ye shall not lack gifts to fill thy sacks, nor want occasions of scattering abroad those blessings which, like me, it is your delight to bear to the good and innocent."

No sooner had Santa Claus ended than there was a murmur of applause and a clapping of tiny hands that sounded like the laughing ripple of a mountain rivulet, gurgling over a bed of pebbles. Then the instruments of the band struck up a merry peal amid which rose the humming of a thousand green and gold wings, and the clattering of the feet of ten thousand coursers. Away through the air and over the snow, flying and riding and running, the messengers of Santa Claus spread themselves in all directions over the moonlit city. As they crossed the crystal snows that covered the Common they looked to the eye like a shower of diamonds and emeralds, so glittered their garments of green and their silver helms in the beams of the moon. Their passage through the air and over the snow was attended with a melodious noise like that of a hundred Aeolian harps sounding at once in the evening wind! Their speed was like the lightning! and in a few seconds they had dispersed themselves in every street, avenue, and lane, and alley in the wide, slumbering city. Those that were astride the backs of humming birds, I saw course high in the air, and then dart like shooting stars down the chimney flues. Those that were mounted on steeds entered, at top speed, through the key holes of the doors; while those less lucky ones who were on foot (and who constituted the foot-guard of good Santa Claus) got in underneath the doors; and in poor men's houses made their entrance through broken panes and yawning chinks. And I saw, that by reason of the more numerous openings that were in the poor man's house, and therefore, the more easy access to the interior, which these little messengers of love and charity obtained, that the poor man's roof had a great many more of these blessed guests than that of the rich man!

After they had all disappeared and silence and moonlight only reigned over the city, I turned to observe king Claus, and to admire in his countenance, the benign expression of that benevolence which was planning happiness of so many beings that night; when, to my surprise a flourish of trumpets filled my ears, and amid the martial melody I beheld him with his few attendants that remained, coursing in his chariot with his six winged horses harnessed to it in silken traces, swiftly over the crystal snow in the direction of the state-house! I followed his glittering progress with my eyes and saw him gallop over intervening snow bank and hollow with the speed of an arrow; and when I looked to see the iron fence arrest him (forgetting what a miniature affair his equipage was the whole being so perfectly proportioned), I saw him pass right through between the bars without a whit lessening his speed. Following his glittering course, still, I beheld him next mount the glacis in front of the State House, and then, dashing across the portico, disappear—chariot, winged-horses, musicians, attendants and all—through one of the ponderous key holes of the great door. In a moment afterwards I beheld him reappear in the lofty cupola above the dome; and there surrounded by his train of attendants, he sat, like a monarch upon his throne, awaiting the report of his messengers, with the snow-clad city, which for that night, he governed as the vice-regent of Charity, spread out in the bright moonlight beneath his feet!

[…]

"When thou comest into the house of the cruel creditor," said Santa Claus, "thou shalt take from his wealth all, to a farthing, that he has unjustly wrested from the poor or the unfortunate, leaving him only his honest gains. In like manner shall judgment come to all this night! When thou goest into the prison lead forth the mother's boy and convey him to her arms! When thou comest into the mansion of the Judge, convey thence such provision and coal as the families of the two unfortunate persons he has imprisoned may require, and I will see that from the coffers of the miser their hearts shall be made glad. I'faith! This shall be a right merry Christmas to the poor! and I thank sweet Charity for making me her minister in this loving matter!"

"But, oh, King," said the Page, "didst thou not say that not only the rich were to be involuntary givers to the poor of Christmas gifts, this night, but the poor were to bestow Christmas presents upon the rich! But so far these are gifts only on the one side!"

"What I said I repeat," answered Santa Claus. "The Christmas presents of the rich shall come from the poor. I have a rare Christmas present for that Judge! Thou shalt be its bearer. You said he sighed that he had no children to inherit his riches. Seek out the living babe that lies nestling upon the cold bosom of its dead mother and taking it up gently bear it and lay it in his arms! Such are the gifts the rich shall have from the poor! Now hie thee on thine errands of mercy and love for thou hast much on hand to do!"

[…]

"Lo! now, oh king," said Charity addressing Santa Claus, "Equity ruleth over this mighty city. From the rich hath been taken that, and only that, which was surplus to their wants, and it is given to him whose need was farthest removed from the rich man's fullness; for every rich man hath his poor man assigned him in the councils of Equity. There is now no more a poor man, nor a rich man in the city! The wail of want is hushed, and the guilt of the wealthy hoarder-up of gold (which contains life) exists no more! In a few moments thy messengers will return. Then, thyself, go and with me, behold in person the sweet fruit of this night's doings. Enter with me the abodes of those from whom thou hast taken, and convey them, in dreams to the presence of those whom their long idle-lying abundance has made happy.—Take the rich merchant to the glad home of the poor woman his riches have blessed: the landlord to the abode of his cheerful tenant; let the woman of fashion, see the good her jewels have done, and let the hard creditor behold the blessings that have followed the distribution of his ill-gotten gains. Let the Judge see from what a fate thou hast rescued the infant, and the miser witness the good the distribution of his hoarded gold has achieved. Let all from whom their over-abundance or unjust gains have been taken, by my command, behold the effects produced! Let them see the dark abodes of wretchedness become sunny with cheerful comforts! Let them see the tears dried! the smile of peace light up the pale cheek of the widow! Let them all witness the varied scenes of happiness they have created! I will then lay my wand upon their hearts, and they will so love what they see, that the rich merchant shall take more delight in viewing his wealth thus bestowed, than in seeing it around him in statues and paintings! the woman of fashion shall love more to see the bright smiles of the faces of the poor children which her dispersed jewels have caused, than once she delighted in their glitter dispersed over her bosom; for a smile of gratitude is brighter to the eye of the giver than the brightest jewel of Ind!

"I will so touch their hearts with these scenes which thou shalt make them witness in their sleep, that, when they shall wake in the morning, the sweet influences shall remain! The work thou hast done this night shall they do over by day in love and charity, prompted by a desire to enjoy in reality, the happiness to which they have beheld themselves the involuntary contributors in their dreams!"

Caroline H. Butler, "A Visit to the Dominions of Santa Claus", from *The Little Messenger Birds* (BOSTON: PHILLIPS, SAMPSON & COMPANY, 1850).

A VISIT

TO THE

DOMINIONS OF SANTA CLAUS.

Only six more days, and the merry Christmas Bells would sound over the broad earth! Only six more days, and their cheerful peal would send happiness to many hearts? Charity, with glad footsteps, would follow their merry chime to the poor man's cottage, and their cheerful echo call together dear parents, happy children, and kind friends, to celebrate with thankful hearts that blest hour, when the bright little Star in the East told the good shepherds, who sat watching their flocks on the green fields of Bethlehem, that the Holy Child Jesus was born!

Oh, the merry Christmas bells!

Only six more days to merry Christmas, and yet Santa Claus had a great deal to do before he would be prepared to make his annual visits to all the good children. No, not for two or three hundred years, had the kind-hearted old gentleman been so hurried or so happy either, as under this unusual press of business. It always made him happy, when he knew that children were deserving of all the pains he took to please them, and he knew his little friends must have been very, very good since the last Christmas, or he should not now have so much to do; because, although he never failed to visit bad children also, he never troubled his head much about giving them anything, or if he did, it was only something which would make them ashamed of their naughtiness. But, for good children,—oh, what beautiful, beautiful things he had for them!—and day and night he kept his little work-people busy getting them ready.

So Santa Claus was very much hurried, you may be sure, when Christmas was so near, giving orders about the work, and examining all the pretty things, as they were finished, to see that they were strong and good.

He had a little pipe in his mouth, and a pair of spectacles on his funny little nose, although he did not make a practice of wearing them, for he declared he could see just as well as ever he did ; but these spectacles were so very fine, and so very clear, that he could detect the tiniest flaw in the work: so that when Santa Claus put them on, then all the little work-people looked at each other timidly, and some trembled and turned pale, because they knew if their work was not done well, they should be banished to the Dark Room, where they made such ugly things for bad children, as bags of soot and ashes, pots of elbow-grease, sharpened birch-twigs, and put in order cats-o'-nine-tails, which, when properly used, make the most dreadful screaming of any cats in the world!

His cap was of so many bright colors, that it seemed, for all the world, as if he was carrying about ever so many kaleidoscopes on the top of his head.

In his hand he held a curious red book, and in the other a pen made from the bill of a little snow-bird, and then dangling from the button of his queer old-fashioned coat was a little ink-bottle, into which he would now and then dip his pen, and write something in the little red-book. I suppose the names of the children whose beautiful presents he was so carefully examining.

His work-room!—oh, it was larger and handsomer than all the toy-shops of the whole world put together!

It took a great while to walk from one end to the other, and it was so high you could scarcely see the top of it; and all round and round, and one over the other, were great shelves filled with such beautiful things!

Why one would think a group of real living little children were gathered there, so much like life were the large wax dolls, with beautiful long curls falling over their pretty necks, and bright sparkling eyes which could open and shut, and all dressed, too, so finely in pink and blue silk, and laces and gauzes, with little gloves on their tiny hands, and little wee slippers on their cunning little feet.

And then besides all these wax dolls, there were whole shelves full, yes indeed, of other kinds of pretty dolls,—wooden dolls and kid dolls, some with very handsome dresses, too, and a great many others with only a thin fold of tissue paper wrapped around their delicate limbs,—for Santa Claus loved to have little girls ingenious, so sometimes he gave them one of these, that they might cut and make its little dresses themselves. This was a nice idea of the old gentleman's, because it teaches little girls to cut and make their own dresses, perhaps, bye and bye, and to be useful to their mothers, which every good girl will try to be.

And as all these charming dolls would want something to sleep upon, Santa Claus had provided the prettiest little bedsteads, furnished with nice beds and mattresses, fine linen sheets, and rose blankets, as white and soft as the wool on a little lamb's back, and cunning little counterpanes, and pillow-cases frilled so neatly and prettily. Some of these bedsteads had curtains festooned about them,—ah, they looked so tempting, no wonder the lady-dolls often reclined upon these pretty beds! The little dolls, too, had the cunningest straw cradles, and little couches, all covered with soft velvet, for them to lie in. And, when tired of play, they would like to rest themselves, there were all manner of sofas and chairs for them to sit down upon. Then there were little bureaus for their fine dresses, and little tables, and little looking-glasses, and such a variety of crockery, such charming tea-sets, and dinner-sets of beautiful china, all gilt and sprigged with roses and pinks; and nice wooden-ware, so white and clean, and pewter tea-cups and saucers, and coffee urns, and platters, and spoons, and little tin kitchens, and pails, and sauce-pans, so bright you would almost think they were silver.

Ah, don't you wish you had some of them? Well, only try to deserve them, my dear little girl, and you may be very sure Santa Claus will not forget you! Wait for the merry Christmas bells, and see.

Ah, are those live horses capering about in yonder corner, with their arched necks and long flowing manes?

You would surely think so.

And then such splendid gilt coaches, drawn by the handsomest and most mettlesome steeds,—you never saw any so fine,— nor such gay rocking-horses, and beautiful little ponies. Then there are noble great dogs and greyhounds, little curly lap-dogs, with long ears and little pink eyes peeping at you, and lots of cows and sheep, and pigs and geese, and turkeys, and ducks, and hens, and chickens, that can *moo* and *blaa-a,— squeak,—hisse-se,—gobble,—quack,—cut-cut-ke-dar-cut*, and *peep-peep*, too, if they have a mind. And as Santa Claus likes to have his little friends know all about the animals that went with the good Noah into the ark, he has taken pains to collect them all together, that you may see them, from the great elephant down to the little dormouse; nor has he forgotten the pretty white dove that returned to Noah, with the olive leaf in its little bill.

Besides these, there are whips and tops, marbles and balls, whistles, trumpets, guns, swords, and drums.

Ah, don't you wish you had some of them? Be kind and dutiful, then, my dear boy, and you may be very sure Santa Claus will not forget you! Wait for the merry Christmas bells, and see.

On each side of this apartment were two doors, so large it seemed as if a giant only could move them! But what will not Love and Kindness overcome!—and it was these which so gently turned their hinges, that children who deserved them might be rewarded by the treasures they protected.

One of these doors was hung all around with beautiful pictures, and portraits of Mother Goose, who, next to Santa Claus, has done the most to make children happy; and Mother Hubbard, and Dame Wiggens, of Lee, and Dame Trot, Madame Blaize, worthy Mrs. Horner and her daughter Patty, and that remarkable old lady who lived in her shoe with such an interesting little family, an example I am sure for all those who wish to live in large houses, besides portraits of many other justly-celebrated ladies. There were also very correct likenesses of Blue-Beard and Jack the Giant Killer, Tom Thumb, the Three Wise Men of Gotham, the Man in the Moon, and Peter Pumpkin and Peter Piper.

Oh, what happiness for children who love to read, was treasured up within the vast room into which this door opened!

Shelf upon shelf of the nicest and prettiest books, all filled with interesting stories and beautiful pictures, which are written and painted on purpose for them. What encouragement to be good, to receive from kind Santa Claus one of these beautiful books!

The other large door had the most curious netting hanging over it, made of twisted candy red and white, and filled with all kinds of pretty bon-bons, and large bouquets, and wreaths of flowers, all made of sugar, festooned about it.

Now, what do you suppose was in this large room?

Guess.

Why, sugar-plums and candy!

Yes, sugar-plums and peppermints, lozenges and almonds, and lemon-drops, from the floor smoothly carpeted with jujube paste, away up to the ceiling, all studded over with great sugar stars! Not even Stewart himself can make half so fine a display,—although it is said he is a very good friend and customer of Santa Claus; but with all his great storehouse of sweets, he never, no never, can equal those vast heaps of sugar-plums, and the great high pyramids of vanilla, cream, lemon, and strawberry candy, all twisted and braided together so beautifully, and some so transparent you would think they were made of glass!

Now I will tell you about the curious little people whom Santa Claus employs to make all these fine things for good children, and how it is that he knows so well who deserve and who do not deserve to receive a present from him on merry Christmas eve.

Each of these three rooms had a great many little creatures,—oh, so small and so cunning, of all trades at work in them. Little carpenters, with their little hammers and saws,—little masons, with little hods of little bricks,—little painters, with the tiniest brushes and paint-pots,—little cabinet-makers, and little shoemakers *tap-tap-tapping* the little dolls' shoes,—little tailors, little milliners, and little mantua-makers, all so busy!

Then, in the room where the books were kept, were some of the oddest and gravest little men and women, with green spectacles on their noses, perched up on high stools, writing, writing, writing, as fast as they could write, with little pens made from a humming-bird's wing, and the tiny eggshell of a wren for an inkstand; then there was a little printing-press, and a little book-bindery, and just as fast as the wise ones who sat in the high places finished what they were writing, they tossed it to the little printer, who tossed it to the little book-binder, who tossed it again, a beautiful bound book, upon the shelves.

But the prettiest little creatures were at work among the sugar-plums. You would think they were themselves made of sugar, they looked so sweet! How swiftly their little hands rolled out the pretty plums so true and round, and wove and twisted together the slender threads of candy, while others were forming the most beautiful boxes to be filled with *bon-bons*!

Now all around these rooms were hung bright little silver bells, which rang out as clear and sweet as the notes of the skylark, when, at early morning, she springs from the dewy grass, and, on glittering wings, flies up, up, up, into the blue vault of heaven.

You have heard, I dare say, of those little birds that sometimes whisper good and bad tidings in the ear. Did you never hear your mother say:

"Ah, a little bird told me?"

Well, Santa Claus has a great many of these beautiful winged messengers to bring him tidings about good and naughty children, and whenever the flutter of their wings is heard, then the little silver bells *tinkle, tinkle, tinkle*, so sweetly and softly, like the song of the lilly of the valley when the bright rain drops find it hid beneath the green leaves, and kiss its pretty modest head.

If the little birds bring good news, they dart swiftly to the shoulder of Santa Claus, chirruping in his ear a few sweet notes. Then the little bells rejoice too, and ring out cheerily and merrily, while the fingers of the little work-people move faster and faster, because it is such a pleasure, I suppose, to work for good children. And they smile and nod to one another, and caress the pretty little birds that have brought such glad tidings, and as the bells keep merrily chiming, in low sweet voices, they sing:

> Hark, hark,—the merry bells ring!
>
> *Ding, dong, ding,—ding, dong, ding!*
>
> Now our fingers must fly faster,
>
> That will please our kind good master;
>
> Who loves, on merry Christmas night,
>
> O'er chimneys wide to take his flight,
>
> Rewarding all good girls and boys,
>
> With these, our work of pretty toys.
>
> *Ding, dong, ding,—ding, dong, ding!*
>
> Hark, hark,—the merry bells ring!

But when these pretty messenger birds brought tidings of disobedient, undutiful children, then their bright wings grew dull and drooped heavily, and they flew slowly and sadly around, while the little silver bells sighed like the night wind through the branches of the weeping-willows, and a great black raven, which sat perched in one corner, lifted his large wings slowly, and flew off croaking, croaking, to the dark dismal room where the names of bad children were registered.

Only six more days then to Christmas, and as the pretty birds continued to whisper more frequently of good than of disobedient children, Santa Claus was obliged to hurry his little work-people as fast as possible, lest all who deserved a reward might not receive one. For most tenderly does the kind old gentleman love those who are good, and he does not mean that a single one shall be forgotten at happy Christmas time.

"Fifty more dolls to make!" cried Santa Claus, with a cheerful smile.

"Fifty more dolls to make!" echoed fifty little voices, laughing merrily.

"Fifty more dolls to dress!" said the little milliners and mantua-makers, briskly threading their needles.

"Bedsteads, bureaus, and chairs are wanted!" said Santa Claus, rubbing his hands.

"Bedsteads, bureaus, and chairs!" quoth the little cabinet-makers, smiling, and drawing forth their little mahogany boards.

"Thirty more superb rocking-horses, and a dozen chariots!" said Santa Claus, almost dancing for joy, because the little messenger birds had just brought him tidings of so many good boys.

"Thirty more rocking-horses, and a dozen chariots!" laughed the little saddlers and carriage-makers.

Then Santa Claus stepped briskly toward the library of pretty books.

"One hundred more of the choicest and best little volumes must be ready by Christmas eve!" he cried, with a triumphant look.

"*Hem!* ah! yes!—one hundred more books!" and the grave little writers stroked their beards, smoothed down their parchment robes, and dipping their pens in the little inkstands, cast up their eyes in thought, and then faster than little humming-birds among the flowers did their pens dart over the paper. And the little printers busily prepared their types, and the book-binders smiled and unrolled their brightest and prettiest morocco.

Just then the little silver bells began to tinkle softly, and in flew two little messenger birds, and Santa Claus laughed outright when they put their pink bills to his ear, and he heard the good news they brought.

Then he hastened in among the sweet little creatures employed in preparing the nice sugar-plums and candy, and tossing off his gay-colored cap, he scooped it up full of the prettiest plums, and began throwing them about, and pelting the merry little work-people, and tapping them over the ears with long sticks of candy.

"Come, come, go to work, go to work," he cried laughing, "one hundred pounds of candy, and fifty more boxes of the nicest sugar-plums!"—and the order was repeated, in merry tones, by the cheerful little creatures.

"One hundred pounds of candy, and fifty more boxes of sugar-plums!" and immediately they began, like so many busy bees, to collect together their sweets.

After Santa Claus had thus given all the necessary orders within doors, he put on one of the oddest caps was ever seen: it was neither round, or square, or pointed; but looked for all the world just like a broad laugh,—just, in fact, as the merry old gentleman felt, in such charming good humor was he put by the good behavior of little children,—and throwing a mantle of fur over his shoulders, and taking an odd stick in his hand, out he trudged to his beautiful forest, of which I have not yet told you, to see after the cutting down of his Christmas trees.

Oh, how pure and white the snow lay all around him, and sparkling too, as though diamonds and pearls had been crushed and sprinkled over its surface. And as he went along, he could hear the *click, click, click*, of his merry little woodmen, as they worked in the forest.

Still the pretty birds flew about him, and the cheerful chime of the silver bells went with him.

By and by the sound of the little axes came nearer and nearer, and pretty soon Santa Claus arrived on the borders of a large forest,—so large it would take a great many days to pass around it.

And here were growing most beautiful Christmas trees, tall and fair, with branches so charmingly fresh and green as delighted the eye to look upon. And there were hundreds of tiny woodmen, all dressed in forest green, with sprigs of holly in their caps, and bright shining little axes in their hands, and little pruning-knives fastened in their belts, with every other implement necessary to keep this beautiful grove in order. All the year round were the little woodmen busily at work, and never were any trees so tall and straight, or planted in rows so true and perfect,—so true, indeed, that for miles one could look up and down the long colonnades overarched with green, and their base resting on the crisped sparkling snow.

Always, a week before the merry Christmas bells sounded, the ringing of the little axes was heard from morning until night echoing through the forest. And merrily the little woodmen plied their tasks, for they thought with every stroke of the axe, how charming those Christmas trees would look, when all blazing with wax lights, and every green branch bearing some present for happy children.

As soon as the woodmen heard the step of their beloved master, they all threw down their axes, and doffing their caps, waved them over their heads, crying:

"A merry Christmas! A merry Christmas!"

And the little messenger birds circled swiftly around the head of good Santa Claus,—and some perched upon all the odd angles of his cap, and some upon his shoulder, and some clung, with their tiny talons, to the shaggy borders of his fur mantle, while from their throats burst forth the most delicious music, just as in a bright May morning, when beautiful rosy clouds wreathe the eastern sky, and the stars are yet twinkling in the clear blue depths of the heavens, you have heard the early song of the birds at your window,—while floating softly, softly floating on the clear air, came the chime of the silver bells.

Then the little woodmen clapped their hands, and began merrily to sing:

> Hark! the silver bells are ringing,—
> Hark! the joyful birds are singing,
> Happy tidings to us bringing!
> Now hew the branches,—trim with care,
> Knobs nor notches must we leave,
> Cheerily, cheerily we prepare
> For the merry Christmas eve.
>   Hark! the bells ring,
>   Ding,—dong,—ding,
>   Hark! the birds sing,
>   Tirre-r-r-rle—le—ling!

"One hundred more of your finest Christmas trees must be hewn down and trimmed!" cried Santa Claus, with a joyous laugh, lifting a little axe, and striking it into the rind of a beautiful cedar tree.

"One hundred more Christmas trees!" echoed one hundred little woodmen, catching up their axes, and swinging them over their heads,—then, with a merry hurra, one hundred shining blades were buried deep in the slender trunks of one hundred trees, while through the forest aisles rang their cheerful song:

> While the birds sing,
> Ho! work cheerily,
> While the bells ring
> Ho! work merrily,—
>   Cleave the Christmas tree!
> From its branches are gathered
> Pretty gifts that are treasured
>   For those whom the little birds sing.
> Then their eyes will sparkle brightly,
> And their little feet trip lightly,
>   While gaily the Christmas bells ring.
> Ho! strike cheerily,
> While the birds sing,
> Ho! strike merrily,
> While the bells ring,—
>   Cleave the Christmas tree!

Then Santa Claus whistled softly, and immediately a large lion, whose mane seemed made of threads of gold, came walking with great dignity toward him; and as he swept his long tail around, the pure white snow rose in a silver cloud about him. When he came near, he lifted his huge head, and looked up into his master's face, as much as to say,

"Here I am, good master,—what would you with me?"

Then Santa Claus gently patted his long, flowing mane, and said:

"Brave Leo, you must bear me to the Treasure Cave."

Shaking his golden mane joyfully, the lion crouched down, and Santa Claus seating himself upon his back, away they went through the forest glades.

Still the pretty messenger birds flew about

him, and the cheerful chime of the silver bells went with him.

And we may always have the soft chime of silver bells in our hearts, if we will. It is but to "do unto others as we would they should do unto us," and their sweet music will ever dwell with us!

Children who love and fear God, who obey their parents, who are kind and gentle, neither selfish or cruel, carry always with them the soft chime of silver bells! Happy, happy children!

On went the Lion, until at last he stopped before a large cave, the door of which looked like one solid pearl, with hinges of gold. He raised his paw, and struck three strokes upon it, and immediately it opened wide, and in walked brave old Leo, with his good master, Santa Claus, upon his back.

Never was there anything so brilliant as the interior of this cave! It seemed as if all the bright shining stars had here met together, so many hundreds of wax-lights were blazing on every side, and as far as the eye could reach. And oh, such beautiful things as they revealed,—I never could tell you the half!

But as they were all intended for Christmas gifts, many of you will, I hope, receive them, for the practice of those virtues they were intended to reward. For, in letters of gold, were written over some, "A Reward for Obedience;" over others, "For Humility;" others, "Good-nature,"—"Industry,"—"Kindness,"—"Neatness;" besides many other traits of character, which all should strive to possess.

Then Santa Claus sprang off the lion's back, and clapped his hands thrice, and instantly the cave was filled with the most beautiful little beings. Their hair was as the spray of a fountain shimmering in the moonbeams, and as rosy summer clouds, their graceful drapery floated around them. Light as air, they came on rainbow wings, at the summons of Santa Claus, and when he told them of the pleasing errand which brought him there, and that more of those beautiful gifts from the Treasure Cave were required, the glad creatures flew merrily round, singing:

Hither robin, hither wren,
Bear us to the forest green;
Hither goldfinch, hither dove;
Bear us to our work of love.

And immediately the whirr of wings was heard, and in flew a flock of pretty birds, harnessed, by threads spun from the film of a gossamer, to little chariots, made of the inner shell of the nautilus.

Then the little creatures who presided over the Treasure Cave, hastened to fill these beautiful chariots with the most charming things can be conceived; and when they had finished, they lighted little waxen tapers, and placed them in brilliant rows all around the chariots, and each pretty bird caught one up also in its tiny talons.

When all was ready, the graceful little beings folded their bright pinions, and sprang into the chariots, and lightly touching the slender reins, sang:

**Hasten robin, hasten wren,
Bear us to the forest green:
Hasten goldfinch, hasten dove,
Bear us on our work of love.**

Then all the birds spread their wings, and rose up,—up,—up, bearing with them the beautiful chariots; and away, away they soared to the forest green.

And the good lion shook his golden mane, and Santa Claus once more seated himself upon his back, and went forth from the Treasure Cave.

And still the pretty messenger birds flew around him, and the soft chime of the silver bells went with him.

When he reached the forest, it seemed as if bright golden and rose-tinted clouds were resting upon it,—it was the golden and rose-tinted chariots descending among the Christmas trees.

Then, oh, how merrily and how nimbly the little beings worked,—flying from branch to branch, hanging on every stem and bough and quivering spray the beautiful gifts they had brought from the Treasure Cave, and lighting up their dark green branches with the waxen tapers.

Ah, don't you wish one of those beautiful Christmas trees could be placed in your mother's parlor?

Love and obey her then, dear children, and you may be sure Santa Claus will not forget you! Wait for the merry Christmas bells, and see.

When their pleasing task was ended, the cheerful little creatures with the rainbow wings, once more mounted their pretty chariots, singing gaily:

**Home again robin,—home again wren,
Bear us from the forest green;
Home again goldfinch,—home again dove,
We have done our work of love.
Happy children will they be
Who shall win our Christmas tree!**

Then Santa Claus patted the lion's head, and said: "Now, faithful Leo, your task is ended!" and the great creature, resting his head against his master's knee, looked lovingly up into his face with his great subdued eyes, and turning, walked slowly away.

In no way does time fly so swiftly as when employed in doing good actions, and therefore, when Santa Claus came out of the dark green forest, he was surprised to see the stars already shining brightly down from the blue sky, and the soft moonbeams playing around him.

Then he walked briskly homeward, where a good supper was already waiting his return; and such excellent promoters of appetite are exercise and cheerfulness, that the old gentleman made a very hearty meal, and you may be sure he had the soft chime of silver bells in his heart. As soon as he had finished his supper, he lighted his pipe, and with a cheerful smile upon his countenance, and peace in his heart, sat down in the corner of the old-fashioned fireplace.

[…]

CONCLUSION.

You know we left good Santa Claus taking a nap to refresh himself, after his long walk to the Forest Green and the Treasure Cave.

He was very tired, and no doubt soon fell asleep; and he must have slept a long time, too, for when he awoke, there knelt a large beautiful rein-deer before him, with his cold pointed nose resting in the lap of the old gentleman, and his soft black eyes looking up into his face.

"Ah, my brave Swift-of-Foot, what now?" cried Santa Claus, patting his head.

The graceful animal sprang to his feet.

As he did so, the room was filled with the tinkling sound of the little bells which hung around his neck, seeming to say:

To-morrow will be Christmas day!
Haste, dear master, haste away;
All is ready, and we must glide
Over earth and oceans wide.
Then hasten, master, haste away,
To-morrow will be Christmas day!

Then Santa Claus hastily arose and looked from the window, and there, standing at the gate, was his swift gliding sleigh, harnessed the twelve beautiful rein-deer, pawing crusted snow, and tossing their antlers proudly.

Hurrying to and fro, were a great many little people, bearing on their heads, and in their hands, and some over their shoulders, heavy loads of the charming things which had been prepared for happy Christmas and for happy children. Some carried cases of prettily bound books; some hampers of sugar-plums; some boxes of furniture; and others were moving swiftly along pretty baby-houses, in which the lady dolls sat at the windows, looking out upon the fine prospect, while far away, coming from the Green Forest, were seen the tiny woodmen bearing their gaily-lighted Christmas trees.

Santa Claus took his pipe in his mouth, and putting on his shaggy fur coat,—for the air was keen and frosty,—went out with his little red book in his hand, to look after this joyously laden team; and to be certain that not a single child, whose name he had set down on his list, was forgotten.

It took a great many hours to load this singular sleigh, for the more pretty things were placed on it, the more room there seemed to be! An admirable plan, was it not? Else, how could good Santa Claus, at one time, make so many thousands of children happy, if this swift gliding sleigh was not able to carry more than it really appeared to?

But, at last, all was ready, and Santa Claus, with a joyous *"ha! ha!"* sprang in.

The rein-deer arched their beautiful necks, and proudly tossed their high antlers; the pretty messenger birds flew round and round, pouring sweet music from their little throats; and the silver bells rang out on the clear moonlight air, like the songs of the angels who watch over all good children.

Then Santa Claus shook the reins gaily,— and away,—away,—away,—over mountains and meadows,—over hills and plains,— through large cities, and quiet little villages, passed the swift sleigh, freighted with so many beautiful things!

Now, listen for the merry Christmas bells, dear children, and may you all be made happy, by receiving from Santa Claus a portion of the charming gifts which he brings. Then you will say:

"Ah, in my heart how sweetly chime the silver bells!"

Illustration by Alexander Francis Lydon from the London edition of *The Little Messenger Birds*
PUBLISHED BY GROOMBRIDGE AND SONS, C1871.

Susan and Anna Warner, from Carl Krinken, *His Christmas Stocking* (NEW YORK: G. P. PUTNAM & CO., 1853)

Wherever Santa Claus lives, and in whatever spot of the universe he harnesses his reindeer and loads up his sleigh, one thing is certain—he never yet put anything in that sleigh for little Carl Krinken. Indeed it may be noted as a fact, that the Christmas of poor children has but little of his care. Now and then a cast-off frock or an extra mince pie slips into the load, as it were accidentally; but in general Santa Claus strikes at higher game,—gilt books, and sugar-plums, and fur tippets, and new hoods, and crying babies, and rocking-horses, and guns, and drums, and trumpets;—and what have poor children to do with these? Not but they might have something to do with them. It is a singular fact that poor children cut their teeth quite as early as the rich,—even that sweet tooth, which is destined to be an unsatisfied tooth all the days of its life, unless its owner should perchance grow up to be a sugar-refiner. It is also remarkable, that though poor children can bear a great deal of cold, they can also enjoy being warm—whether by means of a new dress or a load of firing; and the glow of a bright blaze looks just as comfortable upon little cheeks that are generally blue, as upon little cheeks that are generally red; while not even dirt will hinder the kindly heat of a bed of coals from rejoicing little shivering fingers that are held over it.

I say all this is strange—for nobody knows much about it; and how can they? When a little girl once went down Broadway with her muff and her doll, the hand outside the muff told the hand within that he had no idea what a cold day it was. And the hand inside said that for his part he never wished it to be warmer.

But with all this Santa Claus never

troubled his head—he was too full of business, and wrapped up in buffalo skins besides; and though he sometimes thought of little Carl, as a good-natured little fellow who talked as much about *him* as if Santa Claus had given him half the world—yet it ended with a thought, for his hands were indeed well occupied. It was no trifle to fill half a million of *rich* little stockings; and then—how many poor children had any to fill? or if one chanced to be found, it might have holes in it; and if the sugar-plums came rolling down upon such a floor——!

To be sure the children wouldn't mind that, but Santa Claus would.

Nevertheless, little Carl always hung up his stocking, and generally had it filled—though not from any sleigh-load of wonderful things; and he often amused himself Christmas eve with dreaming that he had made himself sick eating candy, and that they had a stack of mince-pies as high as the house. So altogether, what with dreams and realities, Carl enjoyed that time of year very much, and thought it was a great pity Christmas did not come every day. He was always contented, too, with what he found in his stocking; while some of his rich little neighbours had theirs filled only to their heart's discontent, and fretted because they had what they did, or because they hadn't what they didn't have. It was a woful thing if a top was painted the wrong colour, or if the mane of a rocking-horse was too short, or if his bridle was black leather instead of red.

But when Carl once found in his stocking a little board nailed upon four spools for wheels, and with no better tongue than a long piece of twine, *his* little tongue ran as fast as the spools, and he had brought his mother a very small load of chips in less than five minutes. And a small cake of maple-sugar, which somehow once found its way to the same depending toe, was a treasure quite too great to be weighed: though it measured only an inch and a half across, and though the maple-trees had grown about a foot since it was made.

***

"Wife," said John Krinken, "what shall we put in little Carl's stocking to-night?"

"Truly," said his wife. "I do not know. Nevertheless we must find something, though there be but little in the house."

And the wind swept round and round the old hut, and every cupboard-door rattled and said in an empty sort of way, "There is not much here."

John Krinken and his wife lived on the coast, where they could hear every winter storm rage and beat, and where the wild sea sometimes brought wood for them and laid it at their very door. It was a drift-wood fire by which they sat now, this Christmas eve,—the crooked knee of some ship, and a bit of her keel, with nails and spikes rust-held in their places, and a piece of green board stuck under to light the whole. The andirons were two round stones, and the hearth was a flat one; and in front of the fire sat John Krinken on an old box making a fish-net, while a splinter chair upheld Mrs. Krinken and a half-mended red flannel shirt. An old chest between the two held patches and balls of twine; and the crooked knee, the keel, and the green board, were their only candles.

"We must find something," repeated John. And pausing with his netting-needle half through the loop, he looked round towards one corner of the hut.

A clean rosy little face and a very complete set of thick curls rested there, in the very middle of the thin pillow and the hard bed; while the coverlet of blue check was tucked round and in, lest the drift-wood fire should not do its duty at that distance.

John Krinken and his wife refreshed themselves with a long look, and then returned to their work.

"You've got the stocking, wife?" said John, after a pause.

"Ay," said his wife: "it's easy to find something to fill it."

"Fetch it out, then, and let's see how much 'twill take to fill it."

Mrs. Krinken arose, and going to one of the two little cupboards she brought thence a large iron key; and then having placed the patches and thread upon the floor, she opened the chest, and rummaged out a long grey woollen stocking, with white toe and heel and various darns in red. Then she locked the chest again and sat down as before.

"The same old thing," said John Krinken with a glance at the stocking.

"Well," said his wife, "it's the only stocking in the house that's long enough."

"I know one thing he shall have in it," said John; and he got up and went to the other cupboard, and fetched from it a large piece of cork.

"He shall have a boat that will float like one of Mother Carey's chickens." And he began to cut and shape with his large clasp-knife, while the little heap of chips on the floor between his feet grew larger, and the cork grew more and more like a boat.

His wife laid down her hand which was in the sleeve of the red jacket, and watched him.

"It'll never do to put that in first," she said; "the masts would be broke. I guess I'll fill the toe of the stocking with apples."

"And where will you get apples?" said John Krinken, shaping the keel of his boat.

"I've got 'em," said his wife,—"three rosy-cheeked apples. Last Saturday, as I came from market, a man went by with a load of apples; and as I came on I found that he had spilled three out of his wagon. So I picked them up."

"Three apples—" said John. "Well, I'll give him a red cent to fill up the chinks."

"And I've got an old purse that he can keep it in," said the mother.

"How long do you suppose he'll keep it?" said John.

"Well, he'll want to put it somewhere while he does keep it," said Mrs. Krinken. "The purse is old, but it was handsome once; and it'll please the child any way. And then there's his new shoes."

So when the boat was done Mrs. Krinken brought out the apples and slipped them into the stocking; and then the shoes went in, and the purse, and the red cent—which of course ran all the way down to the biggest red darn of all, in the very toe of the stocking.

But there was still abundance of room left.

"If one only had some sugar things," said Mrs. Krinken.

"Or some nuts," said John.

"Or a book," rejoined his wife. "Carl takes to his book, wonderfully."

"Yes," said John, "all three would fill up in fine style. Well, there is a book he can have—only I don't know what it is, nor whether he'd like it. That poor lady we took from an American wreck when I was mate of the *Skeen-elf*—it had lain in her pocket all the while, and she gave it to me when she died—because I didn't let her die in the water, poor soul! She said it was worth a great deal. And I guess the clasp is silver."

"O I dare say he'd like it," said Mrs. Krinken. "Give him that, and I'll put in the old pine-cone,—he's old enough to take care of it now. I guess he'll be content."

The book with its brown leather binding and tarnished silver clasp was dusted and rubbed up and put in, and the old sharp-pointed pine cone followed; and the fisherman and his wife followed it up with a great deal of love and a blessing.

And then the stocking was quite full.

***

It was midnight; and the fire had long been covered up, and John Krinken and his wife were fast asleep, and little Carl was in the midst of the hard bed and his sweet dreams as before. The stocking hung by the side of the fire-place, as still as if it had never walked about in its life, and not a sound could be heard but the beat of the surf upon the shore and an occasional sigh from the wind; for the wind is always melancholy at Christmas.

Once or twice an old rat had peeped cautiously out of his hole, and seeing nobody, had crossed the floor and sat down in front of the stocking, which his sharp nose immediately pointed out to him. But though he could smell the apples plain enough, he was afraid that long thing might hold a trap as well; and so he did nothing but smell and snuff and show his teeth. As for the little mice, they ran out and danced a measure on the hearth and then back again; after which one of them squealed for some time for the amusement of the rest.

But just at midnight there was another noise heard—as somebody says,

"You could hear on the roof
The scraping and prancing
of each little hoof,"—

and down came Santa Claus through the chimney.

He must have set out very early that night, to have so much time to spare, or perhaps he was cold in spite of his furs: for he came empty-handed, and had evidently no business calls in that direction. But the first thing he did was to examine the stocking and its contents.

At some of the articles he laughed, and

at some he frowned, but most of all did he shake his head over the love that filled up all the spare room in the stocking. It was a kind of thing Santa Claus wasn't used to; the little stockings were generally too full for anything of that sort,—when they had to hold candy enough to make the child sick, and toys enough to make him unhappy because he didn't know which to play with first, of course very little love could get in. And there is no telling how many children would be satisfied if it did. But Santa Claus put all the things back just as he had found them, and stood smiling to himself for a minute, with his hands on his sides and his back to the fire. Then tapping the stocking with a little stick that he carried, he bent down over Carl and whispered some words in his ear, and went off up the chimney.

And the little mice came out and danced on the floor till the day broke.

"Christmas day in the morning!" And what a day it was! All night long as the hours went by, the waves had beat time with their heavy feet; and wherever the foam and spray had fallen, upon board or stone or crooked stick, there it had frozen, in long icicles or fringes or little white caps. But when the sun had climbed out of the leaden sea, every bit of foam and ice sparkled and twinkled like morning stars, and the Day got her cheeks warm and glowing just as fast as she could; and the next thing the sun did was to walk in at the hut window and look at little Carl Krinken. Then it laid a warm hand upon his little face, and Carl had hardly smiled away the last bit of his dream before he started up in his bed and shouted

"Merry Christmas!"

The mice were a good deal alarmed, for they had not all seen their partners home; but they got out of the way as fast as they could, and when Carl bounded out of bed he stood alone upon the floor.

The floor felt cold—very. Carl's toes curled up in the most disapproving manner possible, and he tried standing on his heels. Then he scampered across the floor, and began to feel of the stocking—beginning at the top. It was plain enough what the shoes were, but the other things puzzled him till he got to the foot of the stocking; and *his* feet being by that time very cold (for both toes and heels had rested on the floor in the eagerness of examination), Carl seized the stocking in both hands and scampered back to bed again; screaming out,

"Apples! apples! apples!"

His mother being now nicely awaked by his clambering over her for the second time, she gave him a kiss and a "Merry Christmas," and got up; and as his father did the same, Carl was left in undisturbed possession of the warm bed. There he laid himself down as snug as could be, with the long stocking by his side, and began to pull out and examine the things one by one,— after which each article was laid on the counterpane outside.

"Well little boy, how do you like your things?" said Mrs. Krinken, coming up to the bed just when Carl and the empty stocking lay side by side.

"Firstrate!" said Carl. "Mother, I dreamed

last night that all my presents told me stories. Wasn't it funny?"

"Yes, I suppose so," said his mother, as she walked away to turn the fish that was broiling. Carl lay still and looked at the stocking.

"Where did you come from, old stocking?" said he.

"From England," said the stocking, very softly.

Carl started right up in bed, and looked between the sheets, and over the counterpane, and behind the head-board—there was nothing to be seen. Then he shook the stocking as hard as he could, but something in it struck his other hand pretty hard too. Carl laid it down and looked at it again, and then cautiously putting in his hand, he with some difficulty found his way to the very toe,—there lay the red cent, just where it had been all the time, upon the biggest of the red darns.

"A red cent!" cried Carl. "O I guess it was you talking, wasn't it?"

"No," said the red cent. "But I can talk."

"*Do you know where you came from?*" said Carl, staring at the red cent with all his eyes.

"Certainly," said the cent.

"I dreamed that everything in my stocking told me a story," said Carl.

"So we will," said the red cent. "Only to you. To nobody else."

Carl shook his head very gravely, and having slipped the red cent into the little old purse, he put everything into the stocking again and jumped out of bed. For the driftwood fire was blazing up to the very top of the little fire-place, and breakfast was almost ready upon the old chest.

But as soon as breakfast was over, Carl carried the stocking to one corner of the hut where stood another old chest; and laying out all his treasures thereon, he knelt down before it.

"Now begin," he said. "But you mustn't all talk at once. I guess I'll hear the apples first, because I might want to eat 'em up. I don't care which of *them* begins."

"A. W. H.", "A Christmas Ballad", *The Book of One Thousand Tales* (NEW YORK: DICK & FITZGERALD, 1858; FIRST PUBLISHED IN *THE SCHOOLFELLOW MAGAZINE*, 1856)

Last night, beside the wood-fire, I dreamed of little Fan,
Till through my dream her footsteps like fairy echoes ran;
And I heard her clear voice singing—"To-morrow, Rosy, dear!
And then one more to-morrow, and Christmas will be here!"

So dreaming in the fire-light of what I could not see,
There slid right down the chimney a visitor to me;
First came a pair of snow-shoes, a hose and doublet gay,
And then a merry, wrinkled face, a queue both long and gray.

▼

Till by the peaked hat-crown, and by the sturdy pack
That, folded in a bear-skin, he wore upon his back;
And by the thong of deer-hide that bound his Lapland shoe,
And by his joyful greeting, old Santa Claus I knew.

I set for him a little chair, good cheer before him spread—
Strong waters out of Holland, and old wine rosy red.
A pudding made in Nuremberg, an English Christmas pie,
And a pipe of old tobacco, but nothing caught his eye.

He looked out at the snow-storm, and sadly looked at me,
Till I said—"Good father Santa Claus, what can the matter be?"
So he heaved a great sigh:slowly, and said, as if he cried,
"Oh, Rosy dear! another day will bring the Christmas tide.

"I have a host of darlings that always wait for me,
And I have a host of children whose eyes I never see;
They haven't any chimneys to hang their stockings in,
Because they have no fire to burn, in homes of shame and sin.

"Nor have they any stockings, through snow and sleet to wear;
Their tiny feet are colder than the pavement cold and bare.
I cannot reach these children, their Christmas never comes!
They have no friends, or comfort, they have not even homes.

"What if the happy faces that shining wait for me
 Could see the homeless little ones that I must never see?
 I'm sure the lonely children would have a Christmas too—
 The happy ones would do for them what I could never do.

"Go sing it to the children! go quickly, Rosy, dear!
 And tell them every stocking shall be fuller every year
 If only with the lonely, the sorrowful, and poor,
 They share the Christmas blessings I scatter at their door."

 So I woke up from dreaming, and Santa Claus was gone,
 But I wrote down his message, and sitting there alone,
 I thought about the weary hearts, and faces pale and worn,
 That never knew the happiness that comes on Christmas morn.

 Ah! darlings of old Santa Claus! all these are children too,
 Go find their poor old houses, and make them share with you,
 They are Christ's little children, their angels see His face,
 And out of heaven he calls you, to stand in His own place.

 Go feed and clothe His little ones, and like the angels fair,
 Sing loud your Christmas carol, and warm the frosty air—
 "Glory to God in heaven! good will and peace to men!
 And peace on earth forever, for Christ has come again!"

Ralph Hoyt, "The Wonders of Santa Claus", *Harper's Weekly*, DECEMBER 26 1857

Chapter 1

Beyond the ocean many a mile,
    And many a year ago,
There lived a wonderful queer old man
    In a wonderful house of snow;
And every little boy and girl,
    As Christmas Eves arrive,
No doubt will be very glad to hear,
    The old man is still alive.

In his house upon the top of a hill,
    And almost out of sight,
He keeps a great many elves at work,
    All working with all their might,
To make a million of pretty things,
    Cakes, sugar-plums, and toys,
To fill the stockings, hung up you know
    By the little girls and boys.

It would be a capital treat be sure,
    A glimpse of his wondrous shop;
But the queer old man when a stranger comes,
    Orders every elf to stop;
And the house, and work, and workmen all
    Instantly take a twist,
And just you may think you are there,
    They are off in a frosty mist.

But upon a time a cunning boy
    Saw this sign upon the gate,
Nobody can ever enter here
    Who lies a-bed too late:
Let all who expect a good stocking full,
    Not spend too much time in play;
Keep book and work all the while in mind,
    And be up by the peep of day.

A holiday morning would scarce suffice
    To tell what was making there;
Wagons and dolls, whistles and birds,
    And elephants most rare:
Wild monkeys drest like little men,
    And dogs that could almost bark,
Watches, that, if they only had wheels,
    Might beat the old clock in the Park.

Whole armies of little soldier folk,
    All marching in grand review,
And turning up their eyes at the girls,
    As the City soldiers do.
Engines, fast hurrying to a fire,
    And many a little fool
A-trudging after them through the streets,
    Instead of going to school.

Tin fiddles, and trumpets made of wood,
    That will play as good a tune
As a Scotch bag-piper could perform
    From Christmas-day till June.
Horses, with riders upon their backs,
    Conches, and carts, and gigs,
Each trying its best to win the race,
    Like the Democrats and Whigs.

Some little fellows turning a crank,
    And others beating a drum:
Little pianos, so exact
    You could almost hear them thrum.
Tea-sets and tables quite complete,
    With ladies sitting around,
Chatting as older ladies do,
    But a little more profound.

Steamboats made to sail in a tub,
    And fishing-smacks ahoy,
And boats and skiffs with oars and sails,
    A fleet for a sailor boy.
Ships of the line, equipt for sea,
    With officers and crew,
Each with a rod cap on his head,
    And a jacket painted blue.

Bold pewter men with pistols armed,
    Like duelists so smart,
Each very wickedly taking aim
    At his little comrade's heart!
And nimble Jacks with stipple joints,
    That when you pull a string,
Will give you an easy lesson how
    To dance the Pigeon Wing.

Ugly old women in a box,
    As some younger ones ought to be,
Which, when the cover is lifted off,
    Fly out most spitefully.
Ripe wooden pears like real fruit,
    Somehow made to unscrew;
Kittens with mice sewed to their mouths,
    And tabby cats crying mew.

Gay humming-tops that spin about,
    And snake a senseless sound,
Like windy representatives
    In Congress often found.
Fine marbles, and rich China-men,
    That you can play from taw,
As lawyers play rich clients down
    The ring-pits of the law.

Bright caskets filled with jewelry,
    Chains, bracelets, pins, and pearls,
All glittering with tinsel, like
    Some fashionable girls.
Delightful little picture books,
    And tales of Mother Goose,
More witty than most novels are,
    And twenty times their use.

But it were an endless task to tell,
    The length that the list extends,
Of the curious gifts the queer old man
    Prepares for his Christmas friends.
Belike you are guessing who he is,
    And the country whence he came.
Why, he was born in Germany,
    And St. Nicholas is his name.

Chapter 2

December's four and twentieth day
    Through its course was almost run,
St. Nicholas stood at his castle door
    Awaiting the setting sun.
His goods ware packed in a great balloon,
    Near by were his horse and sleigh;
He had his skates upon his feet
    And a ship getting under weigh.

For he was to travel by sea and land,
    And sometimes through the air,
And then to skim on the rivers smooth,
    When the ice his weight would bear.
The wind blew keen, and the snow fell fast,
    But not a whit cared he;
For he knew a myriad little hearts,
    Were longing that night to see.

Away he flew to Amsterdam,
    As soon as the sun want down,
And left whole bushels of play-things there,
    For every child in town.

Then he tried his skates on the Zuyder Zee,
    Southwest to Dover's Strait,
Then Southward with his horse and sleigh,
    He was soon at Paris' gate.

He scaled the walls of the Tuileries,
    The children were all retired,
And every stocking. was hanging up,
    As St. Nicholas desired.
In one he put a sceptre and crown,
    In another a guillotine,
And a little man without a head,
    Who King of the French had been.

He paused a while at Notre Dame,
    To see the Christmas shows;
Then with his grand Montgolfier
    Majestically rose,
And from his splendid parachute,
    A shower of bonbons threw,
For all the little ones in France,
    And bade them all adieu.

Then down he drove on the River Seine,
    And on the Biscay bay,
Took ship for famous Dublin town,
    And London on his way.
In Dublin what do you think be left,
    For the hearty Irish boys?
Why, bags of potatoes instead of cakes,
    And shillalaghs instead of toys.

In London he gave them rounds of beef,
    And two plum-puddings a-piece,
Then stepped to Windsor palace of course,
    To see his royal niece.
He gave her a little Parliament,
    Discussing a knotty bill,
And two or three nuts for them to crack,
    And a birch to keep them still.

And now, said he, for St. Petersburg!
    Over the cold North Sea,
And up the Baltic he sped in haste,
    And was there when the clock struck three.
He hied to the palace of the Czar,
    And clambered in at the dome;
A great many stockings were hung around!
    But the folks were not at home.

He gave them little Siberian mines,
    With little men in chains,
Who strove to avenge their country's wrongs,
    And were sent there for their pains.
He left the Emperor a map,
    With Russia cut in four,
As much as to say, great Muscovite,
    Your sway may soon be o'er.

Then down he hastened for Italy,
    To call at the Vatican,
Forgetting, until he had arrived,
    The Pope is a bachelor man.
But he looked in at St. Peter's church,
    And saw the whole town at prayer,
So he left a basket full at the door,
    For all the good children there.

Upon the Mediterranean Sea,
    He boarded his ship again,
And hoisted sail, and steered west,
    To see the Queen of Spain,
And give her a legion of wooden men,
    Equipt from foot to nose,
And a troop of leaden horsemen too,
    The rebels to oppose.

Chapter 3

O'er the Cantabrian mountains wild,
    He hurried to the strand,
To meet his treasure-laden ship,
    There waiting his command.
He scattered beautiful gifts around,
    As he went flying past,
Then put his trumpet to his lips,
    And blew a rousing blast.

Up, up my gallant sailors all,
    Swiftly your anchor weigh,
The wind is fair, and we must sail,
    For far America.
By wind and steam for New Amsterdam,
    Three thousand miles an hour,
Onward he drove his elfin ship,
    With a thousand-fairy power.

Down at the Battery he moored,
    And gave a grand salute,
With cannon charged with sugar-plums,
    And powder made to suit.
Thou he hoisted out a score of bales,
    Of his cakes, and nuts, and wares;
You would have been amazed to see
    The heaps on the ferry stairs.

All's well, all's well! loud voices cried;
    St. Nicholas is here!
How charming many a stocking full
    In the morning will appear.
Now all good little boys and girls
    Shall have a noble treat,
Delightful presents, that will make
    The holidays complete.

Upon the spires of old St. Paul's
    Policemen saw him stand,
Reading his list of ancient friends,
    With his leather bags in hand.
'Tis said he dropt a frozen tear,
    As he looked on the streets below,
And saw what a mighty change has come
    Since Christmas times ago!

Those brave old times when great mince pies
    Were piled on every shelf,
And every Knickerbocker boy
    Might go and help himself.
When Broadway was a path for cows,
    And all the streets were lanes,
And the houses were so snug and quaint,
    With their bull's-eye window-panes;

And low old fashioned door-ways, where,
    The upper part swung in,
The Dutchman could his elbows lean,
    And smoke his pipe and grin.
Then doughnuts were all good to eat,
    And made as big as bricks,
And 'twas not thought unmannerly
    To eat as many as six.

Good simple times, when lad and lass,
    In happy groups were seen,
With sled and skate for winter sports,
    Around the Bowling Green.
When maidens plied the spinning-wheel,
    And idlers were unknown,
And all the up-town people lived
    Below the one-mile stone.

When all were good and went to church,
    And heeded what they heard,
And children never learned to speak
    A bad or saucy word.
With plenty smiling every where,
    Like Christmas every day,
Content and love at every hearth,
    O what rare times were they!

But long before all this was said,
    The stockings were all filled,
And Santa-claus was skating home,
    With his nose a little chilled.
He whistled as he skimmed along,
    Till the day began to dawn,
Then giving a twirl in the frosty air,
    St. Nicholas was gone!

The WONDERS of SANTA-CLAUS.

CHAPTER I.
CONCERNING SANTA-CLAUS.—HIS ASTONISHING CASTLE.—HIS BEAUTIFUL GIFTS FOR ALL GOOD CHILDREN.—AND HIS REAL NAME.

BEYOND the ocean many a mile,
  And many a year ago,
There lived a wonderful queer old man
  In a wonderful house of snow;
And every little boy and girl,
  As Christmas Eves arrive,
No doubt will be very glad to hear,
  The old man is still alive.

In his house upon the top of a hill,
  And almost out of sight,
He keeps a great many elves at work,
  All working with all their might,
To make a million of pretty things,
  Cakes, sugar-plums, and toys,
To fill the stockings, hung up you know
  By the little girls and boys.

It would be a capital treat be sure,
  A glimpse of his wondrous shop;
But the queer old man when a stranger comes,
  Orders every elf to stop;
And the house, and work, and workmen, all
  Instantly take a twist,
And just you may think you are there,
  They are off in a frosty mist.

But upon a time a cunning boy
  Saw this sign upon the gate,
Nobody can ever enter here
  Who lies a-bed too late:
Let all who expect a good stocking full,
  Not spend too much time in play;
Keep book and work all the while in mind,
  And be up by the peep of day.

A holiday morning would scarce suffice
  To tell what was making there;
Wagons and dolls, whistles and birds,
  And elephants most rare:
Wild monkeys drest like little men,
  And dogs that could almost bark,
Watches, that, if they only had wheels,
  Might beat the old clock in the Park.

Whole armies of little soldier folk,
  All marching in grand review,
And turning up their eyes at the girls,
  As the City soldiers do.
Engines, fast hurrying to a fire,
  And many a little fool
A-trudging after them through the streets,
  Instead of going to school.

Tin fiddles, and trumpets made of wood,
  That will play as good a tune
As a Scotch bag-piper could perform
  From Christmas-day till June.
Horses, with riders upon their backs,
  Coaches, and carts, and gigs,
Each trying its best to win the race,
  Like the Democrats and Whigs.

Some little fellows turning a crank,
  And others beating a drum;
Little pianos, so exact
  You could almost hear them thrum.
Tea-sets and tables quite complete,
  With ladies sitting around,
Chatting as older ladies do,
  But a little more profound.

Steamboats made to sail in a tub,
  And fishing-smacks ahoy,
And boats and skiffs with oars and sails,
  A fleet for a sailor boy.
Ships of the line, equipt for sea,
  With officers and crew,
Each with a red cap on his head,
  And a jacket painted blue.

Bold pewter men with pistols armed,
  Like duelists so smart,
Each very wickedly taking aim
  At his little comrade's heart!
And nimble Jacks with supple joints,
  That when you pull a string,
Will give you an easy lesson how
  To dance the Pigeon Wing.

Ugly old women in a box,
  As some younger ones ought to be,
Which, when the cover is lifted off,
  Fly out most spitefully.
Ripe wooden pears like real fruit,
  Somehow made to unscrew;
Kittens with mice sewed to their mouths,
  And tabby cats crying mew.

Gay humming-tops that spin about,
  And make a senseless sound,
Like windy representatives
  In Congress often found.
Fine marbles, and rich China-men,
  That you can play from taw,
As lawyers play rich clients down
  The ring-pits of the law.

Bright caskets filled with jewelry,
  Chains, bracelets, pins, and pearls,
All glittering with tinsel, like
  Some fashionable girls.
Delightful little picture books,
  And tales of Mother Goose,
More witty than most novels are,
  And twenty times their use.

But it were an endless task to tell,
  The length that the list extends,
Of the curious gifts the queer old man
  Prepares for his Christmas friends.
Belike you are guessing who he is,
  And the country whence he came.
Why, he was born in Germany,
  And St. Nicholas is his name.

Julia F. Snow, "Santa Claus's Ball; or, A Plea for the Children", *Harper's Weekly*,
JANUARY 3 1863

SANTA CLAUS'S BALL.

Santa Claus had appointed this November night as a dress-rehearsal for Christmas. It was an occasion when not the Dolls only, but very many others, denizens of Toyland, were expected. All, in fact, who could make it convenient to attend felt it to be a duty to do so. In fact, the invitation was almost peremptory. Santa Claus expected to hear from his spies, the Old Dolls, full accounts of the conduct and behaviour of his little friends the Children, in order that he might know who deserved his rich prize, and who might merit the traditional "rod in the stocking" as the penalty of their misbehavior. He also expected to hear from the same reliable sources what all the mothers, sisters, aunts, and cousins were doing with reference to assisting him; for this information he was accustomed to rely entirely upon the Dolls. They are a very intelligent race of little beings, if one did but know it, and they always sleep with at least one eye open. Consequently, when the children have gone to bed, and the Dolls set in order in the nursery, and the hidden work is taken out, and the mysterious plans of the family talked over, the Dolls have the best possible chance to see and hear it all, and of course their sympathies are interested in the Children, and all that concerns them.

Santa Claus was accustomed to hold this annual festival preparatory to Christmas, in order to know exactly what to do, and what to depend upon.

The gala was held in Santa Claus's favorite winter palace, an immense snow-cave in the side of Mount Hecla. Santa Claus found the climate to agree better with his health than a more southern situation, and likewise he found here, in this sequestered spot, the quiet and seclusion so necessary to the mystery in which he is accustomed to invest his good deeds.

The palace was all of a glow with warmth and light from numerous fires in huge fire-places, whose vent was none less than the great crater of Hecla himself. The cheerful blaze illuminated the glittering ceiling and sparkling walls, and mellowed the atmosphere to almost tropical geniality; while, to restrain the melting of snow and ice, which naturally would have ensued, and which would have greatly incommoded the guests, the palace was placed under a perpetual spell or charm by a certain witch. This witch when young had been a famous beauty, and a great favorite of the good saint, who was a gay bachelor in those days.

Of course she could not preside publicly at his entertainments; but it was more than surmised in Northern circles that his domestic *ménage* owed much to her occasional care. It was positively asserted that if she chose she could tell what had become of a certain geyser, which had mysteriously disappeared of late, and there were not wanting dark hints that it had been placed in his kitchen by her agency, in order that he might enjoy a perpetual supply of hot water for his punch, of which it was feared he was becoming very fond.

It is certain that he has been known to lay his finger aside his jolly red nose, wink oracularly, and indulge in a silent inward laugh and chuckle when the subject has been broached to him. But it is not my business to pry into the domestic concerns of these excellent people, but to give an account of Santa Claus's ball.

The dining-hall was brilliantly illuminated by certain Northern Lights, which had generously volunteered their services for the occasion, and a great number of Shooting-stars were engaged to act as drivers and torch-bearers to convoy the guests to and from the scene of the festivities. It was expected that this evening would witness a *début* of many of the belles and beaux of Toyland, and no pains or expense was spared to make the ball "the affair of the season."

Santa Claus had dispatched his numerous reindeer teams over the American continent to collect his guests; and, lest these accommodations should fail, several Lapland witches had benevolently loaned their broomsticks for the use of such of the company who might prefer them. Jack Frost had done himself more than justice in the upholstery and finishing of the palace, which he could well afford to do, having had the contract from time immemorial. The tables were abundantly spread with viands suited to the tastes and appetites of the guests; while Boreas was engaged to furnish music, assisted by a large deputation of Tin Trumpets and Painted Drums, who were expected to arrive somewhat later in the evening.

Santa Claus had to hear what communications his emissaries might have for him, and this must be attended to before dancing, of course.

The apartments were decorated with hemlock boughs and garlands, brought thither with infinite pains. Ash-berries and holly, with the ancient mistletoe, were tastefully arranged over the walls, and huge sparkling icicles glittered among them in pure and beautiful contrast to the rick dark-green of the evergreens.

The reception-room was thickly carpeted with Iceland moss for the benefit of rheumatic old Dolls, and to enable imprudent young lady Dolls who might have overheated themselves with dancing to resort thither and save themselves a pulmonary attack by inhaling its health-restoring fragrance.

And now, as every thing had been properly attended to, and the arrangements were to his entire satisfaction, the old gentleman, in his best suit of furs, with his pipe laid aside for once, in compliment to the ladies, stood before the great fire-place in the reception-room, with his back to the fire and his coat-tails judiciously drawn on each side, awaiting the arrival of his visitors. He did not have to wait long; for the tinkle of his reindeer's bells were now heard, and the first installment of Dolls soon entered the apartment.

As he expected, they were the invalid guard of the ball, the battered and disabled ones, who had stood one year, at least, of the Nursery campaign, and their battered noses, cracked crowns, and shattered or missing limbs bore evidence to the hard service they had seen.

Polly, the oldest Doll, opened the conversation with grumbling and complaints. She was a very old Doll. Lame and dilapidated, with one arm and a foot gone, and her frock torn half off her shoulders, and her garments soiled and tattered generally, she presented but a sorry appearance.

After extending a courteous welcome to the lame, halt, and blinded party, he lent a listening ear to her grievances.

"If your highness could only know of the goings on in our nursery. Now I don't come here to complain of neglect or ill-usage like some, though I was once a very handsome china Doll, and was dressed and petted as much as the best. Nor do I complain of my broken arm;" and she sadly held up the stump of her once plump and snow-white arm. "But it is not myself," she went on, wiping her remaining eye with a soiled rag of a handkerchief; "it's the Children I'm so sorry for. Why, their mother never comes into the nursery more than once a day, and often not that. Sometimes she sweeps in in splendid carriage-dress just ready for a drive, and just touches the children, with 'There, there! don't touch my dress;' and off she goes, while the Children stand at the window and cry themselves sick to see the carriage go off, in which they very seldom have a ride, and never with mamma, unless she goes to fit them with clothes and hats.

"And when little Mary had the scarlet-fever, she left some tiny pills with Kate, the Irish nurse, and told her to give them so often, and the child would be well enough in the morning. But Mary worried and fretted for mamma, who was away at a grand party, and Katy was sleepy and tired, and she muttered to herself – I heard her – 'What's the use o' bothering wi' the like of this thrash! I'll just be giving the poor thing a dhrop o' suthin' to bring the slape to her eyes.' And she *did* give her something out of a bottle, and Mary never woke up out of that sleep. And they carried her away, and I never saw her again. Mary had me in her little bed all the time, and I know all about it."

"How many children are there left?" asked Santa Claus, blowing his nose very hard.

"Two," answered Polly; "another girl and a teething baby. I know just how many teeth he has, for he tries 'em all on me, and I know the minute one is through."

"Poor little things!" sighed the good saint; "I really do not see how I can help them. Is there no aunt or cousin in the house?"

"Yes. Aunt Sophia and Cousin Bell; but they are entirely taken up with Aid Societies, and Lint Circles, and Hospital visiting, and they have no time for the poor children. Mrs. Harvey, the mamma, is wiser. She gave ten dollars to escape the trouble."

"Not so bad! not so bad!" exclaimed the host. "I rejoice that my friends the soldiers are to fare so well. May the shirts be warm and the turkeys fat that I bring, that is all! I don't suppose there is much chance that my juvenile friends are being calculated upon at all, is there?"

"Not much. I fancy the Soldiers' Christmas box engrosses all their time and attention, and the children always come off second to the public in that house."

"The poor children! the poor children!" put in another doll. "Now where I live there are four little children, and not a rag of new clothes have those poor young ones had this fall or winter, and no prospect of them. And not for lack of money, either. Mamma is away to the Hospital, or the Aid Society, of the Lint Company, or what not, as soon as she gets herself breakfast, and Tommy's face isn't washed, nor Lizzie's hair curled until the middle of the afternoon, when Betty is all done her work. The cook hasn't made a seed-cake this fall, and every thing nice of jellies or fruit, or whatever there is, goes to the soldiers. The children don't know what a kiss or a story is hardly, it's so long since they heard one; and Charlie's shoes have gaped for patches this month, and Molly's hat is a sight to behold."

"Well, but," interposed the saint, "the soldiers are proper subjects for care and kindness. They need jellies and the children don't; and, poor fellows! they have no mothers to wait upon them."

"Small loss if they are like some mothers

I know; but if these mothers don't train and love their own little soldiers at home, there will be another rebellion one of these days."

"Just my notions," mumbled an old nut-cracker. "If the Southron mothers had only cared for their children when they were little instead of always *threatening* to send them to convents or boarding-schools – and finally *doing* it to get rid of the trouble they ought *themselves* to take – South Carolina never would have seceded, and Master Peyton wouldn't have screwed my neck off with rage when he heard of the victory of Fort Donelson."

There was another loud jingle of bells, and a merry load of the aristocrats of Toyland were joyfully ushered in. They were accompanied by a Zouave, whose pretty china head and brilliant red white and blue had evidently dazzled the eyes of all the female portion of the company – all but Miss Josephine. She, the waxen beauty in her silk and blond, her tarlatan and spangles, her embroidery and lace, felt herself entitled to the belleship of the ball-room without a question, and was especially irritated at the company of certain nondescript Dolls, who were exceedingly presumptuous, as she deemed it, in riding in the same sleigh as herself. She was especially conceited on the subject of her birth; for, as she boasted, she was a genuine Parisian, body, complexion, curls, dress, and all; and, moreover, a true Santa Clausian, who had come down standing in Santa Claus's own hands, and was none of your fair-bought, home-made, got-up- any-how affairs. She had been promenaded on the Boulevards, and aired in the Bois de Boulogne, and was bursting with spite that the Zouave, who was, as she alleged, "only bought at a Soldiers' Fair," should not notice her more than he did.

She flirted her tarlatans contemptuously past him, and curtsied to the ground before the host. He greeted her kindly, and courteously inquired the occasion of her clouded brow.

"I can not bear mixed companies," she answered, with ill-concealed disdain.

"But my invitation was peremptory."

"True, and therefore I am here."

"Yet, my pretty Doll, your countenance indicates that you come reluctantly."

The petted beauty burst into tears.

"May I never become human!" she exclaimed. "If my heart is not almost broken with neglect!"

(This is the hoped-for future of Dolls, and with good reason, for the metamorphosis is well authenticated in many cases.)

"Neglect! I suppose the fair Josephine was far above the danger of neglect!" murmured the Zouave.

"It is very well for you, Colonel Ellsworth, to speak in that way," she pettishly replied. "You know that I have lain in the drawer without a breath of air or glimpse of daylight but what comes through the broken lock of my drawer, while you sit in the Doll-chair, the pet and darling of the nursery, and feel yourself Lord Paramount every where. My *worst* trouble, and the cause of all my troubles, is the ambition of my little mistress's parents. Unfortunately she let it out that she was a bright child, and they have shown her no mercy ever since. She goes to school at half past eight every morning. She remains until half past two, then she comes home, eats a lunch, and practices music until four. Then she sews an hour for the aid societies, then her evening meal and lessons from seven till nine, when my poor ten-year-old mistress goes to bed. Every day of the week this is the rule except Saturday, when sewing for the soldiers takes the place of lessons and school, and maybe she gets a short walk in the afternoon.

"Dear Santa Claus, can not you help us? She will die if this goes on. I see and hear this, and it is every word of it true;" and the tears stood again – tender, loving tears – in her waxen blue eyes.

The saint's eyes glowed like sparks under his shaggy eyebrows.

"My Master greatly loved these little ones when he dwelt on the Earth, and if their human parents do not more carefully watch and tend them he will gather the lambs to his bosom again," he murmured softly to himself, as he slowly paced the floor, with his hands contemplatively clasped under his coat-tails.

A brisk-looking jointed Chinese Doll now hopped up to their host, and began to retail both information and grievance in his attentive ear.

She said that she and her friends Hoop and Hoop-stick, Ball and Bat, Battle-door and Shuttle-cock, were under a ban, and were heart-broken at the aspect of things in their residence, which was in Boston. She really did not see how she was going to bear it any longer. Evening study was now the rule, and the poor children went to bed so tired that when they rose in the morning they had no spirits for play at all, neither had they the time. She couldn't remember when they had had time.

Katy was as pale as a ghost trying for the prize for French, and Milly was equally desperate for the Mathematical medal. She stated that her memory couldn't recall when she had been properly undressed and put to bed, and she had quite lost her voice, it was so long since she had been squeezed.

The circle smiled at this, and the Zouave mischievously encircled her waist with his padded arm, to which pressure she responded with an extremely natural "squawk," which proved her bellows in excellent order, and made the Dolls look scandalized behind their fans, and Miss Josephine walked away as haughty as a crowned queen.

"It seems that the Aid Societies do not trouble your house very much," whispered the Zouave, offering his arm for a promenade; "at least you do not oppose them as violently as many do."

"Ah!" sighed the almond-eyed Squaw Lin, accepting the proffered arm with a mollified air, "if all soldiers were like Colonel Ellsworth! But really, if you could only see the wooden German Grenadiers at our house which came home from the last fancy fair –" The rest of the sentence was lost as they sauntered off to try the flavour of an ice *à la Hecla.*

Santa Claus looked after them with a peculiar smile.

"We have all been young once," he sighed. "I had a touch of the complaint many years ago myself."

There were many complaints and much important information brought to Santa Claus that night, to all of which he attentively listened, and promised to use his influence on the side of right, reserving to himself the privilege of judging the merits of the case.

There was almost universal complaint from the city of Dolls that their little mistresses were over-studied, in school and out of school; and although the complaint came selfishly from the Dolls, Santa Claus knew too well the consequences to pass the information in silence. Dull children were in little danger. It was the bright, talented ones, who needed no urging to study at all, to whom the harm happened. Boys could and would get air and exercise somehow; but little girls, bright, studious, lady-like little girls, had no redress if parents did not take up their cause.

Santa Claus had a theory that, if a little girl of ten years old made the clothes for her Doll family, it was about as much sewing as she ought to be expected to do; and if she was studious in school she ought not to be expected to study out of school and give up her play hours. He espoused the cause of the Hoops and Balls, the Battle-doors and Shuttle-cocks, feeling that they had a good work to do, in which the parents ought rather to aid than restrain them.

His "little ones" were especially dear to the saint's heart, and he believed that his little Peter Parlegians had turned out full well as those whose studies were more pretentious. He sadly remembered certain bright little faces that, one Christmas, would peer so curiously and sweetly into the stockings it had been his care to fill for them, who, before another Christmas, had laid their throbbing heads and quivering nerves to rest where school-books should never annoy them more. And he shrewdly opined that if half the amount of study at present exacted was performed in school under the teacher's eye, and with his assistance, the good results mentally would be doubled; and if the time thus saved from study would be devoted to vigorous romping in doors or out, the value to the little students would be wonderful, and the bright eyes and curls might look into well-filled stockings until years insensibly stole away the child's privilege. But Santa Claus sighed deeply when he thought how hopeless was the task of convincing parents of this.

His heart grew still heavier when he thought of the many nurseries unblessed by the constant presence of a mother. Society – gay, bewitching, fascinating society – claimed so many, especially young mothers. "And yet," he reflected, as he promenaded the now nearly deserted reception-room, and the gusty sounds of distant music reached his ears from the dancing-halls, where the Tin Trumpet Band, Boreas conductor, discoursed melody for the multitude of twinkling feet – "and yet this class are not so hopeless after all; for sooner or later sorrow, steadiness, or wisdom come to all, and those gay young creatures turn out pretty well after all; for most generally it is only an excess of animal spirit which passes off in time. It's only a few comparatively – alas that there should be any! – who are incorrigible." But even Santa Claus shook his head as he reflected that so many really excellent, high-principled, kind-hearted mothers find their duties and tastes leading them away from home and the dear faces there, even to the neglect of his darling pets, who so sadly missed the smile, the kiss, the story or romp, the walk or ride with mamma, the sunshine of her presence. And very sad remembrance occurred to him of those who, having no tender drawing out of love of home, found bright fires and lights (such unhallowed ones!) elsewhere, and sweet smiles and brilliant glances, glowing with no holy mother-love, and accepted the wretched substitutes. He loved the poor soldiers; they were his especial care. Many a box of comforts and delicacies had he conveyed to them, and so joyfully, when mothers, sisters, and daughters filled them; but his heart ached for the dear Children whose mothers, in restlessness or ignorance, had neglected them to minister to strangers. He saw in this very neglect, whether from misguided ambition or simply indolence, the one great cause of the Great Rebellion; for, of a certainty, if the Children can obey well, the men will command well, and deserve well the opinion of the world.

The Children of Santa Claus must neither be left to the exclusive care of either Biddy or Dinah. Neither devoted to death upon the school desk, nor impaled by the needles of infanticidal Sewing Societies. The races and romps, the balls and hoops, must resume their rule. Their precious Doll cares and baby housekeeping, the song or story from mamma, the evening frolic with papa, must be reinstated. Bo-Peep and Cock Robin must not be supplanted by Manesea and Davies, nor Jack the Giant Killer by Dumas or De Staël, nor Mother Goose by Watts on the Mind. Not a bit of it. And St. Nicholas swore by his eight favourite reindeer to claim back his own, and bid the children be Children once more.

He resolved that the children of soldiers, either absent or killed, should fare especially well, and their stockings well filled by hook or crook, and re-resolved that within the circle of his influence all faces should be bright and happy – Aid Society or Gay Society to the contrary, notwithstanding.

So he walked along with his hands in his pockets to watch the dancers. They were holding high revel there. Over the glittering floor they flew, waxen beauties, clasped by stalwart Highlander or courtly Louis Quatorze, who had escaped the drawing-room mantles. Bronze knights in armor clinked their mailed heels in time with plump china Dolls. Rag Dolls waddled round in the embrace of India-rubber Zouaves. Wooden Dolls stumped round in the Mazurka with the German Grenadiers. Hideous Gutta Perchas and half naked

Arabs hob-a-nobbed with Walnut witches over their boiling punch; while Jumping Jacks executed frantic polkas with beautiful dancing Dolls; and Chinese Dolls and Crying Babies squalled vigorously, as energetic Harlequins bounced them around in time to the wild music of the Band. The Northern Lights glimmered and flashed, the huge fire-places glowed with fervent heat. The icicles trembled on the garlands, and the weird music played faster and faster, and round and round they flew under its enchantment. The Sister of Charity, her skirts smeared with the ink she had wiped from numerous pens, simpered slily under her big white bonnet, as she touched glasses with a burly Punch, astride a beer cask. She looked abominably knowing as she winked to him that she could, if she chose, reveal what a soldier in camp had written under her supervision. "That is, I sat on the inkstand, and wiped his pen – so I read his letter," and she smiled as a gay young tiger replenished her glass with the hottest of punch.

I should talk forever to describe every thing said and done that night. I shall only hint how certain Dolls, too old to dance and too young to stay at home, formed in a snug whist party, and *en masse* got gloriously fuddled, insomuch that some ventured too close to the fire and were instantly reduced to glowing charcoal; while others, not discerning the difference between a witch's broomstick and a comfortable sleigh, imprudently chose the former, and while in the act of sailing home, singing

"On the bat's back I do fly!"

incontinently tumbled off and were lost in the Arctic ocean, and never heard from more. The younger portion of the company, who drank only ice-water, all got home in perfect safety before cock-crow.

Santa Claus made a speech to the Dolls, in which "he assured the Dolls that he would attend to their grievances, and see to it that they had more of the time and attention of their little mistresses than ever before; also that a flea should be judiciously inserted into the ears of the mothers, to the intent that their assistance and co-operation should be lent to further his plans for a merry Christmas. He added that the soldiers were the fathers of his children, and had been his children themselves, and should receive his especial care and attention. All that could be done for them was right, except when it robbed little ones of their mothers. Like-wise, the children and orphans of soldiers were under his especial care, and he promised to co-operate with all Dolls from Fancy Fairs, to see that they were placed where they would do most good to the children."

He squeezed Polly's remaining hand, and exhorted her to mind the slippery steps, and pinched Josephine's glowing cheek, as she curtsied before him down to the ground and showed her flaxen curls over her waxen beauty; she leaned on the arm of the Ellsworth Zouave, who tenderly wrapped her white opera cloak around her, as he placed her inside the sleigh and took his own seat on the box beside the strolling Star who acted as driver for the nonce.

He comforted Squaw Lin, who looked venomously after them as they departed, with a promise of a splendid gutta percha Uncle Tom, and laughed himself sore to see her look of disgust.

He felt an inward disquiet, though he could not keep his face straight either, as he saw that the Walnuts and Gutta Perchas had had more than was good for them, and more than doubted if all of them would arrive home safe.

He detained the demure Sister of Charity a moment with a whispered hint of caution under her bonnet, and gave her arm a sly pinch as she nodded so violently that she nearly lost her head-gear. There was a secret understanding between them, only to be divulged to you, dear reader.

He watched each guest depart, and the long train of matrons, each escorting a load of merry, sleepy, tired Dolls home to their nursery, streamed across the ebon sky like a procession of sparks from a great conflagration.

They were the happiest Dolls that ever started off to a midnight frolic, and the tipsy ones made their exit singing,

"Wewongohomt'llmo'n'g. 'T'lldayItdoespear!"

Then he went in, lighted his pipe, and sat down to cogitate before his fire till morning. Then he concluded that an account of his ball had better be sent to *Harper's Weekly*, and see if a plea for the Children could not be made through its pages; and I did it for him, and here is the story.

J. B. Greene, *An Adventure of Santa Claus*
(BOSTON: LEE & SHEPARD, 1871)

I.

Greet merry Christmas,—happy children all,
Let mirth and laughter ring throughout the hall,
Droop not in mourning for the dying year,
Which lends such heartfelt and such merry cheer,
In Arctic regions unexplored I roam,
Beyond the glacial ice-clad fields I come,
To join your pleasures in your happy home.
My father, Odin, northern God of War,
Repents the mischief of his eldest, Thor;
Bade me, his youngest, restitution make,
And from his store-house ample presents take;
With Cornucopiæ, and the Peace-pipe bring,
And add new pleasures and full anthems sing.

II.
Where ice and sleet and feathery snow-flake fall,
In silent grandeur stands my ancient hall;
From whence I summons all my joyous band,
With gifts send greeting all throughout the land:
The stars and snow-clouds are my neighbors near,
They send kind greetings to the children dear,
And bade me hasten, nor my foemen fear;
Though foes unnumbered in my path arose,
Yet to my rescue came more friends than foes,
They dogg'd my footsteps to my journey's end,
Yet every foeman drew a stronger friend.

III.
Please give attention and you all shall know,
Who lent their friendship and who proved our foe,
Of those proved recreant from a selfish greed,
And those firm friendships in the hour of need:
For whom prove faithful, steadfast to the end,
Are only worthy to be called a friend.
The Black Fox Squirrel in his wild-wood free,
Bade me to hasten to your Christmas-Tree;
And with the children nuts and apples share,
Dividing freely of his ample fare,—
Applauds the service, and thus urges on,
Bespeaks well ending what is well begun.

IV.
The great White Owl, as beacon of the night,
With words of comfort made my journey light:
For Owl and Owlet ever hovered nigh,
As light as snow-flake through the air they fly;
And through the darkness with their great eyes peer
Gave words of comfort when the foe was near:
They pledged their friendship with a promise true,
To act as pilots all my journey through;
Nor ever listened to a would-be friend,
In vending gossip for some selfish end,—
For well they knew to earn the name of friend,
Was proving worthy, faithful to the end.

V.
The great Grey Eagle lent her ample wings,
High on the cliff her rude strong eyre clings;
O'er mountain torrent, or through highland glen,
Would lead our footsteps to the haunts of men;
Her quick eye gleaming with a lurid flame,
Saw pending dangers long before they came;
For long a leader as a bird of prey;
Knew the short passes of the rugged way—
Knew friends from foes, with pinions set on high;
She knew no bounds beneath the starry sky;
Her watchword: Dauntless,—Fearless,—Ever Free;
A type of courage and true liberty.

VI.
The dark brown Beaver as in times of old,
With his fur coat to shield him from the cold,
Awaits my coming in the drifting snow,
The safest pathway to the streamlets show;
To ford the torrents in the mountain dell
He made rude bridges with the trees he fell:
The sleepy Musk-rat from his rushen bed,
Made no great effort but kind words he said:—
"Beware of thin ice where our huts are made,
In the broad meadow in the gloom of night,
They seem as haycopes to unpracticed sight;
Await a pilot on the dawn of light."

VII.
The Owl said: "Thank ye, for this kindly word,
We have our pilots both on land and flood:
Impending danger as approaching foe,
We send back warning with a thrice cahoo;"
While jetty tresses, Alders, ice-fringed curls,
And Oziers, rubies overlain with pearls;
The full rich herbage hung in graceful furls;
And woodland jewels on the branches hung,
And spake their welcome as from Nature's tongue:
From their sly burroughs by the meadow brook,
Came Mink and Otter from their silent nook:
Though rival fishers in the mountain stream,
Their eyes spake welcome by their kindly gleam.

VIII.
In silent wonder and amazement stood,
A group of Herons near a sheltered wood,—
A sly Fox snatched the foremost of the brood;
But feeling guilty as a secret foe,
He turned affrighted at my loud halloo;
And dropped his plunder of this Christmas night,
And sought his safety in unerring flight;
They not unmindful of this favor shown,
Then served as pilots through each deep lagoon;
For all the swamp-land and the streamlets too,
The lakes and rivers, they had fished them through;
And fords for crossing every place they knew.

IX.
From dense pine forests sheltered from the storm,
Flew flocks of Ravens, and in cloud-like form,
As midnight darkness to the tree-tops flew,
They cawed as caution and as welcome too,—
Though not as skillful as a bird of prey,
As Hawk or Eagle, nor as strong as they,
Their words were "welcome," and their precepts true,
For Bear and Panther and the Grey Wolf too,
Their modes of rapine every one they knew;
They knew their duty, well they took their part,
For they were versed in all the woodland art;
And never faltered or declined to show,
The mountain passes which were free from snow.

X.
The snow-white Rabbit burroughed in the ground,
Set his long ears to catch the distant sound;
Of Bear and Panther prowling on my track,
From rock and cliff the hills re-echo back
Reverberations of the prowling pack;
Which moved by envy fierce and fiercer grew,
And from the tree-tops o'er the trunks they flew,
Till their hot breath full in my face it blew;
And ne'er before was ever wood-land wight,
So nearly fainting from a sudden fright,
As I from danger on this Christmas night.

XI.
Yet none so needy but they have a friend,—
No road so weary but there is an end,—
No night so dreary but the day will dawn,
We greet the sunshine of the coming morn:
Just e'er we yielded to a sad despair,
We heard a whisper on the evening air;—
Then god and goddess of the tangled wood
All armed as archers on the trees they stood,
For leaf and leaflet changed into a god;
Who sent their arrows winging on their flight,
Which pierced the prowlers of this Christmas night,
Made safe my journey and the children's right.

XII.
Birds, like misfortunes, seldom singly fly,
Brood after brood will ever hover nigh;
Thus with our favors though divinely sent;
Not fully ours but for a season lent,—
For looking upwards in the trees were found,
(The leaves mere rustle just a fairy sound,)
Full horns of plenty; they were quickly blown;
Full showers of presents on the ground were strewn,—
For bows and arrows into horns had grown;
Then quickly forward pressed two antlered deer,
Enrobed, warm-coated for the winter drear,
They bore their burdens with a heartfelt cheer.

XIII.
They freely used their lithe limbs for my speed,
To shun fresh impulse of the grey Wolf's greed;
And never arrow quite so quickly flew
Fresh from the bowstring the strong archer drew:—
The stars of heaven would guide me as I fly,
As eyes of angels beaming from the sky;
To light my footsteps to this cheerful hearth
To share your pleasures and enhance your mirth:—
Two fierce Grey Badgers then were kindly sent,
To guard my pathway their full service lent;
Though rather late yet next to kindly deed,
Is kind intention in the hour of need.

XIV.
The wily Possum too, came in at last,
To share the glories of the dangers past;
Thus true to nature;—human nature true—
To claim the honors all to others due:
To act as escort in triumphal train,
When naught of danger or of war, had seen.
The Coon more wily Fox-like than the rest,
Kept at such distance as would suit him best.
Not underrating deeds of daring shown
Or claiming virtues not at all his own,
But spake of fields where greater deeds were done.[38]

XV.
The Possum laughing at this sly old elf;
For well he knew just how it was himself;
That glory, honor, valor, yet to be,
Is more uncertain than futurity.
But more than glory, honor yet to gain,
I thought of leaving this cold bleak domain:—
Across the river's ice-bound bed I glide,
Through wide spread vallies up the mountain side;
With dainty footsteps o'er the heath they tread,
Where droops the daisy o'er the violets head;
Chilled by the frosts of hoary winter drear
Which checks the heart-throbs of the dying year.

XVI.
Then here we meet our social friends at last;
Recount the perils and the dangers past,
Of hopes and joys, and pleasures yet to be;
And plead our friends for widest charity.
Let all feel welcome to a heartfelt cheer,
Let none be strangers, but to hate and fear;
And all make merry, and the old house ring,
With joyous echoes of the song we sing;
May dames and grand-dames, join these pleasures too,
And with the children hope and youth renew,
Let sires and grandsires join the happy train,
And bring back childhood to themselves again.

XVII.
Now up the chimney's narrow throat I glide,
And from the housetops through the snow-drifts stride;
For every household in this cherished land,
Must share some bounty of my favored hand,—
Then pressing onward toward my journey's end,
I bear them with me, every valued friend;
To a large cavern near my ancient hall,
Where equal justice is dispensed to all;
I here assemble all, my friends to show,
How firm my friendship and how fares my foe:—
The honest Beaver and the Musk-rat too,
Must share such favors as the others do;

XVIII.
For Mink and Otters choicest morsels bring,
As Trout and Minnow from the cavern spring;
Where fresh grow cresses for the antlered Deer.
In full abundance for their Christmas cheer;
The Black-Fox Squirrel from my ample store
Shares, and the Rabbit need not hunger more;
Through this long Winter guests of mind remain,
In Spring returning to their haunts again.
This old tribunal formed by Nature's hand,
Where equal justice serves at my command;
Here at my bidding from the cavern wall,
Loose huge sharp fragments on my foeman fall;

XIX.
The famished Eagle would the Panther tear,
And hungry Badger unrelenting Bear;
While Wolf fast pinioned writhing in his ire,
With eyes still gleaming as with liquid fire:
The Owl sits waiting her grim foe expire;
With seeming prudence and with solemn face,
Invokes a blessing with becoming grace,
Then helps the Ravens to the choicest piece;
Which through the archways scream in wild despair,
Their deep jet pinions beat the cavern air,
For age gives flavor to their dainty fare.

38 The copy of this poem owned by the American Antiquarian Society is signed by the author, and Greene himself appears to have added an extra handwritten couplet at the end of this stanza about the cowardly but boastful raccoon: "A new occasion all his friends should see / How great, how brave a fellow he would be."

XX.

Herein we tell you briefly as we end,
How fared my foeman, and how shared my friend.
Here ends the legend, not as briefly told,
How well I journey'd on through heat and cold;
All for your pleasure, yet I fain would show,
For 'tis but justice that my friends should know
When thus encountered, how I treat a foe.
A Merry Christmas and a Happy Year;
We wish you constant and abundant cheer:
May future riches never prove to be
Your greatest trial and adversity:
God speed your pleasures make your burdens light,
Farewell! farewell! we wish you all good night.

Margaret Mason, "Santa Claus", *Our Young Folks*, JANUARY 1872

In his crystal palace in the Polar Sea,
Santa Claus harnessed, in tandem three,
The Ursa Major and the Minor Bear,
With the Flying Horse to lead the pair.
They snuffed the wind of sleet and snow,
They pawed the ground in their haste to go,—
Santa Claus' team in tandem three
At his palace gate in the Polar Sea.

That palace built of ice and snow,
Begun in the ages long ago:
Its walls were laid the very day
The Christ-child in the manger lay;
And all its crystal bells were rung
When first the Bethlehem shepherds sung.

And Santa Claus now, in the Christmas cold,
Gathers his gifts for young and old;
Lights up his palace on every side
And opens the icy shutters wide;
Puts on the frost-work steps a star
To keep the swinging door ajar
And show the way for his tandem three
To find the gate of the Polar Sea.

Because the icebergs are rough and tall,
He takes his course above them all;
And his tandem three, as if at play,
Go dashing down the milky-way!
The Northern lights are blazing high,
'Tis his palace lamps on the midnight sky!
That flash of light is a shooting star,
A spark from the wheel of his rolling car!

'Tis Santa Claus' coming which looks like day,
And fades the stars of the milky-way!
You hear not the sound of the north-wind cold,
But the whiz and whir of his car of gold!

So put out the fires lest they should melt
The Icicle sword in his starry belt;
We'll take a nap, and then we'll see
If Santa Claus brought for you and me
Some wondrous gift, with his tandem three,
From his crystal halls in the Polar Sea.

4.

The Thomas Nast Era

A selection of Nast's Santas

Thomas Nast produced annual Christmas illustrations for *Harper's Weekly* from 1863 until 1886. While Nast's illustrations are threaded through this book at the beginning of each section, four of his most famous Santas from across the decades follow here: Nast's first image of Santa Claus from 1863; the pivotal spread "Santa Claus and His Works" from 1866; Santa Claus at his desk from 1871; and perhaps Nast's most iconic vision of the gift-bringer from 1881, "Merry Old Santa Claus". According to his biographer Albert Bigelow Paine in 1904, Nast's memories of the Christmas traditions of his childhood in Germany helped to shape these famous Santas. Paine narrates: "But on Christmas Eve, to Protestant and Catholic alike, came the German Santa Claus, Pelze-Nicol [often spelled Belsnickel], leading a child dressed as the Christkind, and distributing toys and cakes, or switches, according as the parents made report. It was this Pelze-Nicol—a fat, fur-clad, bearded old fellow, at whose hands he doubtless received many benefits—that the boy in later years was to present to us as his conception of the true Santa Claus—a pictorial type which shall long endure." If, like Paine, we can credit Nast with helping to popularise a standard image for Santa, it's worth noting some idioyncracies remain in his drawings, particularly in relation to Santa's size. Following Moore's model, Nast's Santa was often rather diminutive in stature, though he slowly grew over the decades. After Nast left Harper's Weekly, he collected his seasonal sketches together in a single volume in 1889: *Thomas Nast's Christmas Drawings for the Human Race* (New York: Harper & Brothers). A "Publisher's Note" which introduced that volume attempted to define the particular appeal of these illustrations: "The grotesque and airy fancies of childhood which cling about Santa Claus, as the good genius of Christmas, are reproduced upon these pages, in delightfully imaginative reality by the sympathetic touch of the artist, so that the book is an overflowing feast of true Christmas cheer. [...] It is the bluff, honest Santa Claus of "The Night before Christmas;" the Santa Claus of the reindeer and the sleigh, alighting on the snowy roof, and descending the chimney with his wondrous pack of treasures; the Santa Claus of unsuspecting childhood [...] to whom these pages introduce us. There is no child who cannot understand them, no parent who cannot enjoy them. Mr. Nast is fairly without a rival in this kind. His Santa Claus is old Father Christmas himself, and his welcome will be as general and as hearty as that which salutes the crammed and enchanted stocking on Christmas morning."

▶ **Thomas Nast, "Santa Claus in Camp",** *Harper's Weekly,* JANUARY 3 1863

HARPER'S WEEKLY.

A JOURNAL OF CIVILIZATION.

VOL. VII.—No. 314.] NEW YORK, SATURDAY, JANUARY 3, 1863. [SINGLE COPIES SIX CENTS.
$2 50 PER YEAR IN ADVANCE.

Entered according to Act of Congress, in the Year 1862, by Harper & Brothers, in the Clerk's Office of the District Court for the Southern District of New York.

SANTA CLAUS IN CAMP.—[SEE PAGE 6.]

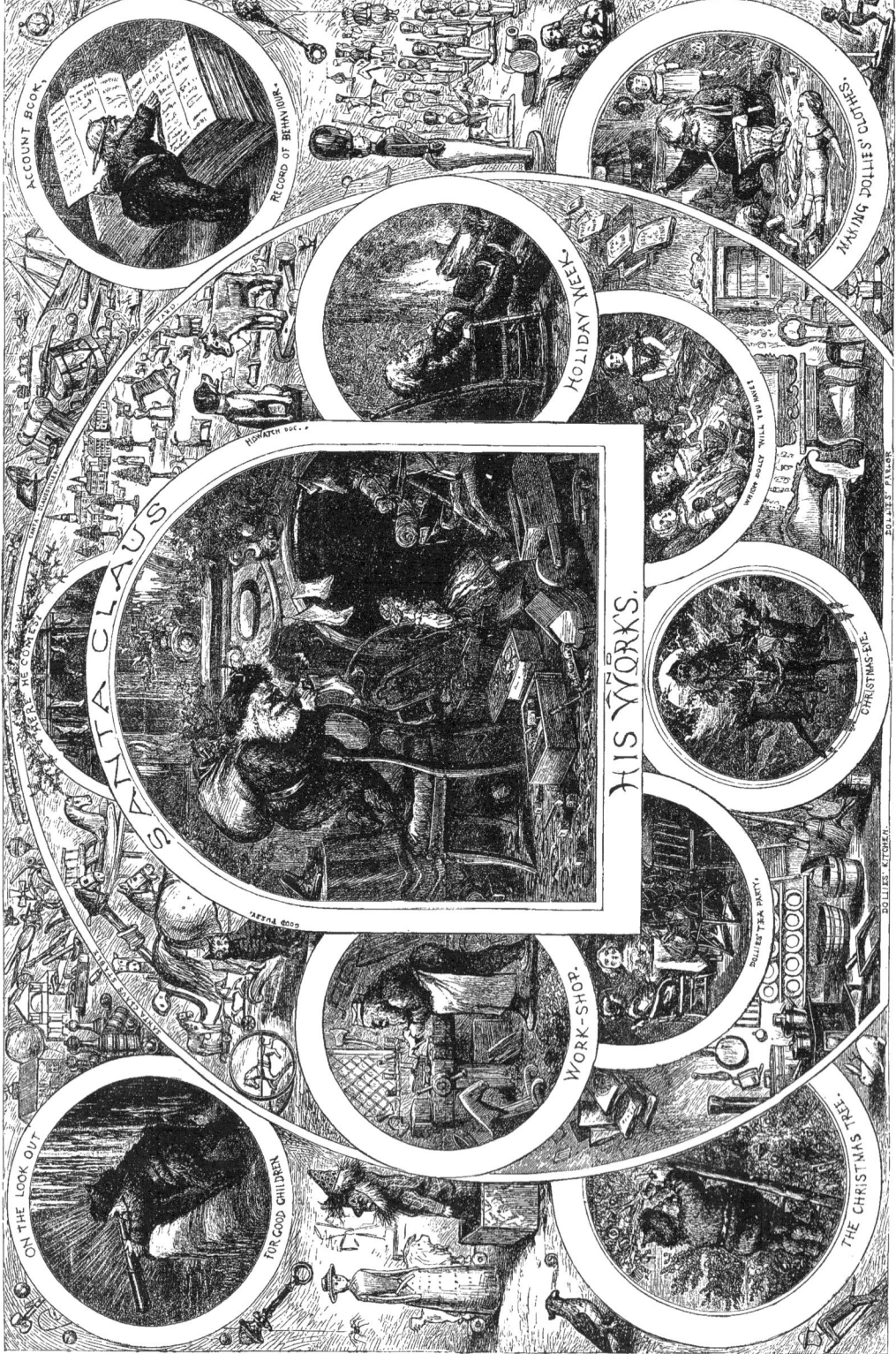

◀ "Santa Claus and His Works", *Harper's Weekly,* DECEMBER 29 1866

▼ "Santa Claus's Mail", *Harper's Weekly,* DECEMBER 30 1871

"Merry Old Santa Claus",
Harper's Weekly,
JANUARY 1 1881

George P. Webster and Thomas Nast,
Santa Claus and His Works
(NEW YORK: MCLOUGHLIN BROS., C1869)

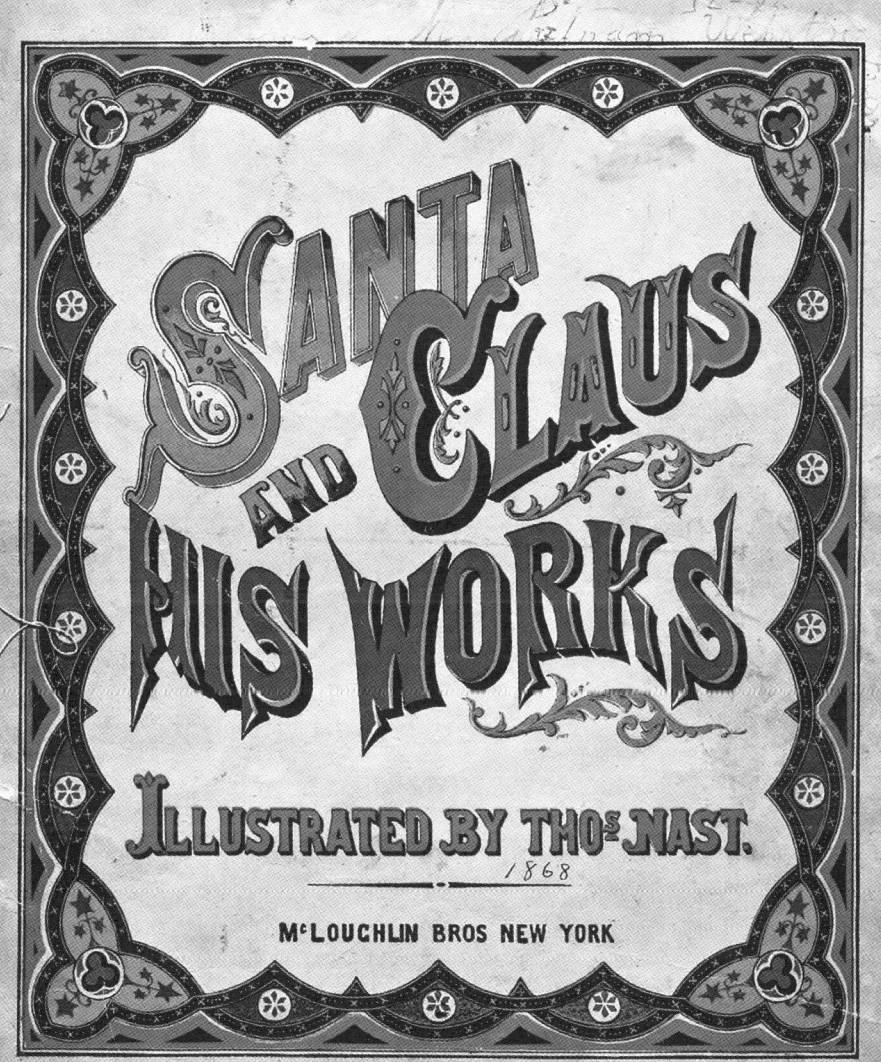

SANTA CLAUS
AND
HIS WORKS.

by GEO. P. WEBSTER

This nice little story for Girls and for Boys
Is all about Santa Claus, Christmas and toys;
So gather around me, but speak not a word—
For I mean what I say, by you all shall be heard.
In a nice little city called Santa Clausville,
With its houses and church at the foot of the hill
Lives jolly old Santa Claus; day after day
He works and he whistles the moments away.

You must know, he is honest, and toils for his bread,
And is fat and good-natured with nothing to dread.
His eyes are not red, but they twinkle and shine,
For he never was known to drink brandy or wine;
But day after day at his bench he is found,
For he works for good children hard, all the year round.
Though busy all day he is happy, and sings
While planning and making the funniest things,
Such as wagons and horses, and dishes and ladles,
And soldiers and monkeys, and little dolls cradles,
With trumpets and drummers, farms, sheep, pigs and cattle,
And he makes the pop-guns and the baby's tin rattle;
Then he takes the new dolls that have long curly hair,
And, setting the table, seats each in a chair,
And he makes them pretend they are taking their tea—
He's the jolliest fellow you ever did see,
And can make a queer codger jump out of a box,
Or will make with his knife a new parrot and fox,
Or sit with his spectacles over his nose
And work all day long making little dolls clothes,
Such as dresses and sashes, and hats for the head,
And night-gowns to wear when they jump into bed;
And garters and socks, and the tiniest shoes,
And lots of nice things such as doll babies use.
(See, the top of his head is all shining and bare—
'Tis the good men, dear children, who lose all their hair.)
With many things more, for I can not tell half—
But just look at his picture, I'm sure you will laugh,

With his dog standing near him, and spy-glass in hand,
He looks for good children all over the land.
His home through the long summer months, you must know,
Is near the North Pole, in the ice and the snow;
And when he sees children at work or at play
The old fellow listens to hear what they say;
And if they are gentle, loving and kind,
He finds where they live, and he makes up his mind
That when Christmas shall come in cold frosty December
To give them a call, he will surely remember;
And he's sure to have with him a bundle of toys
For the nice little girls and the good little boys.
Oh, if you could see him start out with his team
You would doubt your own eyes, and would think it a dream—
Wrapped up in a bear-skin to keep out the cold,
And his sleigh covered over with jewels and gold,
While his deer from the mountains, all harnessed with care,
Like race-horses prance through the cold winter air.
'Tis fun just to watch them and hear the bells tinkle,
E'en the stars seem to laugh and they look down and twinkle.
And the hungry raccoon, and the fox lean and shy
Give a wink as they hear him go galloping by;
For they know by his looks and the crack of his whip,
And his sleigh-load of toys, he is out for a trip.
Then the fox steals the farmer's old goose for his dinner,
Which you know is not right—but the fox is a sinner,
And his morals are bad and his habits are loose,
For he's never so gay as when stealing a goose.

Ah! Here is a picture. Oh, children, just look
At the names of the good little girls in his book,
And a long list of names of the good little boys,
Who never disturb Pa and Ma with their noise.
There is Tommy, who tended the baby with care,
He gets some beautiful books for his share;
And Eliza, just think how bright her eyes will twinkle
When she looks in her stockings and finds Rip Van Winkle.
And Georgie, you know, is the five-year-old dandy—
Won't he strut with his pockets all filled up with candy?
There the old fellow stands with a queer knowing look,
Till he has in his mind every name in the book;
And he would be kind to them all if he could,
But he gives his presents to none but the good.
An army he gives to the boy who is neat,
And never cries when he wants something to eat;
And a farm to the boy who goes smiling to school,
Who keeps out of the mud and obeys every rule;
And all the good girls will get presents, we know,
And the boys who behave will have something to show.
When Christmas Eve comes, into bed you must creep,
And late in the night, when you all are asleep
He is certain to come, so your stockings prepare,
And hang them all close to the chimney with care,
And when in the morning you open your eyes
You will meet, I am sure, a most pleasant surprise;
And you'll laugh and you'll giggle and call to Mamma,
And keep up the noise till you waken Papa—
And of this for one morning will be very nice,
But the rest of the year be as quiet as mice.

How funny he looks as he stands on the round
And gathers the toys that hang far from the ground.
He is large round the waist, but what care we for that—
'Tis the good-natured people who always get fat.
The grumbling wolf who lies hidden all day,
And the fox that at midnight goes out for his prey,
And the serpent that hides in the foliage green,
And all of them ugly, ill-tempered and lean;
But Santa Claus comes in his queer looking hat,
And we know he's good-humored because he is fat.
So when you grow up I would not have you slim,
But large round the waist, and good natured like him.
Just think, if the ladder should happen to break
And he should fall down, what a crash it would make;
And that is not all, for besides all the noise,
It would frighten the dolls and would damage the toys.
I told you his home was up north by the Pole:
In a palace of ice lives this happy old soul,
And the walls are as bright as diamonds that shone
In the cave, when Aladdin went in all alone
To look for the lamp we have often been told
Turned iron and lead into silver and gold.
His bedstead is made of ivory white,
And he sleeps on a mattress of down every night;
For all the day long he is working his best,
And surely at night the old fellow should rest.
He uses no gas, for the glimmering light
Of the far polar regions shines all through the night.
Should he need for his breakfast a fish or some veal,
The sea-calves are his, and the whale and the seal.
Where he lives there is always a cool pleasant air,
Last summer, oh! didn't we wish we were there?
He's a funny old chap, and quite shy, it would seem,
For I never but once caught a glimpse of his team;
'Twas a bright moonlight night, and it stood in full view,
And, so you see, I can describe it to you.

See! Christmas has come, and he toils like a Turk,
And now the old fellow is busy at work—
There are presents for Julia and Bettie and Jack,
And a bundle still left on the old fellow's back,
And if Evrie behaves well and don't tear his clothes,
And quits teasing the cat, why he will, I suppose,
Find on Christmas a horse or a gun or a sled,
All ready for use when he gets out of bed.
But see he has worked quite enough for to-night,
He must fill all the stockings before it is light.
With his queer looking team through the air he will go,
And alight on the roof, now all white with the snow,
And into the chimney will dart in a trice,
When all are asleep but the cat and the mice;
Then will fill up the stockings with candy and toys,
And all without making the least bit of noise.

When the labors of Christmas are over he goes
Straight home, and takes a full week for repose;
And then when the holyday frolics are o'er,
He goes to his shop and his labors once more,
And all the long year with his paints and his glue,
He is making new toys, little children, for you.
So now I must leave you—but stand in a row—
Come Julia, and Bettie, and Louie, and Joe,
And Gracie, and Fannie, what are you about —
Get ready, I say, for a jolly good shout.
Now, three cheers for Christmas! give them, boys, with a will!
Three more for the hero of Santa-Clausville;
When know he is old, and bald headed and fat,
But the cleverest chap in the world for all that,
And jollier codger no man ever saw—
But good-bye, merry Christmas, Hip, Hip, Hip Hurrah!

5.

Dear Santa

Emily Huntington Miller, "Lilly's Secret", *The Little Corporal* (DECEMBER 1865)

Jolly old Saint Nicholas,
Lean your ear this way!
Don't you tell a single soul
What I'm going to say.
Christmas Eve is coming soon,
Now you dear old man,
Whisper what you'll bring to me;
Tell me if you can.

When the clock is striking twelve,
When I'm fast asleep,
Down the chimney broad and black,
With your pack you'll creep
All the stockings you will see
Hanging in a row;
Mine will be the shortest one—
You'll be sure to know.

Johnny wants a pair of skates,
Susy wants a dolly,
Nellie wants a story book,
She thinks dolls a folly.
As for me, my little brain
Never was the wisest,
Choose for me, old Santa Claus,
What you think is nicest.

"Santa Claus's Correspondents", *St. Nicholas,* DECEMBER 1893

SANTA CLAUS's letters begin to pour into the general post-office as early as December 1, and the flow increases daily. Mr. E. P. Jones, of the dead-letter department, who takes charge of all the mail addressed to the merry old gentleman, says he never saw anything like this year's work before. Mr. Jones ought to know, for he has handled Santa Claus's mail for the past twenty years.

A very general notion prevails, Mr. Jones says, among young folks who have occasion to communicate with Santa Claus, that his home is in this city, despite the fact that he is constantly pictured driving a reindeer to a sledge over a snow-bound country covered with fir-trees. For this reason nearly all of his letters go through the local post-office, and are forwarded by Mr. Jones and his able assistants to the Washington dead-letter office, where, it is presumed, they are opened by Santa Claus's private secretary.

The letters come from all over the country. It is curious to note that most of them come from places outside of New York. Perhaps the reason for this is that there are so many Christmas charities in this city that the fear of Santa Claus not putting in an appearance at the appointed time is not so keenly felt here as in some other places.

It is interesting to look over Santa Claus's mail. Of course you cannot open it, any more than you would be allowed to open the mail of any other private or public citizen. The addresses are so curious, and written with such evident pains, and the parenthetical remarks, which are often added as a last reminder on the envelopes, so appealing, and there is such an air of confidence and sincerity about them all, that it is not necessary to examine the contents for entertainment.

Santa Claus, Mr. Jones says, is an idol worshiped by the rich and poor alike, as you would very soon know if you glanced over his mail. The letters come in all sorts of envelopes, and some of them in none at all. There are delicately tinted letters with crests on the back, from children who plead for a pony or a carriage; and there are the letters of another sort, from destitute little ones, who plead with good Mr. Santa Claus for a stocking full of candy or a rattle for the baby. The granting of these widely different requests would afford equal satisfaction to either receiver, as it would, no doubt, to Mr. Claus also.

Eighteen letters for Santa Claus were received at the New York post-office one morning. No two were directed exactly alike. The first was the most direct, and was the only one in which a definite address was given. Here it is:

> MR. SANTA CLAUS,
> 444 Cherry street,
> New York.

This was written in a scrawling hand, but the number was quite plain. It was probably the only one of the lot that did not go directly to the dead-letter office. There was the name, a definite number on a definite street in a definite city, and in the lower left-hand corner was the regular United States two-cent postage-stamp. So the letter was given to the proper carrier, who took it to the Cherry street address. When it came back this legend was stamped in red ink across the face:

> REMOVED: PRESENT ADDRESS UNKNOWN.

There is something realistic in the word "removed". It shows at least that the post-office folks are not skeptical in the belief that Santa Claus *had* his home at 444 Cherry street. If this be true, some young persons will think it was very careless in the old gentleman not to leave his new address. But he is so busy at this time of the year that he may have forgotten it.

One letter, dated at Haverstraw, was addressed like this on a thick, creamy envelope:

> MR. SANTY CLAUS,
> NEW YORK
> CITY
>
> P. S.—If not called for by Xmas, please return.

This was the only one in which Mr. Claus was addressed familiarly. But perhaps he and the writer are old friends, which does not seem improbable, judging from the quality of the envelope and the seal on the back. The letter will have to be sent to Washington with the others, if not called for, owing to the absence of a return address.

The majority of the letters are addressed strangely. There are numerous variations in the spelling of Claus, and not a few, probably Germans, write it with a K. Here are two examples:

> TO DEAR SANTA KLAUS, New York City.

This is dated from Stanfordville, N. Y. It is not quite so fervent as the next:

> DEAR MR. POSTMASTER:
> Bring this to Dear Santa Claus.

Such a touching appeal as this the postmaster thought he could not fail to respond to.

Sometimes, when the envelope is carelessly sealed, or when there is no envelope at all, the missive being held in shape merely by the stamp, it comes apart and the contents are disclosed. Under these circumstances it is, the authorities think, perhaps permissible to read them. Under any other, there would be a manifest impropriety in prying into the confidences of these youngsters.

There was one such letter this morning. It came folded and turned down at one corner, and the stamp was placed so as to hold the folded corner down. It read as follows:

CHITTENANGO, N. Y.

DEAR MR. SANTA CLAUS: I only want a pare of skates for Crissmas and if it aint cold a sled will do My old ones bust. If they aint no snow I would like anything you think of. My mamma says you are poor this year.

Yours truly,

C———N———

"Dear Santa": Letters from Young Readers
The Nursery, DECEMBER 1873

The little boy who got his aunt to write this letter for him wishes to have it appear in "The Nursery," so that Santa Claus may be sure to read it. When it is printed, the little boy says he can read it himself. Here is the letter:—

> DEAR MR. SANTA CLAUS,
> Please, sir, could you not bring me a team of goats next Christmas? I do want them so much! Other little boys no bigger than I am have a pair of goats to play with.
>
> When I ask my mother to get me a pair, she says she will see, but thinks I shall have to wait a little while. Now, dear Mr. Santa Claus, I do not feel as if I could wait.
>
> Besides, ma's "little while" seems like a great while to me, and when I get older I shall have to go to school; but now I could play almost all the time with my little goats, if I had them. Oh, dear! I wish I had them now! I can hardly wait till Christmas. I will be very kind to them, and give them plenty to eat, and a good warm bed at night. Brother Charley says he will get me a wagon, if you, good Mr. Santa Claus, will give me the goats.
>
> Folks say, that, although you are an old man, you love little children; especially little boys with black eyes, and who obey their mother. Well, my eyes are very black; and I love my mother dearly, and try to obey her.
>
> My name is Francis Lincoln Noble: I live at 214, South 8th Street, Williamsburgh, L.I. The house is quite high; but, dear Mr. Santa Claus, I think your nimble deer can climb to the top of it.
>
> You can put the little goats right down through the chimney in ma's room. I will take away the fireboard, so they can come out at the fireplace. Oh, how happy I shall be when I wake in the morning, and see them! I shall say, "Merry Christmas!" to everybody; and everybody will say, "Merry Christmas!" to me.
>
> But dear, good Mr. Santa Claus, if you cannot get to the top of the house to put them down the chimney, please to bring them up the frontsteps, and tie them to the door-knob; and then blow your whistle, and I will run right down to the door; and, dear Mr. Santa Claus, could you not stop long enough for me to say, "Thank you!" for my mother says all good boys say, "Thank you!" when they receive a present?
>
> FRANCIS LINCOLN NOBLE.

"Dear Santa": Letters from Young Readers
The Nursery, JANUARY 1874

What could six-year-old Benny be doing? For half an hour he had been sitting quietly on an ottoman, busy with pencil and paper, only looking up now and then to ask his mamma how to spell a long word.

After a while he came to his mamma for an envelope, and asked her to direct it for him. So mamma wrote on it, at Benny's dictation, SANTA CLAUS, GREENLAND, NORTH POLE. Then Benny sealed his letter, and took it to the post-office.

Two or three days after Benny had posted his letter, his papa came into the parlor, looking very much amused. A mail-agent on the postal-car had found among the letters one directed to Santa Claus, which he had opened. Seeing the signature, and happening to know Benny's papa, the mail-agent had sent the letter to him. Papa had the open letter in his hand. We will read it:—

WINDSOR, NOV. 2.
DEAR SANTA CLAUS,—Next Christmas please bring me a drum, and a pair of rubber-boots, and some oranges, and a pensil that marks red and blue, and one that marks black, and some almonds, and a writing-desk, and a rubber-ball, and some candy, and a pistol that shoots paper caps, and a safe with a frog to swallow the pennies like the one Robbie Kendall has got, and some figs and grapes, and a new sled with Gen. Grant on it; and please bring me some writing-paper and a candy-cane. I liked very much what you brought me last year; but the horses are broken off from the wagon, and the key is lost that winds it up; and Dickie broke the smoke-stack off from my little steamboat.

BENNY HOLBROOK.

Only one word spelled wrong, and all the words printed quite evenly on the lines.

Benny asked his mamma, the other day, if she supposed Santa Claus had got the letter yet.

Of course he had. Mamma sent it to him by a special messenger.

"Dear Santa": Letters from Young Readers
Harper's Young People, DECEMBER 26 1882

Jersey City, New Jersey

I am twelve years old, and have taken your paper for a long time, and like it very much. I send you a letter to Santa Claus, written by my little sister. Perhaps you will think it good enough to print.

Robert D.

Dear Santa Claus,
In your rounds I wish you'd pause
Over the chimney of 135,
And stop there, if you're alive;
Leave me a box of writing-paper large,
And a pair of shoes for my doll named Marge;
A book I would like on your list to set,
The name of it is Fred Bradford's Debt,
You can get it at Cassel, Petter, Galpin, & Co.'s,
739 Broadway O;
I want a little toy caster.
Made of tin, and not of plaster,
And a sharp little penknife;
I had one once before in my life,
But I lost it right away,
So bring it this time in your sleigh.
I want my dolls to have something nice,
Even if it's no more than some little toy mice,
Alice, my oldest, a new dress needs;
Her old one is through with its kindly deeds.
Margie wants a good warm cloak,
Only not black, and quite a long sacque,
I have the fur to trim it for her,
Then very nice tails I know,
And your wife can fix it just so;
I'll put the box up the flue,
And if any one gets it 'twill be you.
But what to get for Emma
I am in a dilemma:
She is such a particular child
She nearly drives me wild.
So get what you think best,
And your judgment I can test.
Otis (the baby) wants a rattle,
If he don't get it I'll have a battle.
And Nettie—what was it she said?
Oh, I know, a new head.
And I want an inkstand, a box, and a pen,
Not a quill from a hen.
But a gold one that shuts up and is gone,
So I can write letters in the early morn.
Now, Santa, please send these things on Christmas-eve,
No sigh you must heave,
But crawling down slowly, take a good look,
And leave them near on chair or book,
Some Christmas soon I hope you'll see
Your little friend,

                                    Cora D.

"Dear Santa": Letters from Young Readers
Harper's Young People, MARCH 29 1881

Huntingdon, Pennsylvania

Mamma helped me print a letter to Santa Claus, and I told him just what I wanted him to bring me. I put my letter in the chimney, and next morning it was gone, and dear old Santa Claus brought me just what I asked him for. I screamed up the chimney, and tried to make him hear me, but he never answered a word.

CHRISIE B. B.

"Dear Santa": Letters from Young Readers
St. Nicholas, APRIL 1900

Here is a young poet who sends us a letter to Santa Claus, and who knows how to make a pun:

ARKANSAS CITY, KAN.
DEAR SANTA CLAUS: How do you do?
And are you very cold?
The air is getting pretty sharp
For you who are so old.

I wear my nice blue mackintosh
Which you gave to me last year.
It isn't worn out the least bit—
How I thank you, Santa dear!

I wish I had some books to read—
I've read my old ones twice.
I think the one about Denise
And her pony "Ned" is nice.

And then, my big doll broke her head;
She needs another one.
She's put away upon the shelf,
And can't have any fun.

To ask you for so many things
Would really be quite mean;
And so I'll simply sign myself
Your loving, true JUSTINE

P. S. The letters that the others write
Perhaps won't be like mine;
But then, my pencil got so cold,
I had to write in "rime."

Justine Fitzpatrick (twelve years old)

Elizabeth Bigelow, "Kitty's Letter", *Ballou's Monthly Magazine,* December 1887

"I don't think Santa Claus is so very good," said Kitty, stoutly, her bit of a forehead all puckered up into a frown, with the hard thinking that had been going on behind it for the last ten minutes. "If he is, why doesn't he carry presents to poor little girls and boys, as well as rich ones? Susy Briggs says he never brought her one in her life, and she don't hang up her stocking now, because she knows he won't come to her house. And it must be because she's poor, and lives in such a mean, little bit of a house. But she can't help it; her father is dead, and her mother can't earn more than enough to keep them from starving. And just because Lily Perkins is rich, and lives in a great, splendid house, Santa Claus carries her dolls and playhouses and books with pictures in them, every Christmas; and last year he brought her a little, truly rabbit, just as white as snow, with pink eyes. And I think Santa Claus is mean!"

Aunt Kate, who had been talking to Kitty about Santa Claus, and telling her that he wouldn't come to fill her stocking unless she were very good, because, being so very good himself he couldn't endure bad children, was reading now, and did not hear a word Kitty said; but Fred, Kitty's brother, who was a great, grown-up boy, almost fifteen, and knew everything, Kitty thought, held up his hands in horror.

"I guess you'll find he won't bring you much, to-night, young lady, after you have talked in this way about him," said Fred.

Kitty looked a little concerned.

"Can he hear me?" she said.

"Hear you! of course," answered Fred, whose greatest delight was in teasing Kitty.

"Well, I'm sorry I said he was mean, because he is good to bring me things," said Kitty, after thinking a while. "But I do wish he would carry Susy Briggs something."

"You might write to him and ask him to; that is, if you knew his postoffice address," suggested Fred.

"Do you know it?" asked Kitty, eagerly catching at the idea.

It would be such a grand thing to write to Santa Claus; and, besides the urgent request in Susy Briggs's behalf, she would like to ask his pardon for calling him mean, for he might be angry, and not bring her any more presents, as Fred said.

"I? Oh, of course I know where he lives," answered Fred; "but I sha'n't tell you, for it wouldn't be of any use for you to send a letter to him this afternoon. He wouldn't get it in time to carry Susy Briggs anything to-night. It's likely that he has started out to buy his presents long before this time; and he won't go home until he has filled all the stockings he intends to—not until broad daylight."

"How do you know that he buys the

presents himself?" she inquired.

"Oh, I saw him last Christmas Eve down in Mace's toy shop," replied Fred.

Kitty's eyes grew round as gooseberries. "You saw him! O Freddy, how did he look? Like the pictures in my 'Kriss Kringle' book?" she cried, breathlessly.

"Yes, a good deal like that, but that picture was taken when he was younger than he is now. He is just as fat and jolly-looking now, as he was then, though; and his cheeks are like two red, shiny apples; and he's got little, twinkling, black eyes, like glass beads. But his hair is getting quite gray," answered Fred, drawing upon his imagination as rapidly as possible.

"Did you speak to him?" inquired Kitty.

"No; he doesn't like to have anybody speak to him. If you ever meet him, you mustn't say anything to him."

"Does he live here, in Wilmington, Fred?"

"Yes, I guess so," answered Fred, who had lost his interest in the conversation suddenly, from having seen some of his comrades going by with skates in their hands.

"Then, if he does, perhaps a letter would get to him before night," persisted Kitty.

"I tell you he has gone out to buy presents before this time. If you want to write to him, you can put a letter on the mantel-piece, and if he comes to put anything in your stocking, maybe he'll see it."

And Fred hung his skates over his shoulder, thrust on his cap and rushed out.

It was better than not to write to Santa Claus at all, to put a letter on the mantel-piece, and run the risk of his seeing it; even then it might not be too late for him to carry something to Susy Briggs. So Kitty got a sheet of paper, and a pen and some ink, and sat down beside the window to write.

She sat for a long time nibbling at the end of the pen with her teeth, and with her forehead all screwed up, just as you have seen people sit, perhaps, when they were coaxing their brains very hard. It wasn't so easy to write a letter to Santa Claus as Kitty had thought it would be. For, besides the printing—Kitty couldn't write—which was very hard, there was the spelling and the composing. Of course, it would never do to write a letter to Santa Claus that was not perfectly correct, and with very polite words in it.

So, after a while, Kitty went and got Fred's big spelling-book, that had all the big words that anybody could think of in it; and then, after a very little more nibbling of her pen and screwing up of her forehead, she wrote the first words of her letter; and, after a great deal of patient labor, and much consulting of the spelling-book, it was, at last, finished to Kitty's mind. And this was the way it ran:—

"DEAR SANTA CLAUS:—I take my pen in hand to write you a letter. I hope you will see the letter on the mantel-piece. I hope you will excuse me for writing you a letter, if you don't like to have people write letters to you, and excuse me if I don't write it very well, for I never wrote a letter before. I write this letter to ask you to forgive me for calling you mean, and I hope it did not make you feel bad. And I write this letter, besides, to ask you to carry Susy Briggs a present to-night. You never do, and perhaps it is because you don't know where she lives. She lives in a little bit of a mean old house in Cherry Lane. I think if you should carry her a new dress, and a good warm shawl, she would like it, because she hasn't got anything but a thin calico dress to wear to school. And if you thought you could afford it, you might carry her a pair of new, high boots, and a pretty, large doll, and a new sled. Because her father is dead, and her mother can't buy her anything. I should like very much to have you bring me a truly rabbit with pink eyes, like the one you carried Lily Perkins last Christmas. Please don't forget to carry the presents to Susy Briggs. Good-bye.
"KITTY BENT."

Kitty folded the letter up and put it in an envelope, and printed Santa Claus's name in very large, plain letters on the outside. Then, being very tired with her afternoon's work, she wheeled the great easy-chair up to the window, and sat down to rest.

It was beginning to grow dark, but the sleighs, with their jingling bells, were flying just as merrily as ever, and there were throngs of people going by on the sidewalk, with their arms filled with bundles; and Kitty thought that everybody seemed in a greater hurry than usual because it was Christmas eve. She wished Fred would come home and take her down to Mace's toy shop, and perhaps she might see Santa Claus. And then she wondered whether she should know him by the picture in her book; she rather thought she should, she remembered so well the expression of his round, good-natured face.

Just then a sleigh came rather slowly along by the window, with an occupant that caught Kitty's eye in an instant. And at the first glance, her heart gave a great thump! For it was a little, old gentleman who sat in the sleigh, and his face was exactly like Santa Claus's in her picture-book—a round, good-natured face, with rosy cheeks and twinkling, black eyes. To be sure, he was not dressed like Santa Claus in the picture, but why wouldn't Santa Claus be as likely to follow the fashions as anybody?

Kitty didn't pause for a second thought, but with her letter in her hand, rushed out of doors. Everybody stared to see a little, bare-headed girl rushing so frantically after a sleigh, but Kitty didn't mind that. The little, old gentleman stopped his horse when he saw her, and Kitty, though she was almost out of breath, managed to gasp out, "Here's a letter for you!" and thrust it into his hand. Then she turned and ran back to the house.

The little, old gentleman looked puzzled; still more so when he read the superscription. But at last he chuckled good-naturedly, a glimmering of the truth seeming to strike him.

"So the child took me for Santa Claus!" he said, to himself; and then he opened Kitty's letter and read it.

"Carry some presents to Susy Briggs, eh?" he said, to himself. "A pretty queer thing to take a forlorn old bachelor like me, who never had anybody to give Christmas presents to, for Santa Claus! Susy Briggs! Well, I don't know but that I may as well take Miss Kitty Bent's advice, and carry her something. Susy—and Briggs, too," he went on, musingly. "It is a little singular; but, of course, it isn't possible that that little sister of mine, who ran off and got married to that poor scamp of a Briggs, should turn up in this little, out-of-the-way place, when I've hunted half over the world for her in the last ten years. No, of course it isn't possible. But I'll carry Susy Briggs some presents for her name, anyway, so that Kitty Bent's faith in Santa Claus needn't be shaken."

So the little old gentleman whipped up his horse, and rode rapidly along until he came to a dry goods store, and then he went in and bought a beautiful, bright-colored, plaid dress, and a nice, warm shawl. Then he went into a shoe store, and bought a nice pair of boots, but he didn't know what size Susy Briggs wore, so he had to guess at it. After that he went into Mace's toy shop, and bought a beautiful great doll, with blue eyes that would open and shut, and curly, flaxen hair.

When he had got all the bundles into his sleigh, he started in search of Cherry Lane. He was a stranger in Wilmington—had come there on business only that morning—and he had to inquire the way, but it was not long before he was knocking at the door of the "little bit of a mean old house." A mean old house it was, indeed; and when the gentleman saw how poor and empty it looked, he began to think he had better not have relied so entirely on Kitty Bent's judgment, but have brought fuel and food, rather than a doll and sled.

He had made up his mind that if the little girl, Susy Briggs herself, came to the door, he would pretend to her that he was Santa Claus, drop the bundles in her arms, and beat a retreat as rapidly as possible. But when little Susy Briggs did come to the door, at the first sight of her face he seemed to forget himself entirely, and stood looking fixedly at her until she was half frightened.

"I—I—Kitty Bent asked me to bring you these—and I want to see your mother!" he stammered, at last, thrusting as many of the bundles as he could into Susy's arms.

Just then Susy's mother appeared in the entry, and what do you think? In an instant, after one startled glance into the gentleman's face, she was sobbing for joy on his shoulder, and he was calling her "Susy". His little sister Susy! while little Susy looked on with wide-open, wondering eyes, thinking her mother must surely be crazy. And she was almost beside herself with delight at finding the brother whom she never expected to see again; and he, on his part, was not less delighted to find the sister whom he had sought for so long in vain. And by-and-by little Susy was as happy as they, understanding that Uncle James, as the strange little gentleman told her to call him, was going to take care of them, and they were never going to be poor any more. He wouldn't consent to their staying in that cold, dreary old house even for one night, but insisted upon their going to the hotel with him, and then they spent a Merry Christmas eve, you may be sure.

And Uncle James didn't forget Kitty Bent, who had been the cause of all their happiness. The next morning, there was brought to the door a large box, with a hole in it to let in the air, with "Kitty Bent, with the respects of Santa Claus," written upon it, and when it was opened, what should it contain but two beautiful, "truly rabbits," with pink eyes!

Kitty was a little bewildered and disappointed, when, the next day, she found that Santa Claus was Suey Briggs's uncle. But, when she understood it all, and learned how much good her letter had done, she was more proud and happy, even, than if it had really been Santa Claus who had read her letter and sent her the rabbits.

6.

Meeting Santa Claus

M. Angier Alden, "Santa Claus in a Dilemma", *Children's New Church Magazine* (JANUARY 1869)

"How many days to Christmas?" asked little Rosa Curlypate of her brother Carl.

"Brother!" said Carl, "don't you know by this time?"

"Why," said Rosa doubtfully, "yesterday it was two days, and so I suppose to-day it is only one day; but is it really Christmas eve this very, very night?"

"Of course," answered Carl, quite indifferently. He was secretly rejoicing in the fact, but he thought it would be foolish to show Rosa how much he cared for Christmas eve.

"Christmas eve," repeated his little sister, "this very night!"

"Yes," said Carl; "is there any thing wonderful in that?" Rosa's eyes looked larger and bluer than ever, and that was very large and blue I can assure you.

"Carl," she said earnestly, "let us go and ask mother to give us a pair of her long stockings to hang up for Santa Claus."

"There isn't any hurry," said Carl, "when it grows dark will be time enough."

"I wish it was dark now," said Rosa, her stock of patience very low.

"It's snowing!" cried Carl from the window where he stood. "Hurrah! I shouldn't wonder if we had a sleigh-ride to-morrow," and he quite forgot Rosa was looking at him with her wide, bright eyes. She ran to the window, and, sure enough, the whole air was thick with the soft white snow-flakes that fell large at first, then finer and finer, until they seemed like one great white sheet of snow whirling about, blinding the men and the horses that ventured out in them.

"Carl," said Rosa, looking very grave, "I am afraid Santa Claus will think he cannot come in such a storm."

"He won't mind it," said Carl, "I guess he rather likes a good, rousing storm. I saw a picture of him once, and he was all covered in snow."

"I know," said Rosa, "he wears a fur cap, and carries all his toys and candy in a great bag on his back; but how does he get down the chimney all safe? Do you see, Carl?"

"Easy enough," said Carl; "he slides right down, without stopping to think."

"What if he should break the toys, or tear the bag?"

"Oh, if he should tear the bag, all the toys would fall down one chimney."

"I wish it might be our chimney."

"So do I," said Carl.

Darkness crept down early, for the storm still raged; the wind rose, and blew the white snow piles higher and higher, till they rose like ghosts all along each side of the road. Carl and Rosa stood by the fireplace, gazing fondly at the two long, limp stockings hanging on either side.

"I hope he won't mind the storm," said Rosa.

Carl's heart sank within him; but he answered bravely, as he had done before, that the harder it stormed the better St. Nick would like it.

"If the dolls should get wet," signed Rosa, "their pretty ribbons would be all spoiled."

"Or the bright colours in the picture books," thought Carl; but he said nothing.

Carl and Rosa had each, little bed-chambers, side by side; they were alike in every way – tiny soft beds, white and fresh, into which they sank every night, and fell asleep almost as soon as their mamma had kissed them and gone down stairs. But this was not a common night; indeed, it was quite an uncommon night, as we shall soon see. The door between the two rooms was always open, and to-night it was very widely open. Presently Carl hear Rosa calling softly,

"Are you asleep?"

"No," replied Carl.

"Can you get to sleep? I can't."

"I don't mean to," said Carl; "I'm going to keep away, and see Santa Claus, when he comes."

"Oh!" said Rosa in surprise. "But you can't see him up here, and how will you know when he comes?"

"We shall hear him in the chimney," called Carl; "and then we'll creep down very softly into the sitting-room, and peep in at him, and see him filling our stockings."

"That'll be nice," said Rosa; but it's so dark, shan't you be afraid? We can't get a light, and how are we going to see him?"

"He'll have a lantern," said Carl, "a great big one."

Just then the door, leading from Carl's room into the hall, opened, and his mother came in. She was going to bed, and she told them they must be quiet, and go to sleep like good children, or Santa Claus would hear them talking and prance off to Minnie Winkie's, who lived next door, and not leave them so much as a stick of maple candy.

After that the children lay very quiet, only now and then conversing in whispers so low that it is doubtful if either of them knew what the other was saying.

All at once, Rosa, who had lain for a long time thinking of what Santa Claus had brought her last Christmas, and what she wished he would bring her this, was roused by some one at her bedside, shaking her and calling, "Come quick, Rosie, he's here."

She had fallen into a doze which, probably, would have ended in a sound sleep till morning, but she knew Carl's voice and was wide awake in a minute. Carl was wrapped in a blanket, and she could see him quite plainly standing beside her.

"Why, how light it is!" she exclaimed.

"Yes, the moon is up," said Carl; "it is not snowing now; but don't stop to talk; take your blanket and put on your stockings and come along."

Rosa was obeying rapidly, when she stopped all at once, and exclaimed in fright,

"What's that noise, Carl?"

"That's Santa Claus roaring in the chimney," said Carl.

It was not the wind, surely, for that was

sinking away, and only moaned feebly, now and then, in the distance; it sounded like a great shouting, and it sounded in the chimney that ran up through Carl's room.

"I heard him chattering on the roof awhile ago," said Carl; "I'd give any thing, if we could see his little reindeer."

"So would I," said Rosa. "I'm ready."

"Step just like a little mouse," said Carl.

Very softly indeed they stole down the long, dark staircase, and pausing outside the sitting-room door, listened intently for a few minutes.

"Peep," whispered Rosa.

Carl pushed the door ajar very gently, and peeped cautiously into the room. He saw only a little glimmer of light among the ashes where the fire had been, and in the moonlight the two long stockings hanging limp and white as they had left them.

"Is he there?" asked Rosa, drawing nearer to Carl, and trying to get a peep too.

Carl made no reply, but advanced slowly and cautiously into the room, followed closely by Rosa.

"Where are you going?" she began to ask; but Carl placed his fingers on his lips as a sign of silence. So she kept very quiet, stepping as he stepped and pausing as he paused. Carl crept behind the great sofa, and Rosa crept after him.

"He can't see us here," said Carl, breathing more freely, "and we can see him, prime, can't we Rosie?"

"Yes; I wish he'd hurry, it's so cold."

"Pull your blanket round you. Here, take part of mine, I ain't cold a bit."

Snuggled closely together, they lay in wait for Santa Claus; four bright eyes gazing earnestly and expectantly through the night shadows in the room to the fire-place.

"He must come pretty soon," whispered Rosa.

"What a howling he does make; I shouldn't wonder if the chimney was too small, and he couldn't get through."

"Oh dear!" said Rosa, "that would be dreadful."

"Hark!" said Carl, starting suddenly.

"Oh what!" cried poor Rosa in fright.

"Don't you hear him?"

"*Hear* him?"

"Calling me: there it is again, 'Carl Curlypate! Carl Curlypate!'"

Sure enough Rosa did hear, or thought she heard, somebody calling, "Carl Curlypate," and the voice came from the chimney, and must be that of Santa Claus.

The children stared at one another in wonder; then Carl said, "I mean to go and ask the old fellow what he wants."

"Carl Curlypate! Carl Curlypate!" called Santa Claus in the chimney.

"Don't go, Carl," cried Rosa timidly.

Unmindful of her entreaties, Carl came out from behind the sofa, and approached the fire-place. Conquering her fear, Rosa, in her anxiety for Carl, followed him closely. The moon, riding high in the fast clearing heavens, looked in at the window, and smiled down on them with her pale yellow light, casting two long, curious shadows on the carpet behind them. Carl looked bravely up the chimney, discovering nothing; but he could hear yet more distinctly Santa Claus calling him.

"I'm here," he shouted at the top of his voice, standing as near under the chimney as he dared.

"My lantern is out," cried the voice in the chimney; "can't you make a light? Build a fire, and thaw out some of this snow that's freezing me."

Carl, without further inquiry, rushed for the wood box; alas! there was no wood, not even a shaving.

"Oh dear!" said Rosa, "what will you do, Carl?"

"Go and get some," said Carl, and opening a little closet he took down his overcoat and put it on, and telling Rosa to shout up the chimney that he would make a fire soon, off he started for the wood shed. Poor little Rosa stood shivering in the fire-place, hardly daring to speak, yet she called faintly to Santa Claus that Carl was coming. Santa Claus kept shouting; but Rosa was so frightened that she could not understand what it was that he wished to say, and she did wish Carl would hurry. He came, at last, with wood and shavings, and soon a large fire was blazing away in the fire-place, streaming up the chimney with its forked tongue of flame. As it burned higher and higher, drops of melting snow fell rapidly down the chimney.

"That's enough," shouted Santa Claus, "put out the fire."

This was not an easy task, for there was no water nearer than the kitchen. Together, however, Carl and Rosa succeeded in reducing to blackness and smoke the bright blaze they had just created.

"Are you an honest little boy?" shouted Santa Claus.

"I guess I am," Carl answered; "Uncle Parley thinks so, and grandma too."

"And the little girl is honest too, isn't she?"

"She's my sister," shouted Carl, as if, in his opinion, that were proof positive.

"I've got caught in this stupid chimney," shouted Santa Claus; "it's too narrow. I've got to cut a hole in the bottom of my pack, and let the toys out, before I can get any farther, and I don't want you to run off and hide any of them. Do you hear?"

"Yes," shouted Carl, "cut away; we ain't going to touch a thing."

Presently they heard a quick, sharp slash, and tumble and thump, down into the fire-place, came heaps of beautiful play-things, and books, and candy, and every thing that ever any little girl could dream of or desire.

"Arn't you coming too?" shouted Carl, after this strange shower had come to a partial close.

"I can't seem to get clear," groaned Santa Claus; "there's a great doll's bureau in the top of my pack that won't start any way, except when I push it up. I can't get down this narrow chimney."

"I'll let you in at the window," shouted Carl.

"All right," replied Santa Claus, "you're a bright boy. I'll be there in a trice."

Sure enough he was; the children had managed to open a window, between them, when, in popped Santa Claus. How he got there they never knew; for they did not see any chariot, nor so much as the tiny hind hoof or Dasher or Vixen.

"Whew!" cried that individual, throwing off his almost empty pack, and shaking his queer little body. "I'm cramped all over. I didn't know but I was destined to spend all night, and perhaps the whole of my life – which, under the circumstances, would not have been prolonged – in that black, crooked chimney. If it hadn't ha' been for this good, naughty little boy, I don't know what I should have done," and he surveyed Carl with his bright, black eyes that danced about merrily under the shade of his heavy fur cap; for he was clad all in fur, just as he is seen in the picture books.

"I don't like to have little boys, or little girls," nodding at little Rosa, "trying to catch a sight of me. I don't like it, I say," and he stamped his funny little foot emphatically. "But I'm glad you did it, little boy, I'm glad you did it. You are a brave little boy, and a good little boy, and now I want you and the little girl to help me fill my sack again. It's late, you see, and I've got ever so many chimneys to slide down and stockings to fill. I'm afraid there'll be some long faces tomorrow morning as it is."

The children, after the first feelings of awe and wonder had worn away, began to help busily in refilling the long sack. Rosa mended the slit in it, with a thread and needle given her by Santa Claus; and it was surprising how quickly and neatly it was don't; you would never know that there had been a slit to mend.

As they put the toys and the candy back into the bag, Santa Claus talked, and the children listened and looked, for Santa Claus had relighted his big lantern, and set it on the centre table, and had built a great fire in the fire-place, after scooping out the playthings. It was warm and light, and the three had a merry time together. Santa Claus told them stories, just like the stories in his picture books, only a great deal better; he gave them candy, too, as much as they wanted, and filled a great box with it for them to eat the next day. He gave them great, red apples, and nuts, and oranges, and figs, and raisins, and to Carl a little sugar lion, and to Rosa a little sugar dove.

By and by, when the pack was full again and Santa Claus ready for a start, he told both the children to shut their eyes while he filled their stockings, and not to look in them until morning, unless they wanted him to come back and carry off stockings and all. They did as he bade them, and kept their eyes shut until they heard him whistle three times, when, opening them, Santa Claus, lantern and all, were gone. Outside the window they could hear him laughing, and Rosa declared she saw the "eight tiny reindeer" cantering on to Minnie Winkie's roof; but Carl could not see any thing, especially, as at the moment he was looking, the moon went behind a cloud; so he thought Rosa could not see any thing, and would not allow that she did.

Back in their little beds they crept, as softly as they had left them, and when their mamma came in the morning, to wish them "Merry Christmas," to her great surprise, she found them sound asleep.

"What! sound asleep!" she exclaimed. "Why are you not up, examining your stockings, to see what Santa Claus has brought you?"

The children roused up and looked around them, expecting to find themselves surrounded with candies and other presents; and they looked up to their mother with astonishment when they could not find them.

"Where are they?" asked Carl, with a surprised and puzzled air, which his mother mistook for the confusion of not being more than half awake.

"Where are they? Why, in your stockings, of course."

The children now jumped up, and ran down stairs as quick as they could, fearing that Santa Claus, and the presents too, might all be a dream.

The moment Rosa caught sight of the stockings, and saw them swelling with their contents, she cried out, "They are full! They are full! Only see! And here is the very bureau I wanted right under them."

"And here are my tin soldiers, and the farmyard," shouted Carl. "Hurrah for Santa Claus! Stockings full, and these things besides."

The stockings were soon emptied, and in the toe of each one was a little note from Santa Claus himself, saying that next Christmas eve he would bring the thing they most desired, only they mustn't try to lay awake to look at him. And if any little girl or boy would like to know what he brought to Carl, let him think what he himself would wish for; or if any little girl feels curious to learn Rosa's choice, she can write a little to Miss Rosa Curlypate, politeness of Santa Claus, and drop it into her own stocking on Christmas next, and when she gets an answer, if it is not too much of a secret between little Rosa and good old Saint Nicholas, she will know all about it.

Anne R. Arran, "A Night With Santa Claus", *Our Young Folks,* JANUARY 1871

Come, little ones, you have outromped the sun. Look! he throws you a good-night kiss, and says, "Heigh-ho! we've had a merry day, little folks; but there's fun left over for to-morrow, and unless you want me to catch you napping in the morning, you had better go to bed."

Now, if the horses are put up in the stable and the dolls tucked into the play-house within five minutes, you shall have a story to dream about.

Well done! Now, Charley, tell Bridget to bring us more coal and make a bright fire. Draw all the little chairs close up,—so, with aunty in the middle, holding this curly mite on her lap. Ah! is not this a cosey party? See how the flames play hide-and-go-seek through the bars, and how merrily they dance on the walls!

Not very long ago, and not very far from here, lived a little boy named Robby Morgan. Now I must tell at once how Robby looked, else how will you know him if you meet him in the street? And I assure you that the boy to whom such a wonderful thing happened is *worth* knowing. Blue-eyed was Rob, and fair-haired, and pug-nosed, just the sweetest trifle, his mamma said; but that small nose had a story of its own to tell: "I know I'm only a mite of a nose on a mite of a boy, but I won't be snubbed by any of you long sharp fellows." If ever nose meant to do its whole duty through thick and thin, that little turn-up of Rob's did. There you have my hero's face, and as faces are but pictures of hearts, until people grow up and teach their eyes and lips to tell wrong stories, you may know about what kind of a boy Rob was. There was a world of mischief and pluck, of goodness and naughtiness, jumbled together in that little heart; but after all there was more *love* than anything else,—love for mamma and papa, Uncle George and—Santa Claus! Ah! now we have come to the story indeed! You know you often nibble away at the crust of a piece of cake, thinking "It isn't so very good after all," until all at once you bite into a raisin; so we have nibbled off the crust of my story, and here we are among the raisins! Santa Claus, childhood's blessed saint, to begin with!

Well, the day before Christmas, Rob thought it would be a fine thing to run down Main Street and see what was going on; so after dinner his mamma put on his fur cap and bright scarf, and filled his pockets with crackers and cookies, telling him to be very polite to Santa Claus if he should happen to meet him.

Off he trotted, merry as a cricket, now a skip, now a slide, longing to turn a somerset in the snow, yet fearing that the Recording Angel, who keeps a sharp lookout on little boys at Christmas time, might pop out from a tree-box and convict him on the spot. At every corner he held his breath, half expecting to run into Santa himself; but nothing of the sort happened, and he soon found himself before the gay windows of a toy-shop.

There he saw a spring hobby-horse, as large as a Shetland pony, all saddled and bridled, too,— lacking nothing, in fact, but a rider. Rob pressed his nose against the glass, and tried to imagine the feelings of a boy in that saddle. He might have stood there all day, trying to conceive that bliss, had not a ragged little fellow pulled his coat, piping out, "Wouldn't you jist like that pop-gun mebbe!"

"Catch me looking at pop-guns!" said Rob, shortly, feeling that their very mention was a direct insult to the hobby-horse; but when he saw how tattered the boy's jacket was, he said more softly, "P'raps you'd like a cooky."

"Try me wunst!" said the shrill little voice.

There was a queer lump in Rob's throat as he emptied one pocket of its cakes and thrust them into the dirty, eager hands. Then he marched down the street without so much as glancing at that glorious steed again.

Brighter and brighter grew the windows, more and more full of toys, till at last our boy stood, with open eyes and mouth, before a great store lighted from top to bottom, for it was growing dark. Rob came near taking off his cap and saying, "How do you do, sir?"

To whom? you ask; why, to an image of Santa Claus, the size of life, holding a Christmas-tree filled with wonderful fruit. It would have puzzled a painter to find colors as bright as Rob's eyes and cheeks were then. Soon a happy thought struck him: "Surely this must be Santa Claus's own store, where he comes to fill his basket with toys! What if I were to hide there and wait for him?" As I said, he was a brave little chap, so he walked straight into the store with the stream of big people. Everybody was busy; mammas were looking at playthings, papas were pulling out their purses, clerks were tying up parcels, and errand-boys were scampering to and fro as if they had lost their wits, and were bent on finding them. No one had time to look at our mite of a Rob. He tried in vain to find a quiet corner, till he caught sight of some winding stairs that led up to the next story. He crept up, scarcely daring to breathe till he reached the top.

What a fairy-land! Toys everywhere! Oceans of toys! Nothing but toys! excepting one happy little boy! This was the wholesale department. Ask mamma what those troublesome big words mean.

Rob came nearer losing his wits than ever in his life before, and indeed I think such a playroom excuse enough. Think of fifty great rocking-horses in a pile; of whole flocks of woolly sheep and curly dogs, with the real bark in them; stacks of drums; regiments of soldiers armed to the teeth; companies of firemen drawing their hose-carts; no end of wheelbarrows and velocipedes!

Rob screwed his knuckles into his eyes, as a gentle hint that they had better not play him any tricks, and then stared with might and main.

The room was lighted just brightly

enough to show its treasures, yet the far corners were so dim as to give quite a mysterious air to the baby-jumpers and great dolls, lying so stiff and still in rows upon the shelves. But what were those things across the room staring at him so fixedly? Nothing but masks, of course; he had played with one many a time at home, but that was quite different from facing such a host of those grinning, frowning faces. Their grimaces and scowls were meant for him, that was clear! All the big noses seemed to be snuffing at him with great relish, as giants always do before putting little boys in to roast, thought Rob. The jaws of a black bear especially had just opened to gobble him up. Altogether he was growing very uncomfortable when he thought he heard a footstep on the stairs, and fearing to be caught he hid behind a baby-wagon. No one came, however, and as he felt rather hungry, he took out the remaining cakes and had a fine supper.

Why didn't Santa Claus come?

Rob was really getting sleepy. The bustle below was only a faint murmur above, and so soothing that he stretched out his tired legs, and, turning one of the woolly sheep on its side, pillowed his curly head on it. It was so nice to lie there, looking at the ceiling hung with toys, the faint hum of voices in his ears, and sleepily thinking that, if he cared to, he might jump up and mount the finest horse or beat the biggest drum in that great room. The blue eyes grew more and more heavy, the place took on a misty look, the sounds became fainter. Rob was fast asleep.

The evening wore on; papas and mammas were on their way home loaded with mysterious parcels. The clerks and errand-boys, too, seized their caps and left the store in high glee,—only one man stayed to guard it. He went up stairs to turn down the lights, but in his hurry did not notice the little boy so snugly stowed away behind the carts.

Midnight! The bells rang loud and clear, as if they had great news to tell the world. What noise is that besides the bells? And look, O look! who is that striding up the room with a great basket on his back? He has stolen his coat from a polar bear, and his cap, too, I declare! His boots are of red leather and reach to his knees. His coat and cap are trimmed with wreaths of holly, bright with scarlet berries.

Good sir, let us see your face,—why! that is the best part of him,—so round and so ruddy, such twinkling eyes and such a merry look about those dimples! But see his long white beard,—can he be old?

O, very, very old! eighteen hundred and seventy years! Is not that a long life, little ones? But he has a young heart,—this dear old man,—and a kind one. Can you guess his name? "Hurrah for Santa Claus!" Right!—the very one.

He put his basket down near Robby, and with his back turned to him shook the snow from his fur coat. Some of the flakes fell on Rob's face and roused him from his sleep. Opening his eyes, he saw the white figure, but did not stir or cry on it. He knew him in a twinkling, though to his sleepy eyes he looked more like a nice plump angel than anything else. Very quiet he lay, not daring to speak a word lest the vision should vanish. But, bless his big heart! *He* had no idea of vanishing till his night's work was done. He took a large book from his pocket, opened to the first page, and looked at it very closely.

"TOMMY TURNER," was written at the top, and just below was a little map,—yes, there was Tommy's heart mapped out like a country. Part of the land was marked good, part of it *bad*; some of the people were called civilized and some savage. Here and there were little flags to point out places where battles had been fought during the year,—like the flags in the atlas, you know. Some of them were black, and some white; wherever a good feeling had won the fight there was a white one. Love and Hate had a dreadful tussle in Tommy's heart one day, but Love won the field, and Santa Claus in triumph reared a white flag on the very spot. In another place a black one showed where selfishness and generosity fought over an orange, but self—that wicked old general who kills and enslaves so many good impulses—carried off the orange. He had to pay roundly for it now, however, for Santa Claus shook his head grimly when his eye fell on it,—then he seemed to be counting.

"Tommy Turner," said he aloud,—"six white flags, three black; that leaves only three presents for Tommy; but we must see what can be done for him."

So he bustled about among the toys, and soon had a ball, a horse, and a Noah's ark tied up in a parcel, which he tossed into the basket.

Name after name was read off, some of them belonging to his little playmates, and you may be sure Rob listened with his heart in his mouth.

"Robby Morgan!" said Santa Claus.

In his excitement that small boy nearly upset the cart, but Santa was so busy with his map that he did not notice it.

"One, two, three, four, five, six, seven"— Rob's breath came very short—"*whites*!"

He almost clapped his hands.

"One, two, three, blacks! Now I wonder what that little chap would like,—here's a drum, a box of tools, a knife, and a menagerie. If he hadn't run away from school that day and then told a lie about it, I'd give him a rocking-horse."

Rob groaned in anguish of spirit.

"But, bless him! he's a fine little fellow, and perhaps he will do better next year if I give him the horse."

That was too much for our boy. With a "hurrah!" he jumped up and turned a somerset right at Santa Claus's feet.

"Stars and stripes!" cried he; "what's this?"

"Come along, I'll show you the one," was the only answer Rob gave, tugging at the fur coat with all his might.

Santa Claus suffered himself to be led off to the pile of horses. You may believe that Rob's sharp eyes soon picked out the one with the longest tail and thickest mane.

"Well, he beats all the boys ever I saw, back to the year one! What shall I do with the little spy?" soliloquized Santa Claus.

"O dear Santa Claus!" cried Robby, hugging the red boots, "do just take me 'long with you; I'll stick tight when you slide down the chimbley."

"Yes, I guess you will stick tight—in the chimney, little man."

"I mean to your back," half sobbed Rob.

Santa Claus can't bear to see little folks in trouble, so he took the boy in his arms, and asked him where he wanted to go.

"To Tommy Turner's, and O you know that boy in the awful old jacket that likes pop-guns," was the breathless reply.

Of course he knew him, for he knows every boy and girl in Christendom; so a pop-gun was added to the medley of toys. Santa Claus then strapped Rob and the basket upon his back, and crept through an open window to a ladder he had placed there, down which he ran as nimbly as a squirrel.

The reindeers before the sledge were in a hurry to be off, and tinkled their silver bells right merrily. An instant more, and they were snugly tucked up in the white robes, an instant more, and they were flying like the wind over the snow.

Ah! Tommy's home. Santa Claus sprang out, placed the light ladder against the house, and before Rob could wink—a good fair wink—they were on the roof making for the chimney. Whether it swallowed him, or he swallowed it, is still a puzzle to Robby. He only had time to wonder, on the way down, if young avalanches felt so, taking their first slide.

Tommy lay sleeping in his little bed and dreaming, doubtless, of a merry Christmas, for his rosy mouth was puckered into something between a whistle and a smile.

Rob longed to give him a friendly punch, but Santa Claus shook his head; so they filled his stocking and hurried away, for empty little stockings the world over were waiting for that generous hand.

On they sped again, never stopping until they came to a wretched little hovel with only a black pipe instead of a chimney sticking through the roof.

Rob thought, "Now I guess he'll have to give it up," but no, he softly pushed the door open and stepped in. On a ragged cot lay the urchin to whom Robby had given the cookies. One of them, half-eaten, was still clutched in his hand. Santa Claus gently opened the other little fist and put the pop-gun in it.

"Give him my drum," whispered Rob, and Santa Claus without one word placed it near the rumpled head.

How swiftly they flew under the bright stars! How sweetly rang the bells! When Santa Claus reined up at Robby's door he found his little comrade fast asleep; so he laid him tenderly in his crib, and drew off a stocking which he filled with the smaller toys; the rocking-horse he placed close to the crib, that Rob might mount him betimes on Christmas morning.

A kiss, and he was gone.

P. S. Rob's mamma says it was all a dream, but he declares, indignantly, that "it's true as Fourth o' July!" and I prefer to take his word for it.

Meeting Santa Claus

Edward Eggleston, "The House of Santa Claus: A Christmas Fairy Show for Sunday Schools", *St. Nicholas*, DECEMBER 1876.

After appropriate introductory exercises, a teacher rises in his place and speaks in substance as follows:

TEACHER. Mr. Superintendent, I see some very pleasant decorations here, but no presents or refreshments for the scholars. I move that a committee of three be appointed to go up to Fairyland and inquire of Santa Claus. I would like to know why this Sunday-school has been left out.

ANOTHER TEACHER. I second that motion.

[Superintendent puts this question to vote, and declares it carried, in due form.]

SUPERINTENDENT. I would appoint—let me see—girls are better at coaxing than boys, I think—I will appoint **X.**, **Y.**, and **Z.** [calling the girls by their real names], who will please come forward.

[**X.**, **Y.**, and **Z.** rise from their places in their several classes, and come forward to the superintendent.]

SUPERINTENDENT. Girls, you see we are without any candy or anything of the sort for our scholars. Old Santa Claus has forgotten us. He never did so before. Now I want you three to proceed to Fairyland and see if you can find him. Tell him we must have something. Don't come down without something. We can't have all these children disappointed. [The committee proceed by the steps to the stage. They stop to examine the first pumpkin face.]

Z. What a strange face! Wonder who it is!

Y. One of Santa's tricks, I suppose.

X. They do say that he's full of fun. But this must be his house. Let's find the door. [All proceed to the front.] Here it is.

Y. Isn't it cute? I'd like to live here.

Z. And play dolly-house?

X. Here's a door-bell. Santa Claus has all the latest improvements, I declare.

Y. Ring it.

Z. No, don't; I'm afraid.

X. Pshaw! Santa never hurts anybody. Don't you see his name over the door? [Rings. After a pause.] I wonder he don't answer. Maybe he isn't at home.

Y. Gone sleigh-riding, as sure as I live!

Z. I guess he's gone to bed. Maybe his mama wouldn't let him sit up late.

X. Let's look around, and see what we can find. You two go around that side, and I'll go around this. See if you can't find him in behind the face that's hanging up there.

[**X.** goes to the left, around the house, while **Y.** and **Z.** go around to the right. They proceed timidly to the back of the house, out of sight of the audience, whereupon the dwarfs blow sharp blasts upon their horns, and the girls all rush back to the front of the house.]

X. I'm so scared!

Y. AND **Z.** Oh, dear! I'm so scared!

X. What could it be? Guess old Santa

Claus made that noise just for fun. I wish the superintendent had come himself, or sent some of the boys!

Y. I'll bet the boys would run from that noise. Don't you?

X. Yes. Boys never are as brave as girls, anyhow. But let's go back again, and see what there is there.

Z. I'm afraid.

X. Well, you stay here, and **Y.** will go that way, and I will go this way.

[**X.** again goes to the right, **Y.** to the left. They proceed more timidly than before to the rear of the house, disappearing behind it. The dwarfs blow their horns, the girls reappear, crying out in alarm, and the dwarfs run out after them. The girls hurry back to the front of the house, followed by the dwarfs—one coming round one end of the house, the other round the other. They speak in high, squeaky tones]

FIRST DWARF. What do you want!

SECOND DWARF. What are you doing here?

X. We want Santa Claus. But we did not know there were two Santa Clauses.

[The dwarfs laugh long and loud.]

FIRST DWARF. We are not Santa Clauses. We are the dwarfs that take care of Santa Claus's store-rooms, full of goodies and presents.

SECOND DWARF. But there's nothing left to take care of now. Santa's given away all he had this Christmas.

X. But we must see old Santa. Our Sunday-school has been left without anything, and we want to see good old Claus himself.

FIRST DWARF. But you can't. He's asleep.

SECOND DWARF. He was out all night last night, and now he's tired to death and sleeping like a top. Thunder wouldn't wake him.

X. But we must see him.

Y. AND **Z.** Yes, we must.

SECOND DWARF. If you'd been riding over roofs all night—

FIRST DWARF. And climbing down chimneys—

SECOND DWARF. And filling stockings—

FIRST DWARF. And Christmas trees—

SECOND DWARF. And climbing up chimneys again—

FIRST DWARF. And getting your hands and face all over soot—

SECOND DWARF. And driving reindeer—they do pull—

BOTH DWARFS. I guess you'd be sleepy too.

X. But we must have something for the children.

Y. AND **Z.** We must have something.

FIRST DWARF. There isn't a thing left.

SECOND DWARF. Not a thing.

X. What will the superintendent say?

Y. What will the children say?

Z. What will the infant class say!

X. And what will the deacons say!

Y. AND Z. Yes, what will the deacons say!

BOTH DWARFS. Deacons! Oh, my! Ha, ha! [The dwarfs now give a blast apiece, and retreat into their hiding-places.]

X. Well, I'm going to wake up old Santa Claus.

Y. Maybe he'll be cross.

X. But we must have something. [Rings.] I wonder he doesn't answer.

Z. Ring louder.

X. Well, here goes. [Rings three or four times.]

[Santa Claus, appearing at the top of the chimney, blows his whistle.]

X., Y., AND Z. Oh, dear!

SANTA CLAUS. Who's there? Who rang my bell, I'd like to know? Pity if I can't sleep Christmas night, when I'm tired to death. Who's there, I say?

X. Oh, you dear old Santa Claus! Don't be angry. Some of your little friends have come to Fairyland to see you. Come down.

SANTA CLAUS. Ha, ha, ha! Some of my little friends come to see me! Well, well! [Blows his whistle.] Light up the house, fairies, light up the house. [Whistles again, and then descends the chimney and reappears at the front door. The house is lighted within.] How do you do, girls? How do you do? [Shakes hands all round, and then, with great deliberation, takes a pinch of snuff.] Well, I'm glad to see you. What can I do for you?

X. Why, you see, Santa Claus, our Sunday-school is left without anything this Christmas.

SANTA CLAUS. [Sneezes and uses his bandana.] What? You don't tell me so! What's the name of your school?

X. The ——— Sunday-school.

SANTA CLAUS. Oh, yes! And your superintendent is Mr.———. I know him like a book. I've filled his stockings many a time when he was a little fellow. I don't know how I came to miss that school. But you see I'm getting old and forgetful.

Y. How old are you, Santa?

SANTA CLAUS. Oh, now! Do you think I'd tell you that?

Z. You must be as old as the Centennial.

SANTA CLAUS. Pshaw! I used to fill George Washington's stockings when he was a little boy.

Y. No! Now, did you?

SANTA CLAUS. Of course I did.

Y. What did you put in them?

SANTA CLAUS. What did I put in little Georgie Washington's stockings? Well, now, that's more than a hundred years ago, and an old man's memory isn't strong. I can't remember but one thing.

X. What's that?

SANTA CLAUS. A hatchet.

Y. Oh, my!

Z. That same little hatchet?

SANTA CLAUS. The very same little hatchet. [Laughs.] But I did not give him the cherry-tree.

X. Yes; but we must have something for our school, good Santa Claus.

SANTA CLAUS. But you can't. I've given away all I had, and turned the reindeer out on the mountains to pasture, and the times are so hard that I can't afford to hire a livery team.

X. Yes; but we must have something.

Y. Yes; we must, dear old Santa.

Z. Yes, indeed.

SANTA CLAUS. [Takes snuff and sneezes.] Well, what is to be done? How many scholars have you got this year?

X. About ———.

SANTA CLAUS. So many! Why, you must be growing. I hope you haven't any Christmas bummers among them—folks that come to Sunday-school to get something to eat. I hate that kind.

Y. I don't think we have many of that sort.

SANTA CLAUS. Well, I always did like that school, and now I've gone and forgotten it! I wish something could be done. [Blows his whistle long and loud, and shouts.] Dwarfs, here! Drako, where are you? Krako, come! Wake up! [Whistles again.]

[Enter dwarfs, each blowing his horn.]

SANTA CLAUS. Now, my little rascals, what have you got for the Sunday-school?

BOTH DWARFS. [Bowing very low.] Nothing, my lord.

SANTA CLAUS. [Takes snuff and sneezes.] I don't see that I can do anything for you.

X. But we cannot go back without something. The children will cry.

SANTA CLAUS. Dwarfs, go and look again.

[They go back behind the house as before. After a time they reappear.]

FIRST DWARF. We cannot find a thing.

SECOND DWARF. Not one thing.

SANTA CLAUS. [Takes snuff.] Well, my little friends, this is very embarrassing—very; but I haven't a thing left.

X. But we can't go back. What will the superintendent say? We must have something.

Y. Something or other.

Z. Yes, something.

SANTA CLAUS. I'll go and see myself. [Exit into house. After a considerable delay reenters.] Yes, I find a box of candy, nuts, and pop-corn in the closet.

X., Y., AND Z. Candy, nuts, and pop-corn! Good!

SANTA CLAUS. What have you got to put the things in?

X. Why, we haven't got anything.

SANTA CLAUS. Well, then, the children will have to take off their stockings and let me fill them.

X., Y., AND Z. Oh, Santa Claus! we couldn't, such a cold night as this.

SANTA CLAUS. [Takes snuff, looks perplexed, walks about the stage.] Well, I don't know what to do.

X. Oh, dear!

Y. Oh, dear!

Z. Oh, dear! dear! dear!

SANTA CLAUS. [Starting up.] Now I have it.

X. Have what?

SANTA CLAUS. An idea.

Z. An idea? [Addressing **X.**] What's an idea? Can you put candy into an idea?

X. Be still, **Z.** Let's hear what Santa Claus's idea may be.

SANTA CLAUS. I know who will help me out of this trouble. There's my friend the Fairy Queen.

X. The Fairy Queen!

Y. Oh, my!

Z. Goody! goody! goody!

[Santa Claus blows three blasts on his whistle and listens. The music-box in the fairy bower begins to play.]

SANTA CLAUS. Listen! She's coming!

X. Fairy music!

Y. AND **Z.** Sh-h!

[The fairy comes down from B, skipping and reciting or singing:]
In the secret rocky dell,
There the fairies love to dwell;
Where the stars on dewdrops glance,
There the fairies love to dance.

BOTH DWARFS. [Bowing to Santa Claus.] The Fairy Queen, my lord!

SANTA CLAUS. [Bowing.] Hail, Queen of the Fairies!

X., Y., AND **Z.** [Bowing.] Hail, Queen of the Fairies!

FAIRY QUEEN. [Bowing.]
Hail, Santa Claus! Hail, little friends!
Oh, stocking-filler Santa Claus,
I heard you whistle—what's the cause!
You rough and shaggy children's friend,
Why did you for a fairy send?

SANTA CLAUS. [Taking snuff.] Why, you see, here's a Sunday-school forgotten, ―――― hundred children! I want to give them something. But they haven't got anything to put it in.

FAIRY QUEEN.
How would fairy stockings do?
White or black or pink or blue?

X. Fairy stockings!

Y. Oh, my!

Z. Goody! goody! goody!

FAIRY QUEEN. [Waving her hand toward B.]
Whatever Santa Claus shall say,
That let Fairyland obey.

SANTA CLAUS. [Entering the house and blowing his whistle.] Fill up the stockings, fairies; fill up the stockings.

[The dwarfs enter, this time by the front door, and return, carrying between them a basket full of little pink tarlatan stockings filled with candy, nuts, etc., which are then distributed to the children.]

Lucy Larcom, "Visiting Santa Claus", *St. Nicholas Magazine* (DECEMBER 1884)

"We want to do something for Santa Claus,"
Two little children were saying;
"Let us go and find him, and thank him, because
He is always bringing us beautiful things.
Let us carry him something as nice as he brings."
They laughed, and they went on playing.

"Oh, he lives away over the mountains of snow,"
Said the fair little maid named Lily,
"And the Northern Lights on his windows glow;
But the good Great Bear will show us the way,
And will wrap us up in his fur robe gray,
If we find the journey chilly."

"Let us start in the morning," said Marjorie
(She was little White Lily's sister);
"By two o'clock, or at most by three,
The moon will be rising, and we will go
With our new red moccasins over the snow!"
And Lily said "Yes," and kissed her.

The children were tired, and they both slept sound;
But, almost before they knew it,
They were tiptoeing over the frozen ground,
Over wide white fields where grew not a tree,—
Over the crust of the Polar Sea,—
You never would think they could do it!

"Are we almost there, dear Marjorie?"
Said the breathless little White Lily;
"I am cold and weary as I can be!
I wish we never had started at all!"
And she cuddled under her sister's shawl,
The air was so very chilly.

"Oh, yes; Oh, yes; we are almost there!
Don't you see the North Star shining?
And here is the house of the good Great Bear;
He will surely be kind to us, because
He is second cousin to Santa Claus;
See! he sits at his table, dining."

So the Great Bear asked the children in,
And made them sit down at his table!
A chain of stars hung under his chin,
And a jeweled pointer was in his hand,
By which all the pilgrims to North-Star-Land,
To keep the straight road are able.

"Will you show us the way to Santa Claus?"
They said, after eating and drinking.
"Oh, that is against the Christmas laws,
Which are strictly obeyed in North-Star-Land":
But the Great Bear leaned his head on his hand.
And sat for a moment, thinking.

"He hung up his coat here, an hour ago—
There! drop down into the pocket!
I hear his sledge-bells over the snow;
Oh, don't be afraid! he will treat you well."
They heard a "Halloo!" and before they could tell
How it was, they were off, like a rocket.
How the reindeer flew! how the stars whizzed by!

But the children so close were hidden,
They scarcely could open the edge of an eye;
They could neither speak, nor wiggle, nor wink,
They could only breathe very softly, and think
Of the ride they were taking unbidden.

At last they arrived at Santa Claus' house,
And he, as he threw off his jacket,
Cried, "Wife! did you hear the squeak of a mouse?"
For the children were frightened, and could not keep still:
"Ho! ho! Mrs. Santa. look here, if you will!
Here's a new-fashioned Christmas packet!"

So Santa Claus' wife put her spectacles on,
And came and peeped over his shoulder,
For she thought that her husband clean daft had gone,
His eyes grew so large in his shiny bald head.
"Please do not be vexed with us," Marjorie said,
And Lily exclaimed, growing bolder:

"We wanted to see where you live, Santa Claus!
To thank you, and bring you a present;
But we could not find anything, sir, because,—"
"Why, you've brought me yourselves, dears,
 and now you must stay,
And make Mrs. Santa Claus merry and gay;
No home without children is pleasant."

The children, quite startled and sorely afraid,
A sob and a sigh tried to smother;
But good Mrs. Santa Claus came to their aid,
And said, "Santa, dear, now I can't have them stay!
Such midgets would only be right in my way;
So please take them home to their mother!"

When the reindeer came, with a jingling din,
The children were hardly ready;
They were watching the Northern Lights begin;
But Santa Claus lifted them into his sleigh,
And whipped up the reindeer, and whisked away,
With a chirrup, and "So! be steady!"

And wasn't it fun now and then to stop,
And eagerly wait and listen
For Santa Claus, over a chimney-top,
And ask if the little folks saw him bring
Their presents inside—then, ting-a-ling-ling!
Down, down, where the snow-drifts glisten!

But, somehow, the two little girls never knew,
Neither Marjorie nor White Lily,—
How they were let down their own roof through,
How they came to be sleeping side by side,
In their own little room at the morning-tide,
When the Christmas dawn broke chilly.

But there was a package under each head,
Tied up with a silver label:
And "Cakes from Santa Claus' oven," it read;
And their stockings were full of beautiful things,
Such as nobody else but he ever brings,
Though they call him a myth and a fable.

And when Marjorie tells of going one night,—
And wonders that people doubt her,—
To see Santa Claus, while the star shone bright,
White Lily will open her eyes of blue,
And say, "There's a Mrs. Santa Claus, too;
Or else I have dreamed about her."

Tudor Jenks, "A Gentle Reminder", *St. Nicholas Magazine* (JANUARY 1891)

Time: Christmas morning.
Scene: Vicinity of everywhere. A cold day.

CHARACTERS.
A LITTLE GIRL, who is "not in it."
MR. SANTA CLAUS, a benevolent and well-meaning old gentleman, unusually fond of children.

COSTUMES.
LITTLE GIRL: à la ragbag.
MR. S. CLAUS: Furs and an engaging smile.

(**MR. S. CLAUS** enters during a paper snow-storm, carelessly swinging his empty pack.)

S. C.—My work is done, and now my goal
Is a little north of the old north-pole!

(**LITTLE GIRL** enters "left." Runs after S. C. and catches his coat.)

L.G.—But, Mr. Claus, one moment stay!
Listen, before you hurry away;
Neither in stocking nor on tree
Has any present been left for me!

S. C.—You've no present? That's too bad!
I'd like to make all children glad.
There's something wrong; the fact is clear.
I'm very sorry indeed, my dear.
I brought an endless lot of toys
To millions and millions of girls and boys.
But, still, there are so many about
Some have been overlooked, no doubt!

L. G.—Well, Santa Claus, I know you're kind,
And mean to bear us all in mind.
But I can't see the reason why
We poor are oftenest passed by.

S. C.—It's true, my child. I can't but say
I have a very curious way
Of bringing presents to girls and boys
Who have least need of pretty toys,
And giving books, and dolls, and rings.
To those who already have such things.
'Tis done for a very curious reason
Suggested by the Christmas season:
Should I make my gifts to those who need,
'Twould become a time of general greed,
When all would think, "What shall we get?"
"What shall we give?" they would quite forget.
So when I send my gifts to-day
'T is a hint: "You have plenty to give away."
And then I leave some poor ones out
That the richer may find, as they look about,
Their opportunities near at hand
In every corner of the land.
My token to those who in plenty live
Is a gentle reminder, meaning

    Give!

(*Curtain, and distribution of presents by the thoughtful audience after they reach home.*)

7.

SEARCHING FOR SANTA CLAUS

Meeting Mrs. Claus

"The Marriage of Santa Claus", from *Dick's Recitations and Readings, No. 13*
(NEW YORK: DICK & FITZGERALD, C.1869)

Once Santa Claus sobered and said with a sigh,
While a tear added lustre to each twinkling eye,
"Oh! I'm getting so lonely and weary of life,
I need a companion, or, better, a wife;
But where could I find one to share my joy,
And love, as I love, every girl and each boy."
He thought and he pondered, this jolly recluse,
Then he shouted, "I have it; 'tis Old Mother Goose."
He was off in a jiffy, he whistled, his sled
O'er the snow like the flight of a sky-rocket sped,
And his reindeer snorted, with heads high and haughty,
And trotted along at the rate of two-forty.
So he found the old lady, of course, very soon—
She had just returned from a trip to the moon,
And was fixing her cap, slightly mussed by the ride,
While the cobwebs were thick in the broom by her side.
She was old, she was weazened, she had a great nose,
Yet her eyes were as bright as the plumage of crows,
And her voice, tho' 'twas cracked, had a ring very sweet,
And her dress, tho' 'twas queer, was most awfully neat.
And Santa Claus blushed as he said, "How d'ye do?"
The dame courtesied low, and replied, "Sir, to you."
"Will you have me?" he prays; "my darling, confess."
She hesitates, murmurs, and then whispers, "Yes.
But my children!" she cries, with the usual pause.
"Why, children, I love 'em," said bluff Santa Claus.
"Bring 'em out—where are they? I want 'em!" cries he,
So forth troop they all in a great company.
First comes a fair maiden, and know her we should,
By the wolf and her granny—'tis Red Riding Hood;
While after them, fearfully blowing his horn,
Is Little Boy Blue on his way from the corn;
And the notes of the music he sweetly doth play,

Brings the piper's son Tom from the hills far away.
And then with a jump and a roll down the hill,
With pails and with water bounce poor Jack and Jill.
Their crowns were both broken, and help they implore
From Old Mother Hubbard and Margery Daw,
As well as a nameless man, tattered and torn,
Who is kissing and kissing a maiden forlorn.
And forth from her garden, in a way quite contrary,
With fruits and with flowers, comes sweet Mistress Mary:
Then Simon the Simple returns from the fair,
With the pie-man, most cautious in selling his ware;
While dragging their tails behind flock in the sheep
Of the wandering shepherdess Little Bo Peep.
A very old woman lugs up a great shoe,
And out jump her children, a boisterous crew;
Some sing and some dance, and some of them play
"The Mulberry Bush" and "Rain, rain go away."
But one little boy slinks off in a corner
And munches a pie—'tis greedy Jack Horner;
While poor Tommy Tucker expects some in vain,
And bewails his fate with Tom Grace, who's in pain.
But music has charms, and they list to the song
Of that jolly musician the young Richard Long.
Then Old King Cole and his fiddlers three
Bring up the rear of this vast company,
"They are just what I want," shouts old Santa Claus;
Mother Goose and her children ring out their applause.
"Now all jump aboard—our new home we'll explore;
On my sled there has ever been 'room for one more.'"
With shouts and with laughter they tumbled within,
And wrapped buffalo robes close beneath every chin;
The reindeer they galloped, the moon shone out bright
As they hurried along in its soft silver light;
And the fat, jolly driver chuckled often in glee
At the sight of his wife and his vast family.
And the songs of the children rang out in the air
As they journeyed along, disregarding all care,
Till they reached the great palace and thro' it to roam,
And forever be happy within their new home.

"Mrs Santa Claus and Jessie Brown",
Harper's Weekly, JANUARY 9 1869

You've heard of good old Santa Claus? ay, doubtless, all your life;
Though not of him I'm going to tell, but of his lovely wife,
And pretty little Jessie Brown, an orphan, you must know:
The story it was told to me a long, long time ago.
One stormy night—'twas Christmas-time—when all the children round
Hung up their stockings, knowing well with treasures they'd abound;
Then scampered laughingly to bed, to dream away the night,
Their little hearts all fluttering with gladness and delight.
But there was one poor little girl—her name was Jessie Brown—
Who with her dear grandfather lived here in Brookhaven town;
But he was old and very poor, and oft his tears would fall
Upon the little face of her, his darling one, his all.
This Christmas-eve their scanty meal was eaten in the dark,
Yet Jessie looked as bright and glad as any singing lark;
And when beside her grandpa's knee she lisped her evening prayer
She looked so sweet you would have thought an angel had been there;
Then with the 'good-night' kiss she crept into her 'trundle bed',
And, smiling, asked, "Will Santa Claus come, now mamma is dead?"
"I hope he will", her grandpa said, and turned away his head;
Then, on a nail hung up with care, her stocking soon he spied,
With many a threadbare patch, although to mend it she had tried;
And when he thought her fast asleep he took it from the nail,
And by the fire-light you could see his face looked strangely pale.
His fingers trembled as he sighed, "My precious little dear!
Oh, would I had a thousand crowns! I'd put them all in here."
Then in the stocking dropped some nuts, and hung it up in haste,
And, walking to the door, looked out upon the dreary waste.
But as he looked a beauteous form before him did appear;
It was a lady, but she seemed as from some other sphere.
Her mantle all embroidered o'er with glist'ning flakes of snow;
Her hair like sparking strings of pearls or dew-drops seemed to grow;
Upon her feet were sandals bright of frost-work such as seen
At morn, when glints of sunlight fall upon the blades of green;
And oh! Her eyes they were so bright! like twinkling stars they shone,
As in a gentle, dove-like voice, her errand she made known.

"I am the wife of Santa Claus, and with him came to town,
Because I wishes so much to see sweet little Jessie Brown;
You'll not refuse me, I am sure, an entrance at your door;
The good I give the choicest gifts out of my bounteous store."
Then from her head a string a string of pearls she hastily unwound,
Each pearl a virtue was; their like elsewhere were never found;
And from her pocket forth she drew an hour-glass filled with sand,
That into golden crowns would turn if touched by Jessie's hand.
Then in the stocking, worn and old, she let the jewels fall,
With many other wondrous gifts too numerous to recall,
And filled it up with sugar-plums, the sweetest e'er were known,
And whispered soft in Jessie's ear, "These things are all your own."

A low, sweet whistle then was heard—'twas Santa Claus, they say,
Who, waiting all the while outside, now called his wife away.
To every house they went that night throughout Brookhaven town,
But none such priceless gifts received as little Jessie Brown.

"Why Two Christmases Came in One Year," *Harper's Bazar*, DECEMBER 30 1871:

"Kriss! Kriss!" called Mrs. Santa Claus, as she went out of the house and across the yard. "Now I do wonder where that boy is," she added, looking behind the iceberg that stood like a great frosted hay-rick just in front of the stable door. Kriss was very fond of playing there with his little white bear; but neither boy nor bear was now to be seen. She then peeped into the stable and saw the reindeer in their stalls, but no Kriss was there. "Well," she thought as she turned back, "he can't be far away, and the smell of supper will certainly bring him home." Just as she was going in the door she saw the bear trotting clumsily but quickly off toward the north pole, which is in sight of the house. She went in then, quite easy, for she knew the boy must be somewhere near; and cutting two fine, juicy seal-steaks off the seal in the pantry, she freshened up her fire, and prepared to cook supper. Mrs. Santa Claus never permitted her family to become hungry. They always had four meals a day; but Kriss, who was growing, and needed more food, had his two lunches besides. It certainly was a great pity that neither Sir John Franklin nor Dr. Kane ever happened upon Santa Claus when they explored the polar regions. He is much more hospitable than the Esquimaux, and would have been glad to have entertained and helped them.

His visiting circle is so very small that to see a stranger is quite an event, and there would have been no limit to the kindness he would have shown them. Mrs. Santa Claus goes out still less than her husband; so, although she is obliged to have several new dresses every year, she is never worried by any changes in the fashions. In fact, she cuts the clothes for the whole family just alike. When Santa Claus brings home the skins from his grand hunts, she sorts them into three piles. The largest is for Santa Claus, the next for herself, and the little ones do for Kriss. When the three are together, they are a comical-looking family, for, except in size, there is no difference in them. Another odd thing about them is, that they have but the one name in common. This became very confusing after the child became old enough to run about, as old Santa Claus would often answer the mother's call for the boy, perhaps leaving a toy half finished, and the glue cooling. He finally decided that it would be best to nickname the young Santa, and call him "Kriss Kringle" – a title he himself is known by among the Pennsylvania Dutch. After this there was no farther trouble about names.

But to come back to Kriss upon this particular evening. He was by no means even as far away as his mother had thought, for he had not only seen her, but also had heard her speak. But if she had known where he was, he would have made a quick march out. Over the stable there was a large room, neatly fitted up with shelves and boxes, where Santa Claus kept all his finished toys. Kriss was never allowed to go there without his father; but here he was now, busy as he could be. He was not, as you may perhaps think, playing with the toys, for he did not care for them now: he had so many, and knew all the secrets about them. He had even helped his father put the squeak into the dogs and pigs, and knew just how the strings must be put into the harlequins if they were to jump properly, and how the jugglers and magic lanterns were made, and so was tired of them all. He had just now, however, handled them very extensively, and was still engaged in the same occupation. He had taken out his father's great leather bags, and was busy filling them up with any thing that came nearest to hand. As every thing in the room was finished in good style for Christmas, he had, in spite of his lack of choice, made a pretty collection. His idea in doing this can be very simply explained. It was now near Christmas-time, and there was much excitement and business in the Santa Claus domicile. Santa Claus was hurried with some extra varnishing; and between dressing dolls, making candy and candy bags, and seeing that the Noah's arks and the menageries were properly assorted, Mrs. Santa Claus never went to bed until after twelve o'clock. Little Kriss was, however, a looker-on in this excitement. His parents thought him too little to work, and he did not care to play. Still he wanted a share in the bustle; and the night before, as he lay in his little trundle-bed watching his mother tie sashes upon a whole row of dolls – for she had the latest fashions for them, if not for herself – a bright idea occurred to him. What he wanted to do was to go with his father Christmas-eve to carry the presents to the children; but he knew this would not be permitted. The year before he had accomplished it, for he hid himself among the bags and buffalo-robes in the sledge, and his father never found him until they reached Vermont, and then it was too late to turn back. But there was no hope for him this Christmas, for he knew the sledge would be well searched before his father started. Still he did not despair; and as he lay in his bed this night it flashed across his mind that he might take the deer and sleigh some night before Christmas and have a little trip of his own. He was now acting upon this idea: and so, when he had finished packing the bags, and preparing everything necessary, he smelled the seal-steaks cooking, and, coming out of the stable, went into the house.

His mother was now busy making a walrus hash – for they always had two dishes of meat on the table – and only glanced up to see that he was all safe and right. Soon supper was ready, and the father called in; but although Kriss had but little appetite, he managed, between what he ate and what he stealthily put in his pocket for a midnight lunch, to satisfy his mother. After supper was over his father delighted him by saying that the work was now so nearly done that he thought they might all go to bed early and take a good night's rest. Mrs. Claus rubbed her eyes, and said she would be very glad to do so; and Kriss hypocritically rubbed his also, but truthfully remarked that the sooner they all went to bed the better he would like it.

It was, however, ten o'clock before they were all in bed, and almost eleven before Kriss was safe to start. He had some trouble, too, with the deer; for Vixen, the off-deer, would not let him harness her for some time, and then, just as he was ready to start, he found that Dancer's harness was too tight. However, after some work he made everything ready, lugged down the bags, packed them safely with the tops up, buttoned up his little seal-skin overcoat, drew on his fur gloves, and was off. He drove directly southeast for a time, then turned south, and passed close by the shore of Hudson Bay, and crossed the St. Lawrence, and stopped in Troy, New York. Here he selected a house with a good wide chimney, took out a wax doll, a curly dog, and a candy tiger, and jumped out of the sleigh. It occurred to him at that moment that perhaps there were no children in that house. His father always knew, but how he knew Kriss could not think. Suddenly he remembered that his mother had said that there was warmth in the house where children dwelt; so he laid down the toys, took off his glove, and felt the roof, but it was icy cold. He then jumped into the sledge and drove on, stopping on several roofs to try them, but they were all cold. This, it was plain, was not the way to find out. He then thought he would go down the chimneys and look for the children. At the next house he accordingly left his toys in the sledge, jumped out, sprang down the chimney, and found himself in a large room, where a little baby lay asleep in a crib, and her mother near her in a big bed. He then went back, and getting the toys, laid them beside her. But he soon found that going on such exploring expeditions first was rather tedious work. His father always strapped a bag on his back, as every one knows, but they were all too big for Kriss to carry; so he filled his pockets with little things, stuck as many as possible in his belt, strung some around his neck, and so dressed up, jumped down many and many a chimney.

He was just going to step into the sledge, after many hours of busy work, when he happened to glance up at the sky, and saw that it was nearly day. He had intended going farther, but now had no time. He took out all his toys – but they were almost all gone – placed what he had on a good straight roof, close to the chimney, whipped up his deer, and galloped home. He had expected to have reached home before his parents had awakened, but although he took a short-cut home, he saw the smoke curling up through the keen morning air before he saw the house, and so knew that his mother certainly was up. He managed to drive quietly into the stable, and had just unharnessed the deer, and was about to give them some moss, when a shadow darkened the door; he looked up, and there stood his father! Kriss did not feel very comfortable, but his only course was plain; he followed the never-forgotten example of George Washington under somewhat similar circumstances, and owned up. The only reply Santa Claus made was to tell him to come into the house and get his breakfast. After the meal was over they all sat down around the fire, and little Kriss had to give a full account of his adventures. After he had finished his story, to which his parents listened in perfect gravity, they sent him out to feed the tame bears and walruses, while they talked the subject over. Mrs. Claus sat on one side of the fire-place, Santa Claus on the other. They were silent for a moment; then he looked at her, she looked back at him, and then they both laughed. It certainly was very funny to them, but it would not do to let him go unpunished, or he would travel off whenever he pleased, and perhaps make Christmas once a month. It was easy enough to find something to whip him with, for Santa Claus had some very fine switches all ready for the stockings of bad children; but he never succeeded in inflicting this punishment, for as soon as Kriss began to cry – and he generally started as soon as he saw the switch – his mother always ran and took him away. This being out of the question, after much discussion they concluded to make him keep up the fire in the cave of ice for three months. Santa Claus used to make his glue there, and do various jobs that Mrs. Claus did not like done at the shop; and as the fire had to be kept up regularly, and so needed wood every day, they knew it would be a severe punishment to Kriss, as he hated stated tasks.

But when this sentence was carried into execution it was found that Kriss was bright enough to make fun out of it. He determined, it seemed, that if he had to make fires, they should be big ones; and he piled on the wood until it could be heard crackling and roaring clear to the north pole. The reflection was often seen in the United States, and it set all the learned men to wondering why there should be so many displays of the aurora borealis that year. If they had only known that they were caused by Kriss heaping pine wood upon his father's fire, it would have saved much trouble and more talking.

But the consequences of Kirss's frolic did not stop here. When the people whose houses he visited arose the next morning, they were astonished to find the presents in their rooms. Some of them thought there must be a new fashion regarding the time for Christmas gifts. Others thought they must have made a mistake in the date. One old lady was so flustered that she ran down into the yard and killed her Christmas turkey with her own hands, she was so afraid that it would not be done in time. In one town, where he had been especially liberal, the neighbors ran in and out of each other's houses asking what day of the month it was, consulting almanacs, and wondering what it all meant. The children, however, were perfectly satisfied; and when they received the second instalment of presents from Santa Claus himself at the proper time, they were so delighted that they wished there could be two Christmases every year.

It was funny, to hear of the way Kriss distributed his presents; for as he knew nothing of the several inmates of the house, he bestowed them as they came to hand. He left a solitary old bachelor an ivory rattle and a little crying pussy-cat; a little girl, not yet three months old, had a pair of skates left upon her cradle; a boy of ten found a little white hood and a tiny silver thimble in his room; a severe old maid, who did nothing but knit coarse, hard, but very durable stockings for her little nieces, and who hated games as inventions of Satan, found a set of ten-pins and a backgammon board set out upon her table; a whole family of children had nothing to divide but an empty picture-frame; and a grave old minister was surprised when he went into his study to find a fine little fiddle lying just on top of his half-finished sermon for the next Sunday.

But, puzzle as they might, nobody ever found out the truth of this frolic. As for the toys Kriss left on the roof, I do not know exactly what became of them. Santa Claus looked for them, but in vain; so it would, perhaps, be well to say now that if any boy or girl living in a town northwest of Boston found some toys, one being a walking doll and another a fishing pole, upon a roof close to a chimney, in the winter of 1870, they may know from this account just how they came there.

M. B. Horton, "A New Departure", *Godey's Lady's Book and Magazine* (DECEMBER 1879)

Conspicuous in the memory of one who witnessed the representation of a "New Departure," is the following Christmas event, now given to the readers of the Lady's Book, that they may receive a hint of the fun which they might elaborate for their future enjoyment.

There appeared in the drawing-room of a home well-filled with children, a somewhat startling but majestic figure, who carried upon her shoulders a good-sized pack, and whose dress was of a most fantastic style. Upon her head she did not wear "a wreath of roses," but a lofty pasteboard turban, covered with Turkey-red, and emblazoned with large newspaper letters, spelling "Woman's Rights!" the interjection point, in very red ink, extending from the turban's top to its base.

The female's robe might have been the sequestered ulster of some one belonging to the so-called wiser sex, but made effeminate (so to speak) by belt, hanging velvet pocket, and other little signs of the prevailing feminine style.

There was no trace of finery about the garment which would indicate a weak woman's regard for fashion, only a distinguished and severe "a la Rights mode," which approached the borders of a sterner apparel, while betraying the softer quality of the female taste. There had evidently been considerable stuffing of the manly boot to make it fit the more delicate foot, as wrinkles might be seen around the ankles, significant of space. But on the whole, the appearance of the advocate for a change of base, was alike creditable to her ingenuity and aim.

She came forward into the midst of the merry group, a most unexpected, but not alarming, visitor, and with a stately air and ringing voice declared:

"For about 1800 years that rotund tramp, St. Nicholas, has been enjoying himself hugely on Christmas Eves by wandering here and there with his reindeer and his gifts, making himself greatly popular with both young and old.

"Allow me to say that it is *quite* high time that *Mrs.* St. Nicholas should be allowed some privileges! and if she is not allowed, she will take them!" (Her appearance here was really majestic.)

"Let me announce to you, both young folks and old, that *I* am *Mrs.* St. Nicholas, the sharer of my husband's sorrows over broken toys, but never a sharer in his Christmas joys.

"Plodding on for so long in my retired home, I have inhaled the new atmosphere of the world with a good, long, earnest, and life-inspiring breath—that new atmosphere which makes a woman as capable and vigorous as a man—which starts the pulse of *Mrs.* St. Nicholas, and brings her before you with the determination (planting one foot and then the other with expressive firmness upon the floor) to win your smiles and praises, as *Mr.* St. Nicholas has been accustomed to receive them from the world since the advent of Christmas gifts."

The emphasis upon the *Mr.* and *Mrs.* was most emphatic, as if the two had been altogether too long considered as one, and that one *Mr.* St. Nicholas.

"I appear before you," she continued, in a softer tone, "as a most injured and long-patient woman, now claiming your sympathy for her wrongs. If the old and young Santa Claus could tell their tale, they would give centuries of detail concerning stockings darned, shoe-strings continually tied up, and buttons sewed on, while Mr. St. Nicholas was being petted and praised for his charming liberality at the Christmas holidays—1800 years of dull home life for the one, and a merry tramping all over the world for the other!

"You must certainly wonder at the patience and forbearance which have lasted so long, rather than cherish any surprise that injured woman should at last rebel, and start out alone to seek the road to love and fame.

"The favorite Santa Claus, puffed up with joviality, and reigning like a king at Christmas-time, must share his throne with one who can wear a crown with much more dignity than he. He has made his pretty toys, and has tumbled them down the chimney, all by himself, quite long enough. It's my turn now to win some hearts, and fame, and—poetry. For years and years, I have read

> **'Twas the night before Christmas,
> when all through the house
> Not a creature was stirring,
> not even a mouse**

(repeated with a sarcastic tone), and I am as tired as I can be of it! Of course it must always have been very pretty poetry to Mr. St. Nicholas; he probably thought it lovely; but I really cannot say that I see much poetry in it, when the facts have been all prose to me for all the Christian years."

She now looks around with a most unnatural smile, intended to be both persuasive and fascinating to the youthful eye, and in a corresponding tone of voice, addresses the most susceptible members of the household about her.

"My little dears, you must have some pretty lines written on *Mrs.* St. Nicholas by another year; now, won't you? She might learn to like poetry if it should be all about herself, you know."

Here she returns to her former dignified manner, and with a more determined voice continues:

"I have left your beloved Santa Claus sound asleep, and smiling beautifully at the dream he is probably having of the expected jaunt he is to take when midnight comes. He has his furs, and all his other noted adornments placed in the same careful order for his start, as a young lady would arrange her wedding wardrobe for a grand sensation—that poetry has so puffed him up with self-conceit, and the pictures that go with it have made him so fastidious about his looks.

"He has his sled partly packed, too, but I think he will find a package missing (with a low, cunning laugh, and beginning to unloose her burden from her shoulders). I suppose he had forgotten to stow this package away in his sled, for I found it by his side when he began to snore. I took it from under his great round nose (he is so proud of being called 'round' as if it were a great beauty to be the shape he is), and although he happened to smile in his sleep as I did it, he little dreamed that with it I was going to steal his welcome at the Browns'." She laughed in quite a womanly way at the capital joke she had played upon the unconscious genius of the hour, and commenced unfastening the pack which she had placed upon the floor. She muttered to herself as she did so in a kind of aggrieved soliloquy, "Yes, for 1800 years and odd, I have been left at home to pine and drudge. 1800 years and odd! A good long time indeed, for a woman to mind her husband's p's and q's; and I have determined not to stand it after 1878. I mean to mind my own affairs after this all alone by myself, as *Mr.* St. Nicholas has done for 1800 years and odd; and this minding my own affairs shall be after an entirely new fashion, I can assure *Mr.* St. Nicholas. I have been told to mind my own affairs, and I mean to do it.

"I have seen those reindeers frisk away quite long enough, with their driver a-laughing and a-shouting, but never looking back upon his forsaken wife; and it seems to me that he shakes all over more and more with every year, just as if the fun grew deeper and deeper, and the older the Christmas holiday grew the better old folks, as well as the young folks liked it. I cannot shake as he does, and I don't want to, because my mind is above such a foolish habit of showing one's feelings; but I mean to try and enjoy myself just as much as if I had the reindeer to 'whistle and shout, and call them by name—Now Dasher! Now Dancer! Now Prancer! Now Vixen, On Comet! On Cupid! On Dunder and Blixen.'

"Yes, eight of them, and such ridiculous names I never heard!"

She now had everything arranged for the presentation of the gifts in the order of age, as marked on the packages, and started on her round with a most pleased expression, exclaiming, as she looked upon the expectant members of the group, "I can see now what good fun it must have been for Mr. St. Nicholas to watch all your faces as he peeped in at the door early in the morning, after dropping his packages down the chimneys while you were asleep. And he has enjoyed this fun for 1800 years and odd! Now it is my time for a Christmas outing, and a pleasant visit to one of his best families. But you must not look at your gifts until they are all distributed, for I want a continual string of 'Oh's' and 'Ah's,' beginning with the oldest and ending with the youngest. Mr. St. Nicholas has often told me that these exclamations pay for all his work during the year. Now let me present to Mr. John X. Brown, the father of this happy family (I suppose that it is happy, for it certainly looks so), 'a testimonial from his beloved wife through the venerable Santa Claus.' I suppose by this that you have had some communication with Mr. St. Nicholas, Mrs. Brown," addressing the lady of the family, "permit me to hope" (in a very sweet tone) "that Mrs. St. Nicholas may in the future be the faithful almoner of your Christmas bounty." This was hesitatingly constructed, as if a grander sentence than usual with her; but an effort must be made to sustain an intellectual, as well as a personal dignity.

"Ah; I read upon the package these words also; 'In presenting this testimonial to Mr. B., Mrs. B. wishes to have it represent not only her enduring affection for the partner of her etc., etc., but also in a delicate and expensive way illustrate the golden character of the hours which have passed since they first met.' I presume it is a watch," added Mrs. St. Nicholas, with a wise expression, as she presented the package, with studied grace of manner, to the person to whom it was addressed.

Mr. Brown received the gift with a bow, but with a somewhat incredulous expression in his eye, as if his mental sight was wandering over the field of possibility that a mine had been discovered by the partner of his etc., ete., of which he had not been notified. The wife of his bosom might be the partner of his etc., etc., in a poetical way, but when it came to money, she had not a cent of her own, and so where was the partnership? The money for this testimonial must have come out of *his* pocket, or else she had discovered a mine. The poor wives have pockets, but they seem hung out for show, while the husband's are often as carefully guarded from sight. Did you ever watch the expression of a careful husband when he puts his hand into the deep receptacle of his pocket-book, to answer the trembling demand of the partner of his etc., etc., for a little of the husband's funds? But beg pardon; Mrs. St. Nicholas waits.

"I now have the pleasure of presenting to 'Mrs. J. X. Brown an elegant neck-tie from her *devoted* husband,' accompanied by these words: 'This gift of affection has traveled from eastern lands to grace the neck of America's fairest daughter (in Mr. J. X. B's. eyes), and may its lovely lines reflect the varied, but ever bright, experience of our united lives.' I am only too happy to be the bearer of this beautiful token to 'America's fairest daughter in Mr. J. X. B's admiring eyes,'" and Mrs. St. Nicholas was sweetness itself, as she presented the Christmas gift to the mother of the family.

"'To Miss Cynthia B. Brown, from her grateful parents,'" read Mrs. St. Nicholas, with a little shaking of her assumed ease of style, at the peculiar quality ascribed to Miss Cynthia's parents. Ah! yes, it was all clear—she had been only staggered for a moment—'grateful children' and 'ungrateful children' had been so familiar to her in her intercourse with the young, that the notion of confessing to Miss Cynthia B. Brown that her parents were grateful *to her* for anything, struck her as of 'a new atmosphere' indeed. But then, if really of the new atmosphere, it was a beautiful change, and the air *must* be fresher for it! So she continued to read with renewed self-possession, the following words: "'If much has been said and written upon the study of the sciences, surely the domestic range of subjects should claim our faithful attention. Our daughter Cynthia has proved herself worthy of our gratitude by her devotion to the kitchen department; therefore, we present her a ruby ring, of a very rich quality, and as 'sweet' as herself.'"

Miss Cynthia's eyes sparkled as Mrs. St. Nicholas presented the gift, and as her hands received the box which contained the treasure, it was with difficulty she restrained herself from a view of its contents; but she felt bound to respect the wishes of Mrs. St. Nicholas, and wait until the distribution was over.

"'To Miss Mehitable L. Brown, a string of coral beads, the like of which cannot, at the present time, be found in the whole Atlantic ocean. Her affectionate parents hope that her long-expressed desire for this brilliant ornament may now prove most successfully gratified.'"

The young girl smiled most radiantly on the lady of " the new departure," as the gift was presented by her in a more caressing manner, as she approached the youngest branches of the family, and Miss Mehitable, as Miss Cynthia, was obliged to restrain her burning curiosity for a time.

"'To Master Chester Brown, a collection of rare articles for his microscope; specimens for which his affectionate father sought in many out-of-the-way places.'" Master Chester Brown almost sprang from his chair, in his eagerness to grasp the bulky package which must contain so much of what he valued beyond playthings or books; and he rested with forced contentment, having his arms tightly closed over his extensive possessions.

"'To Master Delancy Brown, an extraordinary knife for pocket use. The blade can be turned to almost any account.'"

Master Delancy Brown was only kept from breaking open the package at once, by the warning glance of his mother, and nervously continued to test the firmness of the string, without actually disobeying his mother's warning look.

"'To Miss Pansie Brown, a beautiful Paris doll, which Santa Claus was delegated to purchase at the Paris Exposition.'" Here Mrs. St. Nicholas was evidently much disturbed, and re-read the direction of the package with great and feeling emphasis, much to the astonishment of her hearers. "So! So!" she at last exclaimed. "*Mr.* St. Nicholas was delegated to purchase a doll at the Paris Exposition, was he? And how came *Mr.* St. Nicholas at the Paris Exposition? that is what I should like to know! It must have been at the very time that he told me he was going to Florida for his health. It's just the way I have been deceived by *Mr.* St. Nicholas for the last 1800 years and odd!" But she appeared to brighten up a little as she saw the little girl's delight at the reception of the beautiful doll; and, as this was the last of the gifts, Mrs. St. Nicholas now prepared herself for the smiles and the praises she had taken all this pains to receive.

She took her position in the middle of the room, and, gracefully clasping her hands before her, she beamed upon them all by turns, and then, fixing her eyes upon the father of the family, mildly, but with a little tremor of excitement in her voice, requested Mr. John X. Brown to start the round of "Oh's!" and "Ah's!"

It was a pleasing sight to watch Mrs. St. N's. expressive countenance as the voluminous wrappings of Mr. John X. Brown's package were laid aside one by one, until an—enormous turnip was revealed, most artfully covered upon one side with figures and hands, as the dial of a watch, and having a cord of yellow silk attached as a pocket-chain. One could see the very beginning of the cloud steal over the before glowing countenance of Mrs. N., until it grew into something almost as black as terror, when Mr. B, exclaimed, with startling emphasis: "Well, what is this! Am I to be made a fool of by this idiot woman? What do you mean by this humbugging presentation of Christmas gifts?"

Not a word from the 'new departure!' Would that she had left all things to the old!

"Wife," said Mr. Brown, "give us a sight of your brilliant neck-tie; there may possibly be some mistake about my turnip," he added, with the beginning of a smile.

"And what is this?" exclaims the wife, as she draws from the last fold of her package, a bright bandanna handkerchief, which had been made into a lengthy tie, and fringed elaborately at either end. Mrs. J. X. Brown had too much womanly tact to add any further exclamation to her remark, as it might add fuel to the flame of her husband's interjections, so she forced herself to say, "How very funny all this is!—come, Cynthia, let us see what *dear* Mrs. St. Nicholas has brought to you." (A little ire in the honey.)

The box was opered, and on a bed of cotton soft and white, lay a ruby ring, indeed, very 'rich' and 'sweet' as herself—as rich as flour and eggs could make it, and as sweet as sugar of the best.

The deep brown of the ring of dough might be very tempting to the taste, but not to the eye prepared by hope and expectation for a more valuable Christmas gift. And these repeated disappointments of Mrs. St. N's. victims affected the younger members of the family with terrible fancies of what might be in store for them; and they waited no longer for the order of their going at their several packages, but went at once at the strings and envelopes. All eyes were turned upon the four who were endeavoring to end their anticipations in such quick haste.

Miss Mehitable's string of coral beads, of which 'there could not now be found the like in the wide Atlantic Ocean,' proved to be a string of bright, red cranberries, fine of their kind, but not the kind of necklace coveted by the pretty Hetty, who had already in imagination appeared at the New Year's party, to which she had been invited, in a lovely coral necklace which excited the envy of all who looked upon her. It was a disappointment indeed; but did not equal the grief which Master Chester Brown displayed when the specimens for his high-priced microscope were found to be only the most common forms of coal and roots. He had set his heart upon some rare and wonderful things, and it was almost broken (in a scientific way) by this miserable display.

The younger boy, Master Delancy Brown, never took anything much to heart, and as he had laughed at Chester's disappointment, must consistently laugh at his own; so, when he displayed a large ungainly kitchen knife as suitable for "pocket use," he flourished it about with great glee, and threatened to "turn it to any account" upon the person of Mrs. St. N., much to that "new departure's" consternation.

It was really pitiful to see the shower of tears from baby Pansie's eyes, as she brought to view an ugly doll, as far from the expected elegance of form and style as it could be.

The sympathy of all the loving group was excited to a dangerous degree for Mrs. St. N., as this shower of tears burst from the darling's eyes; and had it not been for the sudden appearance of a new face at the drawing-room door, the speechless and dazed woman would still more have lamented the usurpation of her husband's rights. Instead of the coveted praises and smiles, there were angry frowns; and her consternation had reached its highest point, when lo! a round jolly face peeped in at the door; and then appeared a form shaking with laughter, in almost painful contrast to the gloom that rested on all around.

For a moment the figure paused, but then, coming briskly forward, appeared as the venerable St. Nick himself! He approached his wife (a little shaky about the knees, it might be seen, but this might have been from laughter, not from fear), and exclaimed in his own deep jovial voice:

"How pleased I am in finding you out, my dear. And did you walk? I am really afraid you did, for I was obliged to send the reindeers for a run to get up their spirits for their midnight work, and so they must have been off before you started. I am so sorry! For you could have had them, of course, if I had known that you wanted to take an airing." He rubbed his hands together with a chuckle and a comical expression in his round, bright eyes, so irresistible, that even Mrs. St. N. began to smile.

"And so you thought you would bring the Browns their Christmas presents, did you?"

Again he rubbed his hands together, and laughed so merrily that the room rung with the sound.

"Well, let me see—here are the gifts you brought—Ah! Oh! Why what is this, my dear? Do you mean to say that these are the only contents of your Christmas packs? Why, *Mrs.* St. Nicholas," imitating her own emphasis upon the title, "you must have lost your proverbial good taste—for you have often helped me my dear, by capital hints—or else you must have been deceived by some vile wretch who envied you your expected pleasure."

Metting Mrs. Claus

He burst into another fit of laughter, and patting Mrs. Santa Claus upon the shoulder in a good-natured way, addressed her after the following fashion:

"When *Mrs.* St. Nicholas thinks so much of a remarkable start in the direction of Woman's Rights as to talk about it aloud when she imagines herself alone, that tyrannical Old Nick must look out steadily for his own endangered ways. For you see, my dear, that his right of way has been for years and years over every house-top and down every chimney in all lands; and you can't deny it, can you? after knowing all *about it for 1800 years and odd!*

"Well, I couldn't let you travel over my own route any way, because you see it wouldn't do, when you consider that all the little people in all the bed-rooms of the land are well acquainted with Old Nick, and I am afraid that they would be frightened to see even such a well-dressed" (there was a gurgle in *Mr.* St. Nicholas' throat; not a sign of apoplexy it is to be hoped) "and fine-looking woman as yourself suddenly appear—"

He was at this point of his discourse suddenly interrupted by Mrs. St. N., eager to establish the existence of a new feminine power.

"Yes, 'well-dressed' by *Mrs.* not by *Mr.* Worth." The dignity accompanying this important information was really inimitable.

"Oh! Ah! And is it so? by *Mrs.* Worth— 'well-dressed by *Mrs.* not by *Mr.* Worth'" (no mistake about the gurgle now; it was *not* apoplexy), "I see, I see, fine taste, that *Mrs.* Worth!

"But to go on, my dear, knowing that no argument would show you that mine was the right side of our case, I thought I would fix a budget for you and let you go as you desired.

"St. Nicholas is a very ingenious fellow, as you have discovered; so he put his wits to work to get up something that, perhaps, might cure you of wanting to take away his property of 'smiles and praises.' He finally got up something novel to take to the Browns, and laid the package in a handy place for you. So, while this funny man appeared to sleep the innocent sleep of the benevolent old Christmas traveler that he is, you walked most unhesitatingly into the trap prepared for you, and strode off immediately with a manly air, *a la* old Nick himself, with your pack upon your back. I watched you, dear, with admiring eyes" (another supposed catch in the throat), "and was so very anxious lest you should become fatigued before reaching your journey's end; but I really could not spare the reindeers when I had so much work for them to do this night. It was only when you were out of sight that I fully realized my own unworthiness to receive the 'smiles and praises' of the innocent little folks."

Here he suddenly dropped upon his little fat knees, and, with mock heroic supplication exclaimed:

"Forgive your penitent Nicholas, my own! and he will forget the 'new departure'— the effort to get the start of him on the Christmas journey to the Browns. Doing this, my love, even when he smiled in fancy upon you in his peaceful slumber" (a profound chuckle even in his submissive position).

To which the lady replied:

"Do get up, Mr. St. Nicholas! If you only knew how absurd you look with your little round body down there on Mrs. Brown's best carpet! Well, I suppose I must forgive you" (with a gentle sigh), "there's no help for it. I will forgive, and you will forget—it has been just so for 1800 years and odd—I forgiving all the time, and you forgetting all the time. Ho!" (with a sudden start and radiant countenance), "these things are not to last. I hear that somebody who reads the stars, declares that before another Christmas day comes round, there will be a fresh and mighty start of womankind toward the goal of freedom! Ah, that will be the day and hour for Mrs. N.'s, and others' powers! My dear old Nick, let all the past become a blank, because of that good time coming—my dear old Nick, come to my arms!"

Mr. St. Nicholas jumped up with youthful alacrity, and the two embraced with mutual smiles, while Mrs. N. was heard to say in emphatic undertone:

"As we are one again, let there be no more emphasis between us."

They thus became Mr. and Mrs. St. Nicholas without any underlining of either title.

And after this amiable adjustment of their misunderstanding, St. Nicholas produced the genuine pack which he had prepared for the family of Brown, and the distribution of presents gave at last great satisfaction to all concerned.

Margaret Eytinge, "Mistress Santa Claus",
Harper's Young People, DECEMBER 20 1881

Much you have heard about old Santa Claus,
But naught, I think, of his good-natured wife,
And I must tell you of her, dears, because
In sweet'ning life for you she spends her life.
She's small and plump, her eyes are brown and bright,
And in a cave she lives that's full of toys,
Where, with her servant-elves, from morn till night
She's busy working for the girls and boys.
Yes, quite three hundred days out of the year
Never a single idle hour have they,
For well they know there would be many a tear
Should sugar-plums fall short on Christmas-day.
And oh! and oh! the sugar-plums!
Some brown, some red, and some as white
As snow-flakes when they first alight;
Some holding grapes, some holding cherries,
Some bits of orange, some strawberries,
Some tasting like a peach or rose,
And some that dainty nuts inclose:
Some filled with cream, and some with spice,
And all so very, very nice.
And oh! and oh! the sugar-plums!
Those funny, funny little elves,
They cram the boxes and the drums,
The bags, the baskets, and the shelves;
They heap them high upon the floor,
In closets pack them two miles long,
And when there is no room for more
They sing a jolly elfish song;
And pretty Mistress Santa Claus,
With sugar sticking to her thumbs
And tiny fingers, laughs aloud
To think of that great eager crowd
Of smiling girls and smiling boys
Awaiting for her husband's toys.
And oh! and oh! the sugar-plums!
And now, sweethearts, when merry Christmas comes,
And you greet Santa's gifts with loud applause,
Remember who sent you the sugar-plums,
And give one cheer for Mistress Santa Claus.

Sarah J. Burke, "Mrs. Santa Claus Asserts Herself", *Harper's Young People* (JANUARY 1 1884)

Oh, it's all very fine for that husband of mine
To be courted and praised and invited to dine;
Though late in the day, I'll take while I may
My woman's one privilege of "saying her say."

It's "Santa Claus, dear"—"ah, no, Santa Claus here"
(Pray pardon this poor little tricklesome tear);
Complimentary strife is the breath of his life,
But who ever mentions his desolate wife?

Now I've nothing to say in a slanderous way
Of the man I have promised to love and obey:
He's a jolly old soul, he acts up to his role,
And as husbands go, he may pass, on the whole.

Oh, I'd never have spoken—my heart might have broken,
I'd have died without leaving one remnant of token—
Did a gossip not say in my hearing one day,
"Santa Claus is a bachelor, tieless and gay."

"You mistake," was my cry, with a flash of the eye;
"I'm his patient and hard-working wife, by-the-bye;
And the world I will stun, when the gamut I run
Of all that I've suffered and all that I've done."

My sufferings first. With a heart nigh to burst,
Each Christmas-eve brings me the sharpest and worst;
When equipped for a start, I see him depart,
While my tremulous hands seek my quivering heart.

"Be careful," I say; "you grow stouter each day"
(We women must smile though our heart-strings give way);
Tight-fit chimneys, you know, you must surely forego,
Or be roasted alive by the fire below.

"And, darling," I add, "remember the bad
Attack of bronchitis you recently had;
And button your coat high up in the throat,
And don't cross the streams when the ice is afloat.

"And keep a tight rein on My Lady Disdain—
Look, dear! she is kicking the dash-board again."
But away he has sped, heeding naught I have said,
While visions of widowhood dance in my head.

Is it nothing, I ask, that my husband should bask
In the popular smile, like a belle at a masque,
While I, poor old crone, sit and cower alone,
Tight clasping the fingers I've worked to the bone?

With a nod and a blink he would lead you to think
He had dressed all the dolls ere a weasel could wink;
No; while he's in bed—to his shame be it said—
It is I who am plying the needle and thread.

He goes shopping so grand through the length of the land,
But all matters of tastefulness fall to my hand.
Could he crochet and tat, or trim a doll's hat?
Take his clumsy thumb-measure—now answer me that.

Oh, women, whose days are made radiant with praise,
Whose trumpets are blown on the high and by ways,
Pray stifle your scorn for a woman forlorn,
Who is driven to sounding her own little horn.

Katherine Lee Bates, "Goody Santa Claus on a Sleigh Ride", *Wide Awake* (DECEMBER 1888)

SANTA, must I tease in vain, Dear? Let me go and hold the reindeer,
While you clamber down the chimneys. Don't look savage as a Turk!
Why should you have all the glory of the joyous Christmas story,
And poor little Goody Santa Claus have nothing but the work?

It would be so very cozy, you and I, all round and rosy,
Looking like two loving snowballs in our fuzzy Arctic furs,
Tucked in warm and snug together, whisking through the winter weather
Where the tinkle of the sleigh-bells is the only sound that stirs.

You just sit here and grow chubby off the goodies in my cubby
From December to December, till your white beard sweeps your knees;
For you must allow, my Goodman, that you're but a lazy woodman
And rely on me to foster all our fruitful Christmas Trees.

While your Saintship waxes holy, year by year, and roly-poly,
Blessed by all the lads and lassies in the limits of the land,
While your toes at home you're toasting, then poor Goody must go posting
Out to plant and prune and garner, where our fir-tree forests stand.

Oh! but when the toil is sorest how I love
   our fir-tree forest,
Heart of light and heart of beauty in the
   Northland cold and dim,
All with gifts and candles laden to delight a
   boy or maiden,
And its dark-green branches ever murmuring
   the Christmas hymn!

Yet ask young Jack Frost, our neighbor, who
   but Goody has the labor,
Feeding roots with milk and honey that the
   bonbons may be sweet!
Who but Goody knows the reason why the
   playthings bloom in season
And the ripened toys and trinkets rattle gaily
   to her feet!

From the time the dollies budded, wiry-
   boned and sawdust-blooded,
With their waxen eyelids winking when the
   wind the tree-tops plied,
Have I rested for a minute, until now your
   pack has in it
All the bright, abundant harvest of the
   merry Christmastide?

Santa, wouldn't it be pleasant to surprise
   me with a present?
And this ride behind the reindeer is the boon
   your Goody begs;
Think how hard my extra work is, tending
   the Thanksgiving turkeys
And our flocks of rainbow chickens — those
   that lay the Easter eggs.

Home to womankind is suited? Nonsense,
   Goodman! Let our fruited
Orchards answer for the value of a woman
   out-of-doors.
Why then bid me chase the thunder, while
   the roof you're safely under,
All to fashion fire-crackers with the lighting
   in their cores?

See! I've fetched my snow-flake bonnet, with
   the sunrise ribbons on it;
I've not worn it since we fled from Fairyland
   our wedding day;
How we sped through iceberg porches with
   the Northern Lights for torches!
You were young and slender, Santa, and we
   had this very sleigh.

Jump in quick then? That's my bonny. Hey down derry! Nonny nonny!
While I tie your fur cap closer, I will kiss your ruddy chin.
I'm so pleased I fall to singing, just as sleigh-bells take to ringing!
Are the cloud-spun lap-robes ready? Tirra-lirra! Tuck me in.

Off across the starlight Norland, where no plant adorns the moorland
Save the ruby-berried holly and the frolic mistletoe!
Oh, but this is Christmas revel! Off across the frosted level
Where the reindeers' hoofs strike sparkles from the crispy, crackling snow!

There's the Man i' the Moon before us, bound to lead the Christmas chorus
With the music of the sky-waves rippling round his silver shell —
Glimmering boat that leans and tarries with the weight of dreams she carries
To the cots of happy children. Gentle sailor, steer her well!

Now we pass through dusky portals to the drowsy land of mortals;
Snow-enfolded, silent cities stretch about us dim and far.
Oh! how sound the world is sleeping, midnight watch no shepherd keeping,
Though an angel-face shines gladly down from every golden star.

Here's a roof. I'll hold the reindeer. I suppose this weather-vane, Dear,
Some one set here just on purpose for our teams to fasten to.
There's its gilded cock, — the gaby! — wants to crow and tell the baby
We are come. Be careful, Santa! Don't get smothered in the flue.

Back so soon? No chimney-swallow dives but where his mate can follow.
Bend your cold ear, Sweetheart Santa, down to catch my whisper faint:
Would it be so very shocking if your Goody filled a stocking
Just for once? Oh, dear! Forgive me. Frowns do not become a Saint.

Metting Mrs. Claus

So our sprightly reindeer clamber, with their fairy sleigh of amber,
On from roof to roof, the woven shades of night about us drawn.
On from roof to roof we twinkle, all the silver bells a-tinkle,
Till blooms in yonder blessèd East the rose of Christmas dawn.

Now the pack is fairly rifled, and poor Santa's well-nigh stifled;
Yet you would not let your Goody fill a single baby-sock;
Yes, I know the task takes brain, Dear. I can only hold the reindeer,
And to see me climb down chimney — it would give your nerves a shock.

I will peep in at the skylights, where the moon sheds tender twilights
Equally down silken chambers and down attics bare and bleak.
Let me show with hailstone candies these two dreaming boys — the dandies
In their frilled and fluted nighties, rosy cheek to rosy cheek!

What! No gift for this poor garret? Take a sunset sash and wear it
O'er the rags, my pale-faced lassie, till thy father smiles again.
He's a poet, but — oh, cruel! he has neither light nor fuel.
Here's a fallen star to write by, and a music-box of rain.

Wait! There's yet a tiny fellow, smiling lips and curls so yellow
You would think a truant sunbeam played in them all night. He spins
Giant tops, and flies kites higher than the gold cathedral spire
In his dreams — the orphan bairnie, trustful little Tatterkins.

Santa, don't pass by the urchin! Shake the pack, and deeply search in
All your pockets. There is always one toy more. I told you so.
Up again? Why, what's the trouble? On your eyelash winks the bubble
Mortals call a tear, I fancy. *Holes in stocking, heel and toe?*

Goodman, though your speech is crusty now and then there's nothing rusty
In your heart. A child's least sorrow makes your wet eyes glisten, too;
But I'll mend that sock so nearly it shall hold your gifts completely.
Take the reins and let me show you what a woman's wit can do.

Puff! I'm up again, my Deary, flushed a bit and somewhat weary,
With my wedding snow-flake bonnet worse for many a sooty knock;
But be glad you let me wheedle, since, an icicle for needle,
Threaded with the last pale moonbeam, I have darned the laddie's sock.

Then I tucked a paint-box in it ('twas no easy task to win it
From the Artist of the Autumn Leaves) and frost-fruits white and sweet,
With the toys your pocket misses — oh! and kisses upon kisses
To cherish safe from evil paths the motherless small feet.

Chirrup! chirrup! There's a patter of soft footsteps and a clatter
Of child voices. Speed it, reindeer, up the sparkling Arctic Hill!
Merry Christmas, little people! Joy-bells ring in every steeple,
And Goody's gladdest of the glad. I've had my own sweet will.

8.

A New Old-Fashioned Christmas

H. C. Dodge, "Santa Claus at the Telephone", *Detroit Free Press,* DECEMBER 21 1890

Hello! I'm Santa Claus to say that with my reindeers, and my sleigh packed as it never was before, I'm coming in a few days more. So leave the chimneys open wide, hang lots of stockings by the side, and have the children sleeping sound before I enter with a bound. Hello! Hello! Just tell the boys about the sugar plums and toys I only bring to those I find have been obedient and kind. The girls are always good, I know, and need no hint to keep them so. And tell the old folks they must be all ready with the Christmas Tree. Hello! I 'most forgot to say that Mrs. Santa Claus, Hoo-ray! is coming too, this time, at least, to help along the merry feast, and see the little faces shine with gladdest Christmas joy divine. She's putting on her things to be ready for the trip with me. A few days more I'll see you. I—Hello! They've shut me off—Good bye!

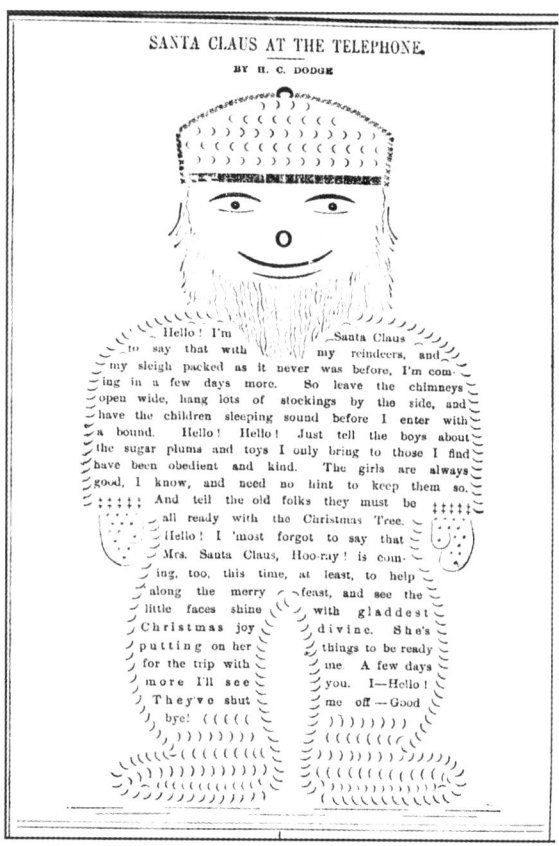

Mary Bissell Waterman, *"Hello! Santa Claus!" or, How a Telephone Upset Christmas*
(UTICA: D, WATERMAN, 1886)

Chapter I.

Santa Claus sat down to the dinner table "as cross as a bear." He never even glanced at his wife to see which of her caps was on her head. And that was a thing Santa Claus was always very particular to notice, so I must tell you about them. Mrs. Santa Claus had three caps. Her "sleeping cap," her "working cap" and her "thinking cap." The first was knit of white cotton yarn, with a small scrimpy crown, fitting close to the head. It had not a pucker or a gather, or frill, or a scrap of trimming on it, and it was tied under her double chin with strings a quarter of a yard wide. When she wore it Santa Claus took off his boots and went around on tip-toe. Her "working cap" was made of stiff cambric, in the shape of a huge inverted candy cornucopia. It had a large, bright yellow bow in front and a larger blue one behind. The high peaked top stood up in a fierce and defiant way. When she appeared in this towering head-dress, Santa Claus always thought best to keep at a respectful distance. So did Sambo the dog, and Jimbo the cat, and Polyanthus the parrot. But the "thinking cap"! Ah! when the good dame placed that on her head, with its full crown and broad frills of soft white mull, and its pretty floating ribbons, then Sambo curled up at her feet, and Jimbo jumped on her lap, and Polyanthus perched on her shoulder, and Santa Claus leaned back in his great arm chair, with his feet on the fender, and chuckled and laughed, and shook his fat sides, the jolliest, happiest old fellow in the world. Because this "thinking cap" covered a great many queer fancies, and wise suggestions, and loving thoughts, which, sooner or later, he was sure to hear about and reap the benefit of. But on this particular day, the day before Christmas, Mrs. Santa Claus was at the dinner table, with her working cap stuck on in a very ferocious and alarming manner. At any other time Santa Claus, seeing this, would have meekly eaten his dinner and gone off to his afternoon nap, without saying a word. But, as I have said before, he was "as cross as a bear." And this is what had caused it. A week before this event occurred, which I am about to relate, Santa Claus had been persuaded into putting a telephone into his winter palace, much to the disgust of his wife. And these were the messages continually flying over the wires:

"Hello! what is it?"

"Please connect with Santa Claus."

"Hello! who is it?" And then would come the answers from Johnny, and Katy, and Nick, and Ned, and Mollie, and Bessie, and Tom, and Rob, and a thousand others. And they were all just alike.

"Dear Santa Claus, I want you to send me for Christmas, a pony, or a donkey, or a big wax doll, or a watch, or a velocipede, or a sled, or a set of real china dishes, or a play house," and five thousand other things. It had kept Santa Claus and his wife very busy answering all these calls, and just as they drew their chairs up to the dinner table, "ting-a-ling-a-ling" went the telephone. "That's the nine hundred and ninety-ninth time that bell has rung this morning," said the dame rather crossly. This was the message that reached their ears—it was a little girl who spoke in a whining, complaining voice, "Dear Santa Claus, you needn't send me such a mean, old present as you did last Christmas. My papa is a very, very rich man and I want a big diamond ring, as big as my mamma's, so that all the little girls in the neighborhood will envy me. Don't give anybody else one. You'll send it, won't you, dear Santa Claus, to Miss Maud Granger, 5th Avenue?"

"No, I won't," he thundered back, and then he shut the telephone with a snap and sat down to his dinner. Do you wonder he was cross?

"I am sick of this business," he said, entirely forgetting what cap his wife had on her head. "I have a good mind to let the children go without a Christmas this year. They are all growing up as selfish as little pigs. What do they think Christmas was made for, I wonder?"

Now, if Mrs. S. had only put on her "thinking cap" before her husband came in, she never, never would have answered her husband as she did.

"You have made them so," she said. "I think it is high time you retired from the business. You are growing old and getting so fat I don't see how you can get down any chimney, even the great old-fashioned ones, and I should think the new-fangled ones would squeeze you to death."

Now, no one likes to be told that he is getting too old and fat to be good for anything, and to intimate dear old Santa Claus was to be held responsible for the naughtiness and piggishness of selfish little boys and girls, when all his life had been spent in trying to make them good as well as happy—why, I think Mrs. Santa Claus ought to have been ashamed of herself; but the mischief was done, and there was no help for it. Santa Claus threw down his knife and fork, jumped up from the table, rushed into the bedroom, flung his boots out of the window, put on his red flannel night cap and green dressing gown, and went to bed.

Now, there was one very queer thing about Santa Claus. When he got so very angry that he wouldn't eat his dinner he always went to bed and slept twenty-four hours and he wouldn't wake up no matter what happened. So Christmas was upset that year, all on account of a naughty girl, a foolish wife, and a telephone.

Chapter II.

Mrs. Santa Claus arose from the table and commenced washing her dishes. She called in Dando. "O Dando, what shall we do? Santa Claus has gone off to bed in one of his awful tempers, and you know what that means. Dear me, he hasn't had one in fifty years. Dando, are Prancer and Dancer, and Dunder and Blixen in the barn?"

"Yes, ma'am."

"Is the sleigh packed full of presents?"

"Yes, ma'am."

"Do you know who they are all meant for? Can you distribute them to the right children?"

"No, ma'am."

Dando stood by the edge of the door ready to pop out suddenly, for Mrs. Santa's high peaked cap was shaking in a threatening and alarming way. He knew what that meant, so he gave his answers in a meek and trembling voice. Sambo had retreated under the sofa, just showing the tip of his black tail, and Jimbo was hidden under a rocking chair, her white nose peeking out. Polyanthus had flown to the top of a high clock in the corner and was talking in her softest voice, "Take care, take care! Top knot's up! Top knot's up!"

Ting-a-ling-a-ling, rang the telephone bell. Mrs. Claus's cap fairly danced on the top of her head with excitement, and she looked around with such an expression that Sambo's tail and Jimbo's nose disappeared entirely, and Polyanthus shut her eyes and pretended she was asleep. Mrs. Santa Claus put the telephone tube to her ear, with a jerk, and waited impatiently for the message. She heard a sweet pleading voice say, "Dear Santa Claus: I am a little lame girl, living in Beggar's Alley. The baker's man said I might telephone from his store. My mamma is sick. Do you ever come to poor little girls' houses? If you would only bring my mamma a new warm blanket, and a cup of hot tea with milk and sugar in it. You needn't bring anything to me. My name is Jenny Gray."

Mrs. Santa Claus stood quite still. The tall cap fell on one side, slowly slipped off her head and dropped quietly to the floor. She gently took down her thinking cap and put it on.

"Dando,"—she spoke so softly that he came in and shut the door behind him. Jimbo purred and Sambo wagged his tail and Polyanthus whistled

"There's a good time coming, boys:
Wait a little longer."

She sat motionless for a few minutes. Then her face brightened and her eyes smiled, and she turned to Dando with such a joyful ring to her voice that Sambo and Jimbo instantly came out from their hiding places and stood on their hind legs, and Polyanthus flew down and settled on her shoulder.

"Dando, bring the sleigh around to the door in less than ten minutes. I am going to run the Christmas business this year. Do you know the children that live in Beggar's Alley?"

"Yes, ma'am," in a loud voice.

"And the children in the Poor House?"

"Certainly, madam."

"And those in the Orphan Asylum?"

"Every one of them, Most Gracious Lady." He put his hand on his heard and bowed very low.

"And, Dando, if you know of any lame, or blind, or sick child in your neighborhood,"—Dando lived in Working Man's Lane—"we'll drop a big bundle there." At this announcement, Dando stood on one leg, then on the other, and finally being unable to restrain his delight any longer, he opened the door and turned a double summersault in the hall. For did not Dando have a little blind daughter, who was so anxious for a music box? And didn't he know of a beautiful one that played five tunes, packed in Santa Claus's sleigh? He was sure the Dame would give it to her.

As this was a new business for Mrs. Santa Claus, of course she didn't have anything suitable to wear.

"I'll dress up in Santa Claus's clothes," she said to herself. So she put on his fur coat, with its fringe of silver bells, and his big fur cap. The coat was so large it wrapped twice around her, and the fur cap kept slipping down over her nose, but she tied it on as well as she could with a red scarf, jumped into the sleigh, with the bells jingling, the dog barking, the cat mewing and the parrot screaming at the top of his voice, "Clackit! Clackit! What a Racket!!"

"What do you suppose Santa Claus will say to-morrow when he wakes up?" said Dando, as he tucked the robes around his mistress and gathered up the reins.

"Dando," she whispered confidentially, "I believe he will really be glad of it. He has been dreadfully worried lately, because it has seemed to him that Christmas wasn't exactly what it ought to be. The rich children have all the good times and the elegant presents, and so many poor children never have anything at all. And Santa Claus can't help it. You know he has nothing of his own to give; other people provide the things, and all he has to do is obey orders and go where he is sent. I am so glad that I don't know where one of those presents belong, but they sha'n't be thrown away. O Dando! the poor children shall have a beautiful time this Christmas!"

And over the hills and through the valleys and into the cities and towns and villages, dashed the sleigh with its loaded treasures, and dear Dame Santa Claus was as happy as a child, and Prancer and Dancer, and Dunder and Blixen, and Sambo and Jimbo, and Polly and Dando were wild with joy, but Santa Claus lay in his night cap and dressing gown, fast asleep.

Chapter III.

Yes, he was sound asleep. When fifty years before he had gone off to sleep in just such a rage, every means that you could think of were used to wake him up, but without success. Bells were rung, and drums were beat, and horns were sounded, and trumpets blown, without doing one particle of good. But what neither bells, nor drums, nor horns, nor trumpets could do, the little telephone up in the corner, did. Because, you see, behind it were the little children.

Oh! that telephone just tingled all over with fun as it kept up a constant ting-a-ling, ting-a-ling, ting-a-ling-a-ling. It knew he couldn't stand that. And sure enough, it woke him up in the middle of the afternoon. He looked at the clock, which stood at the foot of the bed. It was a wonderful timepiece. It not only told the hour of the day, but the day of the week, and the month, and the year of our Lord.

He rubbed his eyes and looked again. There stood the record,

1885, Tuesday, Dec. 24, 4 p.m.

So he had only slept four hours. He turned over in bed and covered himself up and tried to go to sleep again, but it was useless. The telephone hadn't the slightest idea of allowing that thing to go on. It rang incessantly. He couldn't sleep, so he rolled out of bed and looked for his boots, which he had thrown out of the window, but a spiteful little gust of wind had blown a snow drift over them and covered them up, and he could not find them. He put on a short coat over his long dressing gown and a pair of slippers and went out into the dining-room. As soon as he opened the door the telephone bell stopped ringing. He called for his wife, for Dando. No answer. He rushed out to the barn. Sleigh, reindeer, and presents all gone; no sign of Christmas anywhere. He went back into the house. It all came over him. The hundreds of thousands of disappointed children that would wake up Christmas morning. He sprang to the telephone and rang it furiously.

"Hello! I'm Santa Claus. Connect me with everybody. At once! This instant! Immediately!"

Ting-a-ling-a-ling-a-ling. In every house and store and office, except in Beggar's Alley and such places, sounded the call, and fathers and mothers, and uncles and aunts, as well as the children, heard the message. Santa Claus was in such a state of mind that he didn't exactly know what he did say, but these short, jerky sentences went over the wire in such quick confusion that everybody was nearly distracted.

"Dear little children. My wife has run off with my sleigh. And Dando, too. Taken all your presents with her. Can't find my cap, or my fur coat, or my seven-leagued boots. She don't know who the presents belong to. She will give them to all the beggars and sick children all over the world. She always said she would do it if she ever got the chance. Dear children, won't you send me word that you will be willing to go without your Christmas presents this year? It shall never happen again. I'm nearly crazy."

He shouted so loudly that not only the papas, mammas, uncles and aunts heart this dreadful announcement, but it reached the ears of newsboys, and boot-blacks, and rag pickers, and street sweepers, and one impudent little rag'muffin threw up his cap and yelled, "Three cheers for the old woman!" and such a "Hurrah" you never heard before and never will again.

After Santa Claus sent off his message he sat down by the fire. But his head was so bewildered that without knowing what he was about he took down his wife's thinking cap, which hung by the fire place, and put it on hind side before. Now, if he had only put it on right, it would have straightened out his mind instantly, for it was a peculiarity of this cap, that whenever anybody put it on, Dame Santa Claus's queer fancies and loving thoughts popped into the head that wore it, but as he had it on hind side before, these thoughts and fancies were in a good deal of a jumble.

"I wish my wife would come home," he said to himself. Suddenly the door opened and there she stood, with her eyes as big as dinner plates, she was so astonished, first to find him awake, and then to see her thinking cap perched on the top of his bald head, with the cape in front and the frills behind.

"Santa Claus, what are you doing with my cap on your head?"

"What are you doing with my cap on your head?" He tried to speak in a gruff voice, but she looked so funny in his fur coat and cap that he laughed and laughed, and I don't know but he would have kept on until this day, if "Ting-a-ling-a-ling" hadn't sounded through the room. The children were sending in their answers.

"We'll give up our Christmas for the poor children."

"Yes, dear Santa Claus, we'll do it."

"We are so glad!"

"Yes." "Yes." "Yes." "Yes." From New York and Boston and Philadelphia and Chicago and San Francisco and all over the world came back the loving and generous responses. He told his wife all about it in two seconds, and the great tears of joy rolled down their cheeks, and he shouted, "I knew the children weren't growing up little selfish pigs." Then he caught his wife around the waist, as well as he could on account of the fur coat, and her lace cap fell over his left ear, and his fur cap slipped on to the back of her head, and together they danced the merriest jig that was ever danced on Christmas Eve. And Sambo and Jimbo followed suit, to the tune which Polyanthus was whistling at the top of his voice:

"There's a good time coming, boys,
A good time coming."

And so it proved. For the papas and mammas, and uncles and aunts, who had heard all this telephone talk, managed somehow so that the little generous hearts found beautiful presents in their Christmas stockings, and the blind girl had the music box, and the lame girl's mamma her blanket, and hot tea, and heaps of other things, and Beggar's Alley and the Orphan Asylum and the Poor House and the Hospitals and the newsboys and boot-blacks, and rag pickers and street-sweepers were all remembered.

Just as the clock struck twelve that night, ting-a-ling-a-ling went the telephone for the last time, and little Maud Granger's voice said, "It is all right, this time, dear Santa Claus, but next year I hope you will lock up your wife the day before Christmas, so that she can't upset Christmas again." At that they both laughed so loud that it set the bells ringing in all the steeples and the carolers commenced singing in the streets; and the pure white snow shone in the moonlight like frosted pearls, and the icicles hung from the trees like gleaming diamonds, and the sky was as blue as a turquoise, for the dear old earth had decked herself in her loveliest jewels.

"And the Christmas bells began to chime,
    Oh! the beautiful blessed Christmas-time."

Rev. Washington Gladden, "Santa Claus in the Pulpit", *St. Nicholas Magazine* (DECEMBER 1887)

"One and a half for Billington!"

The speaker was standing at the ticket window in the station of the Great Western Rail-way. Evidently he was talking about tickets: the 'one' was for himself, the 'half' for the boy who was clinging to the small hand-satchel, and looking up rather sleepily at the ticket-seller's face.

"When do you wish to go to Billington?" inquired that official.

"On the next train: eleven o'clock, isn't it?" asked the traveler.

"That train does not run Saturday nights; no train leaves here for Billington until to-morrow, at midnight!"

"But this train is marked 'daily' in the guide."

"It was a daily train until last month."

"Well, here's a how-d'ye-do!" said the tall gentleman, slowly; "only three hours' ride from home, on the night before Christmas; and here we are, with no help for it but to stay in Chicago all Christmas day. How's that, my son?"

"It's bad luck with a vengeance," answered the lad, now thoroughly awake, and almost ready to cry. "I wish we had staid at Uncle Jack's."

"So do I," answered his father. "But there is no use in fretting. We are in for it, and we must make the best of it. Run and call that cabman who brought us over from the other station. I will send a message to your mother; and we will find a place to spend our Sunday."

This was the way it had happened: Mr. Murray had taken Mortimer with him on a short business trip to Michigan, for a visit to his cousins, and they were on their return trip; they had arrived at Chicago, Saturday evening, fully expecting to reach home during the night. The ticket-agent has explained the rest.

"Take us to the Pilgrim House," said Mr. Murray, as he shut the double door of the hansom; and they were soon jolting away over the block pavements, across the bridges, and through the gaily lighted streets. It was now only ten o'clock, and the Christmas buyers were still thronging the shops, and the streets were alive with

heavily laden pedestrians who had added their holiday purchases to the Saturday night's marketing, and were suffering from the embarrassment of riches. Soon the carriage stopped at the entrance of the hotel, and the travelers were speedily settled in a second-story front room, from the windows of which the bright pageant of the street was plainly visible.

While Mortimer Murray is watching the throngs below, we will learn a little more about him. He is a fairly good boy, as boys average; not a perfect character, but bright and capable, and reasonably industrious, with no positively mean streaks in his make-up. He will not lie; and he is never positively disobedient to his father and mother; though he sometimes does what he knows to be displeasing to them, and thinks it rather hard to be reproved for such misconduct. In short, he is somewhat self-willed, and a little too much inclined to do the things that he likes to do, no matter what pain he may give to others. The want of consideration for the wishes and feelings of others is his greatest fault. If others fail in any duty toward him, he sees it quickly and feels it keenly; if he fails in any duty toward others, he thinks it a matter of small consequence, and wonders why they are mean enough to make such a fuss about it.

This is not a very uncommon fault in a boy, I fear; and boys who, like Mortimer, are often indulged quite as much as is good for them, have great need to be on their guard against it

Before many moments Mortimer wearied of the bewildering panorama of the street, and drew a rocker up to the grate near which his father was sitting.

"Tough luck, isn't it?" were the words with which he broke silence.

"For whom, my son?"

"For you and me."

"I was thinking of your mother and of Charley and Mabel; it is their disappointment that troubles me most."

"Yes," said Mortimer, rather dubiously. In his regret at not being able to spend his Christmas day at home, he of course had thought of the pleasure of seeing his mother and his brother and sister and the baby; but any idea of their feelings in the matter had not entered his mind. Only a few hours before, in the Murrays' home, Nurse with the happy baby in her arms had said to Charley and Mabel:

"Cheer up, children, and eat your supper. Your papa and Master Mortimer will surely be here by to-morrow."

But Mortimer, so many miles away, had not heard this. Now he glanced up at his father and spoke again:

"When shall we have our Christmas?"

"On Monday, probably. We can reach home very early Monday morning. We should not have spent Sunday as a holiday if we had gone home to-night. Our Christmas dinner and our Christmas tree must have waited for Monday."

"Do you suppose that Mother will have the tree ready?"

"I have no doubt of it."

"My! I'd like to know what's on it?"

"Don't you know of anything that will be on it?"

"N—no, sir."

Mortimer's cheeks reddened at the questioning glance of his father. He had thus suddenly faced the fact that he had come up to the very eve of Christmas without making any preparation to bestow gifts upon others. He had wondered much what he should receive; he had taken no thought about what he could give. Christmas, in his calendar, was a day for receiving, not for giving. Every year his father and mother had prompted him to make some little preparation, but he had not entered into the plan very heartily; this year they had determined to say nothing to him about it, and to let him find out for himself how it seemed to be only a receiver on the day when all the world finds its chief joy in giving.

Mortimer had plenty of time to think about it, for his father saw the blush upon his face, and knew that there was no need of further words. They sat there silent before the fire for some time; and the boy's face grew more and more sober and troubled.

"What a pig I have been!" he was saying to himself. "Never thought about getting anything ready to hang on the tree! Been so busy in school all last term! But then I've had lots of time for skates and tobogganing, and all that sort of thing. Wonder why they didn't put me up to think about it! P'raps they'd say I'm big enough to think about it myself. Guess I am. I'd like to kick myself, anyhow!"

With such discomforting meditations, Mortimer peered into the glowing coals; and while he mused, the fire burned not only before his feet but within his breast as well—the fire of self-reproof that gave the baser elements in his nature a wholesome scorching. At length he found his pillow, and slept, if not the sleep of the just, at least the sleep of the healthy twelve-year-old boy, which is generally quite as good.

The next morning, Mortimer and his father rose leisurely, and after a late breakfast, walked slowly down the avenue. The air was clear and crisp, and the streets were almost as full of worshipers as they had been of shoppers the night before; the Christmas services in all the churches were calling out great congregations. The Minnesota Avenue Presbygational Church, which the travelers sought, welcomed them to a seat in the middle aisle; and Mortimer listened with great pleasure to the beautiful music of the choir and the hearty singing of the congregation, and tried to follow the minister in the reading and in the prayer, though his thoughts wandered more than once to that uncomfortable subject of which he had been thinking the night before; and he wondered whether his father and mother and the friends who knew him best did really think him a mean and selfish fellow.

When the sermon began, Mortimer fully determined to hear and remember just as much of it as he could. The text was those words of the Lord Jesus that Paul remembered and reported for us, "It is more blessed to give than to receive." And Doctor Burrows began by saying that everybody believed that, at Christmas-time; in fact, they knew it; they found it out by experience; and that was what made Christmas the happiest day of the year. Mortimer blushed again, and glanced up at his father; but there was no answering glance; his father's eyes were fixed upon the preacher. The argument of the sermon was a little too deep for Mortimer, though he understood parts of it, and tried hard to understand it all; but there was a register in the aisle near by, and the church was very warm, and he began looking down, and after awhile the voice of the preacher ceased, and he looked up to see what was the matter, and there in the pulpit was —who was it? *Could it be?* It was a very small man, with long white hair and beard, and ruddy cheeks, and sparkling eyes, and brisk motions. Yes; Mortimer had quite made up his own mind that it must be he, when a boy by his side, whom he had not noticed before, whispered:

"Santa Claus!"

This was very queer indeed. At least it seemed so at first; but when Mortimer began to reason about it, he saw at once that Santa Claus, being a saint, had a perfect right to be in the pulpit. But soon this did not seem, after all, very much like a pulpit; it had changed to a broad platform, and the rear was a white screen against the wall; and in place of a desk was a curious instrument, on a tripod, looking something like a photographer's camera and something like a stereopticon.

Santa Claus was standing by the side of this instrument, and was just beginning to speak when Mortimer looked up. This was what he heard:

"Never heard me preach before, did you? No. Talking is not my trade. But the wise man says there's a time to speak as well as a time to keep silence. I've kept my mouth shut tight for several hundred years; now I'm going to open it. But my sermon will be illustrated. See this curious machine?" and he laid his hand on the instrument by his side; "it's a wonder-box ; it will show you some queer pictures—queerest you ever saw."

"Let's see 'em!" piped out a youngster from the front seats. The congregation smiled and rustled, and Santa Claus went on:

"Wait a bit, my little man. You'll see all you want to see very soon, and maybe more. I've been in this Christmas business now for a great many years, and I've been watching the way people take their presents, and what they do with them, and what effect the giving and the taking has upon the givers and takers; and I have come to the conclusion that Christmas certainly is not a blessing to everybody. Of course it isn't. Nothing in the world is so pure and good that somebody does not pervert it. Here is father-love and mother-love, the best things outside of heaven; but some of you youngsters abuse it by becoming selfish and greedy, and learning to think that your fathers and mothers ought to do all the work and make all the sacrifices, and leave you nothing to do but to have a good time."

Just here Mortimer felt his cheeks reddening again, and he coughed a little, and opened a hymn-book, and held it up before his face to hide his blushes.

"So the fact that Christmas proves a damage to many is nothing against Christmas," Santa Claus continued; "but the fact that some people are hurt by it more than they are helped is a fact that you all ought to know. And as Christmas came this year on Sunday, it was my chance to give the world the benefit of my observations, and there couldn't be a better place to begin than Chicago, so here I am."

This last statement touched the local pride of the audience, and there was a slight movement of applause; at which the small boys in front, who had begun to grow sleepy, rubbed their eyes and pricked up their ears.

"There is one thing more," said the preacher, "that I want distinctly understood. I am not the bringer of all Christmas gifts." Here a little girl over in the corner under the gallery looked up to her mother and nodded, as if to say, "I told you so!" "No; there are plenty of presents that people say were brought by Santa Claus, with which Santa Claus had nothing at all to do. There are some givers whose presents I wouldn't touch; they would soil my fingers or burn them. There are some takers to whom I would give nothing, because they don't deserve it, and because everything that is given to them makes them a little meaner than they were before. Oh, no! You mustn't believe all you hear about Santa Claus! He doesn't do all the things that are laid to him. He isn't a fool.

"And now I'm going to show you on this screen some samples of different kinds of presents. I have pictures of them here, a funny kind of pictures as you will see. Do you know how I got the pictures? Well, I have one of those little detective cameras—did you ever see one?—that will take your portrait a great deal quicker than you can pronounce the first syllable of Jack Robinson. It is a little box with a hole in it, and a slide, that is worked with a spring, covering the hole. You point the nozzle of it at anybody or anything, and touch the spring with your thumb, and, click! you have it—the ripple of the water, the flying feet of the racer, the gesture of the talker, the puff of steam from the locomotive, the unfinished bark of the dog. I've been about with this detective, collecting my samples of presents, and now I'm going to exhibit them to you here by means of my Grand Stereoscopic Moral Tester, an instrument that brings out the good or the bad in anything, and sets it before your eyes as plain as day. You will first see on the screen the thing itself, just as it looks to ordinary eyesight; then I shall turn on my aeonian light through my ethical

lens, and you will see how the same thing looks when one knows all about it: where it came from, and why it was given, and how it was received.

"First, I shall show you one or two of those presents that I said I wouldn't touch. Here, for example, is an elegant necklace that I saw a man buying for his wife in a jewelry store yesterday; I caught it as he held it in his hands. There! isn't it a beauty? Links of solid gold, clasp set with diamonds; would you like it, girls?"

"H'm! My! Isn't it a daisy!" murmured the delighted children, as they gazed on the bright picture.

"Don't be too sure!" cried the preacher. "Things are not always what they seem. Look!"

A new light of strange brilliance now lit up the pictures, and every link of that golden chain was transformed into an iron fetter that fastened a woman's wrist,—a woman's wrist that vainly strove to release from its imprisonment a woman's hand. The chain itself was a great circle of women's hands,—wan, cramped, emaciated, pitiful hands,—each one holding a needle, each one clutching helplessly the empty air. Within this circle suddenly sprung to view a little group—a woman, bending by the dim light of a winter afternoon over a garment in her hands, and two pale children lying near her on a pallet covered with rags, while the scanty furniture of the room betokened the most bitter poverty. It was evident enough that the poor creatures were famishing; the hopeless look on the mother's face, as she plied her needle with fierce and anxious speed, glancing now and then at the sleeping children, was enough to touch the hardest heart; a low murmur of pitiful exclamation ran around the room, and there were tears in many eyes.

"She is only one of them," cried Santa Claus. "There are four hundred just like her, working for the man who bought this necklace for his wife yesterday; it is out of their life-blood that he is coining his gold. And to think that such a man should take the money that he makes in this way to buy a Christmas present. Ugh! What has such a man to do with Christmas?" And the good saint shook his fist and stamped his feet in holy wrath. Then the group faded, leaving what looked like a great blood-stain in its place; but that, in its turn, shortly disappeared, and the white screen waited for another picture.

"I have many pictures that are even more painful than this," said the preacher, "but I am not going to let you see any more of them. I only want you to know how the rewards of iniquity look in the aeonian light. There are a few more pictures, less terrible to see, but some of them will be a little unpleasant for some of you, I fear. Here is a basket of fruit; it looks very tempting, at first; but let the true light strike it. There! now you see that it is all decayed and withered. It is really as bitter and disgusting as it now looks. It was given, this morning, by a young man to a politician. The young man wants an office. That was why he made this present. A great many so-called

Christmas presents are made for some such reason. Not a particle of love goes with them. They are smeared all over with selfishness. Christmas presents! Bah! Is this the spirit of Christmas?

"But here is one of a different sort."

A pretty crimson toilet-case now appeared upon the screen.

"Elegant, is it not? Now see how it looks to those who live in the aeonian light."

The crimson plush slowly changed to what looked like rather soiled canton flannel, and the carved ivory to clumsily whittled bass-wood.

"What is the matter with this? I shall not tell you who gave it, nor to whom it was given; it is no real wrong-doing on the part of the giver that makes the gift poor; it is only because the gift represents no effort, no sacrifice, no thoughtful love. In fact, the one who gave it, got the money to buy it with from the one who received it. There are a great many Christmas presents of this sort; it isn't best to say any hard words about them; but you see that they are not, really, quite so handsome as they look. Nothing is really beautiful, for a Christmas present, that does not prove a personal affection, and a readiness to express it with painstaking labor and self-denial. Now I'm going to show you another, which will enable you to get the idea."

It was a little picture-frame of cherry wood, rather rudely carved, that now appeared upon the screen.

"The boy who made this for his mother works hard every day in school and carries the evening papers to help with the family expenses; he carved this at night, when he could gain a little time from his lessons, because he couldn't afford the money to buy anything, and because he thought his mother would be better pleased with something that he himself had made. You think it doesn't amount to much, don't you? Well, now look!"

The transfiguring light flashed upon the screen, and the little cherry frame expanded to a great and richly ornamented frame of rosewood and gold, fit to hang upon the walls of a king's palace; and there, in the space that was before vacant, surrounded by all that beautiful handiwork, was the smiling face of a handsome boy.

The people, old and young, forgot that they were in church and clapped their hands vigorously, Santa Claus himself joining in the applause and moving about the platform with great glee.

"Yes!" he cried, "that's the boy, and that's the beauty of this little frame of his; the boy is in it; he put his love into it, he put himself into it, when he made it; and when you see it as it really is, you see him in it. And that's what makes any Christmas present precious, you know; it comes from your heart and life, and it touches the heart and quickens the love of the one to whom it is given.

"I have a great number of presents of this sort that I should like to show you if I had time. Here, for instance, is a small glass inkstand that a little boy gave his father. It is one of half a dozen presents that he made; it cost only a dime or two, and you think it is not worth much; but now, when I turn the truth-telling light upon it, you see what it is—a vase of solid crystal, most wonderfully engraved with the richest designs. The boy did not make this with his own hands, but he gained every cent that it cost by patient, faithful, uncomplaining labor. He begged the privilege of earning his Christmas money in this way, and right honestly he earned it; leaving his play, whenever he was summoned for any service, without a word of grumbling, and taking upon himself many little labors and cares that would have burdened his father and mother. When he took his money and went out to spend it the day before Christmas, he was happy and proud, because he could fairly call it his own money; and the presents that he bought with it represented him.

"And now there is only one thing more that I shall show you, but that is a kind of thing that is common, only too common, I'm afraid. It is a present that was all beautiful and good enough till it left the hands of the giver, but was spoiled by the receiver. Here it is."

A silver cup, beautifully chased and lined with gold, now came into view.

"A boy whom I know found this in his stocking this morning. He was up bright and early; he pulled the presents out of his stocking rather greedily; he wanted to see whether they had bought for him the things he had been wishing for and hinting about. Some of them were there and some were not; he was almost inclined to scold, but concluded that he might better hold his tongue. But this boy had made no presents at all. He is one of the sort that takes all he can get, but never gives anything. This is what Christmas means to him. It is a time for getting, not for giving. And I want you to see how this dainty cup looked, as soon as it got into his greedy hands."

Again the revealing light fell upon the cup and its beauty and shapeliness disappeared, and it was nothing but a common pewter mug, all tarnished and marred, and bent out of form.

"There!" cried the preacher; "that is the kind of thing that is most hateful to me. It hurts me to see lovely things fall into the hands of selfish people, for such people can see no real loveliness in them. It is love that makes all things lovely; and he who has no love in his own heart can discern no love in anything that comes into his hands. What does Christmas mean to such a one? What good does it do him? It does him no good; it does him harm, every time. Every gift that he gets makes him a little greedier than he was before. That is the way it works with a certain kind of Sunday-school children. They come in, every year, just before Christmas, only because they hope to get something; they take what they can get, and grumble because it isn't more, and go away, and that's the last of them till Christmas comes around again. That's what they think of Christmas. They think it is a pig's feast. Precious little they know about it. I know them, thousands of them! But they never get anything from me,—never! They think they do, but that's a mistake! I don't like to see my pretty things marred and spoiled like this cup. I'm not going to give to those who are made worse by receiving.

"No! I can do better. I can find people enough to whom it is worthwhile to give Christmas gifts because there is love in their hearts; and the gift of love awakens more love. Those who know the joy of giving are made better by receiving. And there are hosts of them, too, millions of them; tens of millions, I believe; more this Christmas than ever before since the Babe was born in Bethlehem; people whose pleasure it is to give pleasure to others; good-willers, cheerful workers, loving helpers, generous hearts, who have learned and remembered the words of the Lord Jesus, how he said, 'It is more blessed to give than to receive.'"

Through all this part of Santa Claus's sermon Mortimer had known that his face was growing redder and redder; he was sure that the eyes of all the people in the church were being fixed on him; he felt that he could not endure it another moment, and he caught up his hat and was going to rush out of the building, when suddenly the voice was silent, and he looked up to see what it meant—and Santa Claus was not there; it was Dr. Burrows again, and he was just closing the Bible and taking up the hymn-book. Mortimer glanced about him and drew a long breath of relief.

As they walked back to the hotel, Mr. Murray asked Mortimer how he liked the sermon.

"Which sermon?" asked Mortimer.

"Why, Dr. Burrows's sermon, of course."

"Oh, yes; I forgot. It was a good sermon, wasn't it?"

"Excellent. What was the text?"

"'It is more blessed to give than to receive.' Wasn't that the way he ended up?" asked Mortimer, brightening.

"It was."

"I thought so."

"Thought so; didn't you hear it?"

"Yes, I heard that. But—I was hearing — something else about that time, and I wasn't sure."

"What else did you hear?"

"Lots. P'raps I'll tell you some time," replied the lad.

Mr. Murray did not press the question, and Mortimer was silent. All that day and the next Mortimer seemed to have much serious thinking to do; he was a little reluctant to take his Christmas presents, and he received them at last with a tender gratitude that he had never shown before.

"It must have been Dr. Burrows's sermon," said Mr. Murray to his wife as they were talking it over the next night. "I didn't think Mortimer could get much out of it; in fact I thought he was asleep part of the time, but it seems to have taken hold of him in the right way. It was a good sermon and a practical one. I'm going to ask our minister to exchange some time with Dr. Burrows."

"I wish he would," said Mrs. Murray.

That was the way Mr. and Mrs. Murray looked at it. But I think that if they had asked Mortimer, Mortimer could have told them that it would be a much better idea to suggest to their minister that he exchange some time with the Reverend Doctor Santa Claus.

"Snap-shots by Santa Claus", *St Nicholas Magazine* (JANUARY 1894)

"I don't see," said Santa Claus, as he took a last look around before going out to climb into the waiting sleigh, "why I shouldn't take my camera with me!" So he picked it up and deposited it on the seat by his side.

Swish!—and away they went, but not so fast as usual, since 'Dunder' and 'Blitzen' were lame, and 'Prancer ' was not well. You know what the genial old gentleman did in the present-giving way, and I mean to tell you only about a few of the pictures he took. He spoiled a good many, for they were all taken by flash-light and in a hurry. But he got one good view of a village church near which lived a favorite little boy and his two sisters; and also a picture of their stockings hanging from the holly-covered mantel.

At another house one little girl woke up when Santa Claus was taking her picture; but she thought next morning it was only a dream, so Santa Claus didn't mind having been seen.

A picture of some snowy chimneys, showing his path to and from the flue, and of the tired reindeer team, also proved successful; but a very timid little girl, and a cross black cat who snarled at Santa Claus, were frightened by the flash-light, and so spoiled their pictures.

Santa Claus took plenty of other pictures, but he doesn't care to show any but these. He says it is fun to take pictures on Christmas eve.

Julie M. Lippman, "A New-Fashioned Christmas", *St. Nicholas Magazine* (JANUARY 1890)

We had been busy talking, for hours, Christmas Eve,
Of all the great improvements until—will you believe?—
I felt quite dull and drowsy, and said, 'twixt yawn and sigh,
"Oh! anything old-fashioned had best pass out and die!"

And then I leaned back smiling and quite self-satisfied,
And closed my eyelids slowly, when, lo! they opened wide
In sheer amaze and wonder, and would you know the cause?
I saw before me standing, the form of Santa Claus.

But, oh! so strange and altered! In clothes of latest style,
And not at all the Santa I'd dreamed of all the while.
But still I recognized him, and said: "I didn't see
You come out from the chimney,—'twas very dull of me."

"The chimney?" said he gruffly, "I beg of you to know
I clamber down no chimneys; I stopped that long ago!"
I said, "Your load was heavy, you're tired; won't you rest?"
"Oh, no," he answered grandly," my goods were all expressed!"

"You must have found it pleasant—the sleighing, sir, I mean.
The roofs are much more snowy than I have ever seen."
"Indeed!"—his air was lofty— "'tis not the present mode
To drive a sleigh. I travel by the elevated road."

'Twas all so strange it chilled me, but still I said, "Now, please,
You won't forget to send us one of your Christmas trees.
The children love you dearly and try to be so good."
He said: "No trees hereafter, I'd have it understood.

"In fact, the time is over for Christmas. I should say
Those very old-time customs have really passed away.
We want the very latest, dear madam, you and I,
And peace, good-will, and Christmas are of a time gone by."

And then he seemed preparing to take his leave and go.
But do you think I let him? I called out bravely, "No!"
I ran to him and begged him, between my sobs and tears,
To leave us blessed Christmas, just as in former years.

To change no little custom; to take no part away;
To leave us dear old-fashioned, beloved Christmas Day.
And then, for just an instant, my eyes were very dim
With tears, and when I cleared them, I saw a change in him:

His face, 'twas round and jolly, his clothes, were as of old,
He had a pack upon his back as full as it could hold.
And as he beamed upon me I heard his reindeer prance.
Then sly old Santa gave me a smile and roguish glance.

"I wish you Merry Christmas!" I thought I heard him say.
And when I tried to answer him, he'd vanished quite away!
But though they say I dreamed it, I know we shall have still
Our dear old-fashioned Christmas, bringing "Peace on earth, good-will!"

9.

Literary Luminaries, Literary Oddities

Frances Hodgson Burnett, "Behind the White Brick", *St. Nicholas* (JANUARY 1879)

It began with Aunt Hetty's being out of temper, which, it must be confessed, was nothing new. At its best, Aunt Hetty's temper was none of the most charming, and this morning it was at its worst. She had awakened to the consciousness of having a hard day's work before her, and she had awakened late, and so everything had gone wrong from the first. There was a sharp ring in her voice when she came to Jem's bedroom door and called out, "Jemima, get up this minute!"

Jem knew what to expect when Aunt Hetty began a day by calling her "Jemima." It was one of the poor child's grievances that she had been given such an ugly name. In all the books she had read, and she had read a great many, Jem never had met a heroine who was called Jemima. But it had been her mother's favorite sister's name, and so it had fallen to her lot. Her mother always called her "Jem," or "Mimi," which was much prettier, and even Aunt Hetty only reserved Jemima for unpleasant state occasions.

It was a dreadful day to Jem. Her mother was not at home, and would not be until night. She had been called away unexpectedly, and had been obliged to leave Jem and the baby to Aunt Hetty's mercies. So Jem found herself busy enough. Scarcely had she finished doing one thing, when Aunt Hetty told her to begin another. She wiped dishes and picked fruit and attended to the baby; and when baby had gone to sleep, and everything else seemed disposed of, for a time, at least, she was so tired that she was glad to sit down.

And then she thought of the book she had been reading the night before—a certain delightful story book, about a little girl whose name was Flora, and who was so happy and rich and pretty and good that Jem had likened her to the little princesses one reads about, to whose christening feast every fairy brings a gift.

"I shall have time to finish my chapter before dinner-time comes," said Jem, and she sat down snugly in one corner of the wide, old fashioned fireplace.

But she had not read more than two pages before something dreadful happened. Aunt Hetty came into the room in a great hurry—in such a hurry, indeed, that she caught her foot in the matting and fell, striking her elbow sharply against a chair, which so upset her temper that the moment she found herself on her feet she flew at Jem.

"What!" she said, snatching the book from her, "reading again, when I am running all over the house for you?" And she flung the pretty little blue covered volume into the fire.

Jem sprang to rescue it with a cry, but it was impossible to reach it; it had fallen into a great hollow of red coal, and the blaze caught it at once.

"You are a wicked woman!" cried Jem, in a dreadful passion, to Aunt Hetty. "You are a wicked woman."

Then matters reached a climax. Aunt Hetty boxed her ears, pushed her back on her little footstool, and walked out of the room.

Jem hid her face on her arms and cried as if her heart would break. She cried until her eyes were heavy, and she thought she would be obliged to go to sleep. But just as she was thinking of going to sleep, something fell down the chimney and made her look up. It was a piece of mortar, and it brought a good deal of soot with it. She bent forward and looked up to see where it had come from. The chimney was so very wide that this was easy enough. She could see where the mortar had fallen from the side and left a white patch.

"How white it looks against the black!" said Jem; "it is like a white brick among the black ones. What a queer place a chimney is! I can see a bit of the blue sky, I think."

And then a funny thought came into her fanciful little head. What a many things were burned in the big fireplace and vanished in smoke or tinder up the chimney! Where did everything go? There was Flora, for instance—Flora who was represented on the frontispiece—with lovely, soft, flowing hair, and a little fringe on her pretty round forehead, crowned with a circlet of daisies, and a laugh in her wide-awake round eyes. Where was she by this time? Certainly there was nothing left of her in the fire. Jem almost began to cry again at the thought.

"It was too bad," she said. "She was so pretty and funny, and I did like her so."

I daresay it scarcely will be credited by unbelieving people when I tell them what happened next, it was such a very singular thing, indeed.

Jem felt herself gradually lifted off her little footstool.

"Oh!" she said, timidly, "I feel very light." She did feel light, indeed.

She felt so light that she was sure she was rising gently in the air.

"Oh!" she said again, "How—how very light I feel! Oh, dear, I'm going up the chimney!"

It was rather strange that she never thought of calling for help, but she did not. She was not easily frightened; and now she was only wonderfully astonished, as she remembered afterwards. She shut her eyes tight and gave a little gasp.

"I've heard Aunt Hetty talk about the draught drawing things up the chimney, but I never knew it was as strong as this," she said.

She went up, up, up, quietly and steadily, and without any uncomfortable feeling at all; and then all at once she stopped, feeling that her feet rested against something solid. She opened her eyes and looked about her, and there she was, standing right opposite the white brick, her feet on a tiny ledge.

"Well," she said, "this is funny."

But the next thing that happened was funnier still. She found that, without thinking what she was doing, she was knocking on the white brick with her knuckles, as if it was a door and she expected somebody to open it. The next minute she heard footsteps, and then a sound, as if some one was drawing back a little bolt.

"It is a door," said Jem, "and somebody is going to open it."

The white brick moved a little, and some more mortar and soot fell; then the brick moved a little more, and then it slid aside and left an open space.

"It's a room!" cried Jem, "There's a room behind it!"

And so there was, and before the open space stood a pretty little girl, with long lovely hair and a fringe on her forehead. Jem clasped her hands in amazement. It was Flora herself, as she looked in the picture, and Flora stood laughing and nodding.

"Come in," she said. "I thought it was you."

"But how can I come in through such a little place?" asked Jem.

"Oh, that is easy enough," said Flora. "Here, give me your hand."

Jem did as she told her, and found that it was easy enough. In an instant she had passed through the opening, the white brick had gone back to its place, and she was standing by Flora's side in a large room—the nicest room she had ever seen. It was big and lofty and light, and there were all kinds of delightful things in it—books and flowers and playthings and pictures, and in one corner a great cage full of love-birds.

"Have I ever seen it before?" asked Jem, glancing slowly round.

"Yes," said Flora; "you saw it last night—in your mind. Don't you remember it?"

Jem shook her head.

"I feel as if I did, but—"

"Why," said Flora, laughing, "it's my room, the one you read about last night."

"So it is," said Jem. "But how did you come here?"

"I can't tell you that; I myself don't know. But I am here, and so," rather mysteriously, "are a great many other things."

"Are they?" said Jem, very much interested. "What things? Burned things? I was just wondering—"

"Not only burned things," said Flora, nodding. "Just come with me and I'll show you something."

She led the way out of the room and down a little passage with several doors in each side of it, and she opened one door and showed Jem what was on the other side of it. That was a room, too, and this time it was funny as well as pretty. Both floor and walls were padded with rose color, and the floor was strewn with toys. There were big soft balls, rattles, horses, woolly dogs, and a doll or so; there was one low cushioned chair and a low table.

"You can come in," said a shrill little voice behind the door, "only mind you don't tread on things."

"What a funny little voice!" said Jem, but she had no sooner said it than she jumped back.

The owner of the voice, who had just come forward, was no other than Baby.

"Why," exclaimed Jem, beginning to feel frightened, "I left you fast asleep in your crib."

"Did you?" said Baby, somewhat scornfully. "That's just the way with you grown-up people. You think you know everything, and yet you haven't discretion enough to know when a pin is sticking into one. You'd know soon enough if you had one sticking into your own back."

"But I'm not grown up," stammered Jem; "and when you are at home you can neither walk nor talk. You're not six months old!"

"Well, miss," retorted Baby, whose wrongs seemed to have soured her disposition somewhat, "you have no need to throw that in my teeth; you were not six months old, either, when you were my age."

Jem could not help laughing.

"You haven't got any teeth," she said.

"Haven't I?" said Baby, and she displayed two beautiful rows with some haughtiness of manner. "When I am up here," she said, "I am supplied with the modern conveniences, and that's why I never complain. Do I ever cry when I am asleep? It's not falling asleep I object to, it's falling awake."

"Wait a minute," said Jem. "Are you asleep now?"

"I'm what you call asleep. I can only come here when I'm what you call asleep. Asleep, indeed! It's no wonder we always cry when we have to fall awake."

"But we don't mean to be unkind to you," protested Jem, meekly.

She could not help thinking Baby was very severe.

"Don't mean!" said Baby. "Well, why don't you think more, then? How would you like to have all the nice things snatched away from you, and all the old rubbish packed off on you, as if you hadn't any sense? How would you like to have to sit and stare at things you wanted, and not be able to reach them, or, if you did reach them, have them fall out of your hand, and roll away in the most unfeeling manner? And then be scolded and called 'cross!' It's no wonder we are bald. You'd be bald yourself. It's trouble and worry that keep us bald until we can begin to take care of ourselves; I had more hair than this at first, but it fell off, as well it might. No philosopher ever thought of that, I suppose!"

"Well," said Jem, in despair, "I hope you enjoy yourself when you are here?"

"Yes, I do," answered Baby. "That's one comfort. There is nothing to knock my head against, and things have patent stoppers on them, so that they can't roll away, and everything is soft and easy to pick up."

There was a slight pause after this, and Baby seemed to cool down.

"I suppose you would like me to show you round?" she said.

"Not if you have any objection," replied Jem, who was rather subdued.

"I would as soon do it as not," said Baby. "You are not as bad as some people, though you do get my clothes twisted when you hold me."

Upon the whole, she seemed rather proud of her position. It was evident she quite regarded herself as hostess. She held her small bald head very high indeed, as she trotted on before them. She stopped at the first door she came to, and knocked three times. She was obliged to stand upon tiptoe to reach the knocker.

"He's sure to be at home at this time of year," she remarked. "This is the busy season."

"Who's 'he'?" inquired Jem.

But Flora only laughed at Miss Baby's consequential air.

"S.C., to be sure," was the answer, as the young lady pointed to the door-plate, upon which Jem noticed, for the first time, "S.C." in very large letters.

The door opened, apparently without assistance, and they entered the apartment.

"Good gracious!" exclaimed Jem, the next minute. "Goodness gracious!"

She might well be astonished. It was such a long room that she could not see to the end of it, and it was piled up from floor to ceiling with toys of every description, and there was such bustle and buzzing in it that it was quite confusing. The bustle and buzzing arose from a very curious cause, too,—it was the bustle and buzz of hundreds of tiny men and women who were working at little tables no higher than mushrooms,—the pretty tiny women cutting out and sewing, the pretty tiny men sawing and hammering and all talking at once. The principal person in the place escaped Jem's notice at first; but it was not long before she saw him,—a little old gentleman, with a rosy face and sparkling eyes, sitting at a desk, and writing in a book almost as big as himself. He was so busy that he was quite excited, and had been obliged to throw his white fur coat and cap aside, and he was at work in his red waistcoat.

"Look here, if you please," piped Baby, "I have brought some one to see you."

When he turned round, Jem recognized him at once.

"Eh! Eh!" he said. "What! What! Who's this, Tootsicums?"

Baby's manner became very acid indeed.

"I shouldn't have thought you would have said that, Mr. Claus," she remarked. "I can't help myself down below, but I generally have my rights respected up here. I should like to know what sane godfather or godmother would give one the name of 'Tootsicums' in one's baptism. They are bad enough, I must say; but I never heard of any of them calling a person 'Tootsicums.'"

"Come, come!" said S.C., chuckling comfortably and rubbing his hands. "Don't be too dignified,—it's a bad thing. And don't be too practical and fond of taking unpractical people down,—that's a bad thing, too. And don't be too fond of flourishing your rights in people's faces,—that's the worst of all, Miss Midget. Folks who make such a fuss about their rights turn them into wrongs sometimes."

Then he turned suddenly to Jem.

"You are the little girl from down below," he said.

"Yes, sir," answered Jem. "I'm Jem, and this is my friend Flora,—out of the blue book."

"I'm happy to make her acquaintance," said S.C., "and I'm happy to make yours. You are a nice child, though a trifle peppery. I'm very glad to see you."

"I'm very glad indeed to see you, sir," said

Jem. "I wasn't quite sure—"

But there she stopped, feeling that it would be scarcely polite to tell him that she had begun of late years to lose faith in him.

But S.C. only chuckled more comfortably than ever and rubbed his hands again.

"Ho, ho!" he said. "You know who I am, then?"

Jem hesitated a moment, wondering whether it would not be taking a liberty to mention his name without putting "Mr." before it: then she remembered what Baby had called him.

"Baby called you 'Mr. Claus,' sir," she replied; "and I have seen pictures of you."

"To be sure," said S.C. "S. Claus, Esquire, of Chimneyland. How do you like me?"

"Very much," answered Jem; "very much, indeed, sir."

"Glad of it! Glad of it! But what was it you were going to say you were not quite sure of?"

Jem blushed a little.

"I was not quite sure that—that you were true, sir. At least I have not been quite sure since I have been older."

S.C. rubbed the bald part of his head and gave a little sigh.

"I hope I have not hurt your feelings, sir," faltered Jem, who was a very kind hearted little soul.

"Well, no," said S.C. "Not exactly. And it is not your fault either. It is natural, I suppose; at any rate, it is the way of the world. People lose their belief in a great many things as they grow older; but that does not make the things not true, thank goodness! and their faith often comes back after a while. But, bless me!" he added, briskly, "I'm moralizing, and who thanks a man for doing that? Suppose—"

"Black eyes or blue, sir?" said a tiny voice close to them.

Jem and Flora turned round, and saw it was one of the small workers who was asking the question.

"Whom for?" inquired S.C.

"Little girl in the red brick house at the corner," said the workwoman; "name of Birdie."

"Excuse me a moment," said S.C. to the children, and he turned to the big book and began to run his fingers down the pages in a business-like manner. "Ah! here she is!" he exclaimed at last. "Blue eyes, if you please, Thistle, and golden hair. And let it be a big one. She takes good care of them."

"Yes, sir," said Thistle; "I am personally acquainted with several dolls in her family. I go to parties in her dolls' house sometimes when she is fast asleep at night, and they all speak very highly of her. She is most attentive to them when they are ill. In fact, her pet doll is a cripple, with a stiff leg."

She ran back to her work and S.C. finished his sentence.

"Suppose I show you my establishment," he said. "Come with me."

It really would be quite impossible to describe the wonderful things he showed them. Jem's head was quite in a whirl before she had seen one-half of them, and even Baby condescended to become excited.

"There must be a great many children in the world, Mr. Claus," ventured Jem.

"Yes, yes, millions of 'em; bless 'em," said S.C., growing rosier with delight at the very thought. "We never run out of them, that's one comfort. There's a large and varied assortment always on hand. Fresh ones every year, too, so that when one grows too old there is a new one ready. I have a place like this in every twelfth chimney. Now it's boys, now it's girls, always one or t'other; and there's no end of playthings for them, too, I'm glad to say. For girls, the great thing seems to be dolls. Blitzen! what comfort they do take in dolls! but the boys are for horses and racket."

They were standing near a table where a worker was just putting the finishing touch to the dress of a large wax doll, and just at that moment, to Jem's surprise, she set it on the floor, upon its feet, quite coolly.

"Thank you," said the doll, politely.

Jem quite jumped.

"You can join the rest now and introduce yourself," said the worker.

The doll looked over her shoulder at her train.

"It hangs very nicely," she said. "I hope it's the latest fashion."

"Mine never talked like that," said Flora. "My best one could only say 'Mamma,' and it said it very badly, too."

"She was foolish for saying it at all," remarked the doll, haughtily. "We don't talk and walk before ordinary people; we keep our accomplishments for our own amusement, and for the amusement of our friends. If you should chance to get up in the middle of the night, some time, or should run into the room suddenly some day, after you have left it, you might hear—but what is the use of talking to human beings?"

"You know a great deal, considering you are only just finished," snapped Baby, who really was a Tartar.

"I was FINISHED," retorted the doll "I did not begin life as a baby!" very scornfully.

"Pooh!" said Baby. "We improve as we get older."

"I hope so, indeed," answered the doll. "There is plenty of room for improvement." And she walked away in great state.

S.C. looked at Baby and then shook his head. "I shall not have to take very much care of you," he said, absent-mindedly. "You are able to take pretty good care of yourself."

"I hope I am," said Baby, tossing her head.

S.C. gave his head another shake.

"Don't take too good care of yourself," he said. "That's a bad thing, too."

He showed them the rest of his wonders, and then went with them to the door to bid them good-bye.

"I am sure we are very much obliged to you, Mr. Claus," said Jem, gratefully. "I shall never again think you are not true, sir".

S.C. patted her shoulder quite affectionately.

"That's right," he said. "Believe in things just as long as you can, my dear. Good-bye until Christmas Eve. I shall see you then, if you don't see me."

He must have taken quite a fancy to Jem, for he stood looking at her, and seemed very reluctant to close the door, and even after he had closed it, and they had turned away, he opened it a little again to call to her.

"Believe in things as long as you can, my dear."

"How kind he is!" exclaimed Jem full of pleasure.

Baby shrugged her shoulders.

"Well enough in his way," she said, "but rather inclined to prose, and be old-fashioned."

Jem looked at her, feeling rather frightened, but she said nothing.

Baby showed very little interest in the next room she took them to.

"I don't care about this place," she said, as she threw open the door. "It has nothing but old things in it. It is the Nobody-knows-where room."

She had scarcely finished speaking before Jem made a little spring and picked something up.

"Here's my old strawberry pincushion!" she cried out. And then, with another jump and another dash at two or three other things, "And here's my old fairy-book! And here's my little locket I lost last summer! How did they come here?"

"They went Nobody-knows-where," said Baby.

"And this is it."

"But cannot I have them again?" asked Jem.

"No," answered Baby. "Things that go to Nobody-knows-where stay there."

"Oh!" sighed Jem, "I am so sorry."

"They are only old things," said Baby.

"But I like my old things," said Jem. "I love them. And there is mother's needle case. I wish I might take that. Her dead little sister gave it to her, and she was so sorry when she lost it."

"People ought to take better care of their things," remarked Baby.

Jem would have liked to stay in this room and wander about among her old favorites for a long time, but Baby was in a hurry.

"You'd better come away," she said. "Suppose I was to have to fall awake and leave you?"

The next place they went into was the most wonderful of all.

"This is the Wish room," said Baby. "Your wishes come here—yours and mother's, and Aunt Hetty's and father's and mine. When did you wish that?"

Each article was placed under a glass shade, and labelled with the words and name of the wishers. Some of them were beautiful, indeed; but the tall shade Baby nodded at when she asked her question was truly alarming, and caused Jem a dreadful pang of remorse. Underneath it sat Aunt Hetty, with her mouth stitched up so that she could not speak a word, and beneath the stand was a label bearing these words, in large black letters:

"I wish Aunt Hetty's mouth was sewed up, Jem."

"Oh, dear!" cried Jem, in great distress. "How it must have hurt her! How unkind of me to say it! I wish I hadn't wished it. I wish it would come undone."

She had no sooner said it than her wish was gratified. The old label disappeared and a new one showed itself, and there sat Aunt Hetty, looking herself again, and even smiling.

Jem was grateful beyond measure, but Baby seemed to consider her weak minded.

"It served her right," she said.

"But when, after looking at the wishes at that end of the room, they went to the other end, her turn came. In one corner stood a shade with a baby under it, and the baby was Miss Baby herself, but looking as she very rarely looked; in fact, it was the brightest, best tempered baby one could imagine."

"I wish I had a better tempered baby. Mother," was written on the label.

Baby became quite red in the face with anger and confusion.

"That wasn't here the last time I came," she said. "And it is right down mean in mother!"

This was more than Jem could bear.

"It wasn't mean," she said. "She couldn't help it. You know you are a cross baby—everybody says so."

Baby turned two shades redder.

"Mind your own business," she retorted. "It was mean; and as to that silly little thing being better than I am," turning up her small nose, which was quite turned up enough by Nature—"I must say I don't see anything so very grand about her. So, there!"

She scarcely condescended to speak to them while they remained in the Wish room, and when they left it, and went to the last door in the passage, she quite scowled at it.

"I don't know whether I shall open it at all," she said.

"Why not?" asked Flora. "You might as well."

"It is the Lost pin room," she said. "I hate pins."

She threw the door open with a bang, and then stood and shook her little fist viciously. The room was full of pins, stacked solidly together. There were hundreds of them—thousands—millions, it seemed.

"I'm glad they are lost!" she said. "I wish there were more of them there."

"I didn't know there were so many pins in the world," said Jem.

"Pooh!" said Baby. "Those are only the lost ones that have belonged to our family."

After this they went back to Flora's room and sat down, while Flora told Jem the rest of her story.

"Oh!" sighed Jem, when she came to the end. "How delightful it is to be here! Can I never come again?"

"In one way you can," said Flora. "When you want to come, just sit down and be as quiet as possible, and shut your eyes and think very hard about it. You can see everything you have seen to-day, if you try."

"Then I shall be sure to try," Jem answered. She was going to ask some other question, but Baby stopped her.

"Oh! I'm falling awake," she whimpered, crossly, rubbing her eyes. "I'm falling awake again."

And then, suddenly, a very strange feeling came over Jem. Flora and the pretty room seemed to fade away, and, without being able to account for it at all, she found herself sitting on her little stool again, with a beautiful scarlet and gold book on her knee, and her mother standing by laughing at her amazed face. As to Miss Baby, she was crying as hard as she could in her crib.

"Mother!" Jem cried out, "have you really come home so early as this, and—and," rubbing her eyes in great amazement, "how did I come down?"

"Don't I look as if I was real?" said her mother, laughing and kissing her. "And doesn't your present look real? I don't know how you came down, I'm sure. Where have you been?"

Jem shook her head very mysteriously. She saw that her mother fancied she had been asleep, but she herself knew better.

"I know you wouldn't believe it was true if I told you," she said; "I have been BEHIND THE WHITE BRICK."

Mary E. Wilkins Freeman, "Santa's Narrow Escape", a composite of its appearances in *The Sunday News* (DETROIT), DECEMBER 25 1892; *The Cleveland Leader,* DECEMBER 25 1892; *The Courier-Journal* (LOUISVILLE), DECEMBER 25 1892; *The Inter-Ocean* (CHICAGO), DECEMBER 25 1892.

Nanny Chrysanthemum lived in a reformed city. Some five years before the time of this story a great reformer had come of age there and directly revolutionized everything.

The day after he was twenty-one and qualified to have a voice in public affairs, a city council had been called for the purpose of changing persons' last names. The Reformer argued that, whereas, in the first place, back in the dark ages people were named from their own occupations and peculiarities and those of their fathers, and the names were quite appropriate, now they were no longer so, and should be changed. The Reformer was a realist, and believed in having everything as real as possible. "Why," said he, "should a man be called Taylor when there has not been a tailor in his family for ten generations? It is not true and real, and the secret of a perfect city government is truth and reality."

The Mayor and the aldermen had a four days' sitting, for it was a serious matter and took time to decide. The Reformer harangued them from morning until night, and they voted over and over until they got a unanimous yea. They thought it better to sit until they were unanimous, and after that all the citizens carried out the same plan when voting for the city officers. It took a longer time, but they always ended by being unanimous. The council decided to change the name of everybody in the city whose name had not been directly appropriate for five generations. The decision was immediately carried into effect, and made a great commotion, for nearly everybody's name had to be changed.

Generally speaking, the Johnsons were discovered not to have had a John in the family for over five generations, so that it was misleading and untruthful for them to be called the sons of John, and it was the same with the Thomsons and the Williamsons. Then nearly all the names were found utterly unsuited to the occupations of their owners. The Leaches were smiths or bakers, and anything but the doctors from whom the name was derived, and so with the Smiths and the Bakers.

The edict involved a great and arduous searching of family records and old archives. The city clerk had to call in many assistants, who were so covered with dust when they went home at night that their own families did not know them, and they sneezed constantly.

When the researches were finished everyone had to register his new name, and a new directory was published. All the old ones were burnt in the public square one night. All the brass bands in the city played, there was a torchlight procession, headed by the Mayor and the Reformer walking hand in hand, and a general rejoicing.

The Mayor's and the Reformer's names were changed with the rest. The Mayor's name had been King, but no record of a King in the family could be found. There were more barbers than anything else, therefore the Mayor's name was changed to Barber. The Reformer, whose name had been Lord, was now called Tubbs, because there was no lord mentioned in the records, but a great many makers of tubs. Their changes were not very pleasing, naturally, but as the Reformer told the Mayor, they were truly realistic, and therefore they said not a word against them.

However, some people fared better by the exchange of names; now and then a person who had been known by an ignoble and common name got a very pretty one. Nanny Chrysanthemum was one who had been benefited. Her name and her father's name had been Smith, and the records showed not a Smith in the family. Indeed, they could not find records of more than two generations, for Nanny's family had not lived longer than that in the city.

Therefore, since Nanny's father was a florist and a very successful raiser of chrysanthemums, it was decided to name him Chrysanthemum instead of Smith. And as hot-houses, filled with his especial flower, took up nearly all one side of the alley in which he lived, it was also decided to name that Chrysanthemum alley. It had been called Briggs alley after some dead and forgotten person by the name of Briggs, who was not mentioned in any of the records.

There was only one other house in the alley, and there lived another girl just about Nanny Chrysanthemum's age. Her name was Betsey Thread and Needles. Her father kept a thread and needle shop, and had had his name changed from Montgomery, in which there had been nothing appropriate.

Nanny and Betsey could just remember when their names and all the others were changed. They could remember how the postman mixed the letters, and how funny the merchants looked running through the streets with their signs. The signs had to be changed with the names, of course, and all the Thomsons had to trade signs with the Johnsons, and so on. Nanny had privately thought that her own new name was much prettier than Betsey's, but she did not tell her so, for she was a considerate girl. She and Betsey played together every day and were better friends than ever as time passed, and the Reformer went on reforming the city. In the course of five years it was nearly reformed, the Reformer was such an indefatigable worker. The inappropriate names were all changed for appropriate ones, the little girls no longer played make-believe with dolls, and there were no fairy tales published. Everything that was not realistic and where truth could not be demonstrated was prohibited.

The Reformer was very successful in all his enterprises except one. For five years the Reformer has been trying to banish Santa Claus, or rather the idea of Santa Claus. He did not believe there was any real Santa Claus. There had been a strict edict issued that all the mothers of families, and all merchants should bring to the public square on Christmas day all mementoes of Santa Claus, all poems and stories concerning him, all Christmas cards with his likeness thereon, and anything that could serve to remind the children of him. Then there was a great bonfire made and a torchlight procession, headed by the Mayor arm in arm with the Reformer, and all the brass bands in the city played.

Every new Christmas day the edict was reissued, and at last the houses were searched, yet still Santa Claus was not quite banished. The most stringent measures were adopted and one little boy was sent to reform school because he had hidden his little cotton pocket handkerchief with a picture of Santa Claus on it, but it was all to no purpose. Santa Claus was still loved and warmly received in many homes.

On the fifth Christmas the Reformer was quite desperate. He decided that something must be done, and he and the Mayor sat in council over a week, only stopping for meals and sleep. They finally resolved to send out large forces of mounted police, headed by the Reformer, to search all the houses in the city for Santa Claus.

Now Nanny Chrysanthemum had always been very fond of Santa Claus. When the edict was issued she had obediently carried a beautiful Christmas card with a picture of Santa Claus on it and her poem, beginning, "'Twas the night before Christmas," to the public square to be burned, but she had wept when she got home. However, her father, who inwardly sympathized with her, although he dared not say much, went out and bought a pound of candy for her, and that comforted her. And too, she reflected that she had learned the poem by heart, so it was not so much of a loss.

She used to repeat it often to herself, and in five years she had not forgotten one word of it. On the eve of the fifth Christmas she said it over to Betsey Thread and Needles. Nanny's father had been obliged to go away on business and could not be home that night, and that left her all alone, because she had no mother. Her mother had died when she was very small. So Betsey Thread and Needles had come over to stay all night with her.

She and Betsey had locked all the doors and windows very carefully, and now, although it was quite late, they had not gone to bed, but sat before the fire.

The kitchen door was open, and it led directly into the hot-house. They could see a long lane of blooming plants which were mostly chrysanthemums. It was late, generally speaking, for chrysanthemums, but Nanny's father had discovered a secret which enabled him to preserve them in bloom an unusually long time.

It was as if the two girls sat in a little forest of the most brilliant flowers, which gave out a sweet, pungent smell. Betsey Thread and Needles looked frightened when Nanny repeated the Christmas poem about Santa Claus.

"Oh, I wouldn't," said she, looking uneasily at the locked windows on which the frost shone thick and white.

"Why not?" said Nanny.

"Because the mounted police are out, and I am afraid they will hear you."

"They can't," said Nanny, "the windows are shut tight."

"Besides, I don't believe my mother would like it," said Betsey Thread and Needles, whose mother stood very much in awe of the Reformer.

The clock struck twelve and still the girls had not gone to bed. It seemed very lonesome and cold to creep off upstairs to an icy bed in a fireless chamber. It was much more cheerful where they were, so they sat close to the hearth and played checkers.

But about five minutes after the clock struck twelve both Betsey and Nanny jumped so violently that the checker board tipped and all the men and kings rolled off on the floor.

"What's that?" gasped Betsey.

"I don't know," Nanny gasped back, and they looked at each other while their rosy faces grew pale.

They could hear quite plainly a strange, sweet jingle of bells playing a tune like a Christmas chime, and it seemed to be overhead and coming nearer and nearer. Presently they could hear a merry voice shouting, "Ho dancer, ho Prancer."

"It is Santa Claus," said Nanny.

Betsey Thread and Needles jumped up and ran to the door, which she unbolted with trembling fingers. "I am going home," she sobbed.

"Oh don't, he won't hurt us," pleaded Nanny. But Betsey threw open the door and flew out. "The mounted police will come and my mother won't like it," she called back. Nanny shut the door after her and bolted it. Then she stood in front of the chimney and waited, for she knew Santa Claus would come that way. Nanny was a pretty girl, with two long, golden braids hanging over her shoulders, and she wore a gown just the colour of a yellow chrysanthemum. It was cut low in the neck and she had a string of gold beads.

Nanny stood looking up the chimney, and the shouting, "Ho, Prancer; ho Dancer," and the chiming bells, and the stamping boots, sounded louder overhead.

The fire had burned quite low; there was only a bed of coals, but Nanny raked some ashes over them, lest Santa Claus should get burnt.

Presently she heard a commotion, and then her heart jumped when she saw a leg in a furry boot appear just over the crane.

Then, she never could tell just how he

managed it, whether with a leap over the coals, or a somersault, but suddenly Santa Claus stood on the hearth.

He looked very much as her poem had stated, but he had a most beautiful face like a fat cherub, and his yellow locks stood out around it like a half ring of light.

"Where's the other girl?" asked Santa Claus.

"Please, sir, she ran away, sir," answered Nanny, curtseying in trembling terms.

"What did she do that for?" asked Santa Claus.

"Please, sir, she was afraid, sir," answered Nanny, curtseying again.

"I don't see what she was afraid of," said Santa Claus. "I had a handsome present for her in my pack."

Santa Claus swung his pack off his back onto the floor, and began untying it. But Nanny suddenly shouted – she heard the mounted police riding into Chrysanthemum alley.

"What's the matter?" asked Santa Claus.

"The mounted police and the Reformer are coming," Nanny replied, faintly.

Santa Claus tied up his pack with a jerk. "Then I've got to hide, that is all," said he, resolutely. "I can't spend any time with mounted police. I have too many poor children all over the world waiting for me."

Nanny fairly wrung her hands as she looked at Santa Claus and his pack. She couldn't think of any place to hide them. She began to cry, but Santa Claus patted her shoulder. "There, don't you cry," said he. "I know quite well how to manage. I am going to hypnotize them; that means I am going to hide behind my own ideas. You wait."

The mounted police by this time had galloped close to the door. There came a knock which shook the house. Nanny trembled. "Don't you do anything but curtsey, and say, 'if you please,' when they come in," ordered Santa Claus in a whisper, and all the time he was looking about the place with his bright blue eyes.

He spied two very large chrysanthemum pots, and one had nothing at all in it, and one only earth, and no plant. Santa Claus quickly dumped his pack into the empty one, then he got into the other himself, thrusting his furry boots well down into the soft mould.

"Open the door now!" he whispered to Nanny. She opened it, trembling, and there stood the Reformer, and behind him were the mounted police, their eyes shining out of the darkness. The Reformer wore a fur cap, and his beard was white with frost. He also wore a new coat, for the price mark dangled from the buttonhole.

He took a stride past Nanny into the kitchen. "Dismount and follow me," he called back to the police. "I know that Santa Claus is within, for his sleds and his reindeer are on the roof."

Then the police dismounted, and came striding in after the Reformer. Nanny shrank back and stood watching them with big, frightened eyes.

She saw, to her great dismay, the Reformer and the police march straight up to Santa Claus, standing in the chrysanthemum pot. Then she saw with wonder the Reformer first, and then the policemen, sniff at Santa Claus' yellow head exactly as if he were a chrysanthemum. Then she heard and could scarcely believe her ears, the Reformer say: "That is the finest chrysanthemum I ever saw. It is quite remarkable." And all the policemen grunted assent.

But she wondered still more when she saw them all walk up to the great flower pot which held the pack, and untie it, and call it a bag of apples. "These are really extremely fine apples," said the Reformer. "I suppose that you will allow the police and myself to eat some apples?" he asked, turning to Nanny. And she curtsied and said: "If you please, sir." Indeed, she kept curtseying and saying that, at intervals, the more astonished she became.

And she became very much astonished when she saw the Reformer eating a picture book with a great Santa Claus picture on the cover, and calling it a very fine apple, and the policemen eating red leather balls and even chewing away at wooden jumping-jacks, and Noah's arks, and calling them apples.

"It is plain Santa Claus is not here," said the head of the police, and he really succeeded in biting off one foot of a wooden soldier.

"But we saw the reindeer and the sledge on the roof," said the Reformer doubtfully.

"I will send out one of the force to look again," said the head of the police, and he did so. When the policeman who was sent out returned and said there were no reindeer and no sledge on the roof, that there was nothing there but a line of clothes fluttering in the wind, Nanny was so aghast that she curtsied and said, "if you please, sir," very fast, indeed. She knew quite well that there were no clothes there, and she could hear every minute the irregular jingle of the bells and the restless stomping of the reindeers' hoofs.

"Well," said the Reformer to the policemen, "we were mistaken. Santa Claus is not here, and we will continue our search in another direction." He swallowed the last page of the picture book as he spoke, and remarked again that it was a fine apple. Then he and the police went out, all stopping to sniff once more at Santa Claus on the way, and to exclaim again at his being such a beautiful chrysanthemum.

When the police had mounted again, and were heard galloping out of the alley, Santa Claus stepped promptly out of the flower pot and took up his pack, which he tied carefully.

"Now I must be gone," said he, "or I shall not visit all my poor relatives tonight. I have left you a special present, and you can tell the girl who ran away that she shall have her present when she gets over being afraid of me. Now, I am going. Merry Christmas to you!"

With that there was a swift rush, and a leap, and a fling of furry boots up the chimney. Then Nanny heard the voice shout again, "Ho Prancer, ho Dancer," and all the rest, the bells chimed again in tune, and the reindeers' hoofs scampered over the roof. Then the strange noises all died away in the distance and Santa Claus was gone.

Nanny locked the door and went to bed. The next morning she found a young chrysanthemum growing in the pot where

Santa Claus had stood, and when her father came home she showed it to him, and told him the whole story.

"That is the special gift," said her father, examining it. "This is a new chrysanthemum, and it will make our fortune." And so, indeed, it turned out. When the chrysanthemum blossomed, never one had been seen like it before. The great delicately fringed blossoms were the silvery blue colour of the Arctic snow fields under the midnight sun, and they made the fortune of Nanny and her father.

▼▶ Willa Cather, "The Strategy of the Were-Wolf Dog", *The Home Monthly* (DECEMBER 1896)

This is a tale of the bleak, bitter Northland, where the frost is eternal and the snows never melt, where the wide white plains stretch for miles and miles without a tree or shrub, where the Heavens at night are made terribly beautiful by the trembling flashes of the Northern lights, and the green icebergs float in stately grandeur down the dark currents of the hungry polar sea. It is a desolate region, where there is no spring, and even in the short summers only a few stunted willows blossom and grow green along the rocky channels through which the melting snow water runs clear and cold. The only cheerful thing about all this country is that far up within the Arctic circle, just on the edge of the boundless snow plains, there is a big house of gray stone, where the lights shine all the year round from the windows, and the wide halls are warmed by blazing fires. For this is the house of his beloved Saintship, Nicholas, whom the children the world over call Santa Claus.

Now every child knows this house is beautiful, and beautiful it is, for it is one of the most home-like places in the world. Just inside the front door is the big hall, where every evening after his work is done Santa Claus sits by the roaring fire and chats with his wife, Mamma Santa, and the White Bear. Then there is the dining room, and the room where Papa and Mamma Santa sleep, and to the rear are the work shops, where all the wonderful toys are made, and last of all the White Bear's sleeping room, for the White Bear has to sleep in a bed of clean white snow every night, and so his room is away from the heated part of the house.

But most boys and girls do not know much about the White Bear, for though he is really a very important personage, he has been strangely neglected by the biographers of Santa Claus. But that is often the way of the historians: they concentrate themselves upon a single important figure of a place or time, and forget to mention at all other factors quite as important. Then after a while some one takes up the people whom the historians have left in the dark, and tries to do them long-delayed justice. Now I would consider it quite a sufficient purpose in life and a very considerable accomplishment if I could set the White Bear right with history, and convince the world of his importance. He is not at all like the bears who carry off naughty children, and does not even belong to the same family as the bears who ate up the forty children who mocked at the Prophet's bald head. On the contrary, this bear is a most gentle and kindly fellow, and fonder of boys and girls than any one else in the world, except Santa Claus himself. He has lived with Papa Santa from time immemorial, helping him in his workshop, painting rocking horses, and stretching drum heads, and gluing yellow wigs on doll babies. But his principal duty is to care for the reindeer, those swift, strong, nervous little beasts, without whom the hobby horses and dolls and red drums would never reach the little children in the world.

One evening, on the 23rd of December—the rest of the date does not matter—Papa Santa sat by the fire in the great hall, blowing the smoke from his nostrils, until his ruddy round face shone through it like a full moon through the mist. He was in a happier mood even than usual, for his long year's work in his shop was done, the last nail had been driven and the last coat of paint had dried. All the vast array of toys stood ready to go into the sealskin bags and be piled into the sleigh.

Opposite him sat Mamma Santa, putting the last dainty stitches on a doll dress for a little sick girl somewhere down in the world. Mamma Santa never kept track of where the different children lived; Papa Santa and the White Bear attended to the address book. It was enough for her to know that they were children and good children, she didn't care to know any more. By her chair sat the White Bear, eating his dog sausage. The White Bear was always hungry between meals, and Mamma Santa always kept a plate of his favorite sausage ready for him in the pantry, which, as there was no fire there, was a refrigerator as well.

As Papa Santa bent to light his pipe again, he spoke to the White Bear:

"The reindeer are all in good shape, are they? You've seen them to-night?"

"I gave them their feed and rubbed them down an hour ago, and I never saw them friskier. They ought to skim like birds to-morrow night. As I came away, though, I thought I saw the Were-Wolf Dog hanging around, so I locked up the stable."

"That was right," said Papa Santa, approvingly. "He was there for no good, depend on that. Last year he tampered with the harness and cut it so that four traces broke before I reached Norway."

Mamma Santa sent her needle through the fine cambric she was stitching with an indignant thrust, and spoke so emphatically that the little white curls under her cap bobbed about her face. "I cannot understand the perverse wickedness of that animal, nor what he has against you, that he should be forever troubling you, or against those World-Children, poor little innocents, that he should be forever trying to defraud them of their Christmas presents. He is certainly the meanest animal from here to the Pole."

"That he is," said Papa Santa, "and there is no reason for it at all. But he hates everything that is not as mean as himself."

"I am sure, Papa, that he will never be at rest until he has brought about some serious accident. Hadn't the Bear better look about the stables again?"

"I'll sleep there to-night and watch, if you say so," said the White Bear, rapping the floor with his shaggy tail.

"O, there is no need of that, we must all get our sleep to-night, for we have hard work and a long journey before us to-morrow. I can trust the reindeer pretty well to look after themselves. Come, Mamma, come, we must get to bed." Papa Santa shook the ashes out of his pipe and blew out the lights, and the White Bear went to stretch himself in his clean white snow.

When all was quiet about the house, there stole from out the shadow of the wall a great dog, shaggy and monstrous to look upon. His hair was red, and his eyes were bright, like ominous fires. His teeth were long and projected from his mouth like tusks, and there was always a little foam about his lips as though he were raging with some inward fury. He carried his tail between his legs, for he was as cowardly as he was vicious. This was the wicked Were-Wolf Dog who hated everything; the beasts and the birds and Santa Claus and the White Bear, and most of all the little children of the world. Nothing made him so angry as to think that there really are good children in the world, little children who love each other, and are simple and gentle and fond of everything that lives, whether it breathes or blooms. For years he had been trying in one way and another to delay Santa Claus' journey so that the children would get no beautiful gifts from him at Christmas time. For the Were-Wolf Dog hated Christmas too, incomprehensible as that may seem. He was thoroughly wicked and evil, and Christmas time is the birthday of Goodness, and every year on Christmas eve the rage in his dark heart burned anew.

He stole softly to the window of the stable, and peered in where the swift, tiny reindeer stood each in his warm little stall, pawing the ground impatiently. For on glorious moonlight nights like that the reindeer never slept, they were always so homesick for their freedom and their wide white snow plains.

"Little reindeer," called the Were-Wolf Dog, softly, and all the little reindeer pricked up their ears. "Little reindeer, it is a lovely night," and all the little reindeer sighed softly. They knew, ah, how well they knew!

"Little reindeer, the moon is shining as brightly as the sun does in the summer, the North wind is blowing fresh and cold, driving the little clouds across the sky like white sea birds. The snow is just hard enough to bear without breaking, and your brothers are running like wild things over its white crust. And the stars, ah, the stars, little brothers, they gleam like a million jewels, and glitter like icicles all over the face of the sky."

The reindeer stamped impatiently in their little stalls. It was very hard.

"Come, little reindeer, let me tell you why all your brothers run toward the Polar Sea to-night. It is because to-night the Northern lights will flash as they never did before, and the great streaks of red and purple and violet will shoot across the sky until all the people of the world shall see them, who never saw before. Listen, little reindeer, it is just the night for a run, a long free run, with no traces to tangle your feet and no sledge to drag. Come, let us go, you will be back again by dawn and no one will ever know."

Dunder stamped in his stall, it made him long to be gone, to hear what the Were-Wolf Dog said. "No, no, we cannot, for to-morrow we must start with the toys for the little children of the world."

"But you will be back tomorrow. Just when the dim light is touching the tops of the icebergs and making the fresh snow red, you will be speeding home. Ah, it will be a glorious run, and you will see the lights as they never shone before. Do you not pant to feel the wind about you, little reindeer?"

Then Cupid and Blitzen could withstand his enticing words no longer, and begged, "Come, Dunder, let us go to-night. It has been so long since we have seen the lights, and we will be back to-morrow."

Now the reindeer knew well enough they ought not to go, but reindeer are not like people, and sometimes the things they want most awfully to do are the very things that they ought not to do. The thought of the fresh winds and their dear lights of the North and the moonlit snow drove them wild, for the reindeer love their freedom more than any other animal, and swift motion, and the free winds.

So the dog pried open the door, with the help of the reindeer forcing it from within, and they all dashed out into the clear moonlight and scurried away toward the North like gleeful rabbits. "We will be back by morning," said Cupid. "We will be back," said Dunder. And, poor little reindeer, they loved the snow so well that it scarcely seemed wrong to go.

O, how fine it was to feel that wind in their fur again! They tossed their antlers in the fresh wind, and their tiny hoofs rang on the hard snow as they ran. They ran for miles and miles without growing tired, or losing their first pleasure in it. Their nostrils were distended and their eyes were bright.

"Slower, slower, little reindeer, for I must lead the way. You will not find the place where all the beasts are assembled," called the Were-Wolf Dog.

The little reindeer could no more go slowly than a boy can when the fire engines dash by. So they got the Were-Wolf Dog in the center of the pack and fairly bore him on with them. On they ran over those vast plains of snow that sparkled as brightly as the sky did above, and Dasher and Prancer bellowed aloud with glee. At last there lay before them the boundless stretch of the Polar Sea. Dark and silent it was, as mysterious as the strange secret of the Pole which it guards forever. Here and there where the ice floes had parted showed a crevice of black water, and the great walls of ice glittered like flame when the Northern lights flung their red banners across the sky, and tipped the icebergs with fire. There the reindeer paused a moment for very joy, and the Were-Wolf Dog fell behind.

"Is the ice safe, old Dog?" asked Vixen.

"To the right it is, off and away, little reindeer. It is growing late," said the Were-Wolf Dog, shouting hoarsely.

And the heedless little reindeer dashed on, never noticing that the wicked Were-Wolf Dog stayed behind on the shore. Now when they were out a good way upon the sea they heard a frightful cracking, grinding sound, such as the ice makes when it breaks up.

"To the shore, little brothers, to the

shore!" cried Dunder, but it was too late. The wicked Were-Wolf Dog where he stood on the land saw the treacherous ice break and part, and the head of every little reindeer go down under the black water. Then he turned and fled over the snow, with his tail tighter between his legs than ever, for he was too cowardly to look upon his own evil work.

As for the reindeer, the black current caught them and whirled them down under the ice, all but Dunder and Dasher and Prancer, who at last rose to the surface and lifted their heads above the water.

"Swim, little brothers, we may yet make the shore," cried Dunder. So among the cakes of broken ice that cut them at every stroke, the three brave little beasts began to struggle toward the shore that seemed so far away. A great chunk of ice struck Prancer in the breast, and he groaned and sank. Then Dasher began to breathe heavily and fell behind, and when Dunder stayed to help him he said, "No, no, little brother, I cannot make it. You must not try to help me, or we will both go down. Go tell it all to the White Bear. Good bye, little brother, we will skim the white snow fields no more together." And with that he, too, sank down into the black water, and Dunder struggled on alone.

When at last he dragged himself wearily upon the shore he was exhausted and cruelly cut and bleeding. But there was no time to be lost. Spent and suffering as he was, he set out across the plains.

Late in the night the White Bear heard some one tapping against his window and saw poor Dunder standing there all covered with ice and blood.

"Come out, brother," he gasped, "the others are all dead and drowned, only I am left. For this night the treacherous Were-Wolf Dog came to us and with enticing words lured us to go with him toward the Pole, promising to show us the Northern lights brighter than we had ever seen them before. But black Death he showed us, and the bottom of the Polar Sea."

Then the White Bear hastened out in his nightcap, and Dunder told him all about the cruel treachery of the Were-Wolf Dog.

"Alas," cried the White Bear, "and who shall tell Santa of this, and who will drag his sleigh to-morrow to carry the gifts to the little children of the world? Empty will their stockings hang on Christmas morning, and Santa's heart will be broken."

Then poor Dunder sank down in the snow and wept.

"Do not despair, Dunder. We must go to-night to the ice hummock where the beasts meet to begin their Christmas revels. Can you run a little longer, poor reindeer?"

"I will run until I die," said Dunder, bravely. "Get on my back and we will go."

So reluctantly the White Bear got on Dunder's back, for bears cannot run themselves, and they sped away to the great ice hummock where the animals of the North all gather to keep their Christmas.

The ice hummock is a great pile of ice and snow right under the North Star, and all the animals were there drinking punches and wishing each other a Merry Christmas. There were seals, and fur otters, and white ermines, and whales, and bears, and many strange birds, and the tawny Lapland dogs that are as strong as horses. But the Were-Wolf Dog was not there. The White Bear paid no heed to any of them, but climbed up to the very top of the huge ice hummock. Then he stood up and cried out:

"Animals of the North, listen to me!" and all the animals ceased from their merry making and looked up to the ice hummock where the White Bear stood, looking very strange up there, all alone in the star light, with his night cap still on.

"Listen to me," thundered the White Bear, "and I will tell you such a tale of wickedness and treachery as never came up among us before. This night the wicked Were-Wolf Dog, who is ever raging in his black heart against the innocent World-Children, came to the reindeer of Santa Claus and with enticing words lured them Northward, promising to show them the great lights as they never shone before. But black Death he showed them, and the bottom of the Polar Sea." Then he showed them poor bleeding Dunder, and told how all the tiny reindeer had been drowned and all the treachery of the Were-Wolf Dog. And all the animals were very indignant and ashamed that one of their number should be guilty of such a thing. And the big whale flapped his tail, and all the bears growled.

"Now, O animals," the White Bear went on, "who among you will go back with me and draw the sleigh full of presents down to the little World-Children, for a shame would it be to all of us if they should awaken and find themselves forgotten and their stockings empty."

But none of the animals replied, for though they felt sorry enough for what had been done, they all loved their freedom and to race over the star-lit snow, and were loath to give it up even for the snug, warm stables of Santa Claus.

"What," cried the White Bear, "Is there not one of you who will take this reproach from us and go back with me to the stables of Santa Claus and take the place of our brothers who are dead? A warm stable shall each of you have, and your fill of clean dry moss-feed, and snow water to drink."

But the animals all thought of the wide plains and the stinging Northwind and their scampers of old, and hung their heads and were silent. Poor Dunder groaned aloud, and even the White Bear had begun to despair, when there spoke up a poor old seal with but one fin, for he had fallen into the seal fishers' hands and been maimed. He had been drinking too much punch, and he spoke thickly, but he had a good heart, that old crippled seal. "It wrings my heart, brothers, that you should be silent to such a call as this, when for the first time since Christmas began it seems that the little children of the world will not get their presents. I am only an old seal who have been twice wounded by the hunters, and am a cripple, but lo, I myself will go with the White Bear, and though I can travel but a mile a day at best, yet will I hobble on my tail and my one fin until I have dragged the sleigh full of presents to the World-Children."

Then the animals were all ashamed of themselves, and the reindeer all sprang forward and cried, "We will go, take us!" So the next day, a little later than usual, Santa Claus wrapped himself in his fur lap robes, and seven new reindeer, headed by Dunder, flew like the winged wind toward the coast of Norway. And if any of you remember getting your presents a little late that year, it was because the new reindeer were not used to their work yet, though they tried hard enough.

L. Frank Baum, "A Kidnapped Santa Claus", *The Delineator* (DECEMBER 1904)

Santa Claus lives in the Laughing Valley, where stands the big, rambling castle in which his toys are manufactured. His workmen, selected from the ryls, knooks, pixies and fairies, live with him, and every one is as busy as can be from one year's end to another.

It is called the Laughing Valley because everything there is happy and gay. The brook chuckles to itself as it leaps rollicking between its green banks; the wind whistles merrily in the trees; the sunbeams dance lightly over the soft grass, and the violets and wild flowers look smilingly up from their green nests. To laugh one needs to be happy; to be happy one needs to be content. And throughout the Laughing Valley of Santa Claus contentment reigns supreme.

On one side is the mighty Forest of Burzee. At the other side stands the huge mountain that contains the Caves of the Daemons. And between them the Valley lies smiling and peaceful.

One would think that our good old Santa Claus, who devotes his days to making children happy, would have no enemies on all the earth; and, as a matter of fact, for a long period of time he encountered nothing but love wherever he might go.

But the Daemons who live in the mountain caves grew to hate Santa Claus very much, and all for the simple reason that he made children happy.

The Caves of the Daemons are five in number. A broad pathway leads up to the first cave, which is a finely arched cavern at the foot of the mountain, the entrance being beautifully carved and decorated. In it resides the Daemon of Selfishness. Back of this is another cavern inhabited by the Daemon of Envy. The cave of the Daemon of Hatred is next in order, and through this one passes to the home of the Daemon of Malice—situated in a dark and fearful cave in the very heart of the mountain. I do not know what lies beyond this. Some say there are terrible pitfalls leading to death and destruction, and this may very well be true. However, from each one of the four caves mentioned there is a small, narrow tunnel leading to the fifth cave—a cozy little room occupied by the Daemon of Repentance. And as the rocky floors of these passages are well worn by the track of passing feet, I judge that many wanderers in the Caves of the Daemons have escaped through the tunnels to the abode of the Daemon of Repentance, who is said to be a pleasant sort of fellow who gladly opens for one a little door admitting you into fresh air and sunshine again.

Well, these Daemons of the Caves, thinking they had great cause to dislike old Santa Claus, held a meeting one day to discuss the matter.

"I'm really getting lonesome," said the Daemon of Selfishness. "For Santa Claus distributes so many pretty Christmas gifts to all the children that they become happy and generous, through his example, and keep away from my cave."

"I'm having the same trouble," rejoined the Daemon of Envy. "The little ones seem quite content with Santa Claus, and there are few, indeed, that I can coax to become envious."

"And that makes it bad for me!" declared the Daemon of Hatred. "For if no children pass through the Caves of Selfishness and Envy, none can get to my cavern."

"Or to mine," added the Daemon of Malice.

"For my part," said the Daemon of Repentance, "it is easily seen that if children do not visit your caves they have no need to visit mine; so that I am quite as neglected as you are."

"And all because of this person they call Santa Claus!" exclaimed the Daemon of Envy. "He is simply ruining our business, and something must be done at once."

To this they readily agreed; but what to do was another and more difficult matter to settle. They knew that Santa Claus worked all through the year at his castle in the Laughing Valley, preparing the gifts he was to distribute on Christmas Eve; and at first they resolved to try to tempt him into their caves, that they might lead him on to the terrible pitfalls that ended in destruction.

So the very next day, while Santa Claus was busily at work, surrounded by his little band of assistants, the Daemon of Selfishness came to him and said:

"These toys are wonderfully bright and pretty. Why do you not keep them for yourself? It's a pity to give them to those noisy boys and fretful girls, who break and destroy them so quickly."

"Nonsense!" cried the old graybeard, his bright eyes twinkling merrily as he turned toward the tempting Daemon. "The boys and girls are never so noisy and fretful after receiving my presents, and if I can make them happy for one day in the year I am quite content."

So the Daemon went back to the others, who awaited him in their caves, and said:

"I have failed, for Santa Claus is not at all selfish."

The following day the Daemon of Envy visited Santa Claus. Said he: "The toy shops are full of playthings quite as pretty as those you are making. What a shame it is that they should interfere with your business! They make toys by machinery much quicker than you can make them by hand; and they sell them for money, while you get nothing at all for your work."

But Santa Claus refused to be envious of the toy shops.

"I can supply the little ones but once a year—on Christmas Eve," he answered; "for the children are many, and I am but one. And as my work is one of love and kindness I would be ashamed to receive money for my little gifts. But throughout all the year the children must be amused in some way, and so the toy shops are able to bring much happiness to my little friends. I like the toy shops, and am glad to see them prosper."

In spite of the second rebuff, the Daemon of Hatred thought he would try to influence Santa Claus. So the next day he entered the busy workshop and said:

"Good morning, Santa! I have bad news for you."

"Then run away, like a good fellow," answered Santa Claus. "Bad news is something that should be kept secret and never told."

"You cannot escape this, however," declared the Daemon; "for in the world are a good many who do not believe in Santa Claus, and these you are bound to hate bitterly, since they have so wronged you."

"Stuff and rubbish!" cried Santa.

"And there are others who resent your making children happy and who sneer at you and call you a foolish old rattlepate! You are quite right to hate such base slanderers, and you ought to be revenged upon them for their evil words."

"But I don't hate 'em!" exclaimed Santa Claus positively. "Such people do me no real harm, but merely render themselves and their children unhappy. Poor things! I'd much rather help them any day than injure them."

Indeed, the Daemons could not tempt old Santa Claus in any way. On the contrary, he was shrewd enough to see that their object in visiting him was to make mischief and trouble, and his cheery laughter disconcerted the evil ones and showed to them the folly of such an undertaking. So they abandoned honeyed words and determined to use force.

It was well known that no harm can come to Santa Claus while he is in the Laughing Valley, for the fairies, and ryls, and knooks all protect him. But on Christmas Eve he drives his reindeer out into the big world, carrying a sleighload of toys and pretty gifts to the children; and this was the time and the occasion when his enemies had the best chance to injure him. So the Daemons laid their plans and awaited the arrival of Christmas Eve.

The moon shone big and white in the sky, and the snow lay crisp and sparkling on the ground as Santa Claus cracked his whip and sped away out of the Valley into the great world beyond. The roomy sleigh was packed full with huge sacks of toys, and as the reindeer dashed onward our jolly old Santa laughed and whistled and sang for very joy. For in all his merry life this was the one day in the year when he was happiest—the day he lovingly bestowed the treasures of his workshop upon the little children.

It would be a busy night for him, he well knew. As he whistled and shouted and cracked his whip again, he reviewed in mind all the towns and cities and farmhouses where he was expected, and figured that he had just enough presents to go around and make every child happy. The reindeer knew exactly what was expected of them, and dashed along so swiftly that their feet scarcely seemed to touch the snow-covered ground.

Suddenly a strange thing happened: a rope shot through the moonlight and a big noose that was in the end of it settled over the arms and body of Santa Claus and drew tight. Before he could resist or even cry out he was jerked from the seat of the sleigh and tumbled head foremost into a snowbank, while the reindeer rushed onward with the load of toys and carried it quickly out of sight and sound.

Such a surprising experience confused old Santa for a moment, and when he had collected his senses he found that the wicked Daemons had pulled him from the snowdrift and bound him tightly with many coils of the stout rope. And then they carried the kidnapped Santa Claus away to their mountain, where they thrust the prisoner into a secret cave and chained him to the rocky wall so that he could not escape.

"Ha, ha!" laughed the Daemons, rubbing their hands together with cruel glee. "What will the children do now? How they will cry and scold and storm when they find there are no toys in their stockings and no gifts on their Christmas trees! And what a lot of punishment they will receive from their parents, and how they will flock to our Caves of Selfishness, and Envy, and Hatred, and Malice! We have done a mighty clever thing, we Daemons of the Caves!"

Now it so chanced that on this Christmas Eve the good Santa Claus had taken with him in his sleigh Nuter the Ryl, Peter the Knook, Kilter the Pixie, and a small fairy named Wisk—his four favorite assistants.

These little people he had often found very useful in helping him to distribute his gifts to the children, and when their master was so suddenly dragged from the sleigh they were all snugly tucked underneath the seat, where the sharp wind could not reach them.

The tiny immortals knew nothing of the capture of Santa Claus until some time after he had disappeared. But finally they missed his cheery voice, and as their master always sang or whistled on his journeys, the silence warned them that something was wrong.

Little Wisk stuck out his head from underneath the seat and found Santa Claus gone and no one to direct the flight of the reindeer.

"Whoa!" he called out, and the deer obediently slackened speed and came to a halt.

Peter and Nuter and Kilter all jumped upon the seat and looked back over the track made by the sleigh. But Santa Claus had been left miles and miles behind.

"What shall we do?" asked Wisk anxiously, all the mirth and mischief banished from his wee face by this great calamity.

"We must go back at once and find our master," said Nuter the Ryl, who thought and spoke with much deliberation.

"No, no!" exclaimed Peter the Knook, who, cross and crabbed though he was, might always be depended upon in an emergency. "If we delay, or go back, there will not be time to get the toys to the children before morning; and that would grieve Santa Claus more than anything else."

"It is certain that some wicked creatures have captured him," added Kilter thoughtfully, "and their object must be to make the children unhappy. So our first duty is to get the toys distributed as carefully as if Santa Claus were himself present. Afterward we can search for our master and easily secure his freedom."

This seemed such good and sensible advice that the others at once resolved to adopt it. So Peter the Knook called to the reindeer, and the faithful animals again sprang forward and dashed over hill and valley, through forest and plain, until they came to the houses wherein children lay sleeping and dreaming of the pretty gifts they would find on Christmas morning.

The little immortals had set themselves a difficult task; for although they had assisted Santa Claus on many of his journeys, their master had always directed and guided them and told them exactly what he wished them to do. But now they had to distribute the toys according to their own judgment, and they did not understand children as well as did old Santa. So it is no wonder they made some laughable errors.

Mamie Brown, who wanted a doll, got a drum instead; and a drum is of no use to a girl who loves dolls. And Charlie Smith, who delights to romp and play out of doors, and who wanted some new rubber boots to keep his feet dry, received a sewing box filled with colored worsteds and threads and needles, which made him so provoked that he thoughtlessly called our dear Santa Claus a fraud.

Had there been many such mistakes the Daemons would have accomplished their evil purpose and made the children unhappy. But the little friends of the absent Santa Claus labored faithfully and intelligently to carry out their master's ideas, and they made fewer errors than might be expected under such unusual circumstances.

And, although they worked as swiftly as possible, day had begun to break before the toys and other presents were all distributed; so for the first time in many years the reindeer trotted into the Laughing Valley, on their return, in broad daylight, with the brilliant sun peeping over the edge of the forest to prove they were far behind their accustomed hour.

Having put the deer in the stable, the little folk began to wonder how they might rescue their master; and they realized they must discover, first of all, what had happened to him and where he was.

So Wisk the Fairy transported himself to the bower of the Fairy Queen, which was located deep in the heart of the Forest of Burzee; and once there, it did not take him long to find out all about the naughty Daemons and how they had kidnapped the good Santa Claus to prevent his making children happy. The Fairy Queen also promised her assistance, and then, fortified by this powerful support, Wisk flew back to where Nuter and Peter and Kilter awaited him, and the four counseled together and laid plans to rescue their master from his enemies.

It is possible that Santa Claus was not as merry as usual during the night that succeeded his capture. For although he had faith in the judgment of his little friends he could not avoid a certain amount of worry, and an anxious look would creep at times into his kind old eyes as he thought of the disappointment that might await his dear little children. And the Daemons, who guarded him by turns, one after another, did not neglect to taunt him with contemptuous words in his helpless condition.

When Christmas Day dawned the Daemon of Malice was guarding the prisoner, and his tongue was sharper than that of any of the others.

"The children are waking up, Santa!" he cried. "They are waking up to find their stockings empty! Ho, ho! How they will quarrel, and wail, and stamp their feet in anger! Our caves will be full today, old Santa! Our caves are sure to be full!"

But to this, as to other like taunts, Santa Claus answered nothing. He was much grieved by his capture, it is true, but his courage did not forsake him. And, finding that the prisoner would not reply to his jeers, the Daemon of Malice presently went away, and sent the Daemon of Repentance to take his place.

This last personage was not so disagreeable as the others. He had gentle and refined features, and his voice was soft and pleasant in tone.

"My brother Daemons do not trust me overmuch," said he, as he entered the cavern; "but it is morning, now, and the mischief is done. You cannot visit the children again for another year."

"That is true," answered Santa Claus, almost cheerfully; "Christmas Eve is past, and for the first time in centuries I have not visited my children."

"The little ones will be greatly disappointed," murmured the Daemon of Repentance, almost regretfully; "but that cannot be helped now. Their grief is likely to make the children selfish and envious and hateful, and if they come to the Caves of the Daemons today I shall get a chance to lead some of them to my Cave of Repentance."

"Do you never repent, yourself?" asked Santa Claus, curiously.

"Oh, yes, indeed," answered the Daemon. "I am even now repenting that I assisted in your capture. Of course it is too late to remedy the evil that has been done; but repentance, you know, can come only after an evil thought or deed, for in the beginning there is nothing to repent of."

"So I understand," said Santa Claus. "Those who avoid evil need never visit your cave."

"As a rule, that is true," replied the Daemon; "yet you, who have done no evil, are about to visit my cave at once; for to prove that I sincerely regret my share in your capture I am going to permit you to escape."

This speech greatly surprised the prisoner, until he reflected that it was just what might be expected of the Daemon of Repentance. The fellow at once busied himself untying the knots that bound Santa Claus and unlocking the chains that fastened him to the wall. Then he led the way through a long tunnel until they both emerged in the Cave of Repentance.

"I hope you will forgive me," said the Daemon pleadingly. "I am not really a bad person, you know; and I believe I accomplish a great deal of good in the world."

With this he opened a back door that let in a flood of sunshine, and Santa Claus sniffed the fresh air gratefully.

"I bear no malice," said he to the Daemon, in a gentle voice; "and I am sure the world would be a dreary place without you. So, good morning, and a Merry Christmas to you!"

With these words he stepped out to greet the bright morning, and a moment later he was trudging along, whistling softly to himself, on his way to his home in the Laughing Valley.

Marching over the snow toward the mountain was a vast army, made up of the most curious creatures imaginable. There were numberless knooks from the forest, as rough and crooked in appearance as the gnarled branches of the trees they ministered to. And there were dainty ryls from the fields, each one bearing the emblem of the flower or plant it guarded. Behind these were many ranks of pixies, gnomes and nymphs, and in the rear a thousand beautiful fairies floated along in gorgeous array.

This wonderful army was led by Wisk, Peter, Nuter, and Kilter, who had assembled it to rescue Santa Claus from captivity and to punish the Daemons who had dared to take him away from his beloved children.

And, although they looked so bright and peaceful, the little immortals were armed with powers that would be very terrible to those who had incurred their anger. Woe to the Daemons of the Caves if this mighty army of vengeance ever met them!

But lo! coming to meet his loyal friends appeared the imposing form of Santa Claus, his white beard floating in the breeze and his bright eyes sparkling with pleasure at this proof of the love and veneration he had inspired in the hearts of the most powerful creatures in existence.

And while they clustered around him and danced with glee at his safe return, he gave them earnest thanks for their support. But Wisk, and Nuter, and Peter, and Kilter, he embraced affectionately.

"It is useless to pursue the Daemons," said Santa Claus to the army. "They have their place in the world, and can never be destroyed. But that is a great pity, nevertheless," he continued musingly.

So the fairies, and knooks, and pixies, and ryls all escorted the good man to his castle, and there left him to talk over the events of the night with his little assistants.

Wisk had already rendered himself invisible and flown through the big world to see how the children were getting along on this bright Christmas morning; and by the time he returned, Peter had finished telling Santa Claus of how they had distributed the toys.

"We really did very well," cried the fairy, in a pleased voice; "for I found little unhappiness among the children this morning. Still, you must not get captured again, my dear master; for we might not be so fortunate another time in carrying out your ideas."

He then related the mistakes that had been made, and which he had not discovered until his tour of inspection. And Santa Claus at once sent him with rubber boots for Charlie Smith, and a doll for Mamie Brown; so that even those two disappointed ones became happy.

As for the wicked Daemons of the Caves, they were filled with anger and chagrin when they found that their clever capture of Santa Claus had come to naught. Indeed, no one on that Christmas Day appeared to be at all selfish, or envious, or hateful. And, realizing that while the children's saint had so many powerful friends it was folly to oppose him, the Daemons never again attempted to interfere with his journeys on Christmas Eve.

10.

So... Is There A Santa Claus?

Francis Church, "Is There a Santa Claus?", *The Sun* (NEW YORK), SEPTEMBER 21 1897

We take pleasure in answering thus prominently the communication below, expressing at the same time our great gratification that its faithful author is numbered among the friends of The Sun:

> "Dear Editor–I am 8 years old.
> "Some of my little friends say there is no Santa Claus.
> "Papa says, 'If you see it in The Sun, it's so.'
> "Please tell me the truth, is there a Santa Claus?
> Virginia O'Hanlon
> 115 West Ninety-fifth Street

Virginia, your little friends are wrong. They have been affected by the skepticism of a skeptical age. They do not believe except they see. They think that nothing can be which is not comprehensible by their little minds. All minds, Virginia, whether they be men's or children's are little. In this great universe of ours man is a mere insect, an ant, in his intellect, as compared with the boundless world about him, as measured by the intelligence capable of grasping the whole of truth and knowledge.

Yes, Virginia, there is a Santa Claus. He exists as certainly as love and generosity and devotion exist, and you know that they abound and give to your life its highest beauty and joy. Alas! how dreary would be the world if there were no Santa Claus! It would be as dreary as if there were no Virginias. There would be no child-like faith then, no poetry, no romance to make tolerable this existence. We should have no enjoyment, except in sense and sight. The eternal light with which childhood fills the world would be extinguished.

Not believe in Santa Claus! You might as well not believe in fairies! You might get your papa to hire men to watch in all the chimneys on Christmas eve to catch Santa Claus, but even if you did not see Santa Claus coming down, what would that prove? Nobody sees Santa Claus, but that is no sign that there is no Santa Claus. The most real things in the world are those that neither children nor men can see. Did you ever see fairies dancing on the lawn? Of course not, but that's no proof that they are not there. Nobody can conceive or imagine all the wonders there are unseen and unseeable in the world.

You tear apart the baby's rattle and see what makes the noise inside, but there is a veil covering the unseen world which not the strongest man, nor even the united strength of all the strongest men that ever lived, could tear apart. Only faith, fancy, poetry, love, romance, can push aside that curtain and view and picture the supernal beauty and glory beyond. Is it all real? Ah, Virginia, in all this world there is nothing else real and abiding.

No Santa Claus! Thank God! He lives, and he lives forever. A thousand years from now, Virginia, nay, ten times ten thousand years from now, he will continue to make glad the heart of childhood.

Jacob Riis, *Is There A Santa Claus*
(NEW YORK: MACMILLAN, 1904)

"DEAR MR. RIIS:
"A little chap of six on the Western frontier writes to us:
"'Will you please tell me if there is a Santa Claus? Papa says not.'
"Won't you answer him?"

That was the message that came to me from an editor last December just as I was going on a journey. Why he sent it to me I don't know. Perhaps it was because, when I was a little chap, my home was way up toward that white north where even the little boys ride in sleds behind reindeer, as they are the only horses they have. Perhaps it was because when I was a young lad I knew Hans Christian Andersen, who surely ought to know, and spoke his tongue. Perhaps it was both. I will ask the editor when I see him. Meanwhile, here was his letter, with Christmas right at the door, and, as I said, I was going on a journey.

I buttoned it up in my great coat along with a lot of other letters I didn't have time to read, and I thought as I went to the depot what a pity it was that my little friend's papa should have forgotten about Santa Claus. We big people do forget the strangest way, and then we haven't got a bit of a good time any more.

No Santa Claus! If you had asked that car full of people I would have liked to hear the answers they would have given you. No Santa Claus! Why, there was scarce a man in the lot who didn't carry a bundle that looked as if it had just tumbled out of his sleigh. I felt of one slyly, and it was a boy's sled—a "flexible flyer," I know, because he left one at our house the Christmas before; and I distinctly heard the rattling of a pair of skates in that box in the next seat. They were all good-natured, every one, though the train was behind time—that is a sure sign of Christmas. The brakeman wore a piece of mistletoe in his cap and a broad grin on his face, and he said "Merry Christmas" in a way to make a man feel good all the rest of the day. No Santa Claus, is there? You just ask him!

And then the train rolled into the city under the big gray dome to which George Washington gave his name, and by-and-by I went through a doorway which all American boys would rather see than go to school a whole week, though they love their teacher dearly. It is true that last winter my own little lad told the kind man whose house it is that he would rather ride up and down in the elevator at the hotel, but that was because he was so very little at the time and didn't know things rightly, and, besides, it was his first experience with an elevator.

As I was saying, I went through the door into a beautiful white hall with lofty pillars, between which there were regular banks of holly with the red berries shining through, just as if it were out in the woods! And from behind one of them there came the merriest laugh you could ever think of. Do you think, now, it was that letter in my pocket that gave that guilty little throb against my heart when I heard it, or what could it have been? I hadn't even time to ask myself the question, for there stood my host all framed in holly, and with the heartiest handclasp.

"Come in," he said, and drew me after. "The coffee is waiting." And he beamed upon the table with the veriest Christmas face as he poured it out himself, one cup for his dear wife and one for me. The children—ah! you should have asked *them* if there was a Santa Claus!

And so we sat and talked, and I told my kind friends that my own dear old mother, whom I have not seen for years, was very, very sick in far-away Denmark and longing for her boy, and a mist came into my hostess's gentle eyes and she said, "Let us cable over and tell her how much we think of her," though she had never seen her. And it was no sooner said than done. In came a man with a writing-pad, and while we drank our coffee this message sped under the great stormy sea to the far-away country where the day was shading into evening already though the sun was scarce two hours high in Washington:

THE WHITE HOUSE.
Mrs. Riis, Ribe, Denmark:
Your son is breakfasting with us.
We send you our love and sympathy.
THEODORE AND EDITH ROOSEVELT

For, you see, the house with the holly in the hall was the White House, and my host was the President of the United States. I have to tell it to you, or you might easily fall into the same error I came near falling into. I had to pinch myself to make sure the President was not Santa Claus himself. I felt that he had in that moment given me the very greatest Christmas gift any man ever received: my little mother's life. For really what ailed her was that she was very old, and I know that when she got the President's dispatch she must have become immediately ten years younger and got right out of bed. Don't you know mothers are that way when any one makes much of their boys? I think Santa Claus must have brought them all in the beginning—the mothers, I mean.

I would just give anything to see what happened in that old town that is full of blessed memories to me, when the telegraph ticked off that message. I will warrant the town hurried out, burgomaster, bishop, beadle and all, to do honor to my gentle old mother. No Santa Claus, eh? What was that, then, that spanned two oceans with a breath of love and cheer, I should like to know. Tell me that!

After the coffee we sat together in the President's office for a little while while he signed commissions, each and every one of which was just Santa Claus's gift to a grown-up boy who had been good in the year that was going; and before we parted the President had lifted with so many strokes of his pen clouds of sorrow and want that weighed heavily on homes I knew of to which Santa Claus had had hard work finding his way that Christmas.

It seemed to me as I went out of the door, where the big policeman touched his hat and wished me a Merry Christmas, that the sun never shone so brightly in May as it did then. I quite expected to see the crocuses and the jonquils, that make the White House garden so pretty, out in full bloom. They were not, I suppose, only because they are official flowers and have a proper respect for the calendar that runs Congress and the Executive Department, too.

I stopped on the way down the avenue at Uncle Sam's paymaster's to see what he thought of it. And there he was, busy as could be, making ready for the coming of Santa Claus. No need of my asking any questions here.

Men stood in line with bank-notes in their hands asking for gold, new gold-pieces, they said, most every one. The paymaster, who had a sprig of Christmas green fixed in his desk just like any other man, laughed and shook his head and said "Santa Claus?" and the men in the line laughed too and nodded and went away with their gold.

One man who went out just ahead of me I saw stoop over a poor woman on the corner and thrust something into her hand, then walk hastily away. It was I who caught the light in the woman's eye and the blessing upon her poor wan lips, and the grass seemed greener in the Treasury dooryard, and the sky bluer than it had been before, even on that bright day. Perhaps—well, never mind! if any one says anything to you about principles and giving alms, you tell him that Santa Claus takes care of the principles at Christmas, and not to be afraid. As for him, if you want to know, just ask the old woman on the Treasury corner.

And so, walking down that Avenue of Good-will, I came to my train again and went home. And when I had time to think it all over I remembered the letters in my pocket which I had not opened. I took them out and read them, and among them were two sent to me in trust for Santa Claus himself which I had to lay away with the editor's message until I got the dew rubbed off my spectacles. One was from a great banker, and it contained a check for a thousand dollars to help buy a home for some poor children of the East Side tenements in New York, where the chimneys are so small and mean that scarce even a letter will go up through them, so that ever so many little ones over there never get on Santa Claus's books at all.

The other letter was from a lonely old widow, almost as old as my dear mother in Denmark, and it contained a two-dollar bill. For years, she wrote, she had saved and saved, hoping some time to have five dollars, and then she would go with me to the homes of the very poor and be Santa Claus herself. "And wherever you decided it was right to leave a trifle, that should be the place where it would be left," read the letter. But now she was so old that she could no longer think of such a trip and so she sent the money she had saved. And I thought of a family in one of those tenements where father and mother are both lying ill, with a boy, who ought to be in school, fighting all alone to keep the wolf from the door, and winning the fight. I guess he has been too busy to send any message up the chimney, if indeed there is one in his house; but you ask him, right now, whether he thinks there is a Santa Claus or not.

No Santa Claus? Yes, my little man, there is a Santa Claus, thank God! Your father had just forgotten. The world would indeed be poor without one. It is true that he does not always wear a white beard and drive a reindeer team—not always, you know—but what does it matter? He is Santa Claus with the big, loving, Christmas heart, for all that; Santa Claus with the kind thoughts for every one that make children and grown-up people beam with happiness all day long. And shall I tell you a secret which I did not learn at the post-office, but it is true all the same—of how you can always be sure your letters go to him straight by the chimney route? It is this: send along with them a friendly thought for the boy you don't like: for Jack who punched you, or Jim who was mean to you. The meaner he was the harder do you resolve to make it up: not to bear him a grudge. That is the stamp for the letter to Santa. Nobody can stop it, not even a cross-draught in the chimney, when it has that on.

Because—don't you know, Santa Claus is the spirit of Christmas: and ever and ever so many years ago when the dear little Baby was born after whom we call Christmas, and was cradled in a manger out in the stable because there was not room in the inn, that Spirit came into the world to soften the hearts of men and make them love one another. Therefore, that is the mark of the Spirit to this day. Don't let anybody or anything rub it out. Then the rest doesn't matter. Let them tear Santa's white beard off at the Sunday-school festival and growl in his bearskin coat. These are only his disguises. The steps of the real Santa Claus you can trace all through the world as you have done here with me, and when you stand in the last of his tracks you will find the Blessed Babe of Bethlehem smiling a welcome to you. For then you will be home.

"The Spirit of Santa Claus": Nell Nelson of the New York *Evening World*

The Evening World, DECEMBER 17 1891
LIFE CHILLED BY POVERTY.
The Story of a Poor Woman's Fight for Existence.

Here is the skeleton of a story from real life, and if it does not put a little Christmas kindness in your heart then either the spirit of Scrooge possesses your soul or it has been butchered in the telling.

The Broadway cars were flying downtown nose to tail, yet every one was packed to its utmost capacity. Well-to-do and comfortable-looking men were reading the afternoon papers, and pretty women and prettier children were thinking and talking about the holiday shopping.

Stops at Twenty-third and Nineteenth streets lightened the travel, and at Fourteenth the last pretty gloved hand let go its hold on the car strap. The exodus still left enough people to fill the seats, the only occupant of standing room being a mite of a girl, too poor in size and style to attract attention. She leaned against a woman's knees for support and amused herself tying knots in the fringe of an old woollen shawl which had evidently been used as an ironing blanket, judging from the triangles that were scorched on it.

Wearying of the pastime reminded her of her discomfort, and in a thin voice, shrill enough to attract the attention of every one in the car, she asked:

"Mamma, why can't I sit down?"

"That's what I'd like to know," replied a good-natured man, who took her in his arms and placed her in his seat.

The next moment she was on her bare little knees, looking out of the window at the matchless preparations New York makes for the holidays.

Every now and then she would turn, caress the hard-featured woman with her baby fingers and tell her to "Look, look, mamma!"

But there was no response to the child's delight. Without even turning turning her head she would answer:

"Yes, I see," with equivocal impatience.

There was some excuse for her indifference. She had a sleeping child in her arms, that the iron-scorched shawl partially covered. She wore a worthless alpaca dress, a hat out of shape and season, and coarse shoes worn to the uppers. She was a woman cruelly aged by trouble and hardship. There were creases in her face that you could hide a finger in; the mouth was hard set from grim repression; several teeth were gone, and the whole expression of her thin face was a glossary of the resentful and passionate views she took of life.

But you can't expect the people who are miserably cold and hungry and helplessly tied down by misfortune to look patient and pleasant and to smile in the face of a world that is too busy with cap and bells to be bothered.

I haven't a doubt but she hated the very sight of the woman opposite who pulled off a tight glove to reverse the settings of her magnificent rings, and who, as she replaced it, insolently stared at the naked limbs and slippered feet of the window-crazed little girl.

We were alone in the car when it passed Wall street, and I had a flirting acquaintance with Kitty that emboldened me to go and sit by her.

For lack of a better subject we talked Christmas, and the first question showed me my mistake.

"What's Santa Claus going to bring you?" I asked.

"For God's sake," replied the woman, "don't put that nonsense in her head. I have trouble enough already trying to keep bread in their mouths."

"My mamma says there ain't no Santa Claus and there ain't no God," piped the child before she had finished the startling sentence.

By degrees I drew from the wretched woman more hardness of heart than I thought was possible to exist with maternal love. It seemed that she had been up in West Fifty-ninth street to visit her husband, who has been ill in the hospital since September, when he was run over by a truck and injured internally. She lives with her two children in the extreme end of Greenwich street, and their sole support comes from the proceeds of two days' work, Saturday and Sunday.

But here are her words: "I can't leave these children alone for I don't know what might happen to them; besides it is easier to keep them alive than it would be to bury them. Through the week all the women in the house are away, but a friend takes care of them on Saturday and Sunday while I do office cleaning. There is plenty of work and I get $1.50 a day."

"My rent costs me $6 a month, and somehow we manage to keep alive on the rest."

"Keep alive! Is that all?"

"Well," she answered with a sigh, "you can see our fix. She," indicating Kitty, "has no shoes but the slippers she is wearing and neither has a flannel to her back. And then you talk about Christmas presents. It makes me sick.

"You wonder, I suppose, why I don't put these children away and go to work. Well, I'll just tell you why. They are my children, and I propose to keep them with me. I don't mean to let them starve, but if they must die that way why we'll go together."

At Battery place she woke up the younger girl, took Kitty by the hand and left the car. After the long, cold ride from Central Park she was in no humor for moralizing. She gave her address, "for the children's sake," with sullen reluctance, and "guessed it was for some other fool thing."

Unfortunately this poor creature refuses to recognize the kind side of charity. Her prejudices blind her to her own interests. It is awful to be poor, cold, hungry and friendless; to have a husband shut up in a silent ward in a city hospital hovering between life and death, and to lie awake all night listening for the messenger sent to tell you "he is dead" and to "come and get the body," in just so many words.

In such straits and under such circumstances it is easy to understand the mockery of Christmas, prayer and religion.

Before starvation, despair and the blighting chill of Winter the moral beauties pale into utter insignificance.

If you want to convince this sorely tried wife and mother that Christmas kindness is not some other fool thing and that the spirit of Santa Claus is not all 'nonsense' you may send a contribution of a penny or a dime or a dollar to the Fund.

Nell Nelson

The Evening World,
DECEMBER 21 1891
TWO SPECIMEN CHILDREN.
This Is the Kind the Christmas Trees Are For.

It can do no harm to tell the happy creatures of fashion and culture, who at this season of the year render almost divine homage to Verdi and Homer, that the Miserere is being sung and the Iliad suffered by hundreds and thousands of living human characters in the very heart of New York.

The difference between the tragedies in poetry and song and those that are daily enacted in the public streets and squares of this great city is life.

There is no mimicry about the suffering of children in prose. Hunger, rags, hardship and sickness are realities too stern for expression in the delicate colorings of poetry. Poverty does not play at shivering.

She doggedly sets her teeth to stifle the cry in her heart, and forgets her own discomfort in trying to warm the famishing child at her breast.

Let's shift the stage to City Hall Square, and if you can try and recall the biting cold of Thursday afternoon.

It was 4 on the face of every reputable clock in Newspaper Row when I crossed the windy thoroughfare.

Every vagrant tramp had been driven from the rustic benches by his mischievous majesty Jack Frost, and not so much as the boa of a sparrow could be seen.

A park policeman was taking the fresh air at the frost-bound fountain, and shivering, blue-nosed, teeth-chattering, goose-fleshed office clerks and typewriter girls scooted across corners in the direction of the bridge and ferry-boats.

The usual army of suspender merchants, curbstone caterers and dealers in toys and notions had been knocked out of the field almost as soon as the Winter king got his innings.

But young blood is warmer and the baby bread-winners were abroad in their rags and patches of misery.

A pair of frost-bitten, uncanny little creatures were selling papers, and when one of them piped, "Full account of the Christmas Tree," I made a bid for the whole stock of EVENING WORLDS.

I also made his acquaintance and that of his friend, Billy.

Joseph touched my heart, but Billy made it ache. His clothes looked as though they had been chewed. A great bite had been taken out of his shoe and stocking, and his little heel was bare and blue. Just think of it, and a day like Thursday.

Shades of misery!

It sends the cold shivers down my back to write about it.

The poor fellow wore an overcoat, more patches and holes than cloth, held at the neck by a pin and if a shirt covered the thin little chest it was too modest to be seen.

Joseph's garb was better in point of decency; there were patches on his toes and knees and buttons on his jacket, but nothing could be said of its warmth.

He is a lovely child, bony as a quail and as shy, sweet-mannered and quick-witted, and he looks at you with a pair of those begging eyes that are at once eloquent and soulful.

Joseph's chronology is not altogether exact, but it detracts nothing from the role in which he has been cast by Fate.

He is not a regular newsboy. Indeed, members of that respected fraternity have on numerous occasions been known to put rocks in his already flint-lined road. He goes to school during the day, and after hours sell the papers, the profits of which help a little to bay the wolf.

But the story:

"I live in Rivington street; I'm eight years old; I have five brothers and sisters, and my mother's sick in bed. The doctor comes three times a day to give her medicine. My brother next to me stays home to do the work and two of us sell papers."

When asked to give the ages of his little brothers and sisters Joseph said:

"I'm eight years old; one brother is thirteen years, and the other is ten years old, and I got three sisters. The littlest isn't any years old. We only got her Tuesday. The next littlest is fourteen months old and the other is three years."

The poor fellow said his father was up in the State working on a new railroad; that he could not get home more than once in four weeks; that he did not think there was any use in his sisters hanging up their stockings Christmas, and that he didn't want anything anyway.

"I guess we won't have any turkey Christmas 'cause we don't have hardly anything to eat now. Mother's too sick to cook the dinner and all we have is milk and crackers."

Now, if I give you the address of this family who will go and help the sick mother? What clothier will give the boy a suit of clothes, and what boy will subscribe enough to the fund to entertain these six boys and girls at the Christmas Tree?

Billy's story is quite as pathetic. His father is a capmaker by trade, but has no work, and there is not one pair of good shoes in the house. The mother is ill in bed with consumption, and so is the eldest boy, whose earnings were all that made ends meet.

Billy is nine years of age and his sisters eight and three respectively, "can't go out because they have no shoes but broken ones."

"If Santa Claus comes what would you like him to bring you?" I asked.

"Oh, but he won't come," replied the boy, with a sneerful little laugh that was painful to hear. "He never comes. He didn't come last year. There is fifty children in our house, and they all say he won't. Nobody hardly in Suffolk street has Christmas or hangs up their stocking."

These are not hoodlum children. They are thin, sickly faced, half starved, forlorn and stunted, but they are quite as intelligent, sensitive and right-minded as any boy in your family of their age.

They are ten in all. They are bitterly in need of help for the physical and spiritual growth of their natures.

They are coming to the people's Christmas Tree. They will be your guests, pensioners on your bounty and friendliness.

You must help entertain them. You will help, won't you, even if the effort throws you into bankruptcy and throws half a dozen names from your Christmas list of people who do not need favors as a proof of your friendship? For them love is enough. But these children are friendless.

Open your hearts to them, pull out your purse and build up the Fund for their benefit.

Nell Nelson

The Evening World, NOVEMBER 13 1893
FOR CHILDREN'S JOY
Santa Claus is Filling His Bag and Will Soon Be Here

There are thousands of poor children in this town, Brooklyn and Jersey City who owe their acquaintance with Santa Claus to "The Evening World" and its array of charity workers. In each of the past five years these unfortunate little ones have looked anxiously down the weeks that led to the greatest of all Christmas festivals, wondering whether Santa Claus would visit them, and, if he did, what he would bring. They knew his sleigh was packed with good things for the children of the better-conditioned class, and that the large bag on his shoulders bulged with beautiful and costly gifts for the offspring of the rich, but they had large doubts about their own yule time luck, and they speculated apprehensively upon their prospects of haloing Christmas morn with a doll of their own, a delight-giving toy or a palate-tickling package of candy.

Well, somehow or other Santa Claus found them in each of those years. He found some in homes of sorrow, where starvation sat hollow-eyed watching ghoulishly the progress of the festival. He found other temporary unfortunates unable to spare a penny from food to expend upon the fleeting cheer of the day. Hungry little mouths and empty little stomachs greeted his coming on most of the cold hearths of the poor, and eager hands stretched out to grasp the joy-tokens he distributed. Every year from 30,000 to 45,000 children were remembered in this way by the jolly old saint; they were all poor children, the poorest of the poor, to whom Santa Claus's visit was like the dropping in of an angel with slices of heaven's joy to give away. The articles they received filled their little lives with a brightness that blotted out the sorrow and misery of their customary surroundings. It made Christmas as much to them as it could have been to the son or daughter of a King. And all at little individual cost to "The Evening World" readers, who brought about the blissful result, for it was "Evening World" readers, big and little ones, and nearly a hundred thousand of them, whose nickels and dimes and quarters provided the toys and candies and loaded the trees with glistening Christmas fruit.

There have always been seven "Evening World" Christmas trees—five in New York, one in Brooklyn and one in Jersey City. Every cent received from contributors to the Christmas-Tree Fund has been judiciously expended for toys, candies and more substantial gifts. Of course, Christmas wouldn't be Christmas if the little folks didn't have dolls and roller skates and miniature express wagons and boxes of healthy toothsome candy, but mittens, caps, mufflers, stocking, &c., have not been forgotten, so that the tiny beneficiaries of the fund have not only their senses feasted, but comforts provided for their little bodies. Thousands of dollars have been raised for this beautiful charity, and it has been distributed with such capable management and magnificent results that the donor of a few cents had the sweet satisfaction of knowing that his mite carried happiness into one distress-dampened home at least.

The Christmas charity has done so much good in former years that it should be unnecessary to waste much space in appeals. Everybody who has given before must be aware of the blessings that his or her small donation purchased for the numerous wards of Poverty. These people ought to give again without hesitation. There should be no break in the ranks of our vast army of Santa Claus boomers and Christmas universalizers. The "hard times" must not detract from the efficacy of this charity. Some people may be in distress now owing to closed factories and the scarcity of money, but they will get over their troubles soon. Prosperity is brightening up her Aladdin lamp, and it will not be long before they will be distributed among the multitude again. Hard times are never welcome visitors and they are not encouraged to make long stays. Good times, better times, are always on the road, and their unpopular foster brother has to skip by the light of the moon as the more beneficent members of the family approach. No matter though, how much grown folks feel or suffer by the hard times, children should not be caused a pang on Christmas Day by reason of the presence of distress in the community. There must be no hard times for the little folks. Santa Claus knows nothing about destitution and distress. No chimneys should be covered up by woe as he passes. No road to a hungry stocking should be blocked by misery or want on Christmas morning.

Nell Nelson

The Evening World, DECEMBER 25 1893
Distributing the Gifts Provided by 'The Evening World's' Readers

As if to make atonement for the hard times Dame Nature appeared with the most genial smiles this morning, and the day, as mild as in April, has been especially fine for the children of the poor who have depended upon "The Evening World" Santa Claus for their Christmas Joys.

He is a mighty fine fellow, this St. Nick. of "The Evening World," thanks to the generous-hearted readers who contribute to his Christmas fund. He was in seven places at once today, and many thousands of his dearest little children were out bright and early to see him.

Santa Claus has a host of lovely daughters, too, and they helped at the seven "Evening World" Christmas trees with smiling faces and hearts so tender that there were tears in them as they bestowed the good old Saint's gifts upon these bairns from back tenements.

Wan-faced, weary mothers, with toddlings at their skirts and their weak arms full of babies, and gloomy-faced and discouraged fathers came with their little ones, forgotten by Santa Claus at home, but remembered bountifully by the old fellow at these gathering places.

Big girls led little ones and big boys helped their smaller brothers to and their way through the crowds and get to the place where Kris Kringle's girls were distributing Christmas joys.

The readers who have given so generously cannot imagine, till they have had one experience, the amount of work and patience and trouble expended by other gentle-hearted people in preparing these festivals of pleasure for the babies of Poverty Row. Besides the cases and cases of toys, dolls, sheep, pigs, goats, drums, horses, jumping-jacks, whips, Noah's arks, tea sets, kitchen sets, mittens, warm stockings, little coats, jackets, shirt waists, caps and what not, purchased with the fund contributed by the readers and added to by the editor of "The Evening World," there were other cases by the score of toys and gimcracks, clothing, books, candies, crackers, cookies, doughnuts, nuts and the like sent in by dealers who give frequently without so much as a mark to show who was the giver.

All these had to be divided up among the seven trees, five in New York, one in Brooklyn and one in Jersey City, and when it is considered that there were thousands and thousands of gifts to be distributed of toys, surely, and articles of wear when they seemed to be needed, besides a box of candy, nuts and crackers to each poor child, some idea of the work done by these volunteer ladies and gentlemen may be had.

They worked last night till past midnight, then visited the various halls where the Christmas trees took root, dressed the trees and packed and arranged the gifts for this morning's distribution. With two winks of sleep, they were on hand again to distribute the gifts at 8.30 this morning.

Nell Nelson, the bright young woman reporter of "The Evening World," was among the ladies who had supervision of the Christmas tree in Brooklyn. She busied herself in providing the little ones with huge stacks of toys and candy, and sent them away with light hearts and smiling faces.

John Kendrick Bangs, "A Toast to Santa Claus", *A Little Book of Christmas* (BOSTON: LITTLE, BROWN & COMPANY, 1912)

Whene'er I find a man who don't
Believe in Santa Claus,
   And spite of all remonstrance won't
Yield up to logic's laws,
   And see in things that lie about
The proof by no means dim,
   I straightway cut that fellow out,
And don't believe in him.

The good old Saint is everywhere
Along life's busy way.
   We find him in the very air
We breathe day after day—
   Where courtesy and kindliness
And love are joined together,
   To give to sorrow and distress
A touch of sunny weather.

We find him in the maiden's eyes
Beneath the mistletoe,
   A-sparkling as the star-lit skies
All golden in their glow.
   We find him in the pressure of
The hand of sympathy,
   And where there's any thought of love
He's mighty sure to be.

So here's to good old Kindliheart!
The best bet of them all,
   Who never fails to do his part
In life's high festival;
   The worthy bearer of the crown
With which we top the Saint.
   A bumper to his health, and down
With them that say he ain't!

11.

"My Pack Is Ready"

Abby Morton Diaz, "A Letter from Santa Claus to the Children", *Our Young Folks* (DECEMBER 1870)

My dear children—

Did the beautiful summer go and leave you? And did you mourn for the flowers and try in vain to call back the singing birds? How cruel of them to hurry away, just as the dismal winter days came on, when you needed them more than ever!

But pray be comforted, my darlings! For though your summer friends are gone, don't you know who is coming? Somebody who is just starting from the north with a pack on his back, a right jolly Somebody who loves children! And he says to himself, "Ah, 'twill be a long time before the birds and flowers return, a long time before the skies are bright and fields are green again! What will become of the little folks? Something must be done. For if they should go to sleep as the bears do, and sleep till spring, what a dreadful thing it would be!"

And so this Somebody comes round in the very middle of winter, with a noise and a stir and a rowdedow, and wakes them up and sets them laughing and singing and dancing and clapping hands and shouting "Merry Christmas!" "Merry Christmas!" No fear after that of their doing as the bears do, and sleeping till spring!

And, children, the good time draws near, for I am coming, O, very soon. This long time the north-wind has been whistling to me and roaring out to me, "Santa Claus! Santa Claus! Away with you! Tarry no longer! And my little nephew, Jack Frost, pinches me and whispers, "Hurry up! Hurry up! The children are waiting and longing!"

O, I am so glad that you are! 'Tis such a pleasure to be sure of a welcome! To know that so many bright eyes are looking out for me! Bless your little hearts! Santa Claus will be your friend always, always. He'd rather have the children's love than anything else in the whole world.

O yes, I mean to belong to the children, and be on their side, and bring them beautiful things. For don't the grown folks have always dollar bills growing in their pockets, and ten-cent bills and other kinds, that they can spend? But the children, poor little dears, have spent their cents and eaten up the candy! Never mind, darlings! Just get your stockings ready, that's all,—long stockings, short stockings, seamed, plain, white, blue, gray, red, speckled, spotted, striped, footed up, cut down, heeled and toed, poor little flannel ones run together at night, after the washerwoman's work is done, anything, no matter what. And be sure the baby hangs his sock! But no fair to hang rubber boots, or grandpa's long stockings, that come 'way up, they are so hard to fill, and my time is precious. For just think of all I have to do in a single night! And when the stockings are hung, go to bed and set your hearts at rest. No need even to think of what you want most, for Santa Claus knows much better than you do yourselves!

Now, then, I am almost ready. My pack is made up, and I am just putting on my seven-leagued snow-shoes, which step me over the house-tops. I shall come in the dead of the night, with a crack of the whip and a jingling of bells!—though you will not hear me, little dears, for you'll be sound asleep. But in the morning, the joyful Christmas morning, when you see the plump stockings, then you'll know all about it, won't you?

O, the jolly times there'll be taking out the goodies, opening the papers, and turning stockings inside out to get what's in the toe! O, the shouting and clapping! O, the thousands of children that will dance for joy! It makes my old heart dance for joy, too, and the tears of joy overflow, and run down my beard, and there they hang in the long icicles you've seen in my picture, I suppose.

Yes, my pack is ready and I shall not fail you. How could I fail you? Did I ever? You know I never did. It would break my heart to think of all those dear little stockings empty! No, I never was a day behind, and never shall be. I have tried to get for you the very nicest and prettiest things, and I hope, dear children, that you will both give and lend. For selfishness does grieve me so! The little boy to whom I brought that tin trumpet, I believe there was a tassel to it, but may be mistaken, what do you think? He wouldn't let the others blow! And the boy that had the sword, what should he do but want to be the captain every time!

I picked out a bright-eyed little girl, and brought her a stick of candy as large round as a wax-candle, and she only gave away just one little taste! Another child had a picture-book with lions in it, or if they were not lions they were some other animals, and she carried that picture-book to school, and kept showing the covers, but if any little scholar peeped in at the pictures, she shut it up!

Another had a scalloped cake. There was pink candy grated over it, and a big sugar-plum on top. She carried this about in her pocket, and pinched off little bits at a time. When anybody said "Let me taste," she only shook her head and put another pinch in her own mouth. I could tell her name, but 'twould shame her so!

But one blessed little girl took all her goodies and sat awhile on the doorstep, and to every half-starved beggar-child that came along she gave a taste of something nice. O, it did my very heart good to see her!

For I am a friend to all the beggar-children. Yes, I'm thinking of you, you poor sorrowful ones! Lonely orphan, I'm thinking of you! And weak little cripple, I'm thinking of you! Ah, it is sad, it is pitiful! You have no home, but hungry and cold you beg from door to door. Where you sleep nights nobody knows. In some old shed, perhaps, or under the door step, or in a cart. Old Santa Claus can't bring gifts to you darlings, for you have no stockings to hang, and no chimney for him to creep down. But he mourns and weeps for you, and tears of sorrow mingle with the tears of joy! No. Santa Claus cannot bring you beautiful things, but he will whisper in the ears of the happy little children, "Remember the sorrowful ones, who have no home, no friends, and not even a stocking to hang at Christmas Eve!" From your loving friend,

SANTA CLAUS.

◀ **From *A Visit from St. Nicholas***
 (BOSTON: L. PRANG & CO. 1864)

In memory of Peter William Smith (1948-2024),
who took me to see *Santa Claus: The Movie*
at the Wymondham Regal Cinema in 1985.

Professor Thomas Ruys Smith specialises in the study of nineteenth-century literature and culture. He is the author and editor of a wide range of books including, most recently, *The Last Gift: The Christmas Stories of Mary E. Wilkins Freeman* (Louisiana State University Press, 2023).